By the same author

A GUIDE TO PROVENCE

MICHAEL JACOBS

A GUIDE TO
ANDALUSIA

VIKING

:roup
27 Wrights Lane, London W8 5TZ, England
Viking Penguin Inc., 40 West 23rd Street, New York, New York 10010, USA
Penguin Books Australia Ltd, Ringwood, Victoria, Australia
Penguin Books Canada Ltd, 2801 John Street, Markham, Ontario, Canada L3R 1B4
Penguin Books (NZ) Ltd, 182–190 Wairau Road, Auckland 10, New Zealand

Penguin Books Ltd, Registered Offices: Harmondsworth, Middlesex, England

First published 1990

Copyright © Michael Jacobs, 1990

Maps drawn by Reginald Piggott

Filmset in Sabon

Printed in Great Britain by
Richard Clay Ltd, Bungay, Suffolk

A CIP catalogue record for this book is available from the British Library

ISBN 0-670-82139-X

CONTENTS

LIST OF ILLUSTRATIONS

A Esperanza Flores

PREFACE AND ACKNOWLEDGEMENTS

I was sixteen when I first came to Andalusia, and travelling alone for the first time. Andalusia seemed the most exotic place I had ever known, and I remember writing home ecstatically about jasmine-scented patios, Holy Week celebrations, and the mountain scenery near Ronda. I remember too an afternoon which began in a *bodega* near Córdoba. The wine went to my head, a gypsy appeared playing a guitar, and an old man told me of his friendship with the poet García Lorca. This first experience of the pleasant effects of drink ended up near some enchanted castle, which I now like to identify with Almodóvar del Río.

Andalusia has similarly bewitched thousands of travellers, many of whom have later gone on to record their impressions in a suitably flowery vein. I realize now the great extent to which such romantic visions of Andalusia have obscured the region's real identity. Though one of the tourist centres of Europe, Andalusia remains remarkably little known, in terms not only of its countless unspoilt villages and forgotten monuments, but also of vital aspects of its culture.

Much of the enjoyment which I have had in writing this book has been due to the exceptional amount of help and friendship which I have received in Spain. In Madrid, I must thank Maite Brik, Manolo Fernandez, Ian Gibson, Carmen and Tito de la Guardia, and Pepe Llanos; Annie Bennett's hospitality made it difficult for me to leave the city, while Alicia Ríos – '*consultadora gastronomica*' – gave me a marvellous insight into Spanish food, and provided me with contacts in Andalusia that proved to be invaluable. Once I reached Andalusia, my debts soon became too numerous to list fully, and came to include people whom I encountered in town halls, tourist offices, churches, bars, restaurants, shops and museums in every corner of the region. The Junta de Andalucía, the British Council in Seville, Equipo 28, and the Seville office of Longman Penguin España were of great assistance to me, in particular Jerónimo Hernández, José Ramon Moreno, Fernando Olmedo, Rod Pryde, Cristina Soler, Javier Verdugo and Judith Wilcox. On the pilgrimage to El Rocío in the spring of 1989 I was adopted by the Hermandad of Umbrete, and was excellently looked after by many people, including Lola Flores, Irene Kappel, Bignia Kuoni, Andrés Modolell, Efraim Pintos, Mariano Zorrilla, and Isabel Zorrilla Vera. Des Brennan, Louise Byfield, Richard Cowan, Geoff Macdonald, Celine Morris, Paul, Janis, Michael and Zoe Stirton, Michael Tamm, Sandro Trevisanello, Jim Urquhart, and Ruth Voggenberger all came to see me in Sanlúcar de Barrameda during the summer of 1988, and helped in various ways. In the course of my stays and travels in Andalusia I benefited also from the kindness and company of Juan Carlos Alonso, David Baird, Javier Barral, Jerónimo Castañeda, Carlo and Anne Chinca, Richard Days, Angel Díaz, John Dillon, Francisco González Gómez, Anchi and Lupe Flores, Cuci González de Caldas, Javier Landa, Paco, Pisco and Sergio Lira, Rosa Martínez, Bigoña Medina, Carlos Ortega, Aurelio and Federico Patanchon, Encarnación Peinado Martínez, Alfonso Rios, Miguel Rodriguez Baeza, Cesar Rodriguez Campos, Matthias Roskoschek, Francisco Salazar Romero ('Curro'), Jean and Hamo Sassoon, Rosario Schlatter, José Schwartz Mosco, and José Luis Valdivia. Above all I am indebted to Esperanza Flores, whose generosity was quite exceptional, and through whom I came to know Andalusia incomparably better than I would otherwise have done.

I owe a distant debt to D. E. Brown and Dr Ernst Sanger, both of whom taught me Spanish and helped greatly to foster my early enthusiasm for the country. I must also thank David and Mariagrazia Jacobs, Mic Cheetham of Anthony Sheil Associates, and the staff both of the Spanish Institute in London and of Viking/Penguin, especially Eleo Gordon and Annie Lee. Jackie Rae, once again, made an immeasurable contribution through her helpful criticisms and unfailing support.

I

THE LAND AND ITS PEOPLE

Andalusia seems at times less of a real place than an invention of poets and story-tellers. Situated at what was once the end of the known world, it faces both the Mediterranean and the Atlantic and is protected on three sides by a mountain wall formed to the north by the Sierra Morena and to the west and south by the Cordillera Cantábrica. The Moors referred to the region as the 'Yesira Andalús', 'The Island of Andalusia', and indeed its boundaries of sea and wild mountains effectively cut off the place from the rest of Spain. As with many a mythical land, the often daunting natural frontiers of Andalusia shield an interior famed for its abundant natural resources, luxuriant sensuality, and formidable history. For on the other side of these mineral-encrusted mountains, at the very heart of Andalusia, stretches the fabulously fertile basin of the Guadalquivir, the former homeland of what is traditionally Europe's oldest if also most elusive civilization, that of Tartessus.

Tartessus itself remains to this day hidden like some inland Atlantis, and the land of its people, the Tartessians, only begins to acquire a firmer historical identity following the arrival in Spain of the Phoenicians, the Carthaginians, the Greeks, and, most significantly, the Romans. The Romans ruled over the south of Spain for nearly 400 years, and called the region Betis after their name for its largest river, the Guadalquivir. Under the domination of the Moors, which began in the eighth century AD, Betis became part of al-Andalus, a name which was once fancifully thought to derive from the Vandal hordes who moved into 'Vandalusia' in the wake of the Romans. Southern Spain was divided by the Moors into the kingdoms of Seville, Córdoba, Jaén and Granada, the latter being the last of the Moors' Spanish possessions, falling to the Christians in 1492. After that date the term

3

Andalusia to describe these former kingdoms came to be current, though to begin with this was not an official expression, nor did it have any administrative meaning. In the late eighteenth century Spain adopted a provincial structure, and in 1834 the provinces of Andalusia were established more or less in their present-day form, each one of these named after its most important town: Almería, Cádiz, Córdoba, Granada, Huelva, Jaén, Málaga, and Seville. After the death of Franco in 1975, opposition to centralist government led to the Spanish regions acquiring a much greater degree of autonomy than hitherto, and in 1981, some time after the other regions, Andalusia acquired its own Parliament, based in Seville, and local regional government, the Junta de Andalucía. In contrast to Catalonia and the Basque Country, few people in Andalusia have ever seriously considered a complete break from the rest of Spain. The irony of this is that Andalusia is not only the Spanish region with the strongest geographical identity, but also – in the eyes of many people – the one with the most idiosyncratic culture.

'Spain is different,' ran a famous tourist slogan of the 1940s. But if Spain is different, Andalusia is even more so, for throughout history travellers who have crossed its borders have experienced a feeling of moving away from Europe and entering another continent. 'Once across the Sierra Morena,' observed Théophile Gautier on a visit to Spain in 1840, 'the landscape changes completely . . . you feel truly in some other place; you are aware of having left Paris once and for all.' For him, as for most travellers to Andalusia, the change was seen in terms of an abrupt transition between Europe and Africa. It is often said that Africa begins with the Pyrenees, but it would be more accurate to claim that Africa begins with the Sierra Morena. Eight centuries of Moorish presence in Andalusia have clearly left their mark, on such diverse aspects of the region as the architecture, the place names, the food, and even the physical types. In addition to all this are the remarkable geographical similarities between the two places. The Cordillera Bética belongs to the same geographical formation as the Atlas Mountains in Morocco; furthermore, much of the flora and fauna of Andalusia is essentially African in type, for instance its palm trees, cacti, and the extraordinary pine tree called *pinsapo*, a relative of the Riffia cedar from Ketawa in Morocco, to be found in Europe only in Andalusia's Serranía de Ronda. Yet to define the exotic character of Andalusia purely in African terms is to oversimplify. Andalusia is neither Europe nor Africa but a potent mixture of the two. It is the proverbial meeting-ground of East and West, with, moreover, a strong suggestion of yet another continent. When the Guadalquivir river reaches the sea, having formed with its estuary the only significant gap in Andalusia's near continuous mountain wall, it looks not to Africa or the rest of Europe, but across the Atlantic to America. From the Guadalquivir Columbus set off on his first journey to the New World, thus establishing the river for a while as the main point of departure and arrival for those plying between the two continents. Andalusia was now no longer at the end of the world, but at its centre. Reciprocal influences between Andalusia and Latin America were understandably enormous, and it is not surprising that the Columbian novelist Gabriel García Marquez could note on a recent visit to Andalusia how much the character of the region reminded him of his native country.

Travellers to Andalusia have often described their arrival here in euphoric terms. The place was seen as a promised land, made more so by the inhospitable countryside which came beforehand. The main overland route to Andalusia crosses the plains of La Mancha, possibly the dreariest landscape in Spain, and an area once known for its poor, infertile look. 'La Mancha,' wrote a Moroccan ambassador in 1690, 'is above all a supremely dry country in relation to Andalusia; it is almost entirely lacking in water, its earth is scorched, and its villages are to be found in a primitive state, the very opposite of what you find in Andalusia.' For Gautier and countless other travellers who have journeyed south across La Mancha, the first sight of the Sierra Morena has always been an exciting one. 'Behind that line of purple mountains,' exclaimed Gautier, 'was hidden the paradise of my dreams.' Approached from this side, Gautier's paradise had its gates, the Pass of Despeñaperros, the only breach in the Sierra Morena's 300-mile wall. This is the traditional entrance to Andalusia, so much so that all the idiosyncratic and diverse phenomena of the region are sometimes covered by the oblique term, 'Despeñaperros por abajo', 'below Despeñaperros'.

The route through Despeñaperros is as dramatic as the one across La Mancha is dull, and takes you through a gorge hemmed in by pine-covered slopes erupting into frenetically projecting outcrops of bare rock. The gorge opens out into the Guadalquivir valley, affording a monumental panorama over a rolling landscape studded with olive trees. Surveying the view, which extends beyond the valley to the distant peaks of the Cordillera Bética, Gautier was reminded of the visionary landscapes of the English painter John Martin. This same view, according to Gautier's contemporary Chateaubriand, so overwhelmed the French troops under Marshal Soult that they saluted it with their guns. Descending into the valley, your eyes will be dazzled in the spring months by a sparkling, jewel-like encrustation of poppies and other flowers. And as in representations of Paradise, there are clusters of palm trees and – for most of the year – an uninterrupted blue sky so vivid in hue that even those living in other parts of Spain feel moved to comment on it.

'Andalusia intoxicates like alcohol and opium,' wrote the Seville poet Luis Cernuda. 'If I was ever asked what Andalusia means to me,' he said elsewhere, 'if I was asked what single word sums up the thousand sensations, suggestions and possibilities that unite the radiant surface of Andalusia, I would say: happiness.' 'I wandered around ancient Betis,' recalled Chateaubriand, 'where the poets had located happiness.' The Roman geographer Strabo likened the Gaudalquivir valley to the Elysian fields, and emphasized, as writers always have done, the exceptional way in which Andalusia has been favoured by nature. Olives, vines and wheat brought great prosperity to the region in ancient times, as did the abundance of its fish, tuna from the coast near Cádiz and caviar from the sturgeons that once swam up the Guadalquivir being exported all over the Roman Empire. Not least was Andalusia's mineral wealth, which was exploited long before the Romans and once gave the region a reputation comparable to that of El Dorado: the first known mention of Tartessus is a line in the Old Testament referring to the 'mineral-laden ships of Tarshish'. The image of natural abundance which hangs over Andalusia like a cornucopia was furthered by the Moors, who introduced new elements such as cotton and silkworms and instigated remarkably sophisticated systems of irrigation that are still partially functioning. To them, too, Andalusia was a paradise, and their loss of the region and eventual expulsion from it has often been described in terms of the expulsion of Adam and Eve in the Bible. Long after the departure of the Moors, Andalusia maintained a reputation as the Spanish region most endowed with natural resources, and traveller after traveller has used the word 'paradise' to evoke the place's charms. 'When we entered Andalusia,' recollected a Polish royal traveller, Jacob Sobieski, in 1611, 'our senses, tired after the monotonous desert we had crossed, were amply restored by the beauty, joy and abundance of products of this country . . . I thought I was in a Paradise.' 'Andalusia,' wrote the French visitor Étienne de Silhouette in 1750, 'is the best part of all Spain, the most fertile, the richest, in short the one in which all of Nature's gifts have been best distributed.' 'The land overflows with oil and wine,' commented Richard Ford in his celebrated guidebook to Spain of 1845. All these views were summed up in 1848 by a Spanish writer, Cuendía, who suggested that the Pass of Despeñaperros was the frontier which separates 'the land of men from the land of gods'. And yet the more fulsome the praise becomes for Andalusia over the centuries, the more ironic the praise so often seems. The irony was in many cases fully intended.

The pass of Despeñaperros has been seen not just as the gates of Heaven, but as those of Hell. Andalusia has managed, paradoxically, to combine an image of great wealth and fecundity with one of extreme poverty: in modern times Andalusia, together with the neighbouring region of Extremadura, has been regarded as the poorest part of Spain. The marked discrepancy which has developed since the seventeenth century between Andalusia's economic potential and its economic reality has prompted sad reflections from travellers. The French agriculturalist of the late eighteenth century, the Baron de Bourgoing, after having evoked Roman Betis as a 'magic land in which happiness and abundance flourished', wrote that 'modern Betis could be the same, and yet, despite its beautiful sky and estimable and varied crops, it only inspires nostalgia'.

The beauty and the tragedy of Andalusia was the subject of a well-known article of 1905 by the Spanish essayist and novelist Azorín. This article, entitled *La Andalucía Trágica*, begins with a description of a train journey between Madrid and Seville. After crossing La Mancha at night, the traveller wakes up in the morning in the Guadalquivir valley. Looking out of the window he is immediately enchanted and soothed by what he sees, for, in contrast to the harshness of central Spain, the landscape in front of him is of an 'inexpressable sweetness'; when he reaches Seville, the voluptuous and carefree character of the city almost overwhelms him. All this serves as a prelude to a description of 'tragic Andalusia', an Andalusia which he finds in the small town of Lebrija, sixty-three kilometres to the south of Seville. Here he is struck by how empty the place seems, by how the streets are deserted, and by how only a handful of sad people fill the town's social club. Unemployment, normally high, has reached a drastic level, thanks to phylloxera in the neighbouring vines of Jerez. Few can afford to go out, or even have the energy to do so. People are literally dying of hunger. A local doctor provides the traveller with frightening statistics of death from malnutrition and tuberculosis. 'I don't know what the solution to our problem is,' says the doctor, 'all that I do know is that we cannot go on living like this. We are not living, we are dying.' The conditions of Andalusia's rural poor as described by Azorín in 1905 were scarcely to change for much of this century, and were to lead from the 1920s onwards to an exodus away from the country to the cities, and away from Andalusia itself. By the 1970s, when the exodus began to be curbed, Andalusia had come to be known as the emigration capital of Spain, and had suffered a severe demographic crisis: the region's rural population, which at the beginning of the century had exceeded the urban population, was now reduced to almost half of the latter. In recent years Andalusia's economy has finally begun significantly to improve, and once-poor areas such as Almería have changed beyond recognition and even begun to attract back former emigrés. None the less, disturbing statistics can still be quoted; for instance, there are more cases of leprosy in Andalusia than anywhere else in Europe, and Seville has a higher rate of unemployment than any other European city.

'The sky and earth are good,' goes an old Andalusian proverb, 'that which lies in between is bad.' Incompetence, corruption, greed, and the persistence of a ridiculous feudalism have joined forces to minimalize the untold natural advantages of Andalusia, and to ensure that what prosperity there has been has benefited only the very few. 'It has indeed,' wrote Richard Ford, 'required the utmost ingenuity and bad government of man to neutralize the prodigality of advantages which Paradise has lavished on this highly favoured land, and which, while under the domination of the Romans and Moors, represented an Eden, a garden of plenty and delight . . .' It is generally agreed that it was the expulsion of the Moors which contributed more than any other factor to the economic decline of Andalusia. The new Christian settlers, brought into Andalusia after 1492, represented only a fraction of the Moors who departed, and were hardly sufficient in number, or even willing enough, to look after the lands that the latter had so lovingly cultivated. As early as 1525 the Venetian ambassador Andrea Navagero lamented the ruinous state of countless gardens and plots of land that the Moors had been forced to abandon at Granada. The Moors, Navagero noted, had a remarkable ability to grow trees and plants, and to transform even the most meagre pieces of land into gentle, perfumed gardens with constant flowing water; the Spaniards meanwhile were 'not very industrious, and neither cultivate nor sow the land with any good will, but prefer instead to go to war or to the Indies to make their fortune.'

Of all the Moors' many gifts, it was their genius at irrigation which was to be most beneficial to them in Andalusia. The sun which lends the region such a smiling aspect for so much of the year is also a relentless, unremitting force which has dried out the land and created throughout Andalusia's history severe periods of drought. Zouch Turton, an English traveller of the 1870s, ridiculed the notion of Andalusia as the garden of Spain by saying that the only plants that flourished here of their own accord were the aloe and the Barbary fig, and that almost everything else had to be brought, planted and watered. The problem of water has been a constant one in Andalusia up to the present day, and was referred to in 1965 in a speech delivered by Franco at Huércal-Overa, a desolate town in the middle of Almería, Andalusia's most arid and desert-like province: 'These lands,' the dictator shouted, 'are crying out for water, water, water.' Yet under the Moors, even Almería flourished. This fact was seized upon by the Catalan writer and socialist Juan Goytisolo, who in 1959 brought out two controversial studies of poverty in Almería, *La Chanca* and *Campos de Níjar*. Reflecting on the lunar-like landscape of Almería, he wondered to what extent this was the cause of the region's poverty and to what extent the result of the expulsion of the Moors and the neglect of their irrigation systems.

Lack of water has by no means been the only problem affecting settlers in Andalusia. The Andalusian climate is one of extremes, long periods without rain being followed by intensive downpours that have often brought on severe flooding, particularly in the Guadalquivir basin; it is known that the weather in Andalusia went through an especially changeable period in the early years of the seventeenth century, and that this undoubtedly consolidated the decline of the region's economy. Then there is the notorious wind called the Levante, which seems to blow almost constantly around the coast of Cádiz and has a popular reputation for causing insanity. Against such factors not even the skills of the Moors could be of much avail. Nor could their impressive achievements hide the extraordinary fact that – according to a recent survey – 47 per cent of Andalusia, this so-called 'Garden of Spain', is totally unsuitable for agriculture. But the main problem which has troubled Andalusia has nothing to do with weather or geography, but rather with the much thornier and still unresolved issue of the ownership of the land.

The enormous potential rewards of Andalusia's land have come only too rarely into the hands of those who have worked or lived on it. Andalusia's most profitable enterprises have been more often than not run by foreigners, the sherry industry being a well-known example of this. British merchants have been based in Jerez and the neighbouring sherry towns of El Puerto de Santa María and Sanlúcar de Barrameda since the Middle Ages, and the names Gordon Byass, Harvey, Osborne, Terry and so on testify to this day to the British domination of the trade. The British, too, together with the Belgians and the French, have played the major role in the region's mining industry. While the Belgians and the French controlled respectively the lead mines in Almería province and the now exhausted coal mines in Peñarroya (Córdoba), the British were for a long while the beneficiaries of Andalusia's oldest and most famous mining concern, the copper mines of Río Tinto. A British syndicate bought the mines from the Spanish government in 1871 for a sum far less than their intrinsic value, and within a few years had achieved a leading position in the world market for copper and sulphur. The mines, which Franco often referred to as an 'economic Gibraltar', recently reverted back to Spanish ownership, but by then the Río Tinto Zinc Company had been able to expand its activities well beyond Europe, and was gaining notoriety for its involvement in Bolivia and South Africa. The Río Tinto mines are by no means the worst example of foreign exploitation of Andalusia's wealth. A far more disturbing and insidious phenomenon than this has been foreign involvement in the property boom of the Costa del Sol. The building companies that have transformed the once desperately poor coast between Gibraltar and Almuñecar into what is generally described as a concrete jungle are mainly foreign-owned, as are the burgeoning estate agencies. What is more, many of the nearby inland villages are also becoming overrun by foreigners, many of whom, often without work permits, have taken up property speculation and other entrepreneurial activities.

The uneven distribution of Andalusia's wealth has been evident above all in agriculture, which is the traditional base of the region's economy. Agricultural oppression has always been symbolized here by the land structure of the *latifundium* or large estate. This structure has characterized other Spanish regions, most notably Castille and Extremadura, but whereas in these other places it declined in the early years of this century, in Andalusia it has prevailed to this day. The large estates of 200 hectares (494 acres) still represent only 1.4 per cent of the region's farms and yet continue to occupy over half the farmland. The *latifundium* remains as integral to the image of Andalusia as *flamenco* or bull-fighting. The word is Latin in origin, though the first *latifundia* might possibly date back to the Tartessian period. In any case, it was not until the Roman occupation of Spain that the *latifundium* was to acquire what was later to be one of its most common features, namely an absentee landlord. When living in Rome, the Andalusian-born philosopher Seneca did not make his money purely from Stoicism; he seems also to have received an ample revenue from his property outside Córdoba. Another such landlord was one Marius, who gave his name to the Sierra Morena (a derivative of the Sierra Mariana) through owning there a vast estate later confiscated by the Emperor Tiberius.

The Roman fiscal system and the Vandal hordes of the subsequent period destroyed the Roman *latifundia*, but these were reconstituted during the Middle Ages, the estates being given out as gifts to the feudal lords who had assisted the Spanish monarchs in their fight against the Moors. The majority of today's big estates, however, date from the nineteenth century and were formed by the sale of the corporate landed property held by the church and the municipalities. These sales were intended as a gesture of reform, as a way of widening the range of ownership and helping the landless. In the end, of course, they just had the effect of strengthening the position of the wealthy few, as these were the only people who could afford the newly available land. The landed élite and their allies formed a powerful oligarchy, which was able to block all the various attempts at land reform that were proposed from the mid eighteenth century onwards and accept only those reforms that were to be beneficial to them.

At the centre of the *latifundium* is the *cortijo*, a group of farm buildings surrounded by a relatively small, well cultivated area; the rest of the estate is traditionally divided up between wheat, grazing land and fallows. The surviving *cortijos*, all dating from after the seventeenth century, comprise a brilliantly white complex of buildings neatly arranged around a courtyard and dominated by a bell tower and a large gate; a fringe of luxuriant tropical vegetation, or even the nearby placing of a palm tree, lends to these places an added exotic quality. Grander and much less common versions of the *cortijos* are the *haciendas*, the equivalent of Roman or Palladian villas, places that combine a farm and a country home; magnificent examples of these are to be found in the province of Seville, for example the Hacienda Torquemada outside Bollullos de la Mitación.

Generally speaking, the more important the landlords, the less time that they have spent on their estates. Visits of leading aristocrats to their *latifundia* have been major events in local history. The Hispanist Gerald Brenan recalled in his book *The Spanish Labyrinth* (1943) how a visit made by the Duke of Alba in the 1920s to his estate near Córdoba took on almost the character of an African safari, the Duke equipping himself with tents and a convoy of lorries. When the landlords have directly worked their estates they have usually done so by putting an overseer in charge of the *cortijo*. Sometimes, however, they have preferred to rent out their land, one of the advantages in the past of doing so being that they did not have to pay taxes on the property or spend money maintaining or improving it. The overseers of the *cortijos* and those who have rented these places, the *labradores*, have traditionally been portrayed as unattractive figures, hard on their employees, and often betrayers of their own class. They frequently took on the role of *caciques*, political bosses who manipulated and even falsified local electoral results.

Lower down the social scale from the *labradores* come the *peletrines*, men to whom the former would sometimes rent out the poorest or more distant parts of the estates. At the very bottom of the scale are the *braceros* or day-labourers, Andalusia's vast landless proletariat who to this day constitute one of the region's great social problems. The *braceros* are employed on a seasonal basis, which means that for much of the year they are redundant. They have never had their homes on the estates, but have lived in villages or towns often many miles away: this fact largely accounts for the emptiness of so much of the Andalusian countryside. When working on the estates, their employers have generally put them up, but in conditions that have often been pitiable. Blasco Ibañez, in his novel *La bodega* (1894), a study of a famous workers' strike in Jerez in 1892, describes how up to 100 labourers and their families would be made to sleep on the floor of a long room called the *gañaría*; they would be fed purely on the cold garlic soup known as *gazpacho*, except at harvest time, when they would be given beans.

Andalusia's large and hungry landless proletariat, faced with huge estates and absentee landlords, *caciques* and ruthless employers, frequently rebelled. The Andalusian countryside has known periods of social unrest since at least the fifteenth century, but from the late nineteenth century right up to the Civil War of 1935/8 it was almost constantly troubled. Anarchism was particularly strong here and, according to some historians, became closely associated with Messianism, its message often being spread by itinerant lay preachers such as one Salvotea, a saintly figure heroized by the *braceros*. The great symbol of Andalusia's struggling rural population is the village of Fuente Obejuna, today a sad and slightly sinister place in the desolate northern half of Córdoba province. On 23 April 1476 the villagers rose up against their tyrannical lord, Fernán Gomez, Comendador of the Order of Calatrava. An early account of the incident relates how they stormed his palace, threw him out of the window, finished him off with lances and swords, then dragged his body to the main square, where it was hacked to pieces by men and women alike; later the village refused to single out any individual culprits but assumed collective responsibility for what had happened, thus giving rise to a popular saying, '*Fuente Obejuna lo hizo*' ('Fuente Obejuna did it'). This rebellion, which was one of several in the history of the village, is remembered today largely through its being turned into a drama of honour and revenge by the seventeenth-century playwright, Lope de

Vega. *Fuenteovejuna* (1612–14), perhaps Lope de Vega's best-known work, was performed in the village in 1933 under the direction of the poet García Lorca. The production was staged in contemporary costume in front of the late fifteenth-century parish church which was built on the site of the Comendador's palace. Shortly before it was due to start, one of the actresses noticed a man wildly pacing up and down in the courtyard of the town hall. She was later told that the man was 'a dangerous anarchist', and was being kept under surveillance until the end of the play, just in case its contents incited his political feelings. With the help of Lorca she obtained his release. In gratitude for this the public surged on to the stage at the end of the production, thus apparently confirming the authorities' fears about the emotive qualities of the play: for a while Lorca was even afraid that the crowd would lynch the local *caciques*.

In 1979 a leading left-wing Andalusian journalist, Antonio Ramos Espejo, paid a visit to the village of Fuente Obejuna and found that the basis of local discontent had remained fundamentally unchanged over the centuries. The seventy-year-old mayor, questioned by Ramos Espejo on the subject of land ownership, replied: 'There are those who have a lot, and those who have nothing. There's nothing in between. It's either the landowner or the day labourer.' Of the 56,311 hectares of land falling within the territory of the village, 22,300 were possessed by only twenty-one owners. The plight of the day-labourer was highlighted by the startlingly high level of emigration, the population of the village having dropped from 19,378 in 1940 to just over 7,000 in 1979.

'Andalusians,' cried the writer Blas Infante, 'rise up; seek land and liberty.' The demand for land has been a constant one throughout Andalusia's history, though many agrarian reformers from the time of Charles III's enlightened agricultural minister, Aranda, have argued that the deep-rooted popular desire for a *reparto* or share-out of the land does not represent a very practical solution to the problem of land ownership. Large areas of the *latifundia* consist of poor pasture which would never prosper as peasant farms; other areas are suitable only for monoculture and would require only two bad years of drought to force the peasant owner to sell them. The idea of a *reparto* has been dropped completely by Spain's present Socialist government. In 1984 this government introduced an agrarian reform law – the first of its kind since 1932 – which did not call into question the actual ownership of the land, but stipulated instead that the farming rights of badly used land should be temporarily taken over and given, under contract, to co-operatives. As for the day-labourers, their position has improved considerably with the introduction of state support for the months in which they are not working. None of these reforms, however, satisfy the demands of the workers' union known as the S O C (Sociedad de Obreros Campesinos), a radical organization in the tradition of Andalusian anarchism, but with an admixture of pacifist and ecologist ideals. One of the main centres of this movement is the village of Marinaleda, in the easternmost part of the province of Seville.

Marinaleda is a small village in the middle of flat, wheat-growing country. It has a modern, undistinguished and fairly prosperous appearance, and bears the characteristically tasteless marks of recent civic improvements, such as an over-neat row of flower beds along the main street. There is nothing to hold the visitor's attention save for the name of the village square – Plaza de Libertad – and the banner flying over it, which bears the symbol of a dove and the words TIERRA DE LIBERTAD. On the square stands the Casa de Cultura, a worker's club, inside which you will find a portrait of a bearded, intensely serious young man standing in a field and addressing a group of admiring peasants. I thought the picture to be a representation of Jesus Christ in a modern setting, but it turned out to be of the man whom I had come to the village to meet, the village schoolteacher and mayor, Juan Manuel Sanchez Gordillo.

Thanks largely to Sanchez Gordillo, Marinaleda has a reputation as one of the most politically radical villages in the south of Spain, if not in Europe: its percentage of communist voters is virtually the highest on the continent. Sanchez Gordillo first caught the public eye in 1980, when he organized in Marinaleda 'a hunger strike against hunger'. More recently he has taken up forcibly occupying nearby large estates. The estate he has been in since February 1988 belongs to one of Andalusia's largest landowners, the Duke of Infantado, and is about sixteen kilometres from the village. This is where I was able to track him down. Attached to a post at the entrance of the estate were the words, 'ESTA TIERRA ES NUESTRA MARINALEDA', 'This land is our Marinaleda.' On the long drive up to the *cortijo* I passed a group of villagers carrying hoes and rakes, the women dressed in black. They could have been straight out of a communist poster of the 1930s, and this impression was reinforced by the political badges they were all wearing. The scene outside the *cortijo* itself was more like a film set, the car I was in adding an incongruous note to what appeared to be a re-creation of a pre-war agrarian strike. Dark, unshaven men and their families lay around in a large circle as if waiting for instructions. In the middle of all this prowled the leonine and instantly recognizable figure of Sanchez Gordillo, wearing a Tolstoyan suit and a red sash. He addressed me in a slow, solemn voice, with no trace of a smile. I could not help feeling, confronted by such a manner and appearance, that I was in the presence of one of the Messianic figures who toured the Andalusian countryside in the nineteenth century. He talked of the inadequacy of the present agrarian reforms, of the great extent of the Duke of Infantado's properties, and of how the land in Andalusia continued to be in the hands of the very few. As he spoke, he gestured to a bucolic backdrop of shimmering wheatfields stretching towards the pale profile of distant mountains.

It is easy to romanticize Sanchez Gordillo, just as it is easy to romanticize the poverty, landlessness and exploitation that he has devoted his energies to eradicating. Tragedy and suffering are as integral to the traditional, stereotypical image of Andalusia as are joy and plenty. Travel writers have always loved to emphasize this dichotomy, which for many is symbolized in the clash between the blindingly white walls of Andalusia and the jet black grilles of their windows, or in the division of a bull-ring into *sol* and *sombra*, sun and shade. 'Sol y Sombra' is the title of the chapter on Andalusia in Jan Morris's highly popular *Spain* (1st edition, 1964), a chapter in which it is even hinted that this poverty, 'borne without grievance', is picturesque: 'For one must admit that the earthiness of Spain, which is the cousin of backwardness, is often very beautiful to experience.' The poverty of Andalusia has to a certain extent become part of its tourist appeal, and it could even be argued that the interest shown by Goytisolo in what he terms the 'third-world' conditions of Almería was a fundamentally romantic one, for the primitive qualities that impressed him here were those that later made this sophisticated city-dweller fall in love with Morocco. Poverty in a southern, backward and preferably rural setting has seemed exotic to many. However, these same people would be unlikely to find glamour in Andalusia's recently built areas of urban deprivation, such as Seville's dangerous and graffiti-scrawled suburb of Tres Mil Viviendas. The poverty in such places has nothing specifically Andalusian about it, and is little different to that found in the distinctly unexotic inner cities of Britain and America. This is a poverty which does not conform to the tidy and essentially poetic notion of *sol y sombra*.

The emphasis on the 'sun' and 'shade' of Andalusia is a reflection of how Spain itself has generally been characterized, as a land of extremes, of austerity and sensuality, passion and honour, grandeur and decay, fantasy and common-sense. Hyperbole, the great sin of travel writing, has at times been ludicrously present in the literature on Spain. 'It has so long and annually been considered permissible,' wrote Richard Ford in 1845, 'when writing about romantic Spain, to take leave of common sense, to ascend on stilts, and converse in the Cambysean vein, that those who descend to common-place matter-of-fact, are considered not only to be inaesthetic, unpoetical and un-imaginative but deficient in truth and power of observation.' And what is true of Spain in general is doubly so of Andalusia, for this region has long been thought of as the distillation of all things Spanish. Almost everything that we consider 'typically Spanish' is Andalusian in origin, from bull-fighting to *flamenco*. Andalusia is a compendium of every cliché that has ever been written about Spain, clichés that were wittily summarized in Mario Praz's wonderfully perverse and scabrous *Unromantic Spain* (1928):

Old Spanish towns languorous beneath the warm sun and the scent of orange blossoms, castellated mansions and Moorish arabesques, a proud people hugging fierce passions beneath their cloaks, guitars and castanets, donkeys and courteous peasants, long white roads and snowy ribbed sierras, quaint old market squares, narrow streets with bal-conies atop and animated *paseos*, gardens everywhere, swimming in the sun.

The Andalusians are rightly angered by the cliché-ridden image of their region which is still promoted abroad. Yet this image has been as much the creation of their own writers as of foreign ones. For instance, the tediously sentimental plays written early this century by the Quintero brothers portrayed Andalusia as a land of endless gaiety and frivolity, while the works of the contemporary and widely successful gypsy playwright and director, Salvator Távora, represent the region misleadingly as a place which has known only suffering and oppression. The Andalusian writer who has done most to influence general attitudes towards Andalusia both in Spain and abroad has undoubtedly been García Lorca. Lorca, in a talk which he gave about his most popular collection of poems, *El Romancero Gitano* or *Gypsy Ballads*, stressed how this book was 'anti-folklore, anti-local colour, and anti-*flamenco*', and that it contained 'not one short jacket, suit of lights, wide-brimmed hat or Andalusian tambourine'. However, though Lorca's Andalusia is radically different from that of his lightweight contemporaries, the Quinteros, it drew on and strengthened all the clichés conveyed by the passionate chords and anguished wails of *flamenco* music. This is the Andalusia of the tragic, solitary gypsy, the Andalusia of *cante jondo* or 'deep song', a cry of pain from the mysterious, distant past, a cry heard in the wind which rustles through the olive trees, stirring up the passions that lie imprisoned behind barred windows, and permeating the very soul of the Andalusian people.

The clichés about Andalusia cannot always be ridiculed like this, and indeed are generally difficult to avoid and express much which is true. None the less, they provide only the most limited view of the region. *Flamenco*, bull-fighting and gypsies are vital components of Andalusian culture, but not the only components; similarly Andalusia has its smiling and tragic faces, but it also has a wide range of moods in between. For a place which Ford was already describing in 1845 as 'the most popular destination for travellers to Spain', and which has since become one of the main tourist centres of Europe, it is surprising how little known Andalusia remains. The fact that Ford's own *Handbook* contains what is still, nearly 150 years later, the best guide and general introduction to Andalusia is itself testimony to this. Our ignorance of Andalusia is reflected not just in our preconceptions of the place but in our knowledge of its towns, villages and landscapes. Most of Andalusia is as yet remarkably unspoilt, and away from the coast and main towns you will find countless villages that have maintained folk and crafts traditions over the centuries, and where the tourist is still a welcome novelty. Travelling here should make you wary of generalizing too much about the character of the place. Andalusia constitutes a geographical and cultural identity of enormous individuality, and yet its apparent unity is belied by the startling variety of parts that make up the whole.

The size and emptiness of Andalusia will soon impress themselves on the traveller. The largest region in Spain, as large as a small country such as Hungary, Portugal or Switzerland, Andalusia is also the least densely populated area in Europe, having seventy people per square kilometre as opposed to 600 in Britain. Much of the terrain is wild and mountainous, and travel within the region has not always been easy. The main lines of communication have always been along the Guadalquivir valley. Those arriving in Andalusia by sea generally landed at Cádiz, and, up to the mid nineteenth century, would often continue their journey by sailing up the Guadalquivir to Seville. The main route connecting Seville with the rest of Spain was nicknamed by Lope de Vega 'the silver route', for it was along here that there once was transported to Madrid all the bounty from the Indies. Passing through Córdoba, the route follows the Guadalquivir almost up to its source in Jaén province, before turning abruptly north towards the Pass of Despeñaperros. Before beginning to silt up in the course of the six-teenth and seventeenth centuries the river was navigable up to Cór-doba, thanks to the Romans, who once dug channels to prevent the water level from dropping. As for the road from Seville to Despeñaper-ros, this was excellently modernized during the reign of Charles III, and was supplemented after 1870 by a railway. The coming of the railway to Andalusia in the late nineteenth century greatly improved links with places off the main Guadalquivir axis such as Huelva, Algeciras, Ronda, Málaga, Granada and Almería. However, anyone travelling to those parts had still to expect a long and often arduous journey. Málaga, which through its airport has today become the most popular point of arrival in Andalusia, was known until as late as the 1960s for its poor road communications with the rest of its province. Almería meanwhile is perhaps the most isolated major town in Spain. The railway link with Madrid was built principally to serve the mining industry, and, well into this century, travellers from Almería to the Spanish capital preferred to sail west to Cartagena or Murcia, and then make their way from there. The once notoriously bad inland route west from Almería was improved only in the 1970s, but it still takes ten hours to travel by road from Almería to Seville.

Travellers have loved to emphasize the adventurous nature of an Andalusian journey. The first thrills usually came while crossing Despeñaperros, and were inspired as much by jubilant feelings on arriving in Andalusia as by the reputation of the Pass as a dangerous place. Travellers of the Romantic period evoked at such length the savage, primitive aspect of Despeñaperros that they almost all overlooked the fact that the road they were on, built in 1779 by the French architect Le Maur, was, with its tunnels, hairpin bends and parapets, one of the great marvels of modern engineering: the Baron de Bourgoing described it in 1808 as 'one of the finest high roads in Europe'. The landscape took on for these travellers an exaggerated, wild appearance because they came here with heads filled with tales of wolves, and, above all, bandits. Andalusia was one of the notorious bandit areas of Europe, and banditry ended up by being one of the region's great attractions. Banditry here goes back at least to the time when gangs of Moors took to the roads to escape from their Christian persecutors, and reached its heyday during the eighteenth and early nineteenth centuries with the important trade in smuggled tobacco and other goods from Gibraltar. The empty, remote character of so much of Andalusia was a major contributory factor in the spread of banditry, which was concentrated largely in the mountainous and little populated areas of the region, above all in and around the Sierra Morena, the Alpujarras and the Serranía de Ronda.

The blatant social injustice expressed by Andalusia's land structure has also been suggested as a major cause of banditry. By the nineteenth century the Andalusian bandit had certainly gained popular fame as a latterday Robin Hood, a friend and helper of the poor and a sworn enemy of the landlord and the *cacique*. He was seen as an essentially noble figure who had been driven into crime through justifiable outbursts of passion. One such person was José Ulloa Tragabuches, a Ronda bull-fighter in the school of the celebrated Pedro Romero (see page 156), who had been forced into banditry and to abandon a promising career after killing his adulterous wife in a passionate fit. The most legendary of Andalusia's bandits was José María Hinojosa Cabacho, known as El Tempranillo. Born in 1805 in Jauja (Córdoba), a fishing village on the banks of the river Genil, he was only thirteen when he killed a man during the pilgrimage festivities to the nearby hermitage of the Fuensanta. Why he did so is not clear, though in the various popular books and films that have dealt with his career the motives have always been presented as honourable ones: that he was avenging either the murder of his father, or an attempt to take away his fiancée, or even the dishonouring of his mother. At all events, José María ran off and joined a notorious gang called the 'Niños de Écija' (the 'Children of Écija'), and later established his own headquarters in the Cave of Los Organos, which is visible from the Despeñaperros road. He made travellers pay protection money to ensure a safe journey, but also earned respect for his courteous treatment of his victims and his consideration of the poor. In 1828 he declared that the 'king rules in Spain, but I rule in the *Sierra*', and four years later the king acknowledged his noble reputation by granting him a royal pardon. An English traveller called George Dennis described him as five feet tall and with bow legs, but to Mérimée, the author of *Carmen*, he was a handsome, dashing figure, which is how he was portrayed by the English artist John Lewis. He died in 1835, and his tomb can be seen in the village cemetery of Alameda (Córdoba), just to the south of Jauja; his gun is in the possession of a local family.

Not all bandits were so kind or civilized as José María was reputed to have been. White crosses marking the sites of roadside murders were numerous in the mountainous districts of Andalusia, and indicated that the dangers in travelling here were not purely figments of the Romantic imagination. However, as Ford noted, Romantic travellers vastly exaggerated the dangers so as to give added drama to an account of their adventures. It should be said that of the hundreds of travellers who wrote up their Spanish journeys, only one, a certain James Slidell, actually experienced a bandit attack, and this did not happen in Andalusia but in La Mancha. Travellers took a perverse delight in the feeling of danger, Disraeli even claiming that his fear of being assaulted on a journey in the Serranía de Ronda had raised his spirits enormously. To be deprived of danger came sometimes as a great disappointment, as Hans Christian Andersen found out when travelling across the Sierra Morena under the protection of armed soldiers: 'I felt myself so thoroughly safe that I was suddenly seized with a desire to witness a slight encounter with banditti. The whole country seems as if formed for it . . .' Andersen went on to relate an apocryphal story about Alexandre Dumas in which the Frenchman, before coming to Spain, had sent a cheque for 1,000 francs to a bandit chief, asking him to arrange an attack on his party, on the condition, however, that no physical danger was to be run.

In the 1870s banditry began gradually to die out in Andalusia, thanks to the successful measures taken by the then Governor of Córdoba, Julián de Zugasti y Saenza, later the author of the first serious study of Andalusian banditry. The man generally thought to be the last Andalusian bandit was Juan Mingolla Gallardo, nicknamed 'Pasos Largos' or 'Long Steps'. Born near Ronda in 1874, he was finally incarcerated in a penitentiary in El Puerto de Santa María in 1932. Here, suffering from tuberculosis, he almost ended his days, but he managed to escape and died in a more worthy manner, shot while firing against the Guardia Civil in 1934. 'Is it true?' asked Gerald Brenan on a train journey across the Sierra Morena in 1949, 'that there are bandits in the Sierra?' 'You bet there are,' replied his Spanish travelling companion. 'All those rocks and peaks you see are full of them.' In fact the man was not really referring to bandits at all but to the 'Reds' who after the Civil War had hidden from the authorities in the same caves that had been used by the bandits. The legend of banditry lived on a long time in Andalusia, and as late as 1986 gullible travellers could still apparently be fooled by it. On a lonely road in Huelva, two policemen with a sense of humour stopped an English car and interrogated its driver, the poet Ted Walker. They warned him of brigands along the road, but Walker paid no attention to this until, shortly afterwards, a group of sinister men in checked shirts and broad-belted corduroys blocked his way. Walker thought that his time had come, but it turned out that these men were merely employees of the Río Tinto Mining Company, and they were stopping him because of dynamiting ahead.

The rebuilding of the main road between Madrid and Seville, then the most used highway in Spain, was not the only step taken during the enlightened reign of Charles III to ensure the greater safety of travellers in Andalusia. Proposals were also put forward to populate the empty, lawless lands that lay immediately to the south of the Sierra Morena. Charles III's minister, Pablo de Olavide, administrator of Andalusia, suggested that colonies of foreigners should be established here, foreigners being preferred to Spaniards so as not to depopulate other parts of Spain. Eventually around 6,000 settlers came here, all of them Catholics, the great majority from Belgium and

German-speaking countries but also some from France, Switzerland and Italy, and even a handful from Greece. In charge of recruitment was a Bavarian officer called Johann Kaspar von Thürriegel, who, after serving in the Prussian army, had come to Spain to set up a sword factory. Among those whom he managed to enlist for the colonies was a group of convicts on the point of being shipped to the notorious French penal colony of Guyana. The French government had been glad to get rid of them.

La Carolina, the first village of any size that you come to after Despeñaperros, was the most important of the twelve colonies that were set up by Charles III and Olavide (among the others were La Carlota and La Luisiana, see page 274). As with the other colonies, and in complete contrast to most Andalusian villages, it was laid out on a grid pattern, with wide avenues and neatly-arranged houses. As late as 1818, the English traveller George Ticknor could describe La Carolina as having a prosperous, comfortable appearance, so different to that of the squalid villages that he had just been through in La Mancha. The fortunes of La Carolina, however, had not been as smiling as they had appeared to Ticknor. The Baron de Bourgoing, who had visited the place ten years earlier, considered that a great decline had set in following the disgrace of Olavide in 1775. Olavide, as befitting an Enlightenment reformer, had settled in La Carolina and had begun to witness at close hand his dreams for the place come true. Unfortunately he had great political enemies, and these had arranged to make him fall foul of the Inquisition. The latter, after throwing him into prison and confiscating his property at La Carolina, accused him of possessing prohibited books and of showing no regard to the faith. Condemned as a heretic, he was forced to spend eight years in a monastery reading books on piety. On the pretext of taking the waters in Catalonia, he escaped to France, and after the Revolution retired to the Loire. By then at least half of the foreign settlers in the Sierra Morena colonies had either died or gone home. The heat was unbearable to many of the northerners, though according to the English traveller Swinburne the fatalities were caused mainly by 'eating unwholesome herbs, and drinking too much wine and brandy'. Those who remained married Spaniards, and gradually lost touch with their origins. By Bourgoing's day, a good twelve years had passed since the village had had any German-speaking priest. George

Borrow, during his travels around Spain in the 1830s, came across a family of German descent and was surprised by how they had forgotten the language and all the traditions of their ancestors. That La Carolina had had foreign settlers at all, and that it had been an experimental community of relatively recent foundation, was apparently unknown to one English traveller, William Pitt Byrne, who passed through the place in the 1860s. 'What a quaint old town it was,' he enthused. Pitt Byrne was one of the many travellers who had suffered the intoxicating effects of the Despeñaperros crossing and had come to see everything through an oriental haze. 'The street architecture,' he wrote of La Carolina, 'was, to a certain extent, Moorish, and the mud walls, denuded *ventas*, jealously caged ground floor windows, mysterious arched entrances, and colonnaded *solanos*, contributed to its oriental character.'

The province which you reach at Despeñaperros is that of Jaén, only a three-hour journey by car from Madrid and yet perhaps one of the least-known parts of Andalusia. From La Carolina, as from the many villages in Jaén province with magnificent vantage points, you are confronted by an endless rolling landscape of red and white earth studded with regular lines of olive trees. There are, lovers of statistics might like to know, over 150,000 olive trees in the province, making the place the largest olive-growing district in Spain. No landscape, you might think, could be more Andalusian, and you feel that it is only natural that in the middle of all these olives, in Jaén capital, was baptized one of the Andalusians best known abroad, the guitarist Andrés Segovia. But Jaén province has actually as much of the character of Castile as it does of Andalusia, and this ambiguous position between the two regions seems even reflected in the Moorish name for Jaén, 'Geen', 'the caravan route'. The impressive yet monotonous regularity of the countryside has a note of Castilian sobriety, as do many of the province's towns and villages. The architecture is often heavy and sombre, quite unlike that of other parts of Andalusia. The twin towns of Úbeda and Baeza, two of the finest architectural showpieces of southern Spain, are filled with red stone Renaissance palaces and churches that are completely Castilian in type. Appropriately, the poet, monk and leading exponent of the Castilian mystical tradition, Juan de la Cruz, died at Úbeda, while at Baeza the Seville-born poet Antonio Machado completed in 1917 one of the greatest books of poems ever dedicated to Castile, the *Campos de Castilla.*

While it is difficult to travel in European regions such as Provence or Tuscany without thinking of the painters who have worked there, in Andalusia it is the memories of poets that are everywhere present. In Baeza, the dark little schoolroom where Machado taught has been preserved as a charming, dusty and little-visited memorial to him, and, on the edge of the town, the path where the poet loved to walk has been renamed the Paseo Antonio Machado. Here you will find a statue to Machado, the poet's features turned east towards a landscape which often features in his work, a grandiose landscape rising up into a massive mountain wall formed by the parallel sierras of Cazorla and Segura.

This mountainous expanse, Spain's largest National Park, is the main natural attraction of Jaén province and one of the great wildernesses of Europe, with ibex, deer and lynx. The attractive small town of Cazorla, directly facing Baeza on the lower eastern slopes of the Cazorla range, is now a popular summer resort, and within the National Park are such tourist attractions as nature trails and a wildlife park. Up to the 1950s there were scarcely any visitors at all to this area, and a French geographer, Dr Bide, describing in the Alpine Club Annual of 1902 a climb up to the nearby peak of Mount Sagra, just to the west of the Segura range, relates the great difficulties that he had in crossing this forested and practically roadless part of Spain. Even today it is easy to shake off all other tourists, as you will probably find out if you decide to enter the Park by the rough track which leads up to the mountains from the road south from Cazorla to Quesada (see page 326). Soon you leave behind the ubiquitous olive fields of Jaén – the terrifying extent of which becomes more apparent than ever in the panoramic views to be had from this steeply winding road – and then enter a dense forest of pines. The forest spreads up to the top of the Cazorla range and down into the long narrow valley which separates the range from that of Segura. Descending into this forested, unpopulated valley, you will find yourself near the source of the rushing mountain stream which runs the whole length of it. The world you are in seems more Appalachian than Andalusian, but the stream in front of you turns into the river which once gave Andalusia its name. This is the river the Romans called Betis, and the

Moors renamed Guad-al-Quivir, 'the Great River'. Born in the north-eastern corner of Andalusia, and dying by Andalusia's Atlantic coast, it is a river entirely contained by the region, and the most important river in Spain. The ships that once plied it, laden with the region's abundant products and later with riches from the Indies, turned it into a symbol of Andalusia's wealth and greatness, and as such it has always been praised by poets. In the rock face above its source are inscribed famous lines by the Golden Age poet Luis de Góngora:

> Oh great river, great king of Spain
> with your noble if not golden sands . . .

Góngora came from Córdoba, and these lines are taken from a poem dedicated to his home town and its surroundings. Córdoba province adjoins Jaén, and sees the Guadalquivir valley opening up, the arable lands or *campaña* becoming yet more fertile. Jaén's olive belt expands into this province, and covers much of its southern half, but there are more signs of other cultivation here, for instance great expanses of wheat, brilliant yellow patches of sunflowers, orchards of oranges, cotton fields, and, around Montilla, extensive vineyards. Góngora's poem continues:

> Oh fertile plain, oh soaring hills
> furrowed by the sky and gilded by the day . . .

To Góngora this countryside was Arcadia, and in later life he retired to an isolated property outside Córdoba to find inspiration for his pastoral masterpiece, *The Solitudes*. Another writer to view the Córdoba landscape in terms of a pastoral idyll was the nineteenth-century novelist Juan Valera, who was born and brought up in the town of Cabra, in the south of the province. In his study of the women of Córdoba, *La Córdobesa*, Valera wrote: '. . . the fertile lands of Cabra are a paradise. There, if only mythology was in fashion, we could say that Pamona placed her throne, and, continuing in the same vein, and without the slightest exaggeration, we could add that Pallas has her own throne in the Hermitages [above Córdoba, see page 272], Ceres hers in the fields that stretch between Baena and Valenzuela, and Bacchus his in Los Moriles, the wine of which is far superior to that of all Jerez.' The villages of Cabra, Baena and Doña Mencía, where Valera set most of his novels of provincial life, mark the transition between the Guadalquivir valley and the foothills of Andalusia's southern ranges. They herald what might be called the most classical landscape of Andalusia. From here down into the provinces of Málaga and Granada extends a landscape of wheat- and olive-covered slopes alternating with bare, arid hills and sharp outcrops of rock, the whole intercut with winding ravines lined on their lower slopes with lush vegetation. This is a noble countryside structured like a landscape painting by a seventeenth-century artist such as Poussin, a world in which a pipe-playing goatherd would not seem out of place.

Córdoba province cannot be and has not always been seen in the idyllic light evoked by Góngora and Valera. Even along the Guadalquivir valley, almost up to Seville, there were dangerous desert-like stretches, two of Olavide's colonies, La Carlota and La Luisiana (Seville), being established next to two such notorious areas, the *desiertos* of La Parilla and Moncloa. The sad, lonely quality which many find in Jaén province can also be found in that of Córdoba. The town of Córdoba, with its cheerful white houses and flower-filled balconies, has come for many to express Andalusian gaiety, but the traditional view of the place is that of a melancholy, abandoned town. 'Córdoba, distant and lonely' begins a famous poem by García Lorca. Directly above the town, hugging the northern banks of the Guadalquivir from Jaén province almost up to the town of Seville, looms the range of the Sierra Morena. The slopes above Córdoba, in which are situated the Hermitages mentioned by Valera, are as verdant as those above Florence, but if you go beyond them you will reach one of the saddest districts in all Andalusia. Much of this northern half of Córdoba province is mountainous scrub-land with a scattering of decaying, ugly towns such as Pozoblanco and Peñarroya Pueblonuevo, the latter a once prosperous mining town now left to ruin following the exhaustion of its coal mines by a French company. Just to the west of Peñarroya is the Fuente Obejuna of Lope de Vega fame, while to the north, in the northernmost tip of Andalusia, is the village of Belalcázar, a place of enormous architectural interest but virtually unvisited, its historical monuments collapsing and its population rapidly dwindling (see pages 256–8). In terms of architecture and atmosphere, there is even less of Andalusia in northern Córdoba than there is in Jaén. 'Although Pozoblanco belongs to the province of Córdoba,' wrote Gerald Brenan, 'it cannot be said to lie in Andalusia.

That low step up from the Guadalquivir valley to the *meseta* lands one in an altogether different geographical and ethnic region. Take architecture. The houses with their deep windows and granite lintels look cold and severe . . .'

From Fuente Obejuna a little used road through wild countryside, the C421, heads along the Sierra Morena in a south-westerly direction, into the province of Seville. Almost at the border between Córdoba and Seville provinces, the mountain scenery changes from bare and shrub-covered slopes to others thick with oaks. The landscape is now mellow and welcoming, and the area is in fact a popular weekend and summer retreat for the people of Seville. The transformation which the Sierra Morena undergoes as it enters Seville province is symptomatic of the whole character of this province, which is the very opposite of austere. Seville itself lies just to the south of the Sierra, at the fertile heart of the Guadalquivir basin. The heat intensifies as does the humidity, and at the height of summer not even the night brings any slackening of these conditions. Despite this, Seville and its surroundings have always been thought to encapsulate all the fertility and sensuality of Andalusia. In an essay on Don Juan (1921), Ortega y Gasset reflected that this libertine could not possibly have come from any other part of Spain, and that the environment induced in its inhabitants and visitors a perpetual, half-drunken state. Today the old town of Seville has been enveloped by a large industrial and residential belt, but up to the end of the nineteenth century it stood surrounded by its medieval walls in the middle of a countryside which must have seemed like a great orchard. Dundas Murray, an English traveller of the 1840s, wrote that Seville was the 'Queen of Andalusia', and that 'her presence is aroused [in the visitor] by his entering a cloud of fragrance exhaled by her girdle of orange-groves; so heavy and luscious are the odours of this zone, that the senses feel oppressed.' Given the countless romantic descriptions of Seville such as these, it needed someone as down-to-earth as Richard Ford to point out that the odours that sometimes dominated the town were rather less sweet than those of oranges. In the early nineteenth century, in the interests of improving the navigability of the Guadalquivir, the river was diverted by a channel to the west of the town, and the much admired stretch which divides old Seville from the former separate township of Triana was blocked up at one end, thus turning it into a long stagnant backwater. Even today, in the summer months, romantic feelings inspired by Seville are tempered somewhat by the rank, all-pervasive smells coming from the river.

Just above Seville the Guadalquivir heads away from the Sierra Morena and turns sharply south towards the sea, into which, to use a word of George Borrow, it 'disembogues' at Sanlúcar de Barrameda. Dundas Murray, though enraptured by Seville and its province, could not raise much enthusiasm for the Guadalquivir, particularly in its last stages, when it runs through unrelievedly flat, marshy terrain. He wrote of the stretch below Seville that 'its tide is dull, its water cloudy, its current lingering, and its banks canal-like and low . . . it divests itself by degrees of every feature of beauty till it becomes little else than a mighty drain, meandering leisurely through a vast flat'. Today occasional pleasure boats ply the stretch between Seville and Sanlúcar, and though the journey is tedious at times and very long (up to eight hours if the tide is low), you experience a certain haunting feeling as you gradually leave all villages and houses behind, eventually to pass, on the right bank of the river, a mysterious barrier of pines. The sense of mystery is compounded by the knowledge that behind these pines lies another of Andalusia's famed wildernesses, the Coto Doñana.

'Directly in front,' wrote Dundas Murray, 'was a tract of land that, from its singular contrast to the surrounding scenery, instantly arrested our eyes. "That," said our guide, "is the Coto of San Lucar [Coto Doñana]; it is a *despoblado* [empty area], and extends backwards from the river for seven or eight leagues; a lonely place it is, and as full of deer, wild boars and mountain cats, as the sea is full of fish; vaya! in all Spain there is no better place for game than the Coto of San Lucar."' His interest thus aroused, Dundas Murray felt compelled to visit the place. 'My acquaintance with Andalusia,' he explained, 'having been as yet confined to its ancient cities and still more ancient roads, I was anxious to see something of its wilds; and this desolate expanse of sand and forest – a fragment, apparently, of some African desert, cast by a convulsion of nature on the shores of Spain – was just one of those solitudes with which the province was said to abound, and which I had long desired to explore.'

The Coto Doñana is a roadless expanse of about 67,000 acres, bordered to the south by the Guadalquivir and to the west by the Atlantic. It comprises three main types of terrain. There are the pine forests, which are popularly thought to have provided the wood for the Spanish Armada and which were at one time far more extensive than they are now, having been brutally decimated in the early years of this century. Then there are the sand dunes, so wild and grand that they were even able to provide some of the settings for the film *Lawrence of Arabia*. Finally come the great expanses of marshland and lakes, reduced in the summer months to a sinister desert of cracked mud. As with the Camargue – the geographically comparable wilderness formed by the estuary of the Rhône in the South of France – the Coto Doñana is a Mecca for naturalists. As in Dundas Murray's day, you will find here wild cats, otters, lynx, wild cattle, the occasional wolf, and an abundance of wild boar and red and fallow deer, the Coto being the only place in Spain where red deer live permanently in a lowland area. Flamingo flocks land here in the spring, and you can also see such birds as egrets, kites, bee-eaters, hoopoes, vultures, and, if you are lucky, Spain's rarest bird, the imperial eagle. Among the only signs of human habitation in the Coto are a group of primitive stick and mud dwellings in the forest overlooking the Guadalquivir: these belong to charcoal-burners and to some of the boatmen who ferry people over the river from Sanlúcar. Nearby is a charming neo-gothic summer villa built in the late nineteenth century and known as the Palacio de las Marismillas. But the main residence in the Coto is the isolated former hunting lodge of the Dukes of Medina Sidonia.

For over 500 years the Coto was a hunting reserve to these Dukes, whose family home was at Sanlúcar. Their estate, which was originally known as that of 'Doña Ana' in homage to a wife of one of the Dukes, was first mentioned in a document of 1495 in which the 3rd Duke requested that the people of Sanlúcar obtain 'as many deer and stags as possible' for the restocking of the forest. From the seventeenth up to the nineteenth centuries all the kings of Spain came to hunt here, the most important visit being that of Philip IV in 1624, in whose honour the original hunting lodge, the Casa del Bosque, was enlarged into the present palace. One of the many distinguished guests to have stayed in the palace is thought to have been Goya, who might have painted here his portraits of the *Maja vestida* and *Maja desnuda*. In the 1880s there hunted at the Coto an Englishman called Abel Chapman, later the co-author of *Wild Spain* (1893) and *Unexplored Spain* (1910). These two books were essentially manuals for the hunter, but they were also among the first serious studies of the life of Spain's wildernesses. Chapman was the first to emphasize the importance of the Coto as a causeway for birds migrating between North Africa and the coast of Western Europe; he also published in *The Ibis* of 1884 an article which must certainly have heightened the mystique of this strange area. This article met with incredulity in England, dealing as it did with the sighting in the Coto of wild camels, and aquatic ones at that, which rushed at high speed across the swamps, creating clouds of spray. These camels were not the product of an over-imaginative mind but instead the offspring of a group of eighty camels brought over in 1820 from the Canary Islands to Cádiz by the Marquis of Villafranca. The Marquis's intention was to use these beasts as pack animals and for ploughing, but such was the fear which they inspired and their uselessness with the plough that in the end they were let loose in the Coto, where they successfully bred. Sixty remained in Chapman's day, but by 1950 there were only five, the majority of the camels having been caught and sold off as venison. Though a few more were brought in during the filming of *Lawrence of Arabia*, there are none surviving today.

In 1901 the Coto Doñana was sold by the Medina Sidonias to the 'sherry baron' William Garvey, who supposedly recouped his investment in two years from the selling off of the Coto's pines. Successive purchases reduced the Coto to its present size, and caused growing concern about the future of this wild-life paradise. In 1958 another Englishman, Guy Mountfort, published *Portrait of a Wilderness*, a book which did much to draw world attention to the plight of the Coto. A result of this was the setting up in 1961 of the World Wildlife Fund, which four years later succeeded in persuading the Spanish authorities to turn the Coto into a National Park, thus stopping a projected highway across it and a large holiday camp along its coastline. Today it is possible to swim and even to drive your own car along its long and dirty Atlantic beach, but to visit the interior you are obliged either to take one of the slow and frankly boring Landrover tours organized by the Park authorities, or to ask beforehand for special permission, which is usually granted only to serious naturalists (see page 332). Many a time, lying on the Coto's beach, I was tempted to make illicit forays into the interior, and, one late afternoon, actually did so, only to be turned back five minutes later, not by Park

guards or by soldiers (for the palace is now sometimes used as a retreat for the Spanish president), but by a vicious cloud of mosquitoes.

The Guadalquivir, as it passes by the Coto Doñana, goes alongside
three of Andalusia's provinces: that of Seville gives way to those of
Huelva and Cádiz, which are divided from each other by the river.
Huelva is Andalusia's westernmost province, and extends up to the
Portuguese border. It falls into two distinct geographical areas. Much
of its southern coastal half is flat, sandy country coated with pines,
and very reminiscent of the large, forested coastal stretch of Les
Landes in south-western France; near the Portuguese border you come
to rich strawberry country, a cultivation of recent date which has
turned the town of Lepe – hitherto famous mainly as the butt of many
an Andalusian joke – into one of the wealthiest communities in Spain.
The northern half of the province takes in the western end of the
Sierra Morena, and is almost continuously mountainous and wooded.
At the centre of this district is the beautiful Sierra de Aracena, the
slopes of which abound in pines, oaks, chestnuts, apples, pears and
recently planted eucalyptus trees; pigs thrive on the chestnuts, and the
village of Jabugo produces many of the best hams in Spain. The
mountains throughout northern Huelva are gently rounded and without dramatic features such as tall rocky outcrops or deep gorges.
Their beauty comes from their wild extensiveness and rich mantle of
trees. Arias Montano, a sixteenth-century poet and theologian who
had worked in the Escorial, ended his days in the hermitage of
Nuestra Señora de los Angeles, enjoying one of the finest views to be
had of this landscape, a view made up of an apparently infinite
succession of undulating, dark green silhouettes. A Jesuit missionary
visiting the area in Montano's day was struck by its wild primitive
aspect and the poverty of its inhabitants, whose Spanish was almost
impossible to understand. The villages here, with houses crowned by
quaintly irregular wooden galleries, are silent secretive places hidden
among the trees. Their tourist potential is only now beginning to be
realized, and weekenders have started coming here from Seville,
which is little more than an hour's drive away. More ominously, a
handful of English people have bought houses in the area, believing
this to be one of the most attractive, least spoilt areas of southern
Spain. The English have always been adventurous in their tastes, but
the pioneering few have generally been the vanguard of a large-scale

invasion, and it is quite possible that within a decade or so the quiet villages of northern Huelva will be filled with English voices.

The English have already left their mark on this district, quite literally so. The one major interruption in the forested landscape occurs just below the Sierra de Aracena, and takes the form of a gigantic cavity wrinkled by deep, terraced fissures. The steep slopes, turning at sunset from dusty pink to vermilion, are striped with bright green rivulets that on the oxidization of the iron in their water by contact with the air change colour and form at the bottom of this infernal landscape what appears to be a meandering stream of blood. The river is the Río Tinto or 'Red River', and gives its name to what are perhaps the oldest worked mines in the world. Popular tradition has it that these were the fabled mines of King Solomon, and there is still a section of them known as the Cerro Salomón, a name from which is also derived the names of the nearby villages, Zalamea la Vieja (now known as Nerva), and Zalamea la Real. The Phoenicians and the Romans extensively exploited the mines, but these were afterwards abandoned, and rediscovered only in 1556 as a result of a search for mines instigated by Philip II with a view to replenishing the coffers of the Spanish crown. The search party, led by one Francisco Mendoza, was taken by a local guide to a large cave, in which they found impressive evidence of ancient workings. But for some reason the mines were not reopened until 1724, and even then they were not exploited as successfully as they could have been. This was not to happen until after their sale to the British in 1873.

With the arrival of the British at Río Tinto there begins a curious chapter in the history of Huelva province. The company which bought the mines, though employing local labour, had an engineering and managerial staff which became increasingly British in its make-up, having in 1902 a ratio of sixty-four British members to only six Spanish ones. At the same time a growing rift developed between the two communities. Almost from the start the British at Río Tinto lived largely apart from the Spaniards, constructing on top of a wooded hill a group of tall Victorian villas based on suburban English prototypes, the only difference being that Spanish stone was used instead of English brick; after 1891 this community, known as Bella Vista, was served by a neo-gothic Presbyterian church, with a simple white interior completely at variance with local architectural tastes. The

British community at Río Tinto was referred to by the Spaniards as the 'Colonia Inglesa', and the life they led there was certainly comparable to that of the British colony in India. Spaniards tended to be called disparagingly 'the natives', and were rigorously excluded from Bella Vista, which was protected by guarded gates. The British were actively discouraged from marrying Spanish women, and those that did so were no longer allowed to live within the colony. The one positive British contribution to Spanish life was the introduction of football, but otherwise the traditions that the British brought to Río Tinto must have seemed to the Spaniards at best bizarre, for instance the activities commemorating Queen Victoria's birthday, such as the egg-and-spoon race. Today it is possible to smile at stories of the British rule in Huelva province, but similar stories could easily be told of the British and other foreign communities that from the 1950s onwards have begun to take over the Andalusian coast and the villages behind it.

Contrary to what is often thought, Spain's southern coast is as yet not entirely dominated by foreigners or by high-rise development, and it is still possible to find quiet, little-spoilt and beautiful beaches. The Atlantic coast of Andalusia, the so-called Costa de Luz or 'Coast of Light', has certainly not suffered to the same degree as the adjoining Costa del Sol. The Huelva section of this coast remains popular largely with Spaniards, and is known for its extensive sandy beaches lined with pines: though tourist development is rapidly expanding, there are still beaches where you can be on your own and out of sight of any buildings, for instance the Playa de Canela and the narrow sandbank or *barra* of El Rompido, best reached by boat (see page 250). The coast of Cádiz province begins at Sanlúcar de Barrameda, an enchanting old town with a quite special atmosphere, though with beaches polluted by being at the mouth of the Guadalquivir. The small area which extends east from here to Jerez and south to El Puerto de Santa María is sherry country, and is flat and densely agricultural. The coastline is uninspired, with few trees and no cliffs, but with noisy resorts such as Chipiona and Rota, the latter booming with American voices from its controversial NATO base. South from Rota is Cádiz itself, one of the most animated and beautiful towns of Andalusia, but in the middle of a stretch of coast which combines, inexplicably, intense tourism with heavy industrialization. It is only in the southern half of Cádiz province that the scenery of the Costa de Luz begins again to excite. South of the pretty white coastal village of Conil de la Frontera, flat agricultural country is succeeded by the foothills of the Serranía de Ronda, which fall, uncultivated, down to the sea. The coast between Trafalgar and Tarifa, where the Costa del Sol begins, is one of the most attractive in southern Spain, with pine-covered slopes, steep cliffs, wide empty bays, and sweeping sand dunes (see page 255). Germans and nudists have taken to this coast in increasing numbers, but tourism here is relatively unobtrusive, and there are villages such as Barbate and Zahara de los Atunes where the fishing industry clearly predominates. That this area continues to be so unspoilt is due both to the fact that the Spanish army occupies much of the land between Barbate and Tarifa and to the Levante wind, which is especially notorious here. This wind might create ideal conditions for wind-surfers – and at Tarifa, where the wind is strongest, there is indeed an important wind-surfing school – but it often makes it impossible to lie comfortably on the beach.

The rest of the Andalusian coast, from Tarifa eastwards, is backed by high mountains, the wildness of which forms a striking contrast to most of the coastal resorts below. The Serranía de Ronda covers much of both Cádiz and Málaga provinces, and was one of the areas of Andalusia most admired by Romantic travellers. These limestone mountains are savagely shaped, bare peaks and rocky crags jut out from wild woods and slopes lush with Mediterranean vegetation, villages perch like eagle-nests, and perilous ravines pock-marked with caves open up at every turn. This is classic bandit country, and it is also a landscape which has always greatly appealed to the English, whose tastes have been governed for so long by nineteenth-century notions of the Picturesque. Richard Ford enthused over the dramatically situated town of Ronda, and since then the English have flocked there, even owning for a while its luxurious late nineteenth-century hotel, the Hotel Reina Victoria. More recently the English have begun to buy up houses in the pretty villages that abound in the area. One such place is the spectacular, isolated village of Gaucín, which appears superficially to have changed little since the time when it was a famous bandit's lair. I was walking admiringly through its streets when I noticed a sign in English advertising for a Trivial Pursuit Society. Soon afterwards the Sevillian friend I was with entered a bar and failed to make herself understood, for it turned out that the barman was English. Later a local boy asked if we were both English ('All strangers who come here are,' he said), and then pointed to a street which had only one Spanish family still living in it. At nearby Jimena de la Frontera, someone has quite rightly scrawled in large letters on one of the walls, *'Pronto los Jimenatos serán los extranjeros'* ('Soon the people of Jimena will be the foreigners').

The anglicization of the Serranía de Ronda is at least discreet, which is definitely not the case with the Costa del Sol, the name for the coast in between Tarifa and the frontier of Almería province. The English presence on the coast dates back to 1704, when Sir George Rooke and Sir Clowdisley Shovell hoisted the British flag on the massive Rock of Gibraltar; the Rock has been a British possession ever since. A visit to this place is a curious and potentially depressing experience, for you are suddenly confronted with British food and other products that you might well have come to Spain to forget about, and also with some of the worst and dingiest examples of British architecture and design of *circa* 1960. 'One moment,' wrote Gautier in 1841, 'you were in Andalusia, and the next you are in England. From the Moorish towns of the Kingdom of Granada and Murcia, you land all of a sudden in Ramsgate.' Gautier had finally been jolted out of the oriental reverie which had accompanied him since Despeñaperros, and knew that the time had come for him to go home. He went on caustically to observe: '. . . wherever an Englishman goes to, he lives exactly as he would in London; he needs his tea, his rump steaks, his rhubarb pies, his port and sherry if he is well, and camomile if he is ill.' The truth of this observation is borne out by the crowds of English residents in Andalusia who regularly descend on Gibraltar to do their shopping.

Tourism along the Costa del Sol was at first limited to the town of Málaga, which, with its temperate winter climate, became a popular wintering resort for the English from the early nineteenth century, and had the first English cemetery in Spain (founded in 1830). Outside Málaga the only luxurious hotel on the coast was for many years the Reina Cristina in Algeciras, which was built after the completion of the railway line to the town in 1873. The rest of the coast remained poor and neglected well into this century. 'The Costa del Sol they call this now,' reflected an old man from Mijas, 'the hunger coast is what it used to be.' After the Second World War English residents from Gibraltar took to using the unspoilt beaches between the Rock and Málaga, and in the 1950s parts of the coast became frequented by beatniks; finally, by the early 1960s, Franco's Minister for Tourism, Manuel Fraga, had given the go-ahead for the coast's full-scale exploitation. Today the stretch between Estepona and Málaga is a virtually uninterrupted series of high-rise buildings joined together by one of Europe's busiest and most dangerous roads. The English were at one time clearly in the majority, but other nationalities are now effectively imposing their own cultures, in particular the Germans and the Scandinavians.

East along the coast from Málaga, high-rise development is slightly less obtrusive, and east from Nerja and into Granada province, the resorts become more dispersed as the coastal road winds its way above impressive rocky bays. In recent years foreigners have moved in frightening numbers into the pretty villages such as Cómpeta and Frigiliana that cling to the steep slopes of the Sierra de Tejeda above Nerja; but beyond this range and throughout much of the interior of Granada province, you are again in unspoilt countryside where foreigners are few and far apart. The interior of Málaga province changes considerably from west to east, as the Serranía de Ronda is succeeded by the bleaker slate range of the Sierra Nevada. The picturesque gives way to the surreal, as in the extraordinary twisted rock formations – comparable in shape to those in Arizona's Bryce Canyon – that comprise the National Park of El Torcal above Málaga. The increasingly arid look of much of the interior as you move east towards Almería contrasts with the areas of sub-tropical cultivation along the coast, such as the *vegas* or fertile plains of Málaga and Motril, which luxuriate in oranges, lemons, sweet muscatel grapes, sugar-cane, custard apples and prickly pears.

Granada province is the Andalusian province with the sharpest contrasts, and brings together the full range of Andalusia's scenery from fertile plains to high mountains and eroded wasteland. Granada is situated sixty-seven kilometres to the north of the coast, at the eastern end of a long narrow *vega* which the Moors irrigated and planted with extensive wheat and tobacco fields. The view to the south-east is taken up by the highest peaks of the Sierra Nevada range, Mulhacén and the Pico Veleta, which are snowcapped for most of the year. García Lorca was born in the *vega*, spent much of his life there, and was executed probably in a lonely mountain spot overlooking it. In common with most Romantic travellers to Granada he viewed the landscape with nostalgia, sensing that with the departure of the Moors it had acquired an underlying melancholy. He evoked too in his poetry the enclosed, isolated character of this province, a character which highlights the openness of that of Seville. One of his poems, entitled the 'The Ballad of the Three Rivers', contrasts the navigable Guadalquivir with the Darro and the Genil, two of the rivers that descend from the Sierra Nevada into the *vega*:

> For the sailing boat
> Seville has a passage,
> Through the waters of Granada there row only sighs . . .

The part of the province with perhaps the saddest and most isolated feel to it is the Alpujarra, which lies on the other side of the Sierra Nevada to the *vega*. The easiest approach is to take the main road south from Granada and then head east into it from near the spa resort of Lanjarón. But a far more adventurous and spectacular route is to go over the top of the Sierra Nevada range, a route which is only practicable during the summer months. The peaks of Mulhacén and La Veleta, which are shown rising above Granada's Alhambra in countless picture postcards, have been endlessly admired, but, until recently, only too rarely climbed. When Gautier expressed a wish to go up Mulhacén, his friends from Granada warned him of the dangers, and tried hard, but to no avail, to dissuade him. Today there is an asphalted, well graded modern road which takes you almost to the summit of La Veleta, passing on the way a hideous new ski resort. The old route, which joins the new one about three-quarters of the way up the mountain, is a steep, rocky road just about manageable for those travelling in a strong car: it is still known by its original name, the Camino de los Neveros (the Road of the Snowfields), and was once used almost exclusively by the men who made their living gathering snow to be used for storage and ice-creams. Whatever route you choose, you will be struck by the greyish-brown Icelandic barrenness of the mountain's upper slopes, and the contrast between these and the ever more distant deep green of the *vega* below. From the top of La Veleta you look south over a landscape resembling a dark, crumpled cloth. This is the Alpujarra, an undulating stretch of land in between the Sierra Nevada and the arid coastal ranges of La Contraviesa and Gádor. On clear days, from La Veleta, you can see the Mediterranean and even Africa.

The road descending from La Veleta is unasphalted all the way, narrow, unprotected and definitely not for drivers lacking confidence or a head for heights. The views from the treeless, uncomforting landscape which you have to go through are sublime in the true sense of the word, combining beauty with a tinge of terror. Before the descent proper begins you have to drive underneath the neighbouring peak of Mulahacén, which at 3,482 metres is nearly 100 metres higher than La Veleta, and the highest mountain in Spain; it is named after a Moorish king whose remains are popularly thought to be buried at its summit. As you descend you look directly down to distant Trevélez, famous for its hams and for being one of Europe's highest villages; but the first place you come to, after entering a belt of pine trees, is Capileira, at the top of the green, steeply descending river bank of the Poqueira. This village, and the two immediately below it, Bubión and Pampaneira, have been recently much prettified, and draw most of today's visitors to the Alpujarra. Lower down, the Alpujarra has a dustier look and the villages have a shabbiness and a lack of architectural sophistication reflective of the great poverty which this area has often known.

The Alpujarra is the part of Andalusia where Moorish influence has persisted longest. The place rose to importance under the Moors in the tenth century, when its slopes were terraced and planted with mulberry trees to supply the silk looms of nearby Almería. The Moorish settlers who flocked here during this period were mainly Berbers, who had been used to mountain living in their North African homeland; later, when the Arab population of Andalusia crowded into the Kingdom of Granada, it was above all the Berbers who favoured moving into the Alpujarra rather than into the towns. Even today the Alpujarra villages, in their layout and architecture, can be closely compared with Berber settlements in North Africa. The quaint cube-like houses, with whitewashed stone walls and painted wooden beams, are compactly arranged one above the other, their flat grey stone roofs sometimes acting as terraces to the houses above. The tapestry industry which the Berbers introduced has also been maintained to this day, even though the original geometrical Islamic patterns have been supplemented by lion, eagle and crown motifs from Christian times.

With the taking of Granada in 1492, the last Moorish king, Boabdil, was briefly exiled to the Alpujarra, and many other Moorish refugees came here too. Forcible conversion of the Moors, and other measures later taken against them, led in the sixteenth century to two major revolts in the Alpujarra. The quelling of the second of these, in 1568, resulted in the Moors being finally expelled from the area, their place being taken by settlers from the mountainous districts of Northern Spain. The silk culture was kept up until the early years of this century, but the Alpujarra became a forgotten district of Spain and from the seventeenth up to the late nineteenth century was scarcely visited. The first person to reawaken an interest in the area was the writer Pedro Alarcón, who came from the town of Guadix in eastern Granada and is best known outside Spain as the author of *The Three-Cornered Hat* (1874). In 1874 he published an account of a journey of his to the Alpujarra, a place which he said had been known until only a short while back only to its sons. 'So much was this the case,' he wrote in the book's prologue, 'that there was hardly a map which represented it with any accuracy, and that neither the foreigners who came from London or St Petersburg in search of Moorish associations, nor the Spanish poets who sung of these associations as of a priceless heritage, had ever penetrated into that labyrinth of cliff faces and chasms, in which each rock, each cave, each tree testified to an episode in the Saracen domination.' For nearly fifty years after Alarcón's book appeared, the Alpujarra remained only accessible on foot or mule, but this did not put off a young Englishman, Gerald Brenan, from coming here in 1920 in search of a quiet place to live. He bought a house in the village of Yegen, and kept this until 1934, receiving visits from Bloomsbury intellectuals such as Lytton Strachey and Virginia Woolf. His book *South from Granada* (1957), a record of these years and an excellent account of local history and folklore, finally secured the Alpujarra's international reputation. On his house at Yegen, a plaque commemorates 'the British hispanist who universalized the name of Yegen and the customs and traditions of the Alpujarra'.

At Yegen, which borders on Almería province, there comes into view a strange landscape. Eroded mountains, flat, arid wastes, and outright desert characterize almost the entire south-eastern corner of Andalusia. The northern boundary of this area is formed by Jaén's Sierra de Segura, which on its southern slopes becomes increasingly parched and then descends into a daunting, forsaken plateau. This belongs to Granada province, which in its northern half juts out to create a great wedge of land in between Jaén and Almería provinces. Off the N342, the main road which leads from Granada to the coast of Murcia, this is territory which has been virtually unvisited by the tourist. It is powerfully impressive country featuring ochre to pink expanses into which winding river courses have bitten like acid; along the narrow banks of dried-out streams cling oranges and palms, sheltering from the erosion which has eaten its way through the surrounding landscape. The gaping holes caused by erosion have been converted into cave dwellings, most famously at Guadix, which has a district which brings to mind the fantastically shaped troglodytic village of Goroemi in eastern Anatolia.

Cave dwellings are a notable feature of eastern Andalusia, and Granada province claims to have the highest number of inhabited caves in Europe. These caves were probably lived in during the Moorish period, but the first documented evidence of their habitation does not date until the sixteenth century. Thereafter travellers to Andalusia have rarely failed to comment on these dwellings, and have usually done so with a mixture of romantic fascination and revulsion, believing, quite wrongly, that the caves housed only the dirtiest and most poverty-stricken gypsies. Penelope Chetwode, describing a 1963 visit to Guadix, put matters right on this point: 'I would like above all to make it clear that the word "cave" is not synonymous with "slum" as some people in England seem to think. There are poor people and better-off people and some quite well-to-do people living in troglodyte colonies just as in any of our council estates; and most of the families living in them are of Spanish and not gypsy blood.' There is none the less no getting away from the fact that these caves, however affluent they might sometimes appear, suffer from humidity and lack of ventilation, and that these conditions have bred illnesses such as typhoid and tuberculosis. Since the 1950s the caves have begun slowly to be abandoned.

The desolate scenery of north-eastern Granada is continued into

Almería province, and, on the southern side of the mournful Sierra de los Filabres, turns into Europe's most remarkable desert. Between Tabernas and Sorbas even the reassuring oasis-like vegetation of the river courses dies out. No part of Andalusia looks more African than Almería, though its desert has been exploited by film-makers less for this than for its similarities with America's Wild West: at Tabernas you can visit 'Mini Hollywood', an American town constructed originally for Clint Eastwood's *A Fistful of Dollars* and later used for various other 'spaghetti westerns'. The writer Juan Goytisolo fell in love with the Almería desert on his first visit here in the early 1950s. Stopping for a drink in a bar at Sorbas, he could not contain his enthusiasm any longer. 'It's the most beautiful landscape in the world,' he blurted out. But the barman reacted in a way which Goytisolo had not expected. He stopped what he was doing, stared reproachfully at the writer, and replied in a voice which Goytisolo was never to forget: 'For us, sir, it is an accursed country.'

Almería can be a very depressing province, and this might well be your first impression of the place if you drive to it along the coastal road from Málaga. Adra, the first town you come to across the Almería border, is dirty, modern and menacing. Its inhabitants, so unlike the Andalusians in general, appear to have as little enthusiasm for their town as do its visitors: 'You've landed in a shit-hole of a place,' one surly Adra youth told me. The impression of poverty which Adra and other nearby towns give is a misleading one, however, for the whole ugly stretch of land between here and the coastal town of Almería has become in recent years one of the wealthiest in Spain. This economic miracle has been brought about by what is known as the 'plastic culture', whereby much of the landscape has been covered by large sheets of plastic which both encourage much needed moisture and allow crops to ripen in the middle of winter. This might only be a short-term solution to Almería's problems, as it is feared that eventually the 'plastic culture' will drain the province completely of its scant water resources. In the meantime the newly acquired wealth has been accompanied by numerous psychological problems, and the suicide rate has risen dramatically. To keep up the heightened new productivity requires near constant work, and there is not sufficient time nor are there the proper amenities to allow the people to enjoy the money they have earned. The one major release has been gambling, the stakes of which have become increasingly preposterous, even to the extent of gambling away wives.

Interesting though the town of Almería itself is, it comes as a relief to leave behind all towns and continue east along what now becomes the wildest if also bleakest coast of Andalusia. A mere half hour's drive from Almería is the extraordinary mountainous peninsula known as the Cabo de Gata, where bleached bare rock falls directly into the sea. The road ceases to be asphalted shortly after passing the cape's tip, and between the tiny, little-spoilt resorts of Las Negras and Agua Amarga it disintegrates into a rock-strewn track suitable really only for walkers. The Cabo de Gata has until recently been favoured largely by German hippies, and it is only to the north of here, around the town of Mojácar, that you meet up with the sort of coastal development that typifies most of the Costa del Sol.

Beyond Mojácar, almost before leaving Andalusia, you will pass a sign pointing to Palomares, a name which to many might have a familiar and sinister ring to it. Much of Almería province is how you would imagine the world to have looked like in prehistoric times, as well as how it might appear in the wake of a nuclear disaster. Appropriately enough, at Millares, near Almería town, is the largest Bronze Age site in Europe, while at Palomares there occurred, in January 1966, an accident which could have made the writing of this book unnecessary. An American bomber from the Rota base, fuelling in mid-air, collided against the plane which was helping it. Four bombs, each carrying sixteen times the explosive power of that of Hiroshima, fell near Palomares. Two landed intact, one into a river bed and another into the sea, but the other two directly hit the ground and their detonators went off. Safety devices fortunately prevented the actual plutonium and uranium from exploding, but the damaged bombs led to much radioactive leakage. The two intact bombs were recovered, the one which ended up in the sea bed only after a lengthy search and the help of a fisherman, Francisco Simó, who later received the local nickname, 'Paco of the bomb'. Before this happened, Manuel Fraga, in his capacity as Minister of Tourism and Information, was rushed to the scene and photographed in his bathing costume, bravely putting on a smile in the cold and potentially explosive waters. The future of Andalusia's budding tourist industry could not be jeopardized.

*

Richard Ford considered that no other part of Spain offered so much to the traveller as Andalusia, and the hurried tour of the region on which the reader has been taken over the previous pages has passed through landscapes of almost every conceivable type. Natural variety is reflected in the range of Andalusia's excellent if undeservedly little-known food, and is also matched by the wealth of the region's monuments, for, as Baron Taylor said in 1840, '. . . is not Spain the land of the arts; and is not Andalusia of all Spain that portion which has produced the noblest monuments of artistic excellence and inspiration?' But the fascination which Andalusia has exerted over generations of travellers has often been inspired less by the region's landscapes, products and monuments than by its people. Andalusia is possibly unique among European regions in having an appeal based to a very great extent on a romantic view of its inhabitants. There is something unquestionably exotic and non-European about the looks of many Andalusians, and there is also a deep-rooted paganism in the Andalusian character which is rarely to be found to the same degree elsewhere in Europe. What other European region, for instance, has such a strong and passionate tradition in dancing and singing as Andalusia, or such fanatical and exuberant religious celebrations? However, writers have loved to dwell on these folkloric and obviously picturesque aspects of Andalusian life without giving much serious thought to the mentality behind these activities. The interest taken in the Andalusians has also been a very partial one, an enormous bias having been shown towards marginal figures in Andalusian society, such as bandits, bull-fighters, musicians and gypsies. Moreover, from the time of Gerald Brenan, writers on Andalusia, deeply nostalgic about vanishing rural traditions, have been interested more in the life of Andalusia's villages than in that of its towns. Finally, the foreign view of the Andalusians has been influenced by the fact that the region gave birth to the world's two most famous sexual stereotypes, Carmen and Don Juan.

The study of Andalusian women, wrote a sociologist, David Gilmore, in 1987, 'is probably the most pressing unfinished task in Andalusian ethnography today'. If ethnographers have yet to write much about the women of the region, travel writers, novelists and poets have amply made up for the omission. Long before and long after Mérimée wrote his novella *Carmen* (1845), writers praised the

Andalusian woman as being the most beautiful in all Spain, if not Europe. Byron, who visited Spain in 1809, did much to promote this reputation:

> Oh never talk to me
> of northern climes, and British ladies,
> It has not been your lot to see,
> like me, the lovely girl of Cádiz . . .

Many British travellers, arriving at Cádiz from Britain, left their boats with hopes raised by Byron's poem, and were naturally often a trifle disappointed. George Dennis, who landed at Cádiz in 1839, found that Byron had greatly exaggerated the beauty of the local women, and that the 'darkness of the Spanish complexion contrasted unfavourably with the fair skins of the Devonshire and Cornish damsels'. By the end of his Andalusian stay, however, Dennis had got over his initial disappointment and was writing that 'the Andaluza takes precedence over all the women of Spain in point of beauty, grace and vivacity'. For a compatriot of Dennis, A. C. Andros, the sight in 1860 of a group of young women gliding over the gas-lit *paseo* of Seville had a quite overwhelming effect: 'My susceptible nature,' he wrote, 'is excited to such an alarming extent by the incomparable charms that I should tremble for the vows of celibacy made in dear phlegmatic old England, were my lot ever cast in the sunny climes of Andalusia.'

The physical attributes that made up the beauty of the Andalusian woman were frequently debated, but it was generally agreed that these were elegance of movement, and dark, expressive eyes; a reader of the London Library copy of Dennis's travels entered the debate by illegally pencilling in the margin of the book 'and teeth', and Mérimée encouraged a little-founded belief that Andalusian women were renowned for their small feet. All these various attributes were at any rate accompanied by a reputation for unbridled sensuality, a reputation which apparently goes back to classical times, when the lascivious dancing girls of Cádiz aroused much interest among the Romans. For Dennis, Andalusian women were more obsessed by 'love' than any other women he knew, and 'not pure exalted love but a much baser passion': 'I never was in the company of an Andaluza for ten minutes but the conversation was sure to turn upon *love*, to which she was generally the first to advert, either directly or otherwise.' 'The Andaluza,' Dennis concluded, 'has not the charms of a refined and cultivated intellect; she is little more than a beautiful animal.' The Andalusian woman, stripped of personality, intellect, and even clothes, is the constant subject of the turgid and crudely symbolic canvases of Julio Romero de Torres (1880–1930), to whom a whole dark and gloomy museum is devoted in the artist's native Córdoba. These works, in which the female nude is generally portrayed with great candour and set alongside fully clothed guitar players, bull-fighters or other such male Andalusian stereotypes, might strike the viewer as being little more than high kitsch, but they are immensely popular in Spain and have inspired many a writer, even such an intelligent one as the Sicilian Leonardo Sciascia (see page 271). For the Andalusian poet and Falange supporter José María Pemán, the women of Romero de Torres were expressive of the 'deepest soul of this land of Andalusia'.

When I stayed in Córdoba during the Franco period, the Romero de Torres museum was a popular place for the young men of the town to take newly arrived foreign girls, in whom the men then placed their main hopes of sexual adventure. For much of Spanish history, even up to the death of Franco, the sort of Andalusian beauty who featured in Romero de Torres's imagination tended not just to be unobtainable outside marriage but also protected from the physical advances of men by a code of behaviour unsurpassed in its rigidity anywhere in Europe. The aspect of Andalusian courtship which used to intrigue and amuse foreigners the most was the convention of men standing in the street and addressing or singing to their beloved through the iron grille of the window. Ford wrote that while the aristocracy was gradually abandoning this convention ('either the ladies' hearts are less cold or the nights more so'), the 'lower order continue the old caterwauling plan'; indeed the convention was to be practised well into this century. Of course there were those who maintained that the limitations of such courtship only intensified the erotic passion, and Ford himself noted that 'this metallic diet makes the lover as bold as fire-eating does elsewhere . . .' One of the more erotic scenes in Buñuel's film *That Obscure Object of Desire* was when the Carmen-like eponymous heroine (played alternatively by two actresses to intensify the illusiveness) teases the man who unsuccessfully desires her by writhing naked behind the iron grille to which he desperately clutches. Gerald Brenan, who must have been the last if not the only English writer to court a Spanish woman through window bars, showed how the outcome of such courtship was rather less glamorous than might have been imagined: when he eventually persuaded the exotic woman of his advances to meet him outside her house (in the company, of course, of a chaperone), he discovered that she was a lumpily formed midget who had been speaking to him standing on a chair. Angel Ganivet, a Granada writer of the late nineteenth century, strongly disapproved of the conventions that forced the Andalusian woman to spend so much of her time at home, and found that the cities of Northern Europe, cold and grey though they were, were more cheerful than the ones in Andalusia because the streets, shops and restaurants were filled with women. A society, like that of Finland, where a woman working in a sauna could show not the slightest concern while washing a naked Ganivet, was for Ganivet a more natural one than that of Andalusia (the healthy effects of Finnish society, however, were not sufficient to prevent the writer from eventually throwing himself into the Riva). Ganivet had also to admit that 'where there are no bolts to break, balconies to scale, third parties to bribe, no vigilants to outwit, there could never be a Don Juan Tenorio'.

The legendary figure of Carmen, dark, passionate, mysterious and cruel, meets her match in the tireless and cynical seducer, Don Juan. The original Don Juan was the hero of a play by the seventeenth-century dramatist Tirso de Molina, *The Joker of Seville*, which is sometimes thought to be based on the life of an aristocratic contemporary of the dramatist, Don Miguel de Mañara. The story of the man and his seductions was later taken up, among others, by Molière, Mozart, Dumas and the nineteenth-century Spanish writer Zorilla, and is still so popular in Spain that every year a production of the Zorilla play is put on in almost every Spanish town on All Souls' Day. The Zorilla version is the one chosen because the tone is cheerful, and the ending happy, with Don Juan deciding to reform his ways. However, it is not always so easy to make fun of the Andalusian type whom the Don Juan legend reflects. Andalusian men, like the women of the region, enjoy a reputation for their good looks, but they are also thought to epitomize Spanish machoism at its worst. With the

advent of modern psychology, the extreme machoism to be found in
Don Juan has sometimes been considered as a sign of latent homosexuality. In any case, there is a male type, particularly common in
Seville, who far prefers the company of other men to that of the
women whom he regularly seduces, and who exudes an ambiguous
sexuality. Good-looking and nattily dressed, he is the descendant of
the nineteenth-century *majo* or dandy, a figure who caught the imagination of the Romantic traveller.

While remaining gullible to all the romantic stereotypes of Andalusian society, from the bandit to the *majo*, travellers have maintained
at heart an ambivalent attitude towards the Andalusians. Every cliché
pertaining to Mediterranean peoples has been brought to bear on the
description of the Andalusian character, and the end result has not
always been very appealing. For though southerners are traditionally
passionate, voluptuous and reckless, they are also hysterical, lazy,
ostentatious, boastful and pleasure-loving. The Andalusians have often
been treated as ridiculous figures, just as have the Provençals or the
Calabrians. 'The Andalusians,' according to George Borrow, 'are in
general held in the lowest estimation by the rest of the Spaniards,' a
view with which Borrow was apparently in agreement: 'In a word, the
Andalusians, in all estimable traits of character, are as far below the
other Spaniards as the country which they inhabit is superior in beauty
and fertility to the other provinces of Spain.' Both Ford and Gerald
Brenan held a completely contrary view to this, and stressed in their
writings the great wit and sophistication of the Andalusians. For Ford,
they 'were, and always have been, the most elegant, refined and sensual
[inhabitants] of the peninsula': Brenan, contrasting the 'hard and dour'
peasants to be found in other parts of Spain with their 'lighter, more
mobile' Andalusian equivalent, wrote that 'at heart all Andalusians are
town dwellers, quick, emotional, talkative and artistic'. Numerous
travellers, Ford among them, have compared the Andalusians to the
Irish, and the comparison is an apt one, for the Irish, like the Andalusians, have been the butt of many a joke while at the same time
having a reputation for their sophisticated culture and rich poetic
tradition. Both the Andalusians and the Irish were for Ford 'impression-
able as children, heedless of results, calculatory of contingencies,
passive victims to violent impulse, gay, clever, good-humoured and
light-hearted, and the most subservient dupes of plausible nonsense'.

An Irishman of this century, Walter Starkie, recognized that the 'stage-Andalusian' is as much a figure of Andalusia as the 'stage-Irishman' is of Ireland, for the Andalusians have in general a love of playing up to what foreigners expect of them. Much of their life, it has been suggested, is a charade enacted for the benefit of tourists, and ruthlessly exploitative of every Andalusian cliché. The philosopher Ortega y Gasset, in an essay of 1921 entitled *The Theory of Andalusia*, attempted a radical assessment of the regional character. 'What is admirable, mysterious and profound about Andalusia,' he wrote, 'lies behind that multi-coloured farce which its inhabitants put on for the benefit of its tourists.' With great originality and eccentricity he proceeded to point out the similarities that exist between the Andalusians and the Chinese, similarities that go beyond the fact that Mandarins and bull-fighters both had pigtails. The Andalusians, like the Chinese, have had a history of passive resistance to the many foreign powers who have invaded their land. For Ortega y Gasset this was not a sign of cowardice, but of the inherent sophistication of the two races, both of which have always preferred peace to war, and have attached little importance to the role of the soldier in society. Foreigners, continued Ortega y Gasset, are overcome by the sensuality of the Andalusian climate and become convinced that the Andalusians must be a passionate, hot-blooded race, when in fact it is they themselves who are experiencing such violent emotions. The Andalusians have reacted to their climate in a completely opposite way to the foreigners, expending their emotions in the most economical way possible, developing a Chinese-like stoicism, and a sybaritic, serene contentment with their environment: '. . . instead of forcing himself to live, [the Andalusian] lives so as not to force himself, he makes the avoidance of effort the guiding principle of his existence.' In the end Ortega y Gasset's radical 'theory' of Andalusia turns out to be little more than an ingenious reassertion of the most harmful of all Andalusian clichés, namely that the Andalusians are all lazy.

'Please don't write that the Andalusians spend all their time drinking and enjoying themselves,' insisted a young Sevillian friend of mine at various stages during the research for this book. I am wary about making generalizations about the character of a particular race, but after only a few weeks in Seville I realized that the life I was leading and the people I was with apparently confirmed all the preconceptions about Andalusia that I was hoping to get away from. The woman I was staying with, Esperanza Flores, was a maker of *flamenco* costumes, and the daughter of an exporter of oranges. Her friends sang and danced at every opportunity, and drank in vast quantities. None were religious, though most of them were passionate devotees of the cult of the Virgin of Rocío (see page 159) and never missed any of Seville's important religious occasions. Above all their mentality was quite anarchic, and they gave little thought either to the future or to social responsibility. Esperanza had no bank account, and believed in spending money as soon as she earned it. An after-lunch drink would turn into an evening and night of *cachondeo*, a word, much used in Andalusia, denoting 'riotous fun'. Conversations took the form of endless jokes and funny stories, and vicious mockery of others. I rarely got to bed before dawn.

Esperanza and her friends represented of course only one aspect of Seville society, and an aspect which many of the city's younger inhabitants find increasingly anachronistic. Moreover, Seville is not Andalusia, no matter how much the Sevillians like to think that they represent all that is best and most characteristic about the region. The Andalusians themselves constantly remind you how the character of their people changes not just between one province and another, but between towns and villages, and even between districts of a town. You might be told that the people of Cádiz and Seville provinces are the wittiest in Andalusia, while those from Málaga and Córdoba are, respectively, the most open and boorish. Idiotic behaviour might be excused on the grounds that the person comes from Huelva. The inhabitants of Granada are frequently characterized as reactionary and bourgeois, and few people are happy to admit that they come from Jerez, which is renowned for its snobbery and arrogance. The villagers of Mairena del Alcor are unable to speak clearly, and the men of the Aljarafe are nearly all homosexuals. The upper and lower towns of Sanlúcar de Barrameda produce completely different types of person. And so on. You might easily dismiss all this as nonsense, but there are often good historical reasons to explain these apparently arbitrary assessments.

The difficulties of reaching any straightforward conclusions about the Andalusians are fully revealed as you begin to discuss the racial origins of these people. Who indeed are the Andalusians? The romantic view is that they are essentially Moors, with a strong admixture of Jewish blood. To these races have been attributed a wide range of characteristics, from guiltless sexuality to fantastical imagination, fatalism, underlying melancholy, and large sexual organs; unmistakably Moorish are the facial features of many of today's Andalusians. Yet, according to official versions of history, the Moors were all expelled from Andalusia and the region largely repopulated by Castilians, Galicians, Asturians and others from north of Despeñaperros. The complex ethnic make-up of the Andalusians was furthered by the later influx of settlers from outside Spain. The surviving Germans from the Sierra Morena colonies might soon have lost their languages and traditions, but they left a legacy of blond hair and blue eyes, as have many of the English and Irish who have moved to Spain in growing numbers since the Peninsular War. The marrying between foreigners and Andalusians has often created a strange racial hybrid. I once met the Marqués Carlos Pickman, a descendant of an English family which had founded a famous ceramics factory in Seville in the early nineteenth century. Tall and fair, he had the look of an English aristocrat, and spoke Spanish with an English accent, but English with a Spanish one: he had never lived in England.

Andalusian nationalists like to think that the Christian forces of the so-called 'Reconquest' tore out the cultural roots of their people, and prefer to ignore the racial transformation that Andalusia has undergone since the time of the conquering Christians. This attitude is romantic and unhistorical, but in attempting to explain what it is about Andalusia that makes the place so different from the rest of Spain, it is clearly vital to look into those traces of earlier culture that survived the Christian invasion. In trying to unravel the mystery of Andalusia, you cannot simply stop at the Moors, but are forced to go further and further back in time, past the Vandals, the Romans, the Greeks, the Phoenicians, and further still, back to the legendary civilization of the Tartessians.

2

FROM TARTESSUS TO GRANADA

The cultural roots of Andalusia lie buried in a past which has been distorted by myth and nostalgia. Andalusians and foreigners alike have fancifully imagined that in the formative years of the region's history there was an age of universal prosperity and enlightenment. The Romans identified this golden age with the Tartessians, just as later generations looked back longingly to the time of the Romans. After the sixteenth century writers and travellers began to glorify the period of Moorish domination, and by the nineteenth century the fascination with Moorish Andalusia had grown to such proportions that the Kingdom of Granada, where this civilization enjoyed its final flowering, had acquired a character almost as mythical as that of Tartessus.

The Moorish monuments of Andalusia have for a long time been the main attraction for the sightseer to the region, to such an extent that the monuments of earlier and later periods are as a whole remarkably little known. Few people, for instance, are aware that Andalusia is one of the richest archaeological areas of Europe. The search for Andalusia's ancient and prehistoric past will take you to wild and exceptionally beautiful places, sometimes to territory which seems scarcely to have been disturbed over the centuries. Most of the archaeological sites are poorly signposted, if signposted at all, many have been improperly excavated, and many more probably remain to be discovered; as yet there is no comprehensive catalogue of the sites, nor even any serious guide-book to direct you to them. The neglected condition of most of the sites will appal many a British traveller, and indeed the great difference in personality between the British and the Andalusians is clearly brought out in their respective attitudes towards their past. In Britain the Department of the Environment surrounds even the most minor archaeological sites with green wooden fences and neatly mown grass, establishes admission times and entrance fees, and puts up clearly laid out information panels. In Andalusia I have seen prehistoric dolmens used for storing farm equipment. A more caring approach towards monuments is developing in Andalusia, but in the meantime the future of many of these places is in jeopardy. The consolation is that the romantically inclined can find here an extraordinary continuity between past and present, and experience a sense of awe and wonder which is too often absent from Britain's well-tended sites.

I know of no other prehistoric cave paintings, still accessible to the public, that are so exciting to visit as those of the Cave of La Pileta, high up in the Serranía de Ronda. Even without its paintings, this is a special place: though tourists are coming here in growing numbers, it has yet to be commercialized in the same way as have some of Andalusia's many other famous caves, such as the Cave of Marvels at Aracena or the Cave of Nerja, both of which have been transformed by coloured lighting into what appear to be gaudy film sets. At La Pileta you can easily imagine what the place must have been like when used by prehistoric man, or when first entered in modern times. The cave was 'discovered' in 1905 by a farmer called José Cullon Lobato, and still remains in his family's possession, two of his nephews, José and Eloy, being the official guides. You reach it by climbing up a steep path carved into a calceous rock face, and at the entrance are presented with an old-fashioned gas lamp. There is no other lighting inside, and the tour lasts for over an hour. You are led first into a massive chamber, at the top of which, fluttering around a narrow opening to the sky, you can make out the dark, fluttering forms of literally hundreds of bats. The cave's discoverer had first been alerted to the cave by the sight of bats disappearing into the mountains, and had gone inside not out of curiosity but with a view to collecting bat droppings for his fields. Deep down into the cave he came across prehistoric paintings, and, in later years, as various other chambers were discovered, it became clear that La Pileta contained one of the more extensive series of rock paintings in Europe. You soon lose all sense of direction as you are led up and down, squeezing your way between rocks, slipping on steep watery slopes, and finding at almost every turn wonderfully preserved examples of the art of early man.

The dating of the La Pileta paintings is controversial, though it is generally thought that the beautifully naturalistic portrayals of goats, horses and other animals are of the late paleolithic period, while the near abstract drawings in black that cover in profusion the largest of the painted chambers date from neolithic times. The cave was probably a sanctuary, as caves of such depth would have been impracticable for habitation; at any rate, by the third millennium B C (the end of the neolithic period), humans had begun living in cane huts, and used caves mainly for religious or burial purposes. In 1870 mineral prospectors uncovered in a cave in the northern foothills of the Serranía de Ronda one of the eeriest and most telling examples of neolithic burial practice (see page 260). Immediately inside this cave, the Cueva de los Murciélagos, were three cadavers, one of which had a gold diadem. There were three more beyond, one wearing an esparto grass hat with traces of blood; further still was a group of twelve bodies, arranged in a semi-circle around a woman adorned with a collar of rings from which hung sea-shells. Fifty other bodies lay beyond, some in an apparently semi-mummified condition. Unfortunately the mining company which owned the cave later destroyed much of what was found, thus preventing further investigation. From the available evidence it has been concluded that the cave was the burial chamber of a powerful chief who had himself buried together with his servants and close associates so that he would not feel too lonely in his new state.

The paintings of La Pileta are almost certainly the oldest in Andalusia, and are the only ones known to have been executed deep down in a cave. The other so-called 'cave paintings' in the region are probably of the late neolithic period (c. 2000 B C) and are to be found in what should really be described as rock-shelters. The Abbé Breuil, the distinguished French scholar who studied the cave art of the Dordogne, was responsible in the early years of this century for publicizing two of the more important of these shelters, the Cueva de los Letreros near Vélez-Blanco, and the Cueva del Tajo de las Figuras near Benalup de Sidonia (see pages 353 and 309). The former, situated in an appropriately primeval-looking landscape of arid mountains, is now protected from the graffiti-writer by an iron grille. However, I was strongly recommended in Vélez-Blanco to bring with me a flask of water to throw at the paintings so as to bring out their colours; the present near-illegible state of the paintings is sad evidence of the frequency of this practice. The Cueva del Tajo de las Figuras is the more inaccessible of the two caves, and requires a certain skill at rock-climbing to reach (a rope is provided to help those less sure of foot). Yet even here the water-throwers have been at work, and the paintings are difficult to recognize as the ones described and drawn by the Abbé Breuil. Among the best preserved of the Andalusian shelter paintings are those of Loza Alta near Jimena de la Frontera, which are especially interesting because they include some of Europe's oldest known representations of boats (see page 297). The excellence of their condition, and the freshness of their colours, are due both to their very recent 'discovery' and to the fact that considerable determination and the services of a local guide are needed to get to them. An eight-kilometre climb up a non-asphalted mountain road is followed by a forty-minute trek through forest and undergrowth, eventually to clamber up, pursued by virulent horse-flies, and with legs bleeding, a sheer rock face. I was certainly surprised, having done this walk, to find attached to the shelter a beautifully written notice in Spanish and English, telling the visitor that the paintings are 'said to be over two thousand years old, please do not throw water over them or in any way deface them'. The notice is, and could only have been, the work of an Englishman. It is a solitary and valiant gesture, and you can only hope that it does not have the opposite effect to the one intended: drawing attention to the paintings' importance might be a deterrent in England, but in Spain this appears mainly to incite the potential defacer.

The wealth of Andalusia's prehistoric legacy is evident not just in its cave culture. On the outskirts of Antequera stand three dolmens, the oldest of which, that of Menga, is the largest such monument in Western Europe. First recorded in 1645, it was thought in the last century to be a meeting place for Druids. Dating back probably to the third millennium BC, it consists of a long white chamber formed of gigantic upright monoliths supporting equally massive slabs. Even more impressive, and in fact Andalusia's most extensive prehistoric site, is Los Millares, memorably located in the middle of a sinister, eroded landscape in Almería province. This site has been carbon-dated to around 2340 BC, and is Europe's largest Bronze Age settlement. Built on top of a wide rock escarpment formed by the confluence of two dried-up rivers, it is surrounded today by a vast metal fence and cannot be seen from the road. The site is not officially open to the public, nor in any way promoted, and the passing motorist might well think that a military rather than an archaeological site lies behind the fence. This encouraging evidence that steps are being taken to protect Andalusia's archaeological past is somewhat weakened when you discover that the key to this – one of the world's outstanding pre-historic sites – hangs above the bar in the nearby village of Santa Fe de Mondújar and can be had just for the asking. The key thus acquired, you are allowed to wander at will around the site in the knowledge that in the time you are there, no one else will be able to disturb the haunting peace of the place. The main site lies about a mile from the entrance gate and features a series of tombs in front of a walled citadel, inside which are the ruins of Bronze Age habitations. Finds from the site – many of which are displayed in the small but excellent archaeological museum at Almería – reveal a civilization living not just off hunting as in paleolithic times, but off the breeding of sheep, goats and pigs, vegetable and cereal culture, the manufacture of cheese and lard, and the making of jewellery and basketwork. Some of the finds also indicate commercial relations with other Mediterranean peoples, for instance a pair of ivory sandals believed to be Egyptian.

Who were the people of Los Millares, and who were their antecedents? The Roman scholar Agrippa wrote that the inhabitants of Betis were of African descent, and the earliest skulls to have been found in Andalusia are identical to ones of the same period discovered in Morocco. At the beginning of the Bronze Age it seems Andalusia was infiltrated by people of Cretan and Mycenaean origin, and it has even been suggested that the Spanish bull-fight owes its origins to a bull-cult introduced by these people. They were joined towards the end of the second millen-nium BC by Phoenician traders, who arrived in Andalusia by sea, and by Celtic tribes, who travelled to Spain over the Pyrenees. Greek traders began settling along the Mediterranean coast by 600 BC and were soon followed by the Carthaginians. Finally, the Romans took possession of the whole of Spain by the third century BC.

The term 'Iberian' is used to describe the multi-racial culture which had evolved in Spain by the time of the Romans. The study of Iberian culture began in the late eighteenth century, but it was not until very recent times that any extensive archaeological research on this subj was carried out. The first people to excavate at Los Millares, and at many other Copper and Bronze Age sites in Almería province, were the brothers Henri and Louis Siret, two Belgian mining engineers who settled in the province in the 1880s, building a house for themselves in a desolate place called Las Herrerías. They financed all their excavations by their modest salaries as engineers, and later claimed to have worked on more sites than all the Spanish archaeologists of their day put together. Louis Siret was still living at Las Herrerías in 1933, when Gerald Brenan visited him ('Fifty years at Las Herrerías!' Brenan exclaimed. 'This took some imagining!'). Brenan described Siret as a man 'of slightly crazy enthusiasm', and also found him rather embittered by the way his colleagues had not accepted many of his and his brother's findings. He told Brenan, *'Ce n'est pas une science, l'archéologie, c'est un combat à mort.'* Another eccentric archaeologist of this period, similarly obsessed by Andalusia's Iberian past, was an Englishman called George Bonsor, who worked among other places at the extraordinary necropolis at Carmona and did for western Andalusia what the Sirets had done for the eastern half; he lived in the castle at Mairena del Alcor, which has now a small museum filled with his eclectic collections and a number of impressionist-style landscapes painted by him. But perhaps the craziest of these pioneering archaeologists was the German Adolph Schulten, who devoted most of his working life to the uncovering of the most mysterious aspect of Andalusia's Iberian past, the civilization of Tartessus.

Schulten was convinced that Tartessus was a glorious city-state, the capital of which lay buried under what is now the Coto Doñana. Thirty years of searching for it, however, failed to discover any proof of its existence, and in the end Schulten came to identify Tartessus with the equally elusive ancient city of Atlantis. Other archaeologists have tried with equal lack of success to locate Tartessus in Cádiz, Jerez, Sanlúcar de Barrameda, Huelva and Seville. The search for Tartessus has been one of the most pressing issues in Spanish archaeology this century, but despite numerous excavations, its existence is still testified only by literary rather than archaeological evidence. Furthermore these sources, derived from Phoenician traditions, are hopelessly contradictory and suggest variously that Tartessus was the name of a kingdom, a city, a village, a mountain and even a river (the

Guadalquivir). The one point on which all the sources are agreed is that the place was exceedingly rich in copper, silver and gold.

The Tartessian civilization is generally thought today to have flourished in the Guadalquivir basin, from the latter half of the second millennium BC to around 500 BC, experiencing its greatest periods in the eighth and ninth centuries. The Tartessians were known to have been ruled by a monarchical dynasty, the origins of which belong now to the realm of mythology. The legends tell in fact of two Tartessian dynasties, one of which was headed by Geryon, a peaceful, flock-tending king whose only fault was to have had three bodies and three heads, for which he was killed by Hercules. Geryon's son, Nora, colonized Sardinia, and at this point mythology reflects historical fact, for there existed commercial relations between the Guadalquivir and Sardinia from around 2000 BC. The other Tartessian dynasty begins with King Gargoris, the discoverer of honey, a man whose incestuous relationship with one of his daughters produced a son, Habis. The moment he was born Habis was abandoned to the wilds, where he was nurtured by the very animals who were expected to kill him. After a miraculous childhood, the king finally recognized him as his rightful successor. Habis proved to be a civilizing monarch, who taught his people how to plough with oxen and divided his subjects into seven social classes, the nobility being exempt from work. The legends of Geryon and Gargoris have been seen to throw much light on the real Tartessians. It says much about the ethnic make-up of these people that the two legends bring together Western and Eastern traditions, the tri-formed Geryon being a type of figure frequently found in Celtic mythology, and the Gargoris story having parallels in legends of the Middle East. Furthermore, the picture of Tartessian society which can be formed from the two legends – one which is peace-loving, monarchical, endogamous, well organized and highly sophisticated – is borne out by what is known about Tartessus from the time of its first real monarch, King Arganthonios, who ruled around 1100 BC.

Though Tartessus itself has never been discovered, excavations at places such as Carmona, Niebla and Setefilla have uncovered numerous remains associated with Tartessian civilization. Just outside Andalusia, at Zalamea de la Serena in the Extremaduran province of Badajoz, there was recently found the ruins of a sanctuary dedicated to a goddess of the underworld, a cult which some believe to have been the dominant one of the Tartessians and the precursor of today's Virgin cult, which is very strong in the south of Spain. But the most spectacular discovery connected with the Tartessians occurred in 1958 during the extension of a pigeon-shooting club at El Carambolo, just to the west of Seville. A walled town was revealed, as well as a dazzling horde of gold jewellery, which is now displayed in a darkened room of its own in Seville's Museo Arqueológico, and is a testimony to the proverbial wealth of the Tartessians. So rich is the Andalusian soil in archaeological remains that discoveries continue frequently to be made, for instance the magnificent sculptures from the Iberian sanctuary at Porcuna in Jaén province (see page 292). The hope that one day Tartessus itself might surface is not an altogether forlorn one.

The Tartessians appear to have enjoyed relatively amicable trading relations with the Phoenicians and the Greeks, both of whom had been attracted to Andalusia by its famed mineral wealth. The Phoenicians and the Greeks founded many coastal colonies in Andalusia, the first and most important of which was the Phoenician town of Gadir, later known as Cádiz: though virtually nothing survives of the original Phoenician and Greek settlements, the important influence of these people on Andalusia is shown by the way in which the traditional unglazed pottery of such places as Lebrija and Utrera continues to follow prototypes established by them. In contrast to the Phoenicians and Greeks, the Carthaginians adopted a ruthless and hostile attitude towards the Tartessians; in fact it was probably they who succeeded in destroying the Tartessian civilization, whether as a result of a major military victory or by gaining a monopoly on the trade in minerals. The growing power of the Carthaginians erupted in the third century BC into a great struggle with the Romans to gain control over the western Mediterranean. Following the first Punic War (264–241 BC), the Carthaginians lost Sicily, Sardinia and Corsica to the Romans, and concentrated their forces on south-eastern Spain. The second Punic War (218–206 BC) led to their final defeat, and to the conquering of Spain by the Romans, who by 195 BC had made it clear that they intended to stay. Among those who had sided with the Romans against the Carthaginians were the descendants of the Tartessians, the Turdetanians. The Romans considered the Turdetanians the most civilized of the Iberian peoples, and in the first century AD Strabo was to write that the 'Turdetanians are ranked as the wisest of the Iberians; and they make use of an alphabet, and possess records of their ancient history, poems and laws written in verse that are 6,000 years old.'

The Romans divided Spain at first into two separate provinces: Hispania Citerior, which embraced the whole eastern and northern parts of the peninsula, and Hispania Ulterior, which had Córdoba as its capital. The latter province was soon afterwards divided into Lusitania and Baetica, and at a much later date Hispania Citerior was broken up into the provinces of Gaellaecia, Carthaginensis, and Tarraconensis. The Romans, characteristically, were able to consolidate their hold over the country through a brilliant administrative system and the construction of an efficient network of roads. Their success in Spain was due also to their tolerance of and integration with the Iberian peoples, who were said to have been allowed to live in the same style as their conquerors.

Baetica played a vital role in the trading and commercial history of Roman Spain, and at Monte Testacchio in Rome there is even a great mound built of fragments of olive oil amphorae from this province. The importance of Baetica, however, was not simply a material one, for the place gave birth to Rome's first emperors from the provinces, Trajan and Hadrian, as well as to such outstanding figures in Roman intellectual history as Lucan and Seneca. The legacy of this Roman past is apparent in sites and monuments throughout Andalusia, many of which are scarcely better known than the ones from prehistoric times, and certainly no better treated: the main survival from Roman Seville consists of three enormous columns sunk into a waterlogged, rubbish-strewn hole off the Calle Marmoles. Though Andalusia has no existing Roman monuments quite as distinguished or celebrated, say, as the theatre at Mérida or the aqueduct at Segovia, there are several monuments deserving special mention, for instance the magnificently preserved bridges at Córdoba and Andújar, and the massively built theatre at Ronda la Vieja, which gains additional power from its isolated, hilltop position and splendid panorama over the Serranía de Ronda (see page 328).

Work has recently begun on uncovering the rest of Ronda la Vieja, which like many Roman cities in the peninsula was built next to an earlier settlement. Lack of funds will protract the excavations for many years, but in the meantime there are extensive remains to be seen of other Roman townships in Andalusia. The least well known of these is that of the Castillo de Mulva, which occupies a verdant hillside position and features the ruins of houses, defensive walls, a mausoleum, a forum, and – dominating the site – a large sanctuary (see page 302). Among the most beautifully situated ruins in Spain are those of the former town of Bolonia, which overlook a wild bay hemmed in by a great sweep of dunes and hills; the ruins come right down to a beach which until a few years ago was hardly frequented and even now shows only the most modest signs of tourist development (see page 255). Bolonia in its present ruined state is probably a more romantic place than it once was, and certainly a less pungent one: it used to be a small port and industrial town, and the buildings nearest the shore, below the forum and basilica, contained vats in which tunny and mackerel were marinaded for several weeks in the preparation of a popular fish sauce known as *garum*, the Roman equivalent of Gentleman's Relish. Another of Andalusia's ruined townships is Carmona near Seville. The walls that enclose present-day Carmona, though restored in Moorish times, still keep much of their Roman masonry; but the main Roman remains lie on the ugly outskirts of the town and consist of an overgrown theatre turned towards a block of flats, and, directly behind the theatre, one of Spain's most interesting necropoli. The necropolis has large rock-hewn family tombs built underground and reached by steps; some have traces of ancient painted decoration, another has a statue of an elephant, one even has a bench and table intended for a funerary meal. The site is one of the best maintained in all Andalusia, and has the additional advantage of an excellent small museum of Roman finds.

Only a few kilometres from Seville, at the small and dusty village of Santiponce, are the most famous Roman ruins in Andalusia, those of Itálica. Founded by Scipio in 205 BC next to a Turdetanian settlement, Itálica was the first Roman town in Spain. Originally it was simply a hospital and a small military base, but it soon developed into an important port and, in the first century AD, gave birth first to Trajan and then to Hadrian; Hadrian took particular pride in his native town, and embellished it with many of the buildings that are to be seen today. Falling into ruins in the Middle Ages, it became during the Renaissance a place of pilgrimage for Sevillian humanists, who regarded it as a Spanish Rome. However, vandalism had already begun to take its toll, and by the fourteenth century many of the columns from Itálica had been used in the building of the nearby monastery church of San Jerónimo. In 1595 and again in 1602 terrible floods forced the villagers of Santiponce to move closer to the site, and to use bricks from it for their new houses. A local seventeenth-century poet and archaeologist, Rodrigo Caro, was moved to write a poem:

> These Fabio, oh shame! which you see in front of you
> . . .
> Fields of solitude, withered, silent
> Were once Itálica of Roman fame . . .

Excavations began in earnest at Itálica in the late eighteenth century, but if anything vandalism increased. The French Marshal Soult took away many of the pieces that he found lying around, as did Wellington, and numerous people from Seville anxious to decorate their houses. An English visitor of 1818, George Ticknor, was saddened by what he saw. 'Everything is neglected. The amphitheatre even is falling in every year; the mosaics, as I absolutely saw, are a part of a sheepfold, and, of course, more and more broken up every day, and the only person, I believe, who takes an interest in these curious remains, is a poor advocate of Seville, who comes out here on the feast days, and digs among them with his own hands . . .' Today the amphitheatre has been restored to the extent that ballets and operas are put on here in the summer months, and the mosaics have been moved to the Museo Arqueológico of Seville. The rest of the site is a strange mixture of neglect and tasteless modern additions such as a pseudo-classical colonnade; it is an ugly place curiously lacking in atmosphere. The most moving part of Itálica is away from the official site, and in the centre of the village. Here you will find the theatre, crumbling away, littered with Coca Cola tins, and supporting a picturesque accretion of houses, rather like those that were once attached to Rome's Forum.

By the early fifth century A D, Rome's control of its Spanish provinces had weakened, and soon the Visigothic kings were the undisputed masters of the land, wresting power both from the Romans and other Barbarian tribes; by the late sixth century, the Visigoths had united Spain under a centralized authority, with Toledo as capital.

However, Spain remained heavily under Roman influence, and Romans lived alongside the Visigoths and still held important civic and ecclesiastical positions. This situation was particularly true of Andalusia, to where the Emperor Justinian had even sent Byzantine troops in 572 (they were not expelled until 621). Few traces of Visigothic culture are to be found in Andalusia, and indeed the only important cultural contribution of this period was made by the scholar St Isidore, who established an important school of learning in Seville in the sixth century.

The Visigoths themselves were not a united force, and throughout their stay in Spain were divided by internal conflicts, not least of which was that of religion. At first the Visigoths were separated from the Romans not only by language but also by religion, the Visigothic rulers adhering to a Christian heresy known as Arianism or Unitarianism. After 507, orthodox Trinitarian Christianity became the official Visigothic religion, but a strong, Arian undercurrent persisted, and became associated with the national heritage of the Visigoths. At the same time there was the growing problem of the Jews, who had probably arrived in Andalusia by the end of the first century A D and by Visigothic times had come to represent a major portion of the merchant and artisan classes. In the course of the seventh century the Jews were subjected to increasingly harsh measures, such as confiscation of property, forced baptism, and persecution. In addition to these religious tensions there were grave economic problems, the nobility and the clergy enjoying all the privileges and wealth, and the peasantry being reduced to a state of serfdom; finally came feuds within the nobility itself, and the controversial problem of succession to the throne. Such was the state of affairs in Spain by the early eighth century that the time was ripe for Arab intervention, an intervention probably encouraged by certain Visigothic factors and certainly welcomed by the Jews. The legend goes that it was a Visigothic merchant called Julian who had encouraged the Arabs to come to Spain as a revenge upon the then ruler, Roderick, for having dishonoured Julian's daughter Florinda. Those more likely to have borne such a strong grudge against Roderick were the partisans of Achila, a Visigothic king who had been deposed by Roderick. But the closeness of Spain to Africa, and the legendary wealth of Andalusia, were reasons enough for the Arabs to want to come here.

In recent years it has become fashionable among historians to play down the notion of an Arab 'conquest' of Spain, and to emphasize instead how small were the forces that initially came here from Africa, how easily they took over the country, and how rapidly their religion and customs were assimilated by the indigenous population. These historians argue that all this was possible because of the strong African element already present in the ethnic make-up of the Spaniards, in particular the Andalusians, and the fact that the Arian Unitarian movement has a parallel in an Islamic Unitarian movement. In other words the Arab take-over of Spain was a welcome and logical step, the idea of a ruthless and bloodthirsty military conquest by an alien force being merely an absurd exaggeration put forward by Arab and Christian fanatics from the eleventh century onwards. There is none the less no getting away from the fact that the Arab presence in Spain was in keeping with an Islamic expansionist policy which had made vast progress since the death of Muhammad in the early sixth century.

The successors of Muhammad were known as Caliphs, and these had succeeded soon after their master's death in spreading Islam and in founding a state in Arabia proper, Syria, Palestine, Iraq, Iran and Egypt. Both the religious and political centre of the state was originally divided between the twin towns of Mecca and Medina, but was later moved to the provinces. The powerful Umayyad dynasty established the Caliphate in the Syrian capital of Damascus, and encouraged Islam to spread east to Central Asia and west to the Atlantic. The winning over of the whole of North Africa to Islam was not achieved without its difficulties, but by 701 this had finally been achieved, and the Berber tribes pacified. The path was now clear to move into Spain. In July 710 an officer called Tarīf went with a small force on a reconnaissance trip to Spain, and soon took possession of the peninsula's southern tip, where his memory is preserved in the name of a town with an impressive Arab citadel, Tarifa. Encouraged by the success of Tarīf's mission, a full-scale expedition led by Tāriq Ibn Ziryāb was sent out to Spain in the following year. Tāriq's forces made their headquarters at Gibraltar (the name of which is derived from the Arabic, Jabal Tāriq, or 'Rock of Tāriq'), and went from there to win over most of the peninsula, stopping short of the northern mountains, which were always to remain in Christian hands: it has been said that the Arabs were never truly happy in places where olive trees did not grow.

The early years of Muslim domination of Spain were especially troubled and confusing ones, and matters were not helped by the lack of interest shown in the place in Damascus, which was a good four months' journey away. Al-Andalus was the name given to the whole of Muslim Spain, and the part of it which we now know as Andalusia lacked the administrative unity which it had had during the Roman period, being divided into about fifteen provinces or *coras*. The governing of al-Andalus was left to an emir, a position which to begin with changed hands with bewildering rapidity. During the brief period when Muslim forces spread over the peninsula, power in the land had been shared between Tāriq, and Mūsā Ibn Nusayr, a former governor of North Africa who had sent Tāriq to Spain in the first place and had later joined him there, apparently jealous of the man's success and wishing to have some credit in the victory. Mūsā's son, 'Abd al-'Azīz b. Mūsā, was appointed emir by his father in 714, and he immediately made Seville the capital of al-Andalus. His rule was able and very tolerant, but he was assassinated after only two years. The capital was moved to Córdoba, where it was to remain until the eleventh century, despite being initially a scene of constant intrigues and infighting.

The Muslim occupants of Spain are commonly referred to as 'Moors', a term coined in the Middle Ages to describe the Muslims who stayed on in reclaimed Christian territory; it was and still remains in Spain a term of abuse. The word, derived probably from the North African country of Mauritania, is at any rate a blanket term covering the many different races that make up the Muslim religion. The so-called Moors who came over to Spain in the eighth century consisted not simply of Arabs, but also of Syrians, Egyptians, and, above all, Berbers, who made up the bulk of Tāriq's expeditionary forces of 711; the Arabs represented in fact the minority of the Muslim races in Spain, even if at first they were politically the strongest. Racial tensions between the Spanish Muslims were inevitable, and far more damaging to begin with than any threat from the Christians. They were complicated by opposing factions within the individual races, the situation thus created in eighth-century Córdoba being not unlike that of present-day Beirut. The greatest friction was between the Arabs and the Berbers, who felt quite rightly that the Arabs were discriminating against them. A Berber revolt broke out in North Africa in 740 and soon threatened Córdoba. An army was sent from

Damascus headed by Balj Ibn Bishr, who eventually defeated the Berbers at Córdoba but then took the opportunity to make himself emir. The partisans of the deposed emir were mainly Yemenites or southern Arabs, and they entered a bloody conflict with the soldiers of Balj, who were mainly Qaysites or northern Arabs. Al-Andalus might have come to an end as quickly as it had been created had it not been for the arrival in Córdoba a few years later of a refugee from the Umayyad dynasty in Damascus.

In 750, after a period of grave political, social and economic crisis, the last Umayyad caliph in Damascus, Marwān II, was taken prisoner and executed, thus bringing to an end nearly 150 years of Umayyad rule. The usurping family, the 'Abbāsids, were anxious to destroy any potential future threat from the Umayyads, and arranged that all its members should be treacherously killed at a banquet. As in a fairy tale, however, one of their number escaped, Prince 'Abd al-Rahmān, who, with his faithful servant Badr, then wandered incognito through Palestine, Egypt and North Africa. Drumming up support from the Yemenites, he moved to Spain and built up an army large enough to defeat the Qaysite ruler of Córdoba. In 756, aged twenty-six, the prince became emir of al-Andalus, and the founder of a new Umayyad dynasty, which was to rule until 1031. Under their rule Córdoba became one of the great cities of the world, rivalled in the Muslim countries only by Damascus, with which it was frequently compared. Its greatest period was to come after 929 when 'Abd al-Rahmān II styled himself 'Commander of the Faithful', the legitimate caliph, and in so doing transformed al-Andalus from an emirate into a caliphate.

By and large the period of Umayyad rule in al-Andalus can be characterized as one of prosperity, religious tolerance, relative stability, and intense cultural and scientific activity. The great natural resources of Andalusia were brilliantly exploited, and though the land structure of Andalusia had changed little since the Visigoths, the peasantry were no longer treated like serfs and owed only 20–50 per cent of their crops to their landlords as opposed to 50–80 per cent previously. The Muslims of this period tolerated all those who 'worshipped the Book', and, while extracting poll and land taxes in return for their protection, allowed Catholics and Jews freely to practise their religions. The Catholics of al-Andalus were known as Mozarabs, and, like the Jews, were fully conversant in the Arab language and traditions and could rise to important positions in Muslim society; there were even those Catholics of al-Andalus who joined the Muslims in fighting against their Christian brothers in the north of Spain. Marriage between Muslim men and Christian women was encouraged, the offspring of such unions being called *Muwalladūn* (the Christians of the north referred to these people as renegades). The great majority of the Catholics in al-Andalus, however, became *musālimah*, or Muslim converts, the most important social group in the country in terms both of numbers and their pre-eminence in the country's religious, political and intellectual life. Another group which should be mentioned were the *Saqāliba*, who were originally slaves from Northern Spain, France, Germany and Eastern European countries. Indoctrinated into Arab ways, they came to be trusted by the Umayyad rulers more than the Arabs and Berbers, and were indeed preferred to them as palace employees by 'Abd al-Rahmān III. From their lowly social position they rose to posts of great importance, and acquired large estates.

Though the Umayyads managed to stay in power for so long, and to avert all religious conflict, they were only just able to contain the many internal quarrels provoked by the ever greater social diversity of Muslim Spain. The greatest challenge to Umayyad authority was offered by a *Muwallad* from Ronda called Ibn Hafsūn. His life was a picturesque one, and began, like that of many nineteenth-century bandits, by his killing a man and leading the life of a highway robber in the mountains. Escaping from justice, he went over to North Africa, where he became apprenticed as a tailor. He returned to al-Andalus, and by 880 had gathered together a rebel army with its headquarters at Bobastro, an isolated mountain-top fortress in the northernmost part of the Serranía de Ronda. Exploiting the dissent felt against the Arab rulers of al-Andalus, he attracted an ever-growing number of followers, particularly among his fellow *Muwalladūn*. Various successful campaigns were mounted against him, at the end of one of which, one of his commanders, 'Ayshūn, was crucified with a pig at his right and a dog at his left. Nevertheless Ibn Hafsūn was able to maintain a strong hold over southern al-Andalus, and this did not weaken even after 899, when he converted to Christianity and thereby lost many of his Arab supporters. He died in 917, and his son continued fighting for his cause for a further ten years. His castle at Bobastro was never taken. Today the scant ruins of the place are difficult to locate, but the site is a beautiful and peaceful one, near the end of a small road which climbs its way up through wild and verdant mountain scenery. Immediately below the castle ruins, and a ten-minute walk from the road, stands an enchanting Mozarabic church (see page 241). Built into the rock, this ruined church with its overgrown horseshoe arch and superb views is one of the most romantic sites in all Andalusia. This was Ibn Hafsūn's final resting place.

The negative aspects of Umayyad rule are outweighed by the positive ones, which for many are reflected above all in the cultural and scientific achievements of the period. These achievements must be seen in the context of the whole Muslim world, which in the fields of arts and sciences was far more advanced at this time than Christian Europe: Arab physicians, for instance, were dissecting before the tenth century, whereas European ones only did so after the Renaissance. The specific part which al-Andalus itself played in all this has only rarely been looked at in any serious, critical way, the many who have written on Muslim Spain having generally eulogized the place unreservedly, often with little or no knowledge of Muslim culture and language. At first al-Andalus was in fact a backward place in relation to other Muslim countries, which was perhaps inevitable given its distant provincial status at this time and its initial minority of Arab speakers. The first great figures in the country's cultural and intellectual life were imports from the East, such as the musician Ziryāb, who came from Baghdad in the early ninth century to work at the court of 'Abd al-Rahmān II (822–52): he was famous not only for his minstrel singing and lute accompaniment, but as a pioneer in the arts of hairdressing, perfumes, fashion and cooking (it was he who introduced to Europe an orderly sequence in which dishes should be presented, ending with the dessert).

Not until the second half of the ninth century, when the population of al-Andalus became thoroughly immersed in Arabic ways, did a flourishing of native talent begin to be apparent. In the tenth century Córdoba emerged as a major centre of patronage and learning, with al-Hakam II (961–76) building up in the city one of the great libraries of the world; at the same time the wealthy of Europe descended upon the city to be treated by doctors such as Rhazes, who distinguished measles from smallpox and popularized animal gut for stitching. Few scholars or writers of great originality, however, were produced during this period. Philosophy and jurisprudence (the latter being the fulcrum of Muslim intellectual life) continued to be dominated in al-Andalus by the views of the Arabian jurist Mālik Ibn Anas, who had been an outspoken opponent of all philosophical and religious speculation; his rigid beliefs – the so-called Mālikite orthodoxy – had been adopted in al-Andalus under Hishām I (789–96), and were probably responsible for the relative poverty of philosophic literature in Muslim Spain. Poetry, the main literary form in al-Andalus, was likewise based largely on Eastern models, and recent claims to find in it specifically Spanish features such as an underlying melancholy have not been convincing.

Whereas Córdoba was known for its learning, Málaga became celebrated for singing and Seville for the making of musical instruments. Singing, dancing and lute music were among the great passions of al-Andalus, even though Muhammad had disapproved of these activities. There is a famous account of an Arab traveller, Ahmad al-Yamānī, staying in Málaga around 1016 and being unable to sleep because of the constant sounds of lutes, harps, drums and song. One such night, however, he heard instrumental music of such beauty and mystery that all his anxiety and irritation vanished and he was filled with a great happiness. Then a woman began to sing with 'a voice more brilliant than the flowers after the rain and more pleasant than is the freshness of the embrace to the ardent lover'. Finally he was unable to contain his curiosity any longer, and got up to see where the music was coming from. He soon found himself in a large courtyard, in the middle of which sat about twenty men, holding fruits and drinks. In front of them were slave girls with lutes, tambourines, flutes and other instruments, but they were silent at the time, absorbed, like everybody else, in the music of one of their number, who was accompanying herself with a lute as she sang.

The form which dancing took is not known, but to judge from the many poems describing dancers of the time, it was a highly sensual one. One poem even describes how a slave girl dances to the chords of a lute until finally she slips out of her dress to appear 'like a bud unfolding from a cluster of blossoms'. Sensuality and sybariticism featured prominently in the Romantic image of Muslim Spain, but it would be difficult to form a different impression of this society. Despite the famous libraries of al-Andalus, leisure time here seems not to have been spent in reading and studying, as Muslim religious leaders would have liked, but instead in playing chess, listening to music and poetry, drinking, watching dancing, and indulging in love-making. One of the few themes to which poetry could be devoted was – strangely enough for a Muslim society – wine and its pleasurable effects. But the most popular of these themes was love, which was portrayed in all its guises, but above all in the physical one. Love was an activity expressed by poets in ever more novel and absurd ways. 'Such was my kissing,' wrote one poet, 'such my sucking of his mouth that he was almost made toothless.'

A strong sensuality characterizes much of the architecture of Muslim Spain. There evolved here an architectural style radically opposed to that of the classical tradition, and one which was fundamentally unintellectual in its approach. Instead of producing an architecture based on strict rules of proportions and rational ordering of space, the Muslim architects favoured curiously intangible structures, in which there was much mysterious play of light and shadow, and intricate decorative effects on an unprecedentedly large scale. All these qualities can be seen in the Great Mosque or Mezquita at Córdoba, which was the major architectural work carried out in Spain under the Umayyads, and arguably the most original achievement in Spanish culture of this period.

Originally a modest structure built under 'Abd al-Rahmān I around 780, it was continually enlarged and embellished under successive Umayyad rulers until eventually it was virtually unrivalled in size and splendour in the Muslim world, and indeed was described by early Arab travellers as the greatest mosque ever built. The exterior is relatively severe and ungainly, and gives little idea of the richness within. The European traveller, accustomed to Christian churches with their prominent west portals, might well be perplexed by the Mezquita's apparent lack of an obvious main entrance, and will certainly have no idea of where to turn the moment on entering the building. In a Christian church your eyes would immediately be led down the central nave to the High Altar, but here you are confronted by what has been described unfailingly since the Middle Ages as a 'forest' of marble columns, of which there were originally 1,293. Somewhere in here is the *mihrāb*, or prayer niche indicating the direction of Mecca, but even this is off-centre and difficult to find.

Even the great Catholic structure built within the Mosque in the sixteenth century, after the building had been turned into a cathedral, is almost lost in the forest. Charles V, who had authorized the construction of this later addition, subsequently believed that he had 'destroyed what was unique in the world'. Damaged rather than destroyed, however, would have been a better word, for the place today remains so magical that it is difficult to imagine what it must have been like with all its columns, mosaics, gold decorations and multitude of candles, lamps and copper chandeliers, one of which reputedly held 1,000 lights. Traveller upon traveller has gaped with astonishment inside the Mezquita, and yet the building must have been deeply disconcerting to classical sensibilities. The German art historian, Meier-Graefe, visiting Córdoba in the 1880s, was one of the few people honest enough to express his reservations about the building. Confronted with the forest of columns, this rationally minded and slightly puritanical German scholar was unable, as it were, to see the wood for the trees. 'I can't make head or tail of the mosque,' he wrote. 'The impression is there of course, but I don't know what to do with it and I am not sufficiently enthusiastic to think about it . . . The mosque lacks altogether the living power of *matière*, the multiple quality of intelligible proportions.' What Meier-Graefe considered an intellectual failing, however, was in fact an indication of a radically different religious mentality to that of Christianity. This is a mentality which does not believe in any priestly hierarchy, and consequently sees no necessity in having any rigid structural format in a place of worship. The centre of a mosque is anywhere in the building where you want to pray.

The earliest mosques in the Muslim world were simple square enclosures, with almost bare interiors, but as Islam moved from desert surroundings to urban centres, the structures became more and more sophisticated, with domes, minarets and a profusion of decoration. Islam forbids the representation of the human form, and the religious message of a building was conveyed by inscriptions. These inscriptions became an ever more prominent element in the decoration of a building, and the complex forms of Arab calligraphy seem in turn to have inspired the Muslim craftsmen to create increasingly intricate and extensive decorative motifs to surround them; the skill of Muslim craftsmen, in all materials, was proverbial. The first outstanding examples of Muslim religious architecture are the Rock of the Dome in Jerusalem and the Great Umayyad Mosque in Damascus, which date respectively from the seventh and eighth centuries. Córdoba's Mezquita, like other mosques throughout the Muslim world, has many echoes of these two buildings, but its most noticeable feature is completely without precedent in a mosque, and is a masterly example of the adoption of Western elements to an Eastern setting. This is the superimposition of one row of arches on top of another, so as to double the height of the building. The actual arches, horseshoe in shape as in all Muslim buildings, are probably of Visigothic origin, but the doubling of them is clearly inspired by Roman aqueducts such as that of Mérida.

The other outstanding innovations of the Córdoba Mezquita are in the part added by al-Hakam I in the 960s. The breathtakingly elaborate ornamentation which had come to characterize Muslim art and architecture of this period is here applied to structures of revolutionary complexity. The decorative possibilities of arcading, as revealed in the main body of the Mosque, are exploited to a far greater degree in the *maqsūrah*, or royal gallery of the caliph: in this the arches are interlaced and have small semi-circular segments cut out of them so as to form what are known as poly-lobed arches. In front of the *mihrāb* – a dazzlingly ornate structure in coloured marbles – is a vestibule lined with mosaics and covered with an aetherial dome, supported on vaulting shaped like a star and with openings through which light floods in. In transforming sturdy simple forms such as arches and domes into delicate and fascinatingly complex ones, the architects employed by al-Hakam II greatly encouraged the Muslim trend towards an architecture in which the distinction between structure and decoration becomes ever more blurred.

The many other mosques constructed in Spain during the Umayyad period were either destroyed or ruthlessly converted into churches. As for the once highly praised secular buildings of this period, these have fared little better, and there remain today only a handful of castles – most notably the much restored and enlarged Alcazaba of Almería and the scant ruins of the extraordinary palace of Medina Azahara (al-Zahrā), which ranked with the Mezquita at Córdoba as one of the great wonders of the world. Medina Azahara was begun in 939 and intended as the summer palace of 'Abd al-Rahmān III, who was perhaps the Umayyad ruler to have devoted the most money to architectural work. He is said to have spent over a third of the state revenue on public construction, and the building boom which he instigated at Córdoba was to turn the place by the end of the century into a vast metropolis containing – according to the seventeenth-century Arab historian al-Maqqarī – 1,600 mosques, 900 public baths, 60,300 mansions for the wealthy, 213,077 ordinary homes, and 80,455 shops. These figures are obviously greatly exaggerated (and if true would mean that Córdoba had a population of over a million), but at least they give some idea of how much has been lost.

Sentimental travellers can indulge in dreams of former glory by visiting what is left of Medina Azahara. Lying eight kilometres to the east of Córdoba, it occupies a quiet, isolated site on the lower slopes of the Sierra Morena and has extensive views over the Guadalquivir valley. To describe this place simply as a 'summer palace' is misleading, for it was actually a great architectural complex comprising several palaces, a mosque, gardens, a zoo, an aviary, and manufactories for weapons; its name in fact means 'city of Azahara' (Azahara being probably a favourite mistress of 'Abd al-Rahmān III). Ten thousand workers and 1,500 beasts of burden were supposedly employed in its construction, during which period 6,000 carved stones were used daily. Marble was imported from Almería and Carthage, and engraved basins from Constantinople and Syria; the roof tiles were covered in gold and silver.

In 1009 a rebellion broke out in Córdoba, and rioters pillaged and destroyed Medina Azahara and rendered it uninhabitable. The ruins were gradually buried, and the remaining parts plundered for their stone. 'But for the testimony of historians,' wrote Dundas Murray on a visit to the site in 1849, 'it would be hard to believe that Medina Azahara ever rose from the ground to cover a wide space with sumptuous edifices.' Gerald Brenan came here over 100 years later and found that the ruins were 'scarcely worth seeing, since all the stones were being carried off to build a monastery on the hill.' I first came here in 1968 and was confronted, in what had been the main hall of the palace, with a monumental jigsaw of masonry and plaster-work. Since then the jigsaw has been miraculously put together, and the profusely decorated, reconstructed hall gives an excellent idea of what the building must originally have been like. Moreover, excavations elsewhere in the site continue to reveal more and more of the original complex. The astonishing extent of this complex has become clearer than it has been for centuries.

The fate of Medina Azahara mirrored that of Córdoba after the fall of the Umayyad dynasty. The Umayyads had maintained a strong rule right up to 1009, thanks mainly to a dynasty of chamberlains headed by the brilliant al-Mansūr, who had risen to power after the death of al-Hakam II in 976 and had virtually governed the country single-handed until his own death in 1002. Al-Mansūr's family, the 'Āmirids, fell from favour in 1009, following the reckless, dissolute and over-ambitious behaviour of al-Mansūr's second son, 'Abd al-Rahmān. With their fall, the Umayyad dynasty itself collapsed. The revolts that had led to the sacking of Medina Azahara in 1009 turned into a bloody civil war, which soon reduced al-Andalus to chaos. In 1023 the Umayyads were briefly and half-heartedly reinstated, but they were ousted for good eight years later. Córdoba's days of greatness were finally over. The celebrated library of al-Hakam II had been pillaged and burnt, and the population of the city had begun to decline. In the late twelfth century an Arab traveller, Muhammad al-Edrisi, was to marvel at the splendour of Córdoba and its monuments, and to describe the place as 'the most famous town in all of Spain'. He had to add, however: 'At the time of writing the town of Córdoba has been torn apart by Discord; its situation has been altered by harsh fortune, and its population is no longer large.' Visitors of later centuries, while generally unqualified in their enthusiasm for the Mezquita, had little good to say about the town itself. 'Córdoba,' wrote Dundas Murray in 1849, 'is a very dull place; the life has utterly departed from it, and to roam through its streets is like wandering among the tombs. If any one desires to know what a silent and desolate city is, let him come here.' Murray's contemporary Richard Ford was no more compli-mentary about the town. 'Córdoba is soon seen. This Athens under the Moors is now a poor Boetian place, the residence of local auth-orities ... and a library of no particular consequence: a day will amply suffice for everything.'

With the ousting of the Umayyads in 1031, al-Andalus came to be broken up into twelve small kingdoms or *taifas*, the boundaries of which were based to a large extent on the provinces or *coras* that had been established in the early eighth century. The kingdom of Córdoba was soon outstripped in power and prestige by that of Seville, which under the rule of the 'Abbāsid kings rose to become the most important and populated town of the peninsula. Intense rivalry between the various courts of al-Andalus had a disastrous effect on the political life of the country, and the quarrels were eventually to facilitate the first stages of the so-called Christian 'Reconquest' at the end of the eleventh century. However, what with each court vying to outdo the other in splendour, this rivalry might be held partially responsible for what has been described as the greatest period in the cultural history of al-Andalus.

The eleventh century was above all a period of exceptional writers, in particular poets, the works of whom might well have been a major influence on the troubadours of France. The most versatile of these new writers was the Córdoba-born Ibn Hazm (994–1064), a man sometimes regarded as the first intellectual giant of Muslim Spain. He wrote on numerous topics, in verse and in prose, though perhaps his most popular work was *The Ring of the Dove*, a youthful treatise on love in which he praised the spiritual aspects of love, attacked sexual excesses and recommended continence. Love remained the major preoccupation of the Muslim poets, though whether they followed Ibn Hazm's advice on this matter seems doubtful, to judge by what is known of some of their lives and by the passionate, physical descriptions of love that they put in their works. One of the most distinguished of these poets was Ibn Zaydūn (1003–70) from Córdoba, who in his twenties fell in love with Princess Wallādah, the daughter of the caliph al-Mustakfi. The princess wrote able poetry herself, and enjoyed a life-style which gives an interesting insight into the relative freedom then experienced by women in Arab society: she completely disregarded the veil, regularly frequented the higher circles of Córdoba society, and openly went out at night to meet her lover, Ibn Zaydūn. The two lovers corresponded in poems, until eventually the princess began responding to the attentions of a wealthy, influential man called Ibn 'Abdūs. The rejected poet wrote a particularly vituperative piece characterizing Ibn 'Abdūs as a stupid, vulgar and loathsome creature no better than a fly or mosquito, but this did little to further his own suit, and in fact landed him briefly in jail. Finally freed, he took refuge in Medina Azahara, where he expressed his anguish at losing the princess's love in a poem in which each line ends in 'um'. This is considered one of the finest love poems in the Arab language.

Among the plethora of poets who worked at Seville in the eleventh century, the two best known are Ibn 'Ammār (1031–86) and the poet-king of Seville, al-Mu'tamid (1038–91). The former, a man of humble origin, began his career as a wandering poet composing works in praise of anyone who would pay him. He ended up working at Seville in the court of al-Mu'tamid's father, al-Mu'tadid, for whom he wrote a poem celebrating a recent victory over the Berbers. At the court he became intimate friends with his fellow poet, al-Mu'tamid, but incurred the displeasure of the latter's father, who had him exiled. When al-Mu'tamid himself succeeded to the throne of Seville in 1068, Ibn 'Ammār was reinstated at the court, but the friendship between the two soon began to fall apart, until finally they became political enemies and wrote vicious poems against each other. Ibn 'Ammār was forced to escape to the north of Spain, but al-Mu'tamid had him brought back to Seville, and there, insensible to a poem begging for forgiveness, killed his former friend with repeated blows from an axe. Al-Mu'tamid was himself to have an unhappy end, exiled to Morocco, and composing bitter poems bemoaning his fate as 'a stranger, a captive in the Maghrib'. In better days he had been the ruler of a powerful kingdom, and had celebrated the joys of wine and women. His great love had been one I'timād, separation from whom in the course of his duties as a king had once inspired the lines:

> I am pining because of being separated from you,
> Inebriated with the wine of my longing for you,
> Crazed with the desire to be with you,
> To sip your lips and to embrace you.

The outpouring of poetic talent in eleventh-century Spain reflected a new confidence among the country's poets and a diminishing of once firmly held feelings of inferiority towards the poets of the East. None the less, Eastern models continued to be faithfully imitated, and the subject-matter and verse forms of classical Arabic poetry in Spain remained as rigid as before. What is more, there were those who continued to feel that poetry and scholarship were still not taken seriously enough in Spain, one such person being Ibn Hazm, who once complained that he would have been far better appreciated had he been born outside the country. The one indisputably original and indigenous contribution made by Spain to Arabic poetry took the form of popular verse, of which there were two known types, the *muwash-shah* and the *zayal*. Written in colloquial rather than classical Arabic, simple and spontaneous, and owing nothing to Eastern connections, these two types of verse were frowned upon by most purists and indeed scarcely considered as poetry. Yet, after 1100, when classical Arabic poetry began to decline, the *muwashshah* and *zayal* flourished more than ever, and have even lived on, some say, in the lyrics of *flamenco*.

In considering the poetry of al-Andalus, mention must finally be made of the many great Jewish poets who emerged in Spain after 1000. Whereas the Jewish scholars and philosophers of Spain wrote in Arabic, these poets composed almost exclusively in Hebrew, partly because many of their works were liturgical, and partly because the Hebrew language had a greater flexibility when applied to poetry than it had with philosophy. Though writing in Hebrew, the Jewish poets followed classical Arabic forms of verse, and adopted the same themes. Thus Samuel Ha-Nagid, the first important Jewish poet of Spain, wrote a poem in praise of wine.

> Red in appearance, sweet to the taste,
> Vintage of Spain, yet renowned in the East,
> Feeble in the cup, but, once in the brain,
> It rules over heads that cannot rise again.
>
> The bereaved, whose blood is mixed with his tears –
> The blood of the grape diminishes his fears.
> Friends, passing the cup from hand to hand,
> Seem to be gambling for a precious diamond.*

Ha-Nagid had a remarkable life. Born in Córdoba in 993, he left the town in the course of the troubles following the rebellion of 1009. Settling in Málaga, his skill with Arabic calligraphy reputedly attracted the attention of the vizier Abu al-Kasim Ibn al-Arif, who made him his private secretary. Later, at Granada, he became a vizier himself, and a commander of the king of Granada's armies. No wonder he could once write a poem entitled *The Power of the Pen*, for apparently only one other Jew was ever to command a Muslim army, and that

* From D. Goldstein (ed.), *The Jewish Poets of Spain (900–1250)*, Penguin edition, 1971.

was his son, Joseph. Many of his poems deal with war and bereavement, and his long descriptions of battles in which he was involved are unique examples of Jewish martial poetry in Spain.

Two other memorable Jewish poets were Moses Ibn Ezra and Judah Ha-Levi, both of whom witnessed and suffered from the collapse of the *taifa* dynasties after 1089. Moses Ibn Ezra, who was born no later than 1055, established an early reputation as a poet among the intellectual circles of his native Granada, but was left destitute after the city's devastation by the Berbers in 1090. Reluctant to abandon the town, as many members of his family had done, he stayed on there for a while, but eventually a personal quarrel compelled him to leave for good. His last years were spent in Christian Spain, longing for the physical and intellectual environment of his native town. Judah Ha-Levi, generally regarded as the finest of Spain's Jewish poets, if not the greatest of all post-Biblical Hebrew poets, also spent an important part of his life in Granada, where indeed he befriended Moses Ibn Ezra. After 1090, he appears to have moved first to Lucena, near Seville, and then to Seville itself, before finally going on to Toledo, which had recently been reclaimed by the Christian armies of Alfonso VI. Persecution of Jews in Christian Castile in 1109 sent him back again to al-Andalus, where he stayed in Córdoba. The position of Jews in Spain, in both the Christian and Muslim parts of the peninsula, was becoming increasingly difficult, and Ha-Levi saw the only hope for his people in an eventual return to the Holy Land. In the end he himself decided to leave Spain altogether and go to the Middle East. Friends tried to dissuade him, and he also had his own fears to contend with, as he later set down in a poem:

> He trembles. His tears begin to fall.
> He fears to leave Spain, to travel through the world,
> To embark on board ship, to cross the desert,
> By the lion's den and the leopard's mountain lair.
> He rebukes his friends, and decides to go.
> He leaves his home and lives in the wasteland.

Ha-Levi pobably died in Egypt, though the story goes that he was killed by a Muslim horseman just as he reached the gates of Jerusalem.

Religious intolerance, which had barely existed under the Umayyads, began gradually to take hold of Spain from the late eleventh century onwards, under the influence first of all of the ever growing threat from the Christian north, and then of the fanatical Muslim beliefs held by the two succeeding Berber dynasties who were to rule over al-Andalus in the twelfth and thirteenth centuries. The turning-point in the history of al-Andalus was the capture of Toledo by Alfonso VI in 1085. This marks the beginning of what came to be known as the 'Reconquest', though it was actually a 'Conquest' of lands which after nearly four centuries of Muslim rule were far more Muslim than Christian in their ethnic and cultural make-up. The loss of Toledo was at any rate deeply disconcerting to the *taifa* rulers in the south of Spain, particularly as Alfonso VI had already declared war on Seville. In 1086 the poet king al-Mu'tamid of Seville felt that he had no other option but to invite to Spain a Berber sect which had recently come to power in North-West Africa, the Almoravids.

The situation in North-West Africa in the first half of the eleventh century was roughly comparable to that of al-Andalus at that time, the whole place being divided up into lands ruled by different Berber tribes. One of these desert tribes, the Sanhājahs, visited Mecca around 1039, and on its way back fell under the influence of a religious teacher called Ibn Yasin. This man later established a retreat or *ribāt* for his followers, who became known in consequence as *al-Murābitūn*, from which the word 'Almoravids' is derived. The Almoravids rapidly gained a hold over North-West Africa and in 1062 founded the city of Marrākush (Marrakesh), which they made the capital of their state. After being called over to Spain in 1086 they immediately defeated the forces of Alfonso VI near Badajoz, but then returned to Africa. Summoned again to Spain two years later, their leader Yūsuf Ibn Tāshfīn decided to make an all-out attempt to take possession himself of al-Andalus, and in so doing to secure the cause of Islam. Granada was captured by him in 1089, al-Mu'tamid was deposed and exiled the following year, and one by one all the *taifa* kingdoms fell to the Almoravids.

The success of the Almoravids was due largely to their winning over of the Muslim lower classes through their religious fervour and austerity, and their strong anti-intellectual stance. However, their success was short-lived, for in the early twelfth century another equally fanatic Berber group, the Almohads, began to win over Almoravid territory. The Almohads were Berbers from the Atlas Mountains, and their religious leader was one Ibn Tūmart, who had been born a lamplighter's son in around 1084. Ibn Tūmart styled himself the *Mahdi*, or divinely chosen leader, and his followers were referred to as *Muwahhidūn* (hence 'Almohads') after their leader's advocacy of the concept of the unity or *tawhīd* of God. The man who brought the Almohads to political power was a potter's son called 'Abd al-Mu'min, who in 1147 seized Marrākush and thus brought about the collapse of the Almoravids. The Almohads then moved over to al-Andalus, but they gained possession over the whole country only around 1170, following years of political turmoil. As with the Almoravids, their hold over such a heterogeneous society as that of Spain had been possible only through the fanaticism of their beliefs, and once this fanaticism began to wane, they were left deeply vulnerable. They were to survive in Spain no longer than had the Almoravids, being crushingly defeated by Alfonso VII at Las Navas de Tolosa in 1212. The event, commemorated today by a large and hideous sculptural group on the site, was romantically described by Théophile Gautier as presaging the end of Spain's happiness and prosperity. The natives of al-Andalus, however, cannot have been too saddened by the defeat of the Almohads, whose intervention in their country's affairs had been welcomed by them with far less enthusiasm than had that of the Almoravids. In fact the Spanish Muslims probably felt that they had less in common with the Almohads than they had with the Christians of northern Spain. As more and more of their country came into the hands of the Christians, many of these Muslims were happy to stay on in Christian territory, and were able to carry on with their lives much as before. The Christian conquest of Spain made rapid progress after 1212, and met with little serious resistance. When Seville was taken in 1248, only the western half of Andalusia remained under Muslim control.

The Almoravids and the Almohads have often been portrayed as uncouth and barely literate people, with little interest in the arts and sciences. This is a great exaggeration. Under their rule, standards of scholarship remained as high as ever in al-Andalus, and the country produced two of the outstanding intellectual figures in the history of Islam, the jurist, physician and Aristotelian scholar Averroës, and the Jewish philosopher and theologian Maimonides. None the less, the patronage of literature declined significantly, and few major architectural works were produced. Our knowledge of both Amoravid and Almohad architecture is in fact based largely on what they built in Africa. From these buildings, it could be said that the Almoravids maintained the trend in Islamic architecture towards ever more extensive surface decoration, in complete contrast to the Almohads, who reacted against such decorative excesses and favoured a style of great austerity. However, the latter's architectural masterpiece in Spain, the Giralda tower in Seville (built between 1172 and 1195), is notable as an elegant structure with exquisite ornamentation, and is thought by some to illustrate the civilizing influence of al-Andalus on these people. A virtuoso intricacy of detailing was always to be kept up by the Muslim craftsmen in Spain, throughout the turbulent history of al-Andalus, and long after the Christian conquest of the country. Those craftsmen who worked for the Christians were happily to incorporate Christian motifs into their designs, and also to apply these designs to structures of a radically opposed style. The work of these craftsmen is referred to as *mudéjar*, a term originally used in reference to Muslims who remained in Christian Spain without converting to Christianity (the word is derived from the Arabic *mudajjan*, which means 'permitted to stay on', but also implies 'tamed'). Some of the great buildings of medieval Spain are essentially the work of the *mudéjar* craftsmen, such as the magnificent Alcázar in Seville, a Moorish building transformed in the late thirteenth century into a palace for the Christian king Pedro the Cruel.

By 1248, when most of al-Andalus had been reclaimed by the Christians, the monuments of Muslim Spain that were to have the greatest impact on the Western imagination had yet to be built. That al-Andalus managed to survive at all after 1248, let alone to do so for nearly two and a half centuries, and to create during this period some of Islam's most remarkable works, was an extraordinary achievement due in no small part to the ambitions and clever manoeuvring of a man who claimed Arab descent, Muhammad Ibn Nasr, founder of the Nasrid dynasty. He had come to power during the chaotic years following the collapse of the Almohads, and had created a small state in his native province of Jaén. Jaén fell to the Christian army of Ferdinand III in 1245, after which Ibn Nasr made Granada the capital of a kingdom which extends from just north of the town down to the Mediterranean, and from Tarifa to Almería. The Kingdom of Granada had a precarious existence, being coveted both by the Christians, and by a now powerful tribe in Morocco, the Marīnids. To lessen the Christian threat, Ibn Nasr signed a peace treaty with Ferdinand III in 1245, but this compelled him to swear allegiance to the Spanish kings, pay them an annual tribute, and even to assist them in fighting should the occasion arise. The terms of the treaty put Ibn Nasr in the unenviable position of having to help Ferdinand III in the siege of Seville of 1248, an act which did much to antagonize his fellow Muslims. Later Ibn Nasr had to call in the Marīnids to fight off the Christians, and the help of these Moroccans was further sought by his son and successor, Muhammad II. The Christians could easily have been provoked by these actions into mounting an all-out attack on Granada, but the mountainous terrain of this kingdom, its proximity to Africa, and the usefulness of its tribute money, deterred them from doing so, at least for the time being. Alliance between Granada and the Marīnids might nevertheless have incited the Christians to adopt increasingly severe measures against the Muslims in their own territories. These people began pouring into Granada in ever-increasing numbers, and the population of the kingdom became almost exclusively Muslim.

Under the Nasrids the town of Granada came to draw from Arab travellers the lavish praise which they had once bestowed upon Córdoba. Their praise has been echoed by countless travellers up to the present day, for whereas Córdoba has lost much of what had made it famous, Granada has retained more of its past than any other Spanish town. Built on and around three spurs of the Sierra Nevada, Granada has Muslim houses and monuments dispersed over a wide area. Even in the middle of the bustling lower town, which was radically altered in the late nineteenth century, you will come across such an important Muslim building as the fourteenth-century Casa del Carbón, with its grand, horseshoe-arched entrance way and excellently preserved three-storied courtyard in brick. The building, the only one of its kind to survive intact in Spain, was originally both a warehouse and a place of lodging for merchants, who would set up their tents in its courtyard just as they would have done in one of the caravanserai of the East. Across the road from it is a lively market, which, though a nineteenth-century Moorish pastiche, marks the site of the original market and has much of the character of an oriental bazaar. But the part of town which gives perhaps the best idea of what everyday life was like in Muslim Granada is the hill of the Albaicín. This largely residential area has been much smartened up in recent years, but its maze of steps and alleys and its dense clusters of tiny white houses and hanging gardens remain otherwise much as they were in Muslim times, with even a sufficient amount of noise, smells and animation to give a life-like quality to this vision of the past. To add to the Moorish illusion, a number of Sūfī Muslims have begun to return to the area in recent times (some refer to this phenomenon as the second coming of the Moors), and several Arab tea-rooms and shops selling oriental goods have opened up. Hidden within the warren of the Albaicín are splendid Moorish palaces that are virtually unvisited by the tourist; and by knocking at the door of a modest private house on the Calle Darro you will have a surprise similar to the one you might have had had you stolen Aladdin's lamp. For behind the door, which the house's owner is only too willing to open for you, lie a series of darkened, atmospheric chambers which were once Moorish public baths. Should you come here in the middle of the day, when narrow shafts of brilliant sunlight pierce through the star-shaped openings in the vaults, you might indeed feel that you have entered some Arabian fairy tale.

Predictably, and with wearying regularity, the world of fairy tales has been invoked to describe what are Granada's if not Andalusia's most celebrated monuments, the palaces and gardens of the Alhambra and the Generalife. Seen from the Albaicín, they appear to float on the crest of a verdant hill, their picturesque silhouette highlighted against a backdrop of snowcapped mountains. Towards evening, large groups of tourists climb up to the Albaicín to enjoy the sun setting behind this enchanted apparition. By day the two places are as crowded with visitors as descriptions of them are congested with superlatives. Their appeal is easy to understand – the luxuriance of their gardens, their coolness even at the height of summer, their magnificent setting, their abundance of pools, fountains and running water, and the way in which their architecture positively drips with ornamentation as in some Hollywood re-creation of an oriental scene. They fulfil popular notions of what Paradise must be like, and have been described by writers as if they were the work of angels rather than of real architects, craftsmen and landscape gardeners. From what you can read about them, you might also conclude that they were places dedicated solely to pleasure, but this is really true only of the Generalife, which was intended as a summer retreat. The Alhambra was both a private residence of the Nasrid kings and a vast complex of government buildings. Its finest parts date from the late fourteenth century, and are remarkable for the lightness of their architecture, the complexity of their vaulting, and, above all, for their ornamentation, which, though heavily restored, is more overwhelming in its intricacy than that of any other Moorish monument in Europe. Mario Praz, whose book *Unromantic Spain* contained a cruel and witty attack on Romantic attitudes to the Alhambra, found, perversely, that the end result of all this ornamentation was mind-numbing monotony. Praz might perhaps more profitably have pointed out that this ornamentation was largely executed in the cheap materials of plaster and wood, and that this was evidence that the Nasrids had far less wealth at their disposal than did the Umayyads, who had used in Medina Azahara only the finest marbles and other rich materials. The Alhambra, furthermore, has none of the architectural innovations of Córdoba's Mezquita. Its greatness, like that of Nasrid culture in general, lies in its dazzling synthesis of centuries of Islamic achievement, rather than in any original contribution of its own.

An Arab visitor to Granada in 1465 compared the town in size and in cultural splendour to Damascus, and wrote that 'it is a meeting place of illustrious people, poets, scientists, artists; there are here some of the finest men of our time, grandiose monuments, charming little corners ... with its Alhambra it is one of the great cities of Islam.' 'Yet,' he added ominously, 'the Infidels are close at hand and have taken the greater part of this land of al-Andalus.' Three years previously the Christians had conquered the Rock of Gibraltar, which the famous fourteenth-century traveller Ibn-Battūtah had once described as the 'citadel of Islam'. The loss of Gibraltar accentuated the Spanish Muslims' sense of being cut off from Africa, a feeling which had grown with the decline of Marīnid power in the second half of the fourteenth century. More isolated than ever before, they turned for help to Egypt and then to the Ottoman Empire, but in vain. The end of the Nasrids was spelt in 1481, when their forces rashly seized the castle of Zahara from the Christians. This action made the Spanish monarchs Ferdinand and Isabella resolve to conquer the Kingdom of Granada. They captured Ronda in 1485, Málaga in 1487, Almería in 1489, and in 1492 were at the gates of Granada itself.

The last Nasrid ruler, Abu 'Abdallah, known in Spanish as Boabdil, ignominiously surrendered to the Christians in 1492. Abandoning his beloved Granada, he went first into the Alpujarras, then to the coastal town of Adra, and finally ended up in North Africa. Legend has it that at a place marked today by a large petrol station and a scattering of characterless modern houses, the escaping Boabdil turned around to catch his final glimpse of his beloved Granada, and heaved a great sigh (this place is now known as El Suspiro del Moro, 'the Sigh of the Moor'). 'Weep like a woman,' his mother told him, 'you who have not defended your kingdom like a man.' For many, the collapse of the Nasrid dynasty brought to an end a golden age in Spanish history. Yet, according to official versions of this history, the Golden Age had only just begun.

3

THE GOLDEN AGE

1492 was a momentous year in Spanish history, and at present great preparations are being made to celebrate its fifth centenary. The year which had begun with the surrender of Granada and the consequent unification of Spain under Ferdinand and Isabella was to end with Columbus's pioneering voyage to America, and the claiming of the lands there for the Spanish crown. The new era which the two events heralded has traditionally been described as 'The Golden Age', and not without reason. A period of great economic prosperity, in which gold flowed into Spain from America, turned eventually into a magnificent flowering of the arts. Andalusia was to play the central role in this new Spain, and yet the Andalusians, more than any other Spanish peoples, are prone to look back at 1492 with scepticism. The nineteenth-century chronicler of Spain and her empire, W. H. Prescott, referred to the reign of Ferdinand and Isabella as the most 'glorious epoch in the annals of Spain'. Yet the basis of this glory was a Reconquest, which was not really a reconquest, and a Discovery, which was not a discovery. Both these achievements should really be seen in terms of a brutal subjugation of other peoples, and it is singularly appropriate that the coat of arms of Ferdinand and Isabella should consist of arrows and a yoke. The Golden Age was an age of great paradoxes, and it has become a commonplace among historians to emphasize that the years of Spain's greatness contained the seeds of her decline. Doubtlessly, few people in 1992 will be commemorating Spain's disastrous decision in 1492 to expel the Jews from the country, just as few people of the time would have openly admitted that many of the great protagonists of their age had Jewish blood themselves, including Ferdinand and probably Columbus.

The early years of Columbus's life are shrouded in mystery, and perhaps he later intended them to be so. He is said to have been born in the Italian town of Genoa around 1445, though he was always to write in Spanish, and never to show the slightest pride in his supposed birthplace. His mother was almost certainly a Spanish Jewess, and it has recently been suggested that in Spain Jews were sometimes referred to as 'Genoese', both races being renowned for their avariciousness. In any case, he married in the 1470s the daughter of a Spanish captain, from whom he would inherit numerous maps and nautical instruments, as well as documents relating to various journeys and discoveries that this captain had made. These documents apparently encouraged Columbus in his belief that it would be possible to reach the East by sailing to it across the Atlantic. There is also a story that Columbus had a meeting with a pilot who had actually done this journey by accident, his boat having been swept drastically off course while sailing between Spain and England; his story, related for the first time in a book of 1535, and afterwards frequently repeated, was later omitted in the biography of Columbus written by his son Hernando.

As is well known, Columbus spent many years trying without success to raise money for his Atlantic enterprise. By 1485 his wife had died, his hair had gone prematurely white, and he had just received another serious rebuttal, from the court of Portugal. Undeterred, he went straight from Portugal to Andalusia, hoping to arrange a meeting with Ferdinand and Isabella, who were then residing at Córdoba. His first stop was at Huelva, where his sister-in-law was living. He stayed a few kilometres outside the town, at the monastery of La Rábida, and it was here that he established a friendship with Fray Antonio Marchena, with whom he had lengthy discussions on astronomy, cosmography and philosophy. From La Rábida he went to Seville and made contact with the Duke of Medinaceli, who was able to secure for Columbus his first meeting with the Catholic monarchs. This was not a success, and Columbus was compelled to continue his search for financial backing, approaching, among others, the Duke of Medina Sidonia and Henry VIII of England. In 1491 Columbus was reported to be in a deeply depressed state, and in the autumn of that year he was back at La Rábida.

Few places seem more suited for the relief of melancholy than the charming monastery of La Rábida, which is now the place in

Andalusia most evocative of Columbus's memory. Though situated on the ugly estuary of the Río Tinto, and with views towards the industrial town of Huelva, it is fortunately shielded from its surroundings by a forest of pines and a colourful garden filled with palms and exotic flowers. The monastery was badly damaged after the Lisbon earthquake of 1755, and has been subject to extensive restoration and rebuilding; but it still has a pleasantly homely and intimate character. This character is completely at variance with the murals of Columbus's life painted in one of the monastery's rooms early this century by a local artist, Daniel Vázquez Díaz (see page 290). These works, executed in a highly stylized manner, have epic pretensions, and even include a scene of a monk embracing Columbus which the artist intended as symbolizing the meeting of the medieval and modern worlds.

The voyage which Vázquez Díaz and countless others were so heroically to envisage was finally made possible on the intervention of La Rábida's abbot, Fray Juan Pérez. Pérez had once been a confessor to Isabella, and he wrote her a letter strongly supporting Columbus's project. By the time the letter arrived, early in January 1492, Granada had just surrendered, and the queen was thus well disposed to finance a project which might conceivably further Spain's glory. Shortly afterwards Columbus was at last able to prepare for the journey, and recruited his crew largely from the two villages closest to La Rábida, Palos de la Frontera and Moguer de la Frontera; he chose as the captain of one of the three ships that he intended to take with him a Palos man called Martín Alonso Pinzón, who had a considerable local reputation as a sailor. Columbus was ready to leave at the beginning of August 1492, and enjoyed a farewell supper at La Rábida in the simply furnished refectory, which still survives. He set sail early the next morning from Palos, a place which is described today as 'the cradle of the Americas'. Approached from La Rábida, you have to drive along a road known as the Calle de las Americas, which is lined with ceramic plaques listing the countries that form the Americas. The village itself is a rather characterless place, and two of its few buildings of interest are the house which belonged to the Pinzón family (this is now being turned into a museum) and the modest late gothic church of St George, where Columbus and his crews were blessed on the morning of their departure. They set off from the small bay directly underneath this church, and reached the New World just over two months later. On the return journey Columbus had a serious quarrel with Pinzón, who arrived back in Spain gravely ill and died at La Rábida in March 1483.

Columbus's pioneering voyage brought him not only great fame but also a considerable amount of money, for he had managed to secure before leaving Spain an excellent financial deal should his mission be successful. It says much of Columbus's character that he decided also to keep for himself the large reward which he had offered to the first sailor to sight land; the poor sailor in question afterwards went off to Morocco, where he was never heard of again. Columbus was later to see his mission of colonizing the New World as being divinely inspired, but he had been trained as a merchant, and he remained a merchant at heart. Religious fervour competed in him with a greed which was to lead ultimately to great personal unhappiness. He returned three more times to America, but proved himself inept at administering the lands that he had 'discovered', acquired many ambitious rivals, was deposed as governor, and ended up a disillusioned man in Spain, where he died in Valladolid in 1506. His remains were transferred to Seville's Charterhouse, the ruins of which are now being transformed into the centrepiece for this city's 1492 celebrations; his corpse was brought many years later to Seville Cathedral, given a splendid memorial in the transept, but then re-interred again and shipped off to the West Indian island of San Domingo.

Greed dominated the lives of many of the so-called *conquistadores* or conquerors who followed in Columbus's footsteps to the New World. And these lives, too, often ended sadly. Cortes, the conqueror of Mexico, died an embittered and forgotten man at a village near Seville called Castilleja de la Cuesta, a place remembered today mainly for its biscuits and for being the birthplace of Rita Hayworth. Pizarro, the conqueror of Peru, was killed in that country in 1541, finished off not by the Indians but by his fellow Spaniards, who set upon him with a brutality which had typified his own exploits in the New World. The Spanish conquerors left in America a legacy of violence and lawlessness which has survived to this day. But they were able to settle the continent probably faster than any other European power of the time could have done: the English, for instance, discovered Nova Scotia in 1497, but were not to have any settlement in America until the seventeenth century. The Spaniards succeeded in colonizing and Europeanizing America so quickly because they had spent over 400 years doing exactly this in their own country.

The unification of Spain under Ferdinand and Isabella was accomplished in a spirit of brutal fanaticism. Isabella had an obsession with racial purity, and tried to impose this on a country which had always been exceptionally diverse in its ethnic make-up: even Ferdinand himself had a Jewish mother. Andalusia, the most heterogeneous of all Spanish regions, was consequently the one most affected by Isabella's racial policies. In 1480 the notorious Spanish Inquisition was set up in Seville, and in the following year the first victims of this were burnt at an *auto-de-fe* in this city. Among those persecuted by the Inquisition were homosexuals, the act of sodomy having always been considered one of the gravest offences possible for a Christian: a German traveller visiting Andalusia in the 1490s, Hieronymus Münzer, found in Almería the corpses of six Italian sodomites who had been hung up first by their necks and then by their feet, and, before finally dying, had had their genitals cut off and attached underneath their chins. But the majority of those killed in the name of Christianity were those Jews who had been converted to it. Known as *conversos*, they often came under the suspicion of the Inquisition on the grounds that their conversions had not been genuine. Converted or not, Jews were by now hated figures in Spanish society, and they were still associated with that most despised of professions, money-lending. The Inquisition stirred up popular resentment towards them as a way of strengthening support for Ferdinand and Isabella. As with the exploits of the *conquistadores*, greed too was a major motivation behind the activities of the Inquisition. Anyone falling foul of this body had their property taken away from them, even before guilt could be proved. In this way the church and many of her inquisitors, such as the dreaded Torquemada (himself, ironically, a secret *converso*), acquired great wealth. Much of this wealth was directed towards the Granada campaign, a campaign which was also financed by Jewish backers. Only the converted Jews were allowed to remain in Spain after 1492, and those who failed to disguise their origins stayed on to an increasingly uncertain fate.

The Muslims who remained in eastern Andalusia after 1492 fared

at first rather better than Spain's *conversos*, and indeed had surrendered to the Christians on quite favourable terms. They were
allowed to keep their religion, costumes and traditions on the one
condition that they stayed away from their fortified settlements such
as the Alhambra. The Muslim population of the former Kingdom of
Granada was now about a quarter of a million, a further quarter of a
million having left Spain voluntarily or been killed in the hostilities.
The Christian colonization of this part of Andalusia was by no
means an even one, the southern towns such as Málaga and Marbella
becoming largely Christian, and the eastern half acquiring only small
and isolated Christian communities. Only in the northern towns,
including Granada itself, could *conversos*, Christians and Muslims, be
found in equal numbers. The Muslims of Granada were concentrated
on the Albaicín, and continued to bring wealth to the town with their
trade in raw and patterned silk. The many Western visitors to the
town after 1492 were fascinated by the Muslims and their exotic
costumes, in the same way as are tourists in Morocco today: of
especial interest was what one traveller described as the 'fantastical'
white robes of the women, which trailed down to the ground and
covered the face almost completely. Though the two races were now
strictly segregated, the Spanish Christians continued to adapt to
Muslim ways as they had always done. Christians came to eat much
the same food as the Muslims, learned from them the silk trade, took
up the strange Muslim habit of nibbling at pieces of porcelain, and
even began wearing some of their clothing, to judge from a few
wardrobe inventories of the time. Even the Moorish love of frequent
washing, which the Christians condemned as a sign of promiscuity,
caught on among some of the Andalusian Christians, and the ritual of
the public bath was to remain an important feature of their social life
well into the seventeenth century.

The first Catholic Bishop of Granada after 1492, Fray Hernando de
Talavera, was a tolerant, enlightened man who believed that the
Muslims would gradually assimilate Christianity and should not have
the religion forced upon them. However, political enemies of his and
numerous Catholic fanatics were anxious to discredit him, particularly
in view of growing fears of a Muslim invasion supported from Africa.
The feared rebellion broke out in 1499, following the arrival in
Granada of the fanatical Cardinal Cisneros, who ordered the baptism

of 60,000 Muslims. The revolt broke out in the Alpujarras, but soon spread throughout eastern Andalusia, and was put down only in 1501. The Spaniards afterwards attempted to safeguard Andalusia by capturing the North African towns of Ceuta and Melilla, and have held on to these places to this day. Meanwhile, in Andalusia itself, they threw out all the unconverted Muslims and forced the others to wear Western clothes and speak in Spanish. These last measures were difficult to impose, and seem to have been ignored by most of the Muslims. The Venetian ambassador Andrea Navagero, in a fascinating description of Granada in 1526, described how the converted Muslims (who were referred to as *moriscos*) continued not just to wear their own costumes and speak their own language but also to practise their traditional faith. They held the Christians in utter contempt, which did not surprise Navagero, as he thought that they were terribly treated by the latter. Navagero hoped that the Inquisition would stay away from Granada, and that no more severe measures would be imposed on the *moriscos*, for, in his view, such measures would seriously damage both the prosperity and the beauty of the town. His pleas for tolerance were not to be heeded, for in 1568 Philip II tried to stamp out Muslim culture far more forcibly than before. Another revolt was sparked off, this one breaking out in the Albaicín and then retreating into the Alpujarras, where it was finally quelled in 1571. The cost of this rebellion was the expulsion of all the *moriscos* from Granada and its former kingdom.

When Ferdinand and Isabella marched into the town of Granada in 1492, they did not just have in front of them the task of introducing Christianity and Western customs into a place which had been under Muslim rule for over seven centuries. They were also determined to create in what had been one of the great urban wonders of the Islamic world memorials worthy of the spirit of the Catholic reconquest. This spirit may not in itself have been so admirable, but no one can deny that the works of art and architecture that it inspired were of outstanding quality. Visitors to Granada today see the place essentially as a Muslim city, and yet in the sixteenth century Granada developed also into one of the main Renaissance centres of Europe.

In the creation of Renaissance Granada, a remarkable amount of care was taken not to destroy the major monuments that had been left by the Muslims. Ferdinand and Isabella are known to have had a great love for the Alhambra, and were happy to adapt to the Moorish style of living and to use the place as a palace, just as their predecessors had done with the Alcázar in Seville. The place had in fact been left by the Nasrids in a slightly decayed state, and the Catholic monarchs had had Muslim craftsmen brought in to restore it to its former magnificence. The main new building which was put up in the Alhambra by Ferdinand and Isabella was a Franciscan monastery, built over a former Arab bath and palace belonging, it is thought, to a Nasrid prince; the monastery is now one of the most exclusive of the government-run hotels known as *paradores*. The temptation to create within the Alhambra a massive cathedral which would rise up above the surrounding Infidel structures to proclaim the greater glories of the Catholic church was wisely avoided. Before a cathedral could be built elsewhere in the town, however, a temporary cathedral was established in the Alhambra's mosque, the building in which the first mass of the Reconquest had been celebrated. This mosque, dedicated by the Christians to the Virgin and pulled down in the late sixteenth century to make way for an austere church, was one of the few mosques in Granada taken over by the Christians in the early years of their rule here; most of the other mosques, including the principal one, kept on functioning as before. The Christians also left largely undisturbed the main residential district of the Muslims – the hills of the Albaicín and Alcazaba. The only important building founded by the Catholic monarchs on these hills was the modest convent of St Isabel, which stands on top of the Alcazaba and has a church adorned with a delightful portal in a playful late gothic style. The two monarchs' dreams of a great Christian city were reserved essentially for the lower town of Granada.

The reign of Ferdinand and Isabella saw the emergence of an architectural style known as the plateresque. Derived from *platero*, the word for silversmith, the term was coined to describe the highly intricate decoration to be found in many of the buildings of this period. The actual decorative forms of the plateresque – gothic in the earlier years of the style, and classical in the later ones – are European in origin, but the love of intricacy was a legacy of Spain's Muslim past. Spanish medieval architecture of the late medieval and early Renaissance periods is imbued with a Muslim presence. As the term 'plateresque' suggests, the Spaniards inherited from the Muslims an essentially decorative approach towards architecture. Spain's great gothic cathedrals are not notable for their harmony of proportions, as are those of France, but instead often gain their power from the profusely decorated surfaces and chaotic cluster of rich furnishings: as with the Great Mosque at Córdoba, it is often difficult in a Spanish church to grasp the overall structure, and you are not even given a clear view down the nave, as this is blocked by a sumptuously carved choir. There are specific Muslim borrowings within Spanish buildings, for instance the use of decorative bands of lettering on a large scale. Furthermore, as has already been noted (see page 81), *mudéjar* craftsmen were themselves responsible for wholly Muslim elements within these buildings: among the most popular Spanish ceilings up to the early seventeenth century were the *artesonado* ones, which were *mudéjar* ceilings in wooden inlay imitating traditional Muslim leather-work. But Spanish architecture is one of great contrasts, and along-side the Muslim-inspired love of decorative richness is an inherently Spanish love of the austere. The most elaborate portals are sometimes set against bare slabs of granite, and breathtakingly sumptuous decoration is applied to structures of exceptional severity. In the course of the sixteenth century the austere elements in Spanish architecture were to gain the upper hand, a development which can be seen in its early stages in Granada.

Ferdinand and Isabella envisaged the new cathedral of Granada as dominating the lower town, and as being built, like that of Seville, on the site of the town's main mosque. The mosque was transformed into a church in 1501, but the cathedral itself was not begun until over twenty years later. In the meantime there was erected next to the former mosque a chapel intended to house the tombs of Ferdinand and Isabella. The two monarchs had originally planned to be buried in the church of San Juan de los Reyes in Toledo, but, in 1504, a year before the queen's death, they decided that it would be more fitting to have their mausoleum in the town where they had known their greatest triumph. They chose as their architect for this chapel a man then engaged in work for Toledo cathedral, Enrique Egas, who, like most of the leading architects and artists in Spain at this time, was of Flemish descent. This Flemish generation is associated with what is called the Isabelline or Gothic plateresque, a style of late gothic fantasy in which playful naturalistic detail abounds. San Juan de los

Reyes, the work of the Flemish-born architect Juan Guas, is one of the masterpieces of this style, and its sumptuous and fantastical ornamentation make the Egas chapel at Granada seem rather restrained in comparison. The Granada chapel was not finished until 1527, a good twenty years after the completion of the Toledo church, and though Egas himself was a pronounced gothicist there worked with him younger men of more classical leanings: the chapel's exuberant gothic north portal, which now stands inside the cathedral, contrasts with the more measured, classical archway through which you enter the building from the street. Isabella's own taste was for the charming, minutely executed naturalism of Flemish art, and in the chapel's sacristy can be seen part of her celebrated collection of Flemish paintings. But tastes in Spain had changed considerably since her death in 1505, and her own tomb and that of her husband were the work of an Italian artist, Domenico Fancelli, who favoured a simpler and bolder monument than a Flemish artist would have done. Egas also had the commission to build Granada's cathedral, but after starting on the foundations, he left Granada for good around 1525, thus clearing the way for the classical, Italianate artists and architects favoured by Ferdinand and Isabella's grandson, Charles V.

The lower town of Granada had been a scene of intense building activity since the beginning of the sixteenth century. A massive Franciscan monastery (now a military headquarters) was erected on the site of the demolished Jewish quarter, and a great hospital (now the university) put up outside the town's walls. Numerous other palaces and churches were built, Moorish towers pulled down, abandoned palaces restored, streets widened, and a series of impressive squares created – the Plazas Nueva, de Bibarrambla, and del Principe. Despite the remaining Moorish monuments the lower town of Granada acquired in the sixteenth century a character very unlike that of most other Andalusian towns; its regular street plan, squares and predominance of grey stone buildings bring to mind an Italian Renaissance town rather than any place in Andalusia. Among the more important buildings dating from the early sixteenth century was the church of Santo Domingo, which has a triple arched classical portico covered in frescoes and could easily be mistaken for some Italian creation. Contemporary with this is the enormous Monastery of San Jerónimo, a structure of gothic proportions but classical detailing, designed by two of the leading exponents of the classical style in Granada, the Italian Jacopo Florentino and the great genius of the Spanish Renaissance, Diego de Siloe.

Andalusia was the part of Spain where the gothic style made the least impact. In the case of Granada, it was supplanted almost immediately by the classical style, which was far better suited than the former to express the uncompromising spirit of the New Spain. Granada was never intended as the capital of Spain, but it was in the sixteenth century an important commercial and university town, and a courtly centre invested with a major symbolic role. The man who did most to emphasize this role was the Holy Roman Emperor Charles V. He entered Granada for the first time in 1526, just after marrying Isabel of Portugal in Seville. They were on their honeymoon, and took up residence in the Alhambra. Most people today could hardly dream of a better place for a honeymoon than the Alhambra, but Charles V and his queen had been spoilt by the luxuries of modern life and found the place uncomfortable, and difficult to warm. Isabel was apparently so horrified by her bedroom that she immediately took off with her retinue to the convent of San Jerónimo in the lower town. Many of Charles's courtiers would have liked to have done the same, as they too complained bitterly about their assigned lodgings. When Charles finally decided that he wanted to turn Granada into a permanent residence of the court, he clearly felt that he had to do something about the Alhambra, particularly so as he considered the place totally unsuitable for receiving ambassadors. Both his mother, Juana la Loca, and his grandparents, Ferdinand and Isabella, had urged him not to destroy the Alhambra, and he himself went that year to Córdoba and was horrified by the effects of his allowing a cathedral to be built within the town's Mezquita. In the end Charles V barely touched the main Nasrid palaces, but built alongside these a mighty palace of his own. He entrusted the work to one Pedro Machuca, a man who had received his architectural training in Italy. Machuca made no attempt to create a building which would harmonize with its architectural surroundings, but designed instead an imposing and scarcely ornamented square block containing a colonnaded circular courtyard. This was a building unprecedented in Spain in its classical severity, and also very revolutionary even in an Italian context. When seen alongside the romantically old-fashioned palaces of the Nasrids, it must have struck contemporaries as a powerful statement of the aspirations of Golden Age Spain.

An indication of what was to become of these aspirations is the fact that the building was abandoned before being completed, and, like the Alhambra, was left to decay. Charles V's ambitious plans for Granada were to be forgotten in the course of his subsequent military exploits throughout Europe. Before leaving Granada for ever in 1527, he expressed a wish to be buried in the town's cathedral, work on which had only just begun. Even this wish was to come to nothing, but at least it gave new impetus to the construction of this building, and an opportunity to reassess existing plans for it. Egas's projected cathedral was considered too old-fashioned, and in 1528 the design of the cathedral was taken over by Diego de Siloe. Siloe was an architect and sculptor of Flemish descent whose father, Gil, had been responsible for some of the most exciting works of the Isabelline plateresque, including the overwhelmingly intricate tombs of Juan II and Isabel of Portugal in the Charterhouse of Miraflores outside Burgos. In Diego's own work can be seen a transition from the Isabelline to the classical plateresque, to – in his cathedral at Granada – a classicism as bold and daring as that of Pedro Machuca. In fact so uncompromising were his plans for the cathedral that even Charles V, when he got to hear of them in 1529, began to be worried: Siloe had to go to the emperor to defend himself, and to reassure him of the suitability of having a great classical structure next to the gothic Royal Chapel built by Egas. It comes indeed as a considerable shock to move from this homely chapel into the cathedral proper. You find yourself at first in a towering circular chancel inspired by the Holy Sepulchre in Jerusalem; as you walk towards the nave, the massive size of the place becomes quite overpowering. Throughout the interior runs a giant order of classical columns and pilasters that were originally intended to support barrel vaulting (the present gothic vaulting was an alteration made to Siloe's plan in the late sixteenth century). The whole place is saved from being heavy and oppressive by its spaciousness and by being painted all over a brilliant white. I was once lucky enough to attend High Mass here on Corpus Christi and was able to appreciate the building's theatricality to the full when, to the accompaniment of the cathedral's superb late baroque organ, dazzlingly coloured confetti fell from the incense loft like manna from the heavens. The theatricality of the place, greatly heightened during the baroque period, has often proved too much for the English traveller, and one of these, John Harvey, was not alone in believing that the building was 'one of the world's architectural tragedies, one of the saddest of wasted opportunities'. Such prejudices seem to be echoed by the tourists who today happily crowd into the Royal Chapel but do not even bother to enter the cathedral proper. This is a telling reflection of the neglect from which so many of Andalusia's Golden Age monuments have suffered.

Granada cathedral was just one of a number of cathedrals that were constructed in Andalusia in the wake of 1492. At Córdoba, Almería, Guadix, Málaga and Jaén, lofty new cathedrals rose up in celebration of the triumph of Spain and the Catholic church. For all their lingering gothic elements, all showed an obsessive interest in the new classical style; in common with Granada cathedral, most of these buildings were not to receive their final coating of splendour until the Baroque period. Córdoba cathedral, so derided because of its unfortunate position within the town's Mezquita, is the most unified of these structures, and is a rich and fascinating blend of the *mudéjar* and the classical plateresque. Almería cathedral is heavy and fortress-like, a true bulwark of the Faith; Guadix is grey and austere; Málaga has much of the theatricality of Granada cathedral though it is fussier in its detailing; and Jaén has the most commanding situation of them all, a true giant dwarfing the town below. Diego de Siloe had a hand in the cathedrals of Almería and Guadix, while at those of Málaga and Jaén there worked Siloe's successor as the leading classical architect active in Andalusia, Andrés de Vandelvira.

Vandelvira was a prolific architect, but the bulk of his works are to be found in the twin towns of Úbeda and Baeza, which are richer in Renaissance palaces and churches than almost any other town in Spain. A thriving textile industry brought enormous prosperity to the area in the sixteenth century, and the importance of the towns was increased by Úbeda being the home town of the man who virtually ruled Spain during the first half of the century, Charles V's secretary, Francisco de los Cobos y Molina. This man founded and is buried in what is the most striking of Úbeda's many fine churches, the chapel of the Salvador. Designed by Diego de Siloe but executed by Vandelvira, this is the great rarity in Spain, a Renaissance church built within a very short period of time, little altered in later centuries, and containing most of its original furnishings: the excellence of the architecture is matched by the superlative quality of the furnishings, among which is a powerful retable by Spain's leading Renaissance sculptor, Alonso Berruguete, a pupil of Michelangelo.

Baeza has not any single monument equal in quality to the Salvador, but in many ways it is the more attractive of the two towns, having fortunately been spared the ugly modern development which has grown up around Úbeda. To wander around the quiet and excellently preserved streets of Baeza is to turn the pages of some manual of Renaissance architecture. The delicate classicism of Vandelvira and his followers is everywhere apparent, but the building which claims the visitor's attention most is the extraordinary and fantastical Palacio de Jabalquinto: whether or not this was the work of Juan Guas, the architect of Toledo's San Juan de los Reyes, it is indisputably the most striking example of the Isabelline plateresque in the south of Spain. I was standing admiringly in front of this building when a group of schoolchildren came up to ask me what I was doing. They seemed amazed that any foreigner should take an interest in their town. Baeza's decline into obscurity after the sixteenth century has been quite remarkable, and I found it hard to believe that the school from which these children came – a harmonious classical building adjoining the Palacio de Jabalquinto – had been founded in 1535 as one of Spain's earliest universities.

Another of Andalusia's improbable former university towns is Osuna near Seville. Osuna too is a little-visited place and exceptionally rich in monuments. Hardly a single modern building spoils its perfect sixteenth- to seventeenth-century character, and, what is more, the old buildings give directly on to the countryside. Its two major monuments of the Renaissance rise up on a gaunt hill above the town. One is the old university, which was founded in 1548 and is now also a school. The other is the splendid collegiate church, which has an exquisite classical plateresque portal adorning an otherwise rather severe west façade, and a light and spacious interior. The building has been magnificently endowed with sixteenth- and seventeenth-century furnishings and paintings, but the highpoint of a visit here is the sixteenth-century pantheon of the Dukes of Osuna, which is like a church in miniature, with doll-like choir stalls and jewel-like Renaissance ornamentation.

The monuments of Osuna might be undeservedly little visited, but at least they have been excellently looked after. The same could not be said of the castles of Lacalahorra and Vélez-Blanco. Both places were designed and embellished in the early years of the sixteenth century by Italian architects and craftsmen, and were among the first buildings in Spain in an Italian Renaissance style. The former, situated in a forlorn village fifteen kilometres south of Guadix, stands on top of what seems like a great mound of rubble; its exterior is particularly sturdy and forbidding, but inside is a sumptuous Italian Renaissance courtyard crumbling away. Vélez-Blanco is an even less likely place for Italian Renaissance ideals to have been introduced into Spain, being in the middle of the wild, uninviting landscape of Almería province, in an area which in the early sixteenth century was still inhabited largely by people of Muslim descent. This castle has an elegant and well preserved exterior, and the tourist, not forewarned, might well approach the building with mounting excitement. Inside, however, there is nothing. The celebrated courtyard, with its rich marble decoration by Italian craftsmen, was sold off in 1903, and has since been reconstructed in the Metropolitan Museum of Art in New York.

The glory, the squalor, and the decline of Golden Age Andalusia are illustrated above all in the history of Seville. While Granada and its former kingdom suffered in the sixteenth century from racial strife and major demographic changes, the western half of Andalusia experienced a great surge in prosperity. This was the part of Spain which most benefited from the settlement of the New World, and its thriving centre, well into the seventeenth century, was Seville. Seville had already become Spain's largest city in the twelfth century, and its importance had been recently emphasized by its becoming the headquarters of the Spanish Inquisition. But its fame was finally assured in 1503, when the Spanish court decreed the setting up here of a Casa de Contratacción, a royal agency responsible for the administration of trade and politics in the New World. From now on all ships sailing between Europe and the New World would have to pass through Seville. As a monk was to observe in 1587, 'was not Seville and all Andalusia the furthest point and the end of all land, and now it is the middle to which come the best and most esteemed of the Old World . . . to be carried to the New'. In the early years of the century the exodus to the New World, together with losses from plagues, resulted in a temporary fall in Seville's population. When Andrea Navagero came here in 1525 he found the place to be 'poorly populated and almost in the hands of women'. This situation was soon to change, and between 1530 and 1580 the population doubled to reach an estimated 85,000, which made the town the largest in Europe after Venice and Rome. Seville's boom-town atmosphere attracted people here from all over Spain and Europe. Merchants from Flanders, Germany, England and Scotland settled here, as did many of the *moriscos* who were expelled from Granada in 1570. The racial muddle of Seville was furthered by the influx of mainly black African slaves, who were to turn the place into the second slave capital of Europe (the first being Lisbon). And in the wake of all these people grew up a notorious underworld of thieves, murderers, muggers, swindlers, card-sharps, prostitutes, pimps, entrepreneurs, black marketeers, and all kinds of seekers of fortunes and refugees from justice. A priest of the time described Seville as a *'mare magnum'*, a 'great sea', and criminals referred to the place in their slang as 'Babylonia'. The celebrated Golden Age poet Luis de Góngora addressed Seville as 'great Babylon of Spain, map of all nations'; and the Seville poet, Fernando de Herrera, said, '. . . you are not a city, but a world.' In the sixteenth century Granada acted as the symbolic capital of Spain, and Madrid became the political one; but the economical and cultural one was unquestionably Seville.

'A powerful gentleman is Mr Money,' wrote the cruel satirist Francisco Quevedo, whose smirking, bespectacled face was portrayed by the Seville-born painter, Diego Velázquez. The obsession with money was one which united all the social classes in sixteenth- and seventeenth-century Seville. The traditional image of the aloof Spanish aristocrat refusing to demean himself by involvement in the trading profession has to be forgotten when discussing the Seville of this period. The Seville aristocrat speculated in money no less avidly than the merchants, and, moreover, an increasing number of these merchants – many of whom, incidentally, were secret *conversos* – were able to buy their way into the aristocracy. 'Money,' continued Quevedo, 'is born in the Indies, dies in Spain, and is buried in Genoa.' Sixty to 100 boats a year would bring back the bounty from America, bounty which greatly increased in value after 1560, when a new way was discovered of processing silver. One of the most profitable investments to be made in Seville was to buy a boat or even a whole fleet, but much money was also acquired through the stocking up of these ships for their long journeys, and through exports to the New World. The biscuit business flourished in sixteenth-century Seville, as did more traditional enterprises such as the making of wine and olive oil, vast quantities of which were required for America. Gunpowder was needed for the protection of those working in America and for the safeguarding of the goods that came from there: the Seville suburb of Triana had one of the largest gunpowder factories in Europe, until 1579, when this blew up, causing great loss of life. Less explosive, but no less profitable Seville activities included the making of ceramics and the manufacturing of soap from olive oil (an industry which had been introduced by the Muslims). Nor should one forget the various trades dependent on the mineral wealth of the New World, such as the silversmiths, the jewellery-makers, and those involved in the minting of the metal into coins.

Great fortunes were to be made in Seville, but a high proportion of the population was barely able to subsist. The enormous marginal element in Seville society provided many of the victims for the Inquisition, which further increased this element by depriving of their livelihoods those whom they arrested. The real underdogs were the *moriscos*, who were subject to constant racial harassment and sometimes responded by violence themselves. They stayed closely together, and many of them even lived in those ghettoes that had once been allotted to the Muslims, who had been chased out of the city between 1502 and 1505. In common with slaves and *conversos*, they were strictly excluded from the guilds and thus could take on only unskilled or semi-skilled jobs. One of the common sights in sixteenth-century Seville was that of *morisco* men selling fritters, while their wives sold roasted chestnuts, buttercakes and sweets. These people were often the lucky ones; many others resorted to desperate measures.

Cervantes described Seville as the 'asylum of the poor, and the refuge of the outlaw'. The place abounded in beggars, among whom were so many false cripples that by 1597 a licence was needed to be able to beg. Numerous women took up prostitution, thereby risking the new and dreadful disease of syphilis, which had reputedly been brought over from the New World. Seville's criminal reputation was legendary, and the city has retained it to this day, though with increasingly less justification. In the sixteenth century the risk of assault was so great that everyone carried arms for protection. The part of the city where the silversmiths worked had its own walls and guards, but otherwise the policing of Seville was scant and ineffective. Criminals could easily evade the law by moving into another district of the city, taking sanctuary in the cathedral, or, as a final resort, going to America, which, as Cervantes said, was 'the refuge and shelter of all desperate folk in Spain, the sanctuary of bankrupts, the safe-conduct of murderers, the protection and cover of those gamblers known by the experts in the craft as sharpers, the general decoy of loose women . . .' The picaresque novel, the novel of the wandering rogue or *picaro*, was born in sixteenth-century Spain, and Cervantes was one of the many Golden Age writers to take their inspiration from the low life of Seville. In one of his *Exemplary Stories*, he tells of two impoverished boys who come to Seville, and soon take to thieving, despite initial reservations. 'What's wrong with it?' says the person who persuades them into thieving. 'Isn't it worse to be a heretic or a renegade, or to kill one's father and mother, or to be a solomite [sic]?' One of the boys finally ends up 'shocked by the slackness of the law in that famous city of Seville, where pernicious and perverted people could live almost openly.'

The English writer Laurie Lee, evoking the Seville he had known in the 1930s, spoke of the place as a 'city where, more than in any other, one may bite on the air and taste the multitudinous flavours of Spain – acid, sugary, intoxicating, sickening but flavours which, above all in a synthetic world, are real as nowhere else'. Thanks to a wealth of sixteenth- and seventeenth-century documents and literary accounts, it is possible vividly to experience what the place must have been like in the Golden Age, down to the place's very sounds and smells. Up to 1500, the place had changed little since Muslim times. It had kept the irregular street plan characteristic of a Muslim city, and its white-washed houses had been left plain on the outside, in accordance with Muslim taste. In the course of the sixteenth century, streets were widened, but the irregularity of the layout remained, as it does today. The houses meanwhile were given often lavish exteriors, while retaining what has always been their most enchanting feature – their patios. 'What a pleasure for both the sight and sound is a Seville patio!' enthused the normally rather reticent priest, Padre Alonso de

Morgado, in 1587. These patios were filled, as they are today, with jasmine, rose bushes, orange trees and flower pots containing, in Morgado's words, 'a thousand different kinds of fragrant flowers and plants'. The patios were renowned for their cleanliness, and Cervantes described one as 'so spotlessly clean that it shone as if it had been rubbed with the finest vermilion'. Outside, in the streets, a rather different world awaited you, filthy and foul-smelling. Navagero was impressed by the way the streets were paved with bricks, but most people commented on the way these streets were piled high with rubbish. In 1597 an assistant to the Seville Court of Justice found that the 'conditions in the city are shameful', and that all the streets had 'become little more than dung heaps'. Added to the smells of rubbish was a rather more sinister odour. While the Moors and the Jews had had the sense to bury their dead outside the city, the Christians preferred to do so in shallow graves in the cloisters of the city's monasteries and convents. Through the streets of jasmine-scented Seville wafted in the summer months the odour of decomposing flesh and organs.

Seville was and remains a city of violent contrasts, the beautiful and the ugly, wealth and poverty existing in close proximity. '*Quien no ha visto Sevilla no ha visto meravilla*,' 'He who has not seen Seville has not seen marvels,' is a saying which has been unfailingly repeated by travellers over the centuries. Yet this city, praised for its marvels, has been equally famous for its slums and wastes. Only a few minutes' walk from the cathedral was El Arenal, an area of inhabited swampland in between the city walls and the Guadalquivir. This was one of the famed meeting places for the city's underworld, and it was sometimes referred to as 'El Corral del Arenal' after the name of Seville's largest brothel, which was once to be found here. Another grim and dangerous part of Seville was an area of polluted, marshy land now known as the Alameda de Hercules. Situated in the northern half of the city, this was such an eyesore that in 1574 a nobleman gave money for it to be transformed into a tree-lined promenade or *alameda*. Two ancient columns were re-erected at one end of it, and on these were put statues of Hercules and Caesar. The promenade survives today, though it is no longer the elegant place which was intended: it has reverted back to the dirty, depressing state of the former wasteland, and is in the middle of a part of the city famous for its prostitutes and drug-addicts.

The poor and the rich were roughly divided in the sixteenth century between the northern and southern halves of Seville, and this division remains much the same today. The decline of northern Seville was probably accelerated in the fifteenth century, when the Muslim quarter, or *Morería*, was moved from a favourable situation near the cathedral to the outlying northern parish of San Marcos; this parish later became populated by *moriscos*, and, after them, gypsies. *Moriscos* and gypsies were also to be associated with the suburb of Triana, which lies on the eastern side of the Guadalquivir and is considered by some to be a separate town to Seville. It was until recently a notoriously depressed area, even though many of the city's important industries had once been situated here. Described by Dundas Murray in 1849 as 'the abode of robbers and desperate characters', it had had a reputation since the sixteenth century as a place of heavy crime and lax morals. The irony was that Triana's most prominent building – until coastal floods eventually forced its demolition in the late seventeenth century – was the lugubrious castle of the Inquisition.

'What Seville lacks,' complained one Francisco de Siguenza in 1579, 'is a good central square.' The most important square in the sixteenth century was that of San Francisco, around which were situated the town's main prison and the newly built Mint, High Court and Town Hall; but this was hardly a square to be compared with the monumental public spaces to be found in northern and central Spain, such as Madrid's Plaza Real. The traditional meeting-place in most Andalusian towns had always been the intersection of four streets. Seville also had its cathedral, which acted as an extraordinary magnet for all levels of Seville society and all kinds of activities. On the *gradas* or steps of the cathedral took place many of the Inquisition's *autos-de-fe*, and, for most of the sixteenth century, nearly all the city's business transactions. That the cathedral should be desecrated by commercial enterprise led finally in 1572 to Archbishop Cristóbal de Rojas making a complaint to Philip II; only then was work begun on the construction of the city's Exchange or *Lonja*. Well after the expulsion of its merchants and bankers, the cathedral and its surroundings continued to attract much of the city's criminal milieu. The roughest elements in Seville society were drawn to the Corral de los Olmos – a small square, no longer surviving, in between the cathedral and the Archbishop's palace – where there was a cheap and very popular eating place. The élite of the criminal world gathered instead in the cathedral's charming Courtyard of the Orange Trees (Patio de los Naranjos), which owed much of its popularity to its being within the sanctuary area of the cathedral. Refugees from justice could stay here untouched throughout the day and make their escape at night. So many criminals did this that in 1586 a law was introduced limiting sanctuary within the church to eight days, banning entrance to women, and forbidding gambling to take place.

Today it is mainly tourists who converge in vast numbers on the cathedral, the place being Seville's major attraction along with the neighbouring palace and gardens of the Alcázar. As with the Alcázar, the cathedral complex has parts dating back to Muslim times. After the taking of Seville from the Muslims in 1245, the Christians had used the town's mosque as their cathedral. The fifteenth-century *mudéjar* gateway through which you enter the Patio de los Naranjos has two of the mosque's twelfth-century bronze doors, both of which feature inscriptions from the Koran. But the principal survival of the old mosque is the Giralda (see page 81), a former minaret turned by the Christians into a bell-tower. The elegance of this structure contrasts with the squat, heavy profile of the cathedral itself, a building which Laurie Lee evocatively described as 'hugging the ground like an encrusted turtle'. Begun in 1401, its main body was complete by 1504. A Polish traveller of 1484, Nicolas de Popielvo, found to his surprise that the building was even larger than Cologne cathedral; it has in fact the reputation of being the largest gothic cathedral in the world. The impression on entering the gloomy interior is of enormous space though not of soaring proportions. So dark and vast is the place that you are at first barely aware of its wealth of sixteenth- and seventeenth-century paintings and furnishings. The Golden Age provided the cathedral not only with its greatest works of art, but also with some outstanding architectural additions. Two of the architectural highpoints of the interior are the Great Sacristy, in a classical plateresque style, and the Chapter House, a pioneering elliptical structure designed by Diego de Siloe.

The Alcázar too was splendidly embellished during the sixteenth century, some of the work coinciding with the marriage here of Charles V in 1525. The greatest transformation was to the Moorish gardens, which acquired numerous features of the Italian Renaissance, such as a delicate and perfectly proportioned arcaded pavilion (known as the Pavilion of Charles V), statues and grottoes dedicated to figures of classical mythology, and one of those many light-hearted inventions typical of sixteenth-century Italy – a hydraulic organ. The harmonious combination of Muslim gardening skills and Italian whimsy and inventiveness created in the Alcázar one of Europe's finest gardens. A successful intermingling of Moorish and Renaissance elements can also be found in another remarkable Seville residence, the Casa de Pilatos. Begun around 1480, and completed in the early sixteenth century by Pedro Afán de Rivera, this has many of the enchanting characteristics of the Alcázar with the added charm that it is relatively little visited. Classical arcading, Roman statues, and plateresque ornamentation vie with *mudéjar* craftsmanship, and a Moorish luxuriance and sensuality. Sixteenth-century Seville also saw the construction of many other impressive buildings, ranging from the lavishly ornamented plateresque Town Hall to the austerely classical Exchange, designed by the architect of the Escorial, Juan de Herera. But none of these buildings has the originality of the Casa de Pilatos, and few of them are so unmistakeably Sevillian in character. Appropriately, under Afán de Rivera's grandson, the third Duke of Alcalá, the Casa de Pilatos was to turn into one of the city's main cultural centres.

In the second half of the sixteenth century, long after the city's economic importance had been established, Seville's cultural life began to flourish as it had not done since Muslim times. The beginnings of this renaissance can be seen in the literary gatherings that took place after 1559 in the house of Columbus's great-grandson, Álvaro Colón y Portugal, Count of Gelves. Seville had at this time only a modest, recently founded university college, and in the absence of a full-scale university the meetings in Álvaro's house assumed a particular importance: they were an early example of what was to be a vital ingredient in Spain's cultural life, the *tertulia* or *salon*. Among the writers in this circle were the Humanist scholar and teacher Mal-Lara, and the dramatists Juan de la Cueva and Lope de Rueda, who are among Spain's greatest dramatists prior to Lope de Vega. The most revered poet of the group was Fernando de Herrera, known to his contemporaries as the 'divine'. A great admirer of Petrarch, this shy and retiring man found his Laura in Álvaro's wife, Leonor, to whom he constantly referred in his Petrarch-inspired love poetry. All his poetry is high-flown, rhetorical and rather alien to present-day tastes, but he was a highly influential figure. His commentary on the work of Spain's early sixteenth-century poet, Garcilaso de la Vega, was the most important poetic treatise of the Golden Age; and his own poems, with their striking abundance of words expressing colour, prefigured the works of the great Córdoban poet of the seventeenth century, Luis de Góngora. A totally different poet to Herrera, and a far livelier and more vivid personality, was Baltasar del Alcázar. He too belonged to the Álvaro circle, though he lacked the pretensions of its other members, did not consider his works worth publishing, and made a living as a soldier. Alone among the Seville writers of this time, he displayed in his works the great wit for which the people of Seville are renowned, and their love of good living. His humour and obsession with eating well come together in two of his best-known works. One, *The Comic Meal*, has the poet trying to relate a romantic tale but being constantly side-tracked by the delicious food which he is eating. In the second he describes the three great loves of his life:

> There are three things
> that hold my heart love's captive:
> the fair Inés, raw ham,
> and aubergines with cheese.

Alcázar was also greatly esteemed as a madrigalist, though his reputation as a musician was far eclipsed by that of another member of the Álvaro circle, Francisco Guerrero. Guerrero and his Seville contemporary Cristóbal de Morales were two of Spain's leading polyphonists of the sixteenth century, and their work was noted for its simplicity and spontaneity of inspiration, and its opposition to the exaggerated artifices of Flemish composition. The vitality of the Seville musical world of the sixteenth century – of which two other luminaries were the organist Francisco Peraza and the *vihuela* player Alonso de Mudarra – owed much to the presence in the city of the Biblioteca Colombina, which included the largest group of musical manuscripts in Spain outside the Escorial; the whole library had been amassed by Columbus's son, Hernando, and presented to the city's cathedral after his death.

The great age of Sevillian painting and sculpture was to come, but there were many important artists working here in the sixteenth century. The arts in Seville at the beginning of the century were dominated, as they were throughout Spain, by artists and craftsmen of Northern descent. Lorenzo Mercadente, Miguel Perrin, and Pedro Millán, the sculptor responsible for the naturalistic carvings that decorate the cathedral's exterior, all came originally from France. However, Italian art was coming into fashion, and various Italian artists had started moving to Seville. One of these was Niculoso Pisano, who executed for the north portal of the convent church of Santa Paula a yellow and white terracotta lunette imitative of the works of the Florentine artists, the Della Robbias. The Florentine sculptor Pietro Torrigiano was another and more important arrival to the city. His life had been a restless one ever since he had been expelled from Florence for breaking Michelangelo's nose: he had wandered around Italy and the Netherlands, and had introduced the Renaissance style to England in the tomb of Henry VII in Westminster Abbey. In Seville he carved a kneeling figure of St Jerome (now in the Museum of Fine Arts) which in later centuries was to serve as a maquette for students at Seville's art academy; but his propensity for getting into trouble led to his being denounced as a heretic by the Inquisition and thrown into prison, where he died in 1528.

The greatest painter active in Seville in the early years of the century was Alejo Fernandez, an artist of German origin who had married a woman from Córdoba and taken her name. His art shows Italianate influence in its use of perspective and architectural detailing, but it is essentially Flemish in its intimate naturalism: one of his most charming works is the *Virgin of the Navigators* (now in the Alcázar), in which the virgin protects under her capacious cloak many of the more famous people involved in the colonization of America. A later artist, also torn between Italy and Flanders, was Pedro de Campaña. Born Pieter de Kempeneer in Brussels in 1504, he had been trained as a painter first in Brussels and then in Italy, and had settled in Seville by 1537. In Italy he had fallen heavily under Raphael's influence, though his colouring, landscape backgrounds and naturalistic detailing were always to remain very Flemish in character. The major work in his career was the multi-panelled altarpiece featuring the *Deposition* in the Mariscal Chapel of Seville cathedral: it is a work of great emotional power, yet it was apparently not a success, and the artist afterwards returned in disgust to Brussels.

A fully-fledged Italian style was achieved in the works of the Seville painter Luis de Vargas, who had also spent part of his youth in Italy. Back in Seville by 1551, he later began to frequent the house of Álvaro Colon, and became a true figure of the Renaissance by developing an additional talent as a musician. His retable of the *Genealogy of Christ* in Seville cathedral, and his *Pietà* in the church of Santa María la Blanca, reveal an artist blindly emulating the example of Raphael. One of the Spaniards who most lived up to the Italian Renaissance ideal of the artist was Francisco Pacheco. Born in Sanlúcar de Barrameda in 1564, Pacheco soon moved to Seville and became a central figure in the city's cultural life. His uncle, a canon at Seville cathedral, had been a leading member of the Álvaro circle, and he instead became closely associated with the literary gatherings that superseded Álvaro's in the last years of the century – those held by the third Duke of Alcalá in the Casa de Pilatos. Pacheco believed that the artist should be a person of great learning rather than a mere craftsman, and he himself was a poet, a scholar and the author of a biographical survey of the Seville artists and writers of his day. His own paintings are stiff and academic, and his attempts at mythology and allegory – as can be seen in the Casa de Pilatos – are frankly ludicruous. Yet he was an outstanding teacher of painting, and was to have among his pupils artists whose fame would extend well beyond the frontiers of Seville.

The finest achievements of Spain's Golden Age date mainly from a period of political and economic decline. Despite the great riches coming from America, the money which came into the hands of the State had largely been squandered in expensive military campaigns. The financial crisis which developed in Spain towards the end of the sixteenth century was to have a particularly strong effect on Seville, where it was aided by a major demographic upheaval. Plagues had swept through the city throughout the sixteenth century, though none with greater virulence than that of 1599–1601, which decimated Seville's population. The population had barely had time to recover when, in 1609, all of Spain's *moriscos* were finally expelled from the country. The majority of the *moriscos* were from Seville, and their growing numbers and the separateness of their existence had become of increasing concern to the city's authorities, who were worried that these people might support an invasion from North Africa or even become allies of the English. A law had been introduced limiting the number of *moriscos* to a specific building, and there had even been talk of providing all the *moriscos* with an identity badge. In the end expulsion seemed the only solution. Most went directly to North Africa, but a law prohibiting them to take children under seven to non-Christian lands forced many to go first to Marseille or to other European ports: this was a dangerous undertaking, and there were those who decided simply to abandon their children in Seville. A significant proportion of the *moriscos* were clearly able to evade the expulsion order, for in 1623 a traveller to Seville was to comment on how many 'Moorish men and women' there were in the city; later in the century a Moroccan ambassador was to describe the population of the nearby town of Lebrija as being almost wholly Muslim in origin. The *moriscos* who ended up in Africa were to stick as closely together there as they had done in Spain, and they have done so to this day, retaining also a feeling of superiority to their neighbours.

In the course of the seventeenth century great areas of Seville became emptied of people, and where there had once been houses, orchards were planted. By 1630 Seville had been overtaken by Madrid as Spain's largest city, and in 1649 the place suffered its worst plague ever. The process of decline was accelerated greatly by Seville's notoriously inefficient government (of which Philip III complained), and, above all, by the silting up of the Guadalquivir, which in 1620 forced the Casa de Contratacción to move from Seville to Cádiz. Cádiz prospered while Seville stagnated. Other Andalusian towns also fared rather better than Seville in the seventeenth century, including Granada and other places that in the previous century had been Seville's poor relatives. But Seville remained the cultural capital of Spain, and it was during these years of decline that many of her greatest works of art and architecture were produced.

The baroque period had no less great an impact on the look and character of present-day Andalusia than the Muslim period. The region's wealth of baroque monuments and works of art, and the continuing baroque traditions in craftsmanship and religious art, make Andalusia one of the European capitals of this style. Yet, ironically, most of the travellers who have lavishly praised Andalusia have had only a limited appreciation of baroque art and architecture, in particular the British, whose country is one of the least baroque in the continent. The one aspect of this period's culture to be universally admired is its painting, thanks largely to three artists, Velázquez, Zurburán and Murillo.

The story of Spanish seventeenth-century painting begins in Seville, the churches and monastic institutions of which continued to offer artists in the early years of the century numerous and lucrative commissions. One of the leading painters at the beginning of the century was Juan de Roelas, who had probably been trained in Italy and been influenced by the Venetian painter Tintoretto: his masterpiece, the *Martyrdom of St Andrew* in the Seville Museum, is dark, dramatic, and has that peculiarly Spanish combination of mysticism and acute realism. The renewed realism in Seville art of this time was a reaction against the Raphael-inspired idealism of the preceding period. Strange though this might at first seem, the new realism was advocated principally by Francisco Pacheco, whose studio was by far the most important in the city. Pacheco's dry and academic manner was belied by the advice that he gave his pupils 'to go to Nature for everything'. One of these pupils was Alonso Cano, the most versatile of Spain's great baroque artists. Though born in Granada of Castilian parentage, Cano's early years as an artist were spent entirely in Seville, where he was trained as both a painter and a sculptor. In later life he was to become known also as an architect and draughtsman, and this versatility was to earn him a reputation as 'the Spanish Michelangelo', an artist with whom he had otherwise very little in common. His paintings and sculptures have a quiet, unsensational realism tinged with considerable sentimentality: among his most popular works were his countless Immaculate Conceptions, a subject which had been strongly advocated in Pacheco's studio. The sweet nature of Cano's art was contradicted by a troubled life which gave rise to much malicious gossip. His second wife, whom he had married when she was only twelve, was brutally murdered in 1644, six years after he had moved from Seville to Madrid. The murderer, an unidentified Italian, fled without trace, and suspicion immediately fell on Cano, who was proved innocent only after undergoing torture. During his last years Cano mainly worked for Granada cathedral, and managed also to be ordained a priest there, despite opposition from the ecclesiastical authorities. He died in Granada in 1669, apparently in poverty, and uncommemorated.

In his youth in Seville Cano would have been able to witness at close hand the rapid rise to fame of his fellow pupil at Pacheco's studio, Diego Velázquez. Born in Seville in 1600, Velázquez became apprenticed to Pacheco when he was little more than ten, and was so precocious that he soon surpassed his master. Pacheco recognized the superior gifts of his pupil, but, far from being jealous, he gave him every possible encouragement, and even the hand of his daughter in marriage. It says much of the changing economic situation in Seville that Velázquez, like Cano and many other ambitious artists of the time, tried to further his career by seeking work in Madrid. He paid a brief visit to Madrid in 1622, and painted there a portrait of his fellow Andalusian, the poet Luis de Góngora. In the following year he was recalled to the capital by Philip IV's powerful minister, Count-Duke Olivares, who was himself from Seville. After painting a portrait of the king, Velázquez was appointed court painter and remained based in Madrid for the rest of his life, enjoying a remarkably close friendship with the king. Velázquez is not one of those geniuses whose lives can be embellished by tales of tortured private life and destructive jealousy on the part of others. The ease of his success was comparable to the ease with which he painted, and his was a life which until recently had seemed completely free of discord. In 1983 documents were discovered revealing that on a visit to Rome in the 1640s he had had an affair with a widow called Martha, who had given him an illegitimate son, Antonio. Such details might seem barely relevant, but they serve to show that Velázquez was actually human, something which you might otherwise forget when looking at his art.

When Pacheco urged his pupils to turn to nature for inspiration, he could hardly have imagined such extraordinary naturalism as that shown by Velázquez even in his early teens. Virtually no other artist before or after him has given so life-like a quality to the painted image. The history of art is filled with ridiculous stories of birds pecking at painted cherries, servants mistaking portraits of their masters for the masters themselves, and so on; but in the case of Velázquez such confusion between art and reality seems almost plausible. In the works that he painted in Seville, he used this realism to portray scenes of everyday life, such as an old woman stirring eggs, and an old man selling water to a young boy: these scenes are treated with extreme seriousness, and not with that patronizing humour or sentimentality with which many of Velázquez's contemporaries might have handled such subject-matter. He also painted a handful of religious works during this period, and displayed in these a similarly restrained realism: in two of them he might even have used his wife as the model for the virgin. Velázquez appears to have preferred genre scenes to religious ones, and in two of his Seville works he reduced the religious element to a sketchily portrayed event glimpsed in the background of a contemporary domestic scene.

Unfortunately almost nothing of Velázquez's work can be seen in his native town. In the nineteenth century foreign visitors to Seville stripped the city of many of the paintings that they most admired. Most of Velázquez's genre scenes ended up in British collections, for these were exactly the sort of paintings that the British could appreciate, paintings mercifully devoid of all the morbid religious fervour generally thought characteristic of Spanish art. It is to the Prado in Madrid, however, that the traveller must go to study the full range of Velázquez's art. Here you will see how his style changes between his Seville and Madrid years, how his palette lightens and his brushwork loosens, and how in his last works he achieves the most life-like effects with what seems from close-up a random series of hasty brush-strokes: as an eighteenth-century Spanish critic put it, '. . . you cannot understand [the technique] if standing too close, but from a distance it is a miracle.' The naturalism of Velázquez's late art is endowed with an almost supernatural quality.

Velázquez's works would not have been widely known at the time, as hardly any of them were for public places. Zurburán, on the other hand, painted almost exclusively for churches and religious institutions. Extremaduran by birth, he came to Seville in his teens, studying painting at the same time as Velázquez. The Seville Guild of painters, like the other guilds in the city, was not welcoming to people from other parts of Spain, especially not to those who came from such a provincial backwater as Extremadura. After completing his studies, Zurburán had great difficulties in finding work in Seville, and had to go back for a time to his native town of Fuente de Cantos. Only in 1629, after marrying as his second wife a woman from an influential family, was he finally able to establish himself in Seville; he was to be based here throughout his most successful years. Zurburán's naturalism is of a very different kind to Velázquez's, and has an austerity which has been seen as a reflection of the character of his native region. Simplified and tightly executed forms and figures, set against plain, sombre backgrounds, are given a solemn monumentality. The sturdy simplicity of Zurburán's art is very much to present-day tastes, but it is easy to see how this same quality could once have been interpreted as a sign of naïveté; his art was in fact to go out of fashion even in his lifetime, and it was not until the nineteenth century that its reputation was to be revived and its originality recognized.

Many of Zurburán's paintings remain in Andalusia, but only a fraction of these are in the settings for which they were originally intended. He painted his major works mainly for monasteries and convents, and most of these institutions either fell on hard times in later years or else were dissolved: in either case nineteenth-century collectors, responding to the growing fashion for his art, made every possible effort to acquire the paintings. Two of Zurburán's most important Andalusian commissions were for the Charterhouses at Jerez de la Frontera and Seville. A visit to the former institution greatly helps an understanding of Zurburán's art, even though all his paintings that were once there have long been dispersed. The Charterhouse lies in fertile, undulating countryside several kilometres to the east of Jerez. In the early baroque period its church was given a sumptuously ornate façade and embellished inside; but the greater part of the complex was finished in the late fifteenth to early sixteenth centuries, and is in a gothic style. It is the only Charterhouse still functioning in Andalusia, and you have to be male and get special permission to pass through its gates.

The Carthusian monks are few in number and occupy only a small area of the original vast complex. Unable now to work the large orchard which they own, they dedicate much of their spare time to maintaining the surviving parts of the Charterhouse in a state of spotless cleanliness. The odd monk in his coarse white garment and with shaved head walks silently by, disappearing into the darker recesses of a sharply lit cloister. The atmosphere is of perfect order and complete silence. Zurburán was the ideal artist to produce work for such an environment, and his pictorial style was also excellently suited to portray the austere robes of the Carthusians. The placing of these robes against the artist's characteristic dark backgrounds creates a most powerful effect, as can be seen in Zurburán's panels of saints now in the Museum of Fine Arts at Cádiz. These and a group of other small panels in Cádiz are all that remains in Andalusia of his Jerez altarpiece. In the Museum of Fine Arts in Seville, however, you can see the three large works that Zurburán executed for the Sacristy of Seville's own Charterhouse. The most impressive of these works depicts the moment when the Carthusian bishop St Hugo observes a bowl of meat turning into ashes, thus offering him divine justification of the Carthusian practice of vegetarianism and abstinence. A group of Carthusians are shown in icon-like formation behind a long refectory table. For those lucky few who have been to the Charterhouse at Jerez, memories of the refectory there will come back as you look at this scene, which reveals to the full Zurburán's genius as a painter of simple still-lives in which the humblest object is invested with tranquil dignity. The table is covered in a plain white cloth, and sparingly laid with the same blue and white ceramic bowls and mugs that are still in use in Jerez's Charterhouse today.

The Plague of 1649–50 killed off many of Zurburán's family, including apparently all his children from his second marriage. Finding life hard in Seville in the 1650s, Zurburán finally moved to Madrid, where he died in 1664, not poverty-stricken, as is sometimes said, but certainly in no great state of wealth. His last paintings lack the power of his earlier ones, his technique having lost its former precision in its attempt to imitate the more flowing, vaporous style then in fashion. The master of this style was Bartolomé Murillo, who in the late 1640s had displaced Zurburán as Seville's leading painter.

Murillo's career illustrates how possible it still was for an artist to prosper even in the depressed Seville of the late seventeenth century. He received constant commissions in this, his native city, right up to his fatal fall from scaffolding in 1682, and in 1660 he even founded an institution which had given new dignity to the arts in Seville, an Academy of Painting. After Velázquez's death in 1660, Murillo was indisputably Spain's most renowned painter and was soon to be considered, in the eyes of the rest of Europe, as one of the greatest artists of all time. This reputation was to be maintained well into the nineteenth century and then to fall as quickly as it had risen, his works being dismissed as facile and cloyingly sentimental. Today Murillo is coming more into fashion again, especially now that his own works are being distinguished from those of his numerous and slapdash followers and copyists. The technical virtuosity of his art is undeniable, and even though he is often sweetly sentimental, there is also a darker, more forceful side to his personality. His international reputation was once based mainly on his radiant Immaculate Conceptions, and his genre scenes, which are mainly of pretty-faced beggar boys in picturesque rags. Most of the latter works found their way into British collections, but a large proportion of his religious paintings remains in Seville, and includes some of his most powerful works. The Fine Arts Museum is filled with his paintings, but many others are still in the buildings for which they were originally commissioned, most notably the Cathedral, the Archbishop's Palace, and the churches of Santa María la Blanca and the Caridad. Murillo's *St John of God Carrying an Ill Man*, and *St Isabel of Hungary Feeding the Lepers* deserve special mention, for they show the artist to have been as capable of conveying drama and deep emotion as he was of portraying celestial visions. The two paintings are both in the Caridad, and need really to be seen in the context of this hospital church, a building distinguished not just for its paintings but for being a magnificent sculptural and architectural complex.

The sculpture and architecture of the Andalusian baroque are no less worthy of attention than the region's paintings of this period, and yet they have been ignored by most foreigners, even one as conscientious and open-minded as Richard Ford. The prejudices that are still held against the sculptures of the baroque are strongly connected with a puritanical belief in truth to materials, and a distaste for the religious sensationalism which came to the fore after the Reformation. From the late sixteenth century the favourite medium in Spanish sculpture had been polychromed wood, and this medium was used to create ever more lifelike effects. The first great Seville sculptor in this style was Martínez Montañés, a friend and contemporary of Pacheco, who in fact was responsible for polychroming many of the artist's works. Known in his time as the 'God of Wood', Montañés was famous for his ability to give human semblance to his sculptures, and some of his portrait heads, such as that of St Francis of Borja in the Seville Museum, do indeed seem to be creatures of flesh and blood. The succeeding generation of Seville sculptors persevered in this realistic vein, while at the same time abandoning the restraint which Montañés had always reserved for the gestures and emotions of his figures. The outstanding sculptor of the middle and latter years of the century was Pedro Roldán, whose retable for the altarpiece of the Caridad features a frenetically agitated *Deposition*. It is in the work of Roldán's followers, however, that critics of the baroque see Spanish art descending into out and out vulgarity. Eye-sockets are filled with glass, beads imitate tears, and real clothing and even hair are used. It is certainly wrong to discuss these works simply in artistic terms, for they are much more than mere sculptures, they are images that continue to play a central role in Andalusian life of today. Adorned in different finery for different occasions, paraded through the streets during the region's celebrated Easter processions, they inspire a devotion in people who are not even religious, and are talked about as if they had magical powers. The respective merits of these images are hotly debated, and allegiance to a particular image is often seen as defining someone's personality. The most famous of Andalusia's sculptures is Seville's Virgin of the Macarena, attributed to Roldán's daughter, Luisa. To most foreigners, this Virgin is the epitome of shallowness of emotion and crude artifice, but thousands of Sevillians praise her beauty and mystery, and are moved to tears by the sight of her face. I have even known those who would not dream of living with anyone who does not worship the Macarena above all other images of the Virgin.

The baroque architecture of Andalusia has at times an appeal as visceral as that of much of the region's sculpture, and can leave many distinctly queasy. The baroque style was actually slow to evolve here, and the buildings put up in the first half of the seventeenth century, such as the Convent of the Merced (now the Fine Arts Museum), largely perpetuated the mannered classicism of the preceding century. The feature which makes them unmistakeably Sevillian, and which looks ahead to later developments, is their dazzling colour: the lines of the architecture are accentuated by bright pastel colours, expanses of white plaster alternate with shining ceramics and pink to russet red brickwork. In the last quarter of the century, colour was to combine with ornamental inventiveness to create baroque effects of mesmerizing power. But in many ways the most striking Seville monument of the seventeenth century was a building in a transitional style dating from the middle years of the century. This, the Church and Hospital of the Caridad, has a history as fascinating as its architecture and decoration.

Miguel de Mañara, the founder of the Caridad, was a wealthy aristocrat popularly thought to have been the model for Tirso de Molina's Don Juan. He would actually have been far too young for this, but he was certainly an intriguing figure who, in middle age, decided to live frugally and give away most of his wealth to the construction of a building intended for the care of the poor and sick. Legend has it that he had led a dissolute philandering life until one day, seeing a funeral cortège pass by, he asked who was inside the coffin, and was told that it was himself. Little is in fact known of Mañara's youth, though there is good reason to suppose that he was not very proud of it. The latter half of his life was devoted entirely to his hospital of the Caridad and to self-punishment, and when he lay dying in 1679 he insisted on being treated in the same room as the paupers. His tomb at the entrance to the Caridad church bears, as he had requested, the following inscription, worded with characteristic Sevillian exaggeration: 'Here lie the bones and ashes of the worst man who has ever lived.' Immediately inside the church are two paintings by Valdés Leal that testify to Mañara's obsession with death: one, *In Ictu Oculi*, has a gleeful skeleton standing over a pile of discarded books, and insignia of wealth and power; the other, *Finis Gloriae Mundi*, shows in savage close-up the decomposing, insect-ridden bodies of a cardinal and a soldier. Yet the building itself is by no means sombre. Its principle baroque feature, the superb retable supporting Roldán's *Deposition*, is a joyous, gilded structure with swirling columns. The interior is light and colourful, and the white exterior is inset with large ceramic panels as intensely blue as the Andalusian sky. The architecture and decoration of the Caridad, and the life-story of Mañara himself, are an interesting reflection of the Andalusian mentality, a mentality in which a love of suffering is frequently the obverse of a passion for life.

The paintings, sculptures and other furnishings of the Caridad are integral to the architecture, but they do not overlap with each other and are neatly contained by the regular lines of the building. Towards the end of the century the Andalusian architects went in more and more for shock tactics, and broke down completely the remaining barriers between architecture and the visual arts. Underneath all these buildings' lavish accretions is usually a simple and unoriginal structure, but the initial impact is none the less quite staggering. A foretaste of what is to come is provided by the Seville church of Santa María la Blanca (1751–3), a simple cruciform building made exciting by an extraordinary ceiling of frothing plaster foam. The greatest and most prolific Seville architect of the late seventeenth and early eighteenth centuries was Leonardo de Figueroa, whose many churches for the city, such as the Magdalena and San Luis, revel in ceramics, polychroming, and a plethora of busy, ornamental forms of plateresque derivation. In his frontispiece for the former monastery of San Telmo, these forms seem almost to be pitted against each other in a struggle to be seen, rather like the anarchically behaved traffic which congests the Seville streets. Hurtado Izquierdo, a contemporary of Figueroa's, went in for particularly dramatic ornamentation, and his masterpiece in Seville, the chapel of San José, has a retable resembling a gilded lava flow churning up a flotsam of limbs and architectural bric-à-brac (see page 339).

Outside Seville the main centre of the Andalusian baroque was Granada, and it was in this city's Charterhouse that the style reached a point of ornamental exuberance beyond which it could scarcely go any further. Hurtado worked in the monastery church, producing in the chancel a blaze of gold and coloured marble of enormous theatricality; but it was an unknown architect who was responsible for the building's most startling feature, its sacristy. Entering this from the nave is to be drawn suddenly into a blizzard, from which you emerge reeling and with eyes dazed by the brilliant whiteness. Not a single part of the walls is left undecorated, and many visitors such as Mario Praz have found parallels with the Alhambra, though the intended effect of all this decoration was not to soothe, as in the latter's case, but to exhilarate.

The exhilarating, emotionally charged architecture of seventeenth- and eighteenth-century Andalusia was successfully transposed to Latin America, where its ornamental fantasies gave much inspiration to the native craftsmen. It was an architecture too which travelled far beyond the main cities and often ended up in what are now the humblest of places. Rural Andalusia is rich in lavish monuments of this period, particularly the small towns and villages of the Guadalquivir basin, where the wealthy owners of *latifundia* once had homes. Lucena boasts a Sagrario chapel in the parish church of San Mateo of an ornamental intricacy unsurpassed even in Seville and Granada. Écija has a splendid series of polychromed baroque towers described by Gautier as being in 'sublime bad taste'. Meanwhile, on the magnificent palace-lined street of San Pedro in nearby Osuna you can see the rivetingly bizarre Palace of the Dukes of Gomera, which has an asymmetrical, undulating skyline inspired by the fantastical engravings of German rococo artists. The enchanting small town of Priego de Córdoba, beautifully situated above a ravine, has two of perhaps the most surprising baroque monuments of them all, a great public fountain with mythological statues playing beneath over 100 jets of water, and an unexpectedly large Sagrario chapel overwhelming an otherwise modest parish church. Few structures can have such a claim to be compared to a wedding cake as this circular chapel of soaring proportions and plaster-coated balconies which recent restoration has revealed to be a glistening white. Gerald Brenan doubted whether the showy virtuosity as revealed in this chapel could be the source of 'great art', and Jan Morris, reflecting on both the monuments of Priego de Córdoba and the Charterhouse of Granada, wrote that for her tastes 'they are too flippant, too frothy, and their practitioners stand in relation to the masters of Spanish austerity as a gifted interior designer might stand to the engineer of a pyramid'.

The transition in Andalusia between the baroque and neo-classical periods is shown in the evolution of Cádiz. The Cádiz of ancient fame was by the early seventeenth century a small, inconsequential place, the scant remains of which constitute today a decrepit prostitute quarter in the shadow of the city's cathedral. The importance of Cádiz grew considerably in the course of the century, but it was not until the following century, when the place enjoyed a forty-five-year monopoly of trade with America, that it became a scene of major urban and architectural development. None of the new buildings were of outstanding architectural merit, least of all the massive and clumsy cathedral, which was begun in a heavy baroque style in 1722 and completed in a neo-classical one in 1856. Cádiz none the less grew into a most elegant town, thanks largely to a programme of urban reform carried out after 1775, during the period of governorship by a Spanish general of Irish descent, Alexander O'Neill. The houses, churches and regular street plan of eighteenth- and early nineteenth-century Cádiz have survived to this day, grimy but virtually intact, contained within the imposing encircling walls put up by the French in 1810. Cádiz, today one of the finest and best preserved towns of this period in Spain, impressed and disappointed travellers of the Romantic period by its modernity. Many of these travellers caught at Cádiz their first glimpse of Andalusia, a region to which they had come expecting a journey back in time. Stepping off the boat, they found themselves instead in a city which had the first sewage system in Spain, as well as a sparkling new architecture, some of it imitative of that of Revolutionary France. 'There was nothing of the sombre aspect I had been accustomed in fancy to associate with the streets of Spain,' wrote Dundas Murray on a visit to Cádiz in 1849. 'Every edifice appeared modern and new, or, if ancient, was painted "up to the eyes".'

The contrast between Cádiz and Seville in the early nineteenth century was a striking one. For Dundas Murray Seville was a city locked in a glorious past: 'Her fame in the present day rests upon the traditions of the past, and upon the undoubted signs of a wealth and magnificence which once rolled through her streets.' Murray's English contemporary George Dennis described the vast abandoned cannon factory in Seville and found this to be a poignant reflection of the city's economic decline. Yet in Murray's and Dennis's day there was one industry still flourishing in the city – tobacco. The construction of the city's tobacco factory between 1728 and 1757 had brought new vitality to the city, and had resulted in a building which Dennis was to describe as 'one of the wonders of Seville'. This vast factory, today the city's main university building, contains an apparently endless series of courtyards and is crowned by the monumental figure of Fame blowing her trumpet. It was the last great monument of Andalusia's Golden Age, and it was also a pioneering example of industrial architecture. However, the many tourists who visited the place from the early nineteenth century onwards took increasingly less of an interest in the actual architecture or in the building's industrial implications. These were people who failed to take seriously Andalusia's role in the modern world, and were dreaming instead of a region of mystery and romance, colourful costumes and lascivious dancing, Moorish monuments and voluptuous maidens. The tobacco factory was not for them a factory but a harem, where thousands of sultry beauties lay imprisoned, scantily dressed owing to the great heat, and provocatively behaved. One of these legendary employees was a gypsy woman called Carmen.

4

GYPSIES

The image of Andalusia had changed significantly by the middle of the nineteenth century. The region which had once been one of the economic centres of Europe was by now living mainly off its reputation as an exotic land. This new image had been greatly fostered by a group of people whose origins were mysterious and whose life-style inspired a mixture of revulsion, fascination and sentimentality.

The word 'gypsies' which is used to describe these people covers in fact a large number of different ethnic groups spread today between India, Europe, North Africa and America. Traditionally all these groups lead a nomadic existence, speak variants of the same language, Romany, and make their living through ironmongery, horse-trading and thieving. Their origins have been endlessly discussed, often in a malicious way. Many have identified the gypsies as the accursed descendants of Cain, others have seen them as people condemned to perpetual wandering for having forged the nails of the crucifixion. The most fantastical hypothesis concerns specifically the gypsies of Spain, Southern France and North Africa, who have been related to the Guanches, a people from the Canary Islands sometimes considered to be the last survivors of Atlantis. The eccentric poet rancher of the Camargue, the Marquis Baroncelli-Javon, pursued this hypothesis further after he had invited Sitting Bull and other American Indians to come and visit him in his Provençal home. So struck was he by the similarities between the Indians and the local gypsies that he concluded that all were descended from red-skinned nomads dispersed after the destruction of Atlantis.

The general belief today is that all gypsies were originally from India, and that, after reaching the Bosphorus, some went directly to Europe and others travelled along the southern shores of the Mediterranean, eventually crossing the straits of Gibraltar. The Spanish and Provençal gypsies probably chose the latter route, as they are referred to respectively as *'gitanos'* and *'gitans'*, which are derivatives of the Spanish and French words for 'Egyptian'. There is the complication, however, that the Andalusian gypsies are also often known as *'flamencos'*, or 'Flemings'. Were the gypsies described as such because their colourful costumes were similar to those brought back by Spanish soldiers from Flanders? Or was it because these people came from Central Europe, the Spaniards of the time being unable to distinguish Flemings from Germans? Numerous interpretations of the word *'flamenco'* have been offered, and there is the strong possibility that it has nothing to do with Flanders at all. For instance, it might derive from the Arabic word for a 'fugitive peasant' (*'Felagmengu'*), or even from the supposed flamingo-like appearance of gypsy men, with their brightly coloured trousers clinging to spindly legs (see also page 135).

Whatever their origins, gypsies had first come to Europe by 1425 and by the end of the century had formed considerable communities in Spain. A great many of the Spanish gypsies were drawn to the Nasrid Kingdom of Granada, and sentimentalists have argued that they went there out of an innate preference for the Moors over the Christians. However, Andalusian gypsies supported the Christians after 1481, and might even have forged the projectiles used by Ferdinand and Isabella in the siege of Granada in 1492. In all probability the gypsies were driven largely by opportunistic motives, and at heart cared as little for one nation as for the other.

The gypsies were spared the early stages of the Inquisition, probably because they were too poor to be worth bothering about, rather than as a gesture of good will for their having helped the Catholic monarchs. Isabella certainly had no great love for them, and in 1499 she issued a decree giving them sixty days to stop their wanderings and to find stable employment, or else to be exiled for life. Subsequent Spanish monarchs were to be no less harsh on them. Philip II did not conceive of them as a race but as a 'collection of vicious people drawn from the dregs of Spanish society'; Philip IV saw them as useless Spaniards, and called for their colonies to be broken up. Between 1499 and 1783 at least twelve laws were to be passed limiting their activities and lifestyle. The gypsies did their best to ignore these.

After the departure of the *moriscos* in 1609 the gypsies became the main objects of Spanish racial abuse and hostility. Significantly, the gypsies moved into areas that had once been frequented by *moriscos*, such as Triana in Seville and the Albaicín in Granada, and took over some of the casual unskilled trades that the *moriscos* had vacated. Yet they inspired much greater fear and hatred than the latter had done. They did not share the *moriscos*' concern with personal cleanliness, and lived unwashed in the filthiest surroundings. They were thought capable only of deceit and thieving. 'Gypsies,' wrote Cervantes, 'seem to have been born into the world for the sole purpose of being thieves: they were born of thieving parents, they are brought up with thieves, they study in order to be thieves, and they end up past masters in the art of thieving.' The most feared of Andalusia's infamous highway robbers were gypsies, who were supposed to have no mercy on their victims, and to have none of the nobility of character associated with bandits such as José María. They were quite happy to kill for the smallest amounts of money, because they belonged to a race notorious for its complete lack of scruples and morals.

Much of what was thought about the gypsies was based on the disdain which these people often showed to those not of their race. The nineteenth-century author George Borrow, one of the first to write about the gypsies with both sympathy and learning, noted how among themselves they behaved according to the strictest of moral codes. This was particularly true as regards personal loyalty and sexual behaviour. One of the great myths about the gypsies was that they were extremely promiscuous. Yet they held virginity and fidelity to one's partner to be sacrosanct, and punished terribly those who violated their laws. Gypsy women might frequently appear to behave in a provocative manner towards outsiders, but Borrow insisted that none of them would ever dream of committing an indiscretion. Prosper Mérimée, not surprisingly for the author of *Carmen*, dismissed Borrow's views on gypsy chastity as rather naïve, though he himself had to concede that the women displayed extraordinary loyalty towards their husbands.

Some of the qualities attributed to the gypsies were wholly fanciful. The tendency of the gypsies to work with furnaces and live in caves made many think that they were in league with the devil. Involvement with the black arts was apparently confirmed by their interests in palmistry and by the strange culinary concoctions brewed up in large pots by the women. One of the most unfounded and widespread beliefs about the gypsies was that they practised cannibalism. This belief was the cause of much persecution in seventeenth- and eighteenth-century Spain, and yet there was not a single shred of evidence to support it.

In 1783 Charles III, a true figure of the Enlightenment, tried to dispel many of the prejudices held against the gypsies and to integrate them into Spanish society. He passed a law forbidding the gypsies their costume, wanderings, and language, while at the same time permitting them to choose virtually any profession that they wanted, and penalizing any non-gypsy for refusing both to employ them and to allow them entry into a public place; he also insisted that they were no longer to be referred to as *gitanos* – a word which they have always hated – but rather as 'New Castilians'. Charles III's law came at a time when the gypsy contribution to Spanish culture was beginning to be recognized. The following century saw great changes in Spanish attitudes towards gypsies and in the gypsy life-style itself. Spanish gypsies found a great champion in George Borrow, whose book *The Zincali* (1841) did much to promote tolerance and understanding of them: in other European countries such as Moldavia, gypsies were still being thrown into slavery. In 1889 Spain became the first country in the world to have a special school for gypsy children. It was founded in a cave in Granada's Sacromonte by an eccentric priest called Padre Manjón, a man whom Walter Starkie was to remember in the 1920s as a saintly figure ambling down cactus-lined paths on a donkey. Padre Manjón's small school grew into a large institution, and the priest's belief that the gypsies could be turned into good Catholics helped to pave the way for the gypsy pilgrimage to Rome in 1956 to seek the protection of the Pope.

Spain's gypsies are today more integrated into their country's society than those elsewhere in Europe. Unlike most other gypsies, their first language is not Romany, and they are no longer nomadic, the gypsy encampments that you occasionally see in Andalusia being generally made up of Portuguese gypsies. None the less, the Spanish gypsies have continued to stick closely together and have retained their idiosyncratic culture, contrary to fears that Charles III's 1783 law would deprive them of much of their individuality. Triana is no longer a gypsy suburb, and few gypsies remain in the Albaicín; but there are many other urban areas in Andalusia which are still inhabited largely by gypsies. Two such districts are that of Santiago in Guadix and La Chanca in Almería, both of which have many cave dwellings and are thus considered picturesque by passing tourists. Some of these dwellings are still lived in, but those in Granada's famous Sacromonte are now used by the gypsies only for putting on tourist entertainments. Walter Starkie remembered Sacromonte when its caves were still in everyday use, glowing at night with the fires of countless furnaces, transforming the hillside into 'some island of Vulcan'. Serious flooding in the Sacromonte in 1963 compelled the Granada authorities to move the gypsies to makeshift 'temporary' homes in the suburb of La Chana. They are still there. La Chana, one of Granada's ugliest, poorest and most crime-ridden districts, is typical of many places in Andalusia where gypsies have been forced to live. Romantically inclined tourists might pine for the days of gypsy caravans and gypsy caves. But places such as La Chana serve as a useful reminder that gypsy life is anything but picturesque, and remains in many ways as hard today as it always was.

The fact that gypsies have managed to keep a strong cultural identity despite the constant attempts of others to suppress this is an indication of the strength of gypsy laws, social ties and pride. Secret gypsy tribunals continue to be held, and gypsies still obey unwritten laws of loyalty to the clan. Marriage to a non-gypsy is not encouraged, and those who do so have to make their partners adjust entirely to gypsy ways. Cultural conservatism is further ensured by gypsy parents allowing their children almost total participation in the adult world; the adult appearance and behaviour of these children can be quite disconcerting for the outsider. Underlying, and strengthening the gypsy mentality is a belief in the superiority of gypsies to other beings. The Spanish gypsy still refers to the non-gypsy as '*payo*', which translates as peasant or serf; the exclamation '*ique gitano!*' ('how gypsy-like!') is used meanwhile to express approval of non-gypsy people, acts or things. In the Romany dialect of Spain called Calí, the word 'to know' is '*chanelear*', which means not simply 'to know' but 'to know by intuition'. To some people this is an indication that the gypsy mentality is indeed a more advanced one than that of the *payo*.

The gypsies' contemptuous attitude towards the non-gypsy is an understandable one in view of the prejudices that are still held against them throughout the world. This century they were in fact subject to the worst persecutions in their history, when Hitler sent 400,000 of them to die in the concentration camps. The Spaniards pride themselves on being more tolerant towards the gypsies than any other nation, and fail to recognize how strong their racial prejudices still are. One of the most detailed recent books in Spanish on the subject of gypsies, *Los Gitanos Españoles* by María Helena Sánchez (1977), bears the extraordinary dedication, 'To my father, lover of *flamenco*, although not of gypsies'. A medical research student whom I met in Málaga uncovered three cases of leprosy in parts of the city which were very poor and happened to be largely populated by gypsies. The publication of his research had the effect of ostracizing all gypsy children in Málaga schools.

The hatred which has always been felt against gypsies has been balanced by a tradition of romantic infatuation with them. Cervantes's short story *The Little Gypsy Girl* describes a wealthy aristocrat falling in love with a beautiful gypsy, to whom he proves his love by leaving his family and taking up a gypsy life of wandering and stealing. Cervantes, the nephew of a gypsy, expressed in this story the yearning for the simple gypsy life which has been experienced by many young men of privileged background. The yearning was to become particularly strong from the early nineteenth century onwards, when the gypsy was to acquire a heroic status. Travellers to Andalusia up till then had mentioned gypsies only rarely, and had done so usually in a derogatory way. The Marquis de Layle, visiting the region in 1784, wondered how anyone could put up with them, 'a people . . . who hold nothing sacred, and have neither religion, laws nor strength of character'. Bourgoing, thirteen years later, believed that they should have been 'purged from society a long time ago'. However, by 1830, Gautier was describing the gypsy women of Granada as if they were goddesses: 'Nearly all of them carry themselves so naturally, and with such innate dignity, and they have such ease of posture when sitting, that, despite their rags, filth and poverty, they seem imbued with an awareness of the Antiquity and unsullied purity of their race . . .'

Gautier's romantic attitude towards gypsies was to be shared by a growing number of travellers and writers. The rapid industrial and capitalist expansion of the nineteenth century made the untramelled, unconforming life-style of the gypsies seem increasingly attractive. Many of those who wrote on it had nomadic tendencies themselves, such as George Borrow. Borrow's fascination with gypsies had begun as a child, when he had been allowed a privileged glimpse of a gypsy encampment in Norfolk; his fascination grew in the course of his extensive travels around England, France, Germany, Russia and Spain. He developed a particular empathy for the Spanish gypsies, perhaps because he himself, as an eccentric, wandering Englishman selling Protestant bibles, must often have felt an outcast in this country. The combination of scholarship and romanticism with which he wrote on gypsies was to typify many later studies of these people. In 1888 the Gypsy Lore Society was founded in London with the intention of recording gypsy traditions. Its presidents have included several colourful figures, for example the painter Augustus John and the writer Walter Starkie, both of whom espoused a gypsy life-style. Starkie had had his first encounter with gypsies in Italy at the end of the First World War, meeting there a Transylvanian gypsy musician who became his blood brother. In fulfilment of a pledge that he would one day go and meet this man in Transylvania, Starkie set off on a long journey through Hungary and Romania, earning his living as an itinerant musician. By 1921 he was in the south of Spain, still with his fiddle, and still spending most of his time with gypsies: the outcome of this latter trip was *Don Gypsy* (1936).

In the 1920s and 30s many romantic young travellers journeyed in similar style to Starkie, with little money, and frequently on foot or donkey: many of these ended up, like Starkie, in Andalusia, for example Gerald Brenan and Laurie Lee. These two decades saw also a great surge of writing on gypsies, among which were the works of an American called Irving Brown, who was of gypsy blood himself. Augustus John, Starkie, Brenan and Irving Brown were all in Granada at the beginning of the 1920s. The place had by now become as famous for its gypsies as for its Moorish monuments, and John found that the gypsies here were 'wholly given up to the entertainment of tourists'. The character of Granada's Sacromonte became ever more bogus in the following decades, as indeed did so many other aspects of gypsy life that were exposed to the public. Yet the fascination with the life has lasted to this day, together with numerous romantic preconceptions about it. Jean-Paul Clébert, the author of one of the most

scholarly recent books on gypsies, despises all the sentimental literature on the subject, yet he himself was undoubtedly attracted to it for
sentimental reasons: he has gloried for many years in self-imposed
isolation in the Provençal countryside, and first made his name with a
book on down-and-outs and other social outcasts in Paris, *Paris
Insolite*. If Clébert had written about low life in Seville rather than in
Paris, he would undoubtedly have had a few words to say about
'Lucy'. Lucy is an elderly American woman who for the past thirty
years has lived in Seville, claiming to write a book on the gypsies. She
is well known to those who frequent the Seville bars, and spends
much of her day propped up at one of them. Dishevelled, and always
mumbling to herself, she speaks hardly a word of Spanish but is
understood by everyone. Many of those who talk to her are gypsies,
though whether they seek her company out of genuine affection or
simply in a mocking spirit is sometimes difficult to tell. Whichever is
the case, this enigmatic figure exemplifies an extreme type of gypsy
enthusiast.

No other region in the world has an attraction based to such an
extent on its gypsies as Andalusia. Towards the middle of the nineteenth century, Andalusian gypsies began to realize the tourist potential of their music and dancing, and by the end of the century had
made '*flamenco*' famous throughout Europe and America. They
created a vogue for their flashy '*flamenco*' costumes, and brought new
panache to that traditionally Andalusian art of bull-fighting: in this
century some of the most elegant and exciting of Spain's bull-fighters
have been Andalusian gypsies, for example Joselito, Rafael el Gallo,
and Curro Romero. Numerous writers, musicians and painters have
taken their inspiration from Andalusian gypsy themes, and their
works have in turn done much to promote gypsy fashions: Bizet's
1873 musical version of Mérimée's *Carmen* is a notable example of
this, establishing Andalusia once and for all as the land of the glamorous gypsy. The gypsies have no written tradition, and it has been left
to non-gypsies to invent a gypsy literature. By the late eighteenth
century, pseudo-gypsy ballads had begun to appear in Andalusia; but
it was not until the time of García Lorca that this literary tradition
was to achieve real distinction. The most popular of Lorca's collections of poetry was his *Romancero Gitano* (1928) or *Gypsy Ballads*,
which both drew on gypsy themes and emulated the moving simplicity

of gypsy song. Lorca, who did more than any other writer this century to influence attitudes towards Andalusia, encouraged his readers to look at the region through gypsy eyes.

Flamenco and bull-fighting are the two most obvious aspects of gypsy culture in Andalusia. The fascination with the Andalusian gypsy has much more to it than just an interest in these two activities; it is inseparable from other essential elements of the region's appeal. To travellers nostalgic for Moorish Andalusia, the gypsies have often seemed to represent an unbroken link with this Moorish past. They have a suitably exotic appearance, and had of course until recently lived in districts such as the Albaicín and Triana that had previously been the haunts of *moriscos*; occasionally they had even been referred to as Moors. Gautier fancifully believed the Granada gypsies to be at heart 'Arabs and Muslims', and numerous other visitors to this city, staring across to the Albaicín from the Alhambra, have had their oriental reveries confused with gypsy fantasies. 'In 1921,' wrote Walter Starkie, 'on my first visit to Granada I started the day in the Alhambra in the company of Abenamar, Zaïda, and the heroes and heroines of the Moorish ballads; but I finished it in the caves of the dancing gypsies. Whenever I gazed out of the arched windows of the Alhambra, my mind travelled over to the Albaicín . . .'

The Andalusian gypsy, who has often been thought of as the most beautiful of all gypsies, has also fulfilled travellers' visions of exotic Andalusian beauty: Carmen was after all a gypsy. But more than living up to the ideal physical image of the Andalusian, the gypsy encapsulates those aspects of the Andalusian personality that have most intrigued foreigners. Gypsies are known for their ability to adapt to other cultures, but the amount that they have in common with the Andalusians suggests that the influence has been mutual, and that there is a fundamental empathy between these two peoples.

It is difficult to get to know the gypsies, and foreigners especially have to be wary in their dealings with them. Gypsies generally assume, often rightly, that foreigners are interested in them purely out of an interest in *flamenco* culture. Many promise to accompany foreigners to 'real' *flamenco* events, convince them of their wholly friendly motives for doing so, then extort from them as much money as possible. Even if you are an Andalusian, to be accepted by the gypsies to an extent that a genuine friendship develops is not always easy, and depends to a great degree on your being introduced to them through a *payo* they already trust. One such *payo* is Esperanza Flores, who, as a celebrated maker of *flamenco* costumes, and as someone who once ran one of the Seville bars most popular with gypsies, is a figure well known and much loved in the gypsy world. Through her I got to know more gypsies than I would otherwise have done, but I was also made more aware than before of the ties that link the gypsy with the Andalusian *payo*.

Driving once in a car with Esperanza, I innocently pointed to a large snake which was crossing the road. Without realizing it, I had touched on one of the great superstitious fears common to both gypsies and Andalusians: the very mention of the word 'snake' is meant to bring on bad luck, and the only remedy is to shout out afterwards '*Lagarto*' (lizard). Esperanza and many in her *payo* circle in Seville shared a great number of the superstitious fears of the gypsies, and I had rarely encountered such superstitiousness among urban-living people. Every day I discovered new sources of bad luck, ranging from the colour yellow to a chance encounter with a funeral procession. A terribly unlucky act is to refuse to buy one of the sprigs of rosemary that are constantly being hawked by passing gypsies: not only do you have to buy one, but you also have to keep it afterwards in your house, and only get rid of it by burning. Magic and superstition also play a vital role in both the Andalusian and gypsy attitudes towards religion, along with an obsessive dwelling on death and suffering, and a love of exuberant spectacle. Gypsy rites are perfectly in keeping with the Andalusian brand of Catholicism: the famous pilgrimage to El Rocío (see pages 159–64) is as much a gypsy spectacle as it is a Catholic one, and for over 300 years the church authorities in Granada have employed gypsy dancers and singers in their Easter processions.

The infamous machoism of the Andalusian is matched in its strength only by that of the gypsy. Once I found myself standing at a bar next to a well-known group of male gypsy singers. Esperanza was friendly with all of them, but told me that, as a woman, she could not introduce them to me at that moment, as this would entail breaking into an exclusively male gathering, and thus being contemptuously received. In gypsy society women lead a life completely separate to that of the men, but what is remarkable is that they frequently support their husbands, and far prefer to do so than to see these men working. Such an attitude is in fact common in Andalusia generally, and has certainly worn off on to Esperanza, much of whose life has been spent selflessly looking after men with little money and large drink problems.

Visitors to Andalusia, and to Seville in particular, frequently comment on the amount of time which people appear to spend doing little other than drink, sleep, and enjoy themselves. Such indolence, constantly made fun of by outsiders to the region, reflects a philosophy of life common to both gypsies and Andalusians: some call it by the more dignified name of 'fatalism'. To the gypsy, and to many Andalusians, the ideal in life is to be free, not to be tied down by work, social obligations, or thoughts about the future. To these people, of whom Esperanza is one, the careful way in which most Westerners plan their lives is utterly incomprehensible. In their philosophy, to be practical is to be boring and not to appreciate life to the full. As Irving Brown wrote: 'Gypsies are not content with spending their last cent: in order to be happy they must defy all sense of practicality.' It is a philosophy which leads to great extremes of pleasure and pain. Esperanza once had a birthday in the middle of which she quarrelled with her employer, decided that the job she had was curtailing her freedom too much, and gave it up then and there, thus losing the only secure source of income which she had had in years. Her subsequent reaction was to spend the rest of her birthday getting rid of all her remaining money by an afternoon and night trailing the Seville bars with an ever-growing crowd of friends and acquaintances, whom she lavishly regaled with food and drink. Excessive pleasure is the main way of many Andalusians of coping with sadness, as it is with the gypsies. A gypsy funeral is renowned as an orgy of gaiety.

Social restraints generally prevent Andalusians from behaving with quite the same excessiveness as do the gypsies and Esperanza and her friends. An underlying love of riotous pleasure is none the less shown in the Andalusian obsession with *ferias*. All the social classes are united in these occasions in a whirlwind of drinking, dancing and singing. And to be able to enjoy yourself without the slightest inhibitions about such whole-hearted hedonism, it has been customary since the nineteenth century to dress up for these occasions in *flamenco* costumes.

5

FLAMENCO

The sounds of dancing, plucked strings and plaintive song have echoed through Andalusia's history. The famed sensuality of the dancing girls of Roman Cádiz was taken up in Moorish times by slave girls, whose bodies swayed to the rhythms of tambourines and lutes. The minstrel Ziryab pioneered in Umayyad Córdoba the use of the lute as an accompaniment to singing, and this instrument was further developed by the brilliant musician of sixteenth-century Seville, Alonso de Mudarra. By the eighteenth century a passion for the lute had given way to one for the guitar, and a sensual new dance form had emerged in the fandango. Guitar, song, and dance are the main components of *flamenco*, a type of popular music and dancing which has affected the way we look today both at Andalusia and at Spain itself. *Flamenco* lies at the mythical heart of a region which has constantly been shrouded in myth. It expresses much which is genuinely mysterious about Andalusia, and much which is bogus.

There are many commonly held preconceptions about *flamenco*, which is not surprising given the fanciful, vague, contradictory and purely speculative nature of most of what has been written on it. Probably the greatest of all these misconceptions is the belief that the *flamenco* artist is respecting an age-old tradition. It is one thing to show how deep-rooted is the Andalusian love of music and dance, it is quite another to say that *flamenco* has gradually evolved over the centuries. The composer Manuel de Falla did much to propagate this myth in a short essay which he wrote in 1922 on the origins of what is always considered the purest form of *flamenco* – *cante jondo* or 'deep song'. Falla saw as the three major influences on its development the adoption in Visigothic Spain of Byzantine chant, the Muslim invasion, and the settlement in Spain of numerous groups of gypsies. Walter

134

Starkie added as a fourth influence the festival songs of the Jews, and also suggested – on the basis of a conversation with a Jewish bookseller in Tetuan – that the word *'jondo'* came from the Hebrew *'jon tob'*, which means good day or festival. With García Lorca the discussion of *cante jondo* evaporated completely into hot air, the style becoming a blend of influences in which 'the emotion of history, its lasting light without dates or facts, takes refuge'.

Flamenco, which Lorca once described as 'one of the most gigantic creations of the Spanish people', and which many have characterized as the proverbial soul of Andalusia, probably dates no further back than the late eighteenth century. The word itself is not known to have been used before 1837, and is possibly derived from the eighteenth-century slang for a 'boaster'. Used initially to describe gypsies, the word was only in later years applied to a specific tradition of music and dancing. This tradition was essentially the creation of gypsies, and appears to have begun after 1783, when Charles III issued the edict compelling gypsies to integrate themselves into Spanish society. The place of origin is thought by many to have been the Guadalquivir basin, more specifically a triangular area of land incorporating Seville, Jerez and Cádiz, the three Atlantic-facing towns that are often regarded as the Holy Trinity of *flamenco*. The triangle itself, referred to variously as the 'Tartessian' or 'Golden Triangle', has as much mystery attached to it as that of Bermuda. None the less, scholars have been able to show that almost all the many songs and dances of *flamenco* are native to this area.

The tragic lyrics and tone of much *flamenco* is generally seen to reflect the sufferings of the gypsy people. Understandably the gypsies were anxious initially to keep their songs and dances to themselves, and probably did not understand how outsiders could take an interest in an art of such personal significance. They performed them at their weddings, funerals and baptisms, and at *juergas* or 'sprees', spontaneous gatherings of musicians and musical enthusiasts. *Flamenco* evolved in the homes of gypsies, above all in their *patios*. One of the first *payos* or non-gypsies to describe at length a gypsy festival was the Seville writer Estébanez Calderón, who in 1847 published an account of singing and dancing in Triana, the Seville centre of *flamenco*. Antonio Mairena, one of the finest gypsy singers of recent times, believed that Estébanez Calderón had been made fun of by the gypsies, because many of the latter's observations on their traditions were frankly ridiculous. To this day, gypsies have exploited the gullibility of *payos* to relate all manner of nonsense about their music. A recent example of this was a BBC documentary which purported to show '*flamenco* as it had never been seen before'. Each of the performers interviewed stressed how they were '*gitano puro*' or 'pure gypsy', as if this made incontrovertible everything that they said about *flamenco*. You had the impression that they were enjoying themselves leading the programme's director on, convincing her that she was witnessing *flamenco* in its authentic state.

It is certainly difficult to know what to and what not to believe about *flamenco*. That music runs in the blood of all gypsies is clearly untrue, for only a tiny proportion of gypsies are musicians. But you cannot so easily dismiss the widely held view that only gypsies can successfully perform *flamenco*. I spoke about this with the guitarist Paco Peña, and as a non-gypsy himself he was understandably contemptuous about this point of view, referring me to a book called *Payos Too Know How to Sing*. He himself has an enormous reputation outside Spain, though not, interestingly enough, in Spain itself, where it is sometimes thought that he lacks the feeling which only a gypsy can have. This 'feeling' is obviously not exclusive to gypsies, as one of the most influential of all *flamenco* singers was the half-Italian, half-Andalusian *payo* of the last century, Silverio Franchetti; furthermore, two of the most exciting *flamenco* artists of today are also *payos*, the guitarist Paco de Lucía and the dancer Cristina Hoyos. Yet the fact remains that most of the finest *flamenco* performers are and have been gypsies. The reason for this might not be as mysterious as it seems. *Flamenco* music, with its chromatic inflections and subdivisions, and its free and complex rhythms which do not conform to any regular measurement, is very difficult to transcribe with modern European musical notation. To be able to learn and perform such music, it is obviously a great advantage to have been exposed to it from an early age: a great many of the *flamenco* performers come from musical dynasties that stretch back for decades.

Flamenco depends much on spontaneity and improvisation, yet it also obeys strict rules and conventions that, like the lyrics of the songs, appear mainly to have been formulated in the last century. *Flamenco* singing, to the uninitiated, can seem monotonous and unvarying. The singers or *cantaores* are usually seated, and sing one at a time, the palms of their hands outstretched and shaking, their faces becoming ever redder, and the veins on their foreheads more prominent, until eventually apoplexy seems forthcoming; the same note is often endlessly repeated, and there are frequent shouts of '*Ay*', which often appear to express genuine pain. Those knowledgeable about *flamenco*, the *aficionados*, will usually be able to tell you what type of song the singer is reciting, though I have known people who have listened enthusiastically to *flamenco* most of their lives and are still unable to distinguish between certain of these types. The types fall into two main groups, only one of which, confusingly, is actually known as '*flamenco*'. This group, the *cante flamenco* or *cante chico* ('small song'), includes light-hearted, lyrical songs such as *bulerías*, *alegrías*, *fandangos gitanos* and *malagueñas*. Far more primitive and anguished are the songs in the other group, the *cante jondo* or *cante grande* ('big song'). Two of these songs, the *siguirilla gitana* and the *solea*, are unrelievedly sad (the word '*solea*' is derived from '*soledad*', or solitude), and are considered by all *aficionados* as the greatest works in the *flamenco* repertory. Less common songs in the same group are the *martinetes* and *deblas*, which today are sung completely unaccompanied, and might originally have evolved in the gypsy forges, the beat being provided either by the workings of the bellows or the hammering of the metal. Another type of *cante jondo* is the *saeta*, which is an 'arrow of song' (to use Starkie's words) directed towards the images of a religious procession: the *cantaor* Antonio Mairena first made his name during the Seville Holy Week of 1933, after jumping out of a crowd watching one of the processions and singing so well that the procession was halted and he was carried in triumph around the city's streets. Commonly confused with *flamenco*, though not belonging either to *cante jondo* or to *cante chico*, are those traditional Andalusian or Latin American folk songs that have been greatly influenced by *flamenco*: the most famous of these songs, and the ones that you constantly hear today throughout both Andalusia and Spain generally, are the *sevillanas*.

Flamenco songs are usually accompanied by the tapping of feet (*zapoteo*) or the clapping of hands (*tapoteo*). Audiences frequently join in the clapping themselves, often without realizing that the *tapoteo* is quite an art in itself, and that three people who are good at it can make as much noise as ten novices. For fast rhythms, the middle three fingers of the right hand are used to strike the extended palm of the left, the sound sometimes being supplemented by the clacking of tongues; for a deeper, more hollow sound, suitable to more solemn singing, the palms of both hands are cupped. Essential to any *flamenco* performance are shouts of encouragement, the one most travestied by foreigners being '*¡Olé!*'; other popular exclamations are '*¡Anda!*' ('Bravo!') and '*¡Asi se cante!*' ('That's singing!').

The importance of the guitar in a *flamenco* performance has greatly increased over the years. To begin with the *flamenco* guitar was used as a simple accompanying instrument; but at the beginning of this century, under the influence of the great Rafael Montoya, it was made to adopt some of the techniques of the classical guitar, such as the *tremolo* and the *arpeggio*. The playing of the *flamenco* guitar has become an exceedingly difficult task requiring great skills not only at interpreting composition, but also at spontaneously composing to match the mood of the other performers. *Flamenco* guitarists have created further difficulties for themselves by having kept, out of pride, the traditional *flamenco* practice of resting the guitar on the right thigh: this awkward posture is particularly unsuited to the more classical style of guitar playing developed by Montoya. Another difference between the *flamenco* and the classical guitarist is the use of the *capo*, a moveable bridge whereby the tuning of the guitar can be raised or lowered without having to retune each string.

Whereas the guitarist is often the least acclaimed player in a public performance of *flamenco*, the dancer generally receives most of the attention, especially from the foreigners in the audience. The costumes worn by the women dancers borrow traditional Andalusian street wear of the nineteenth century, such as the *peinetas*, or large combs, and *mantillas*, or fringed shawls; peculiar to gypsy dancers are the polka-dotted fabrics and the trailing frilly dresses known as the *batas de cola*. *Flamenco* dancing involves movement of the hands and torso rather than of the feet, and, in its purest form, rarely requires castanets. The strong, erotic element in the dance is undeniable, though it is of a different kind to that which you find in the dancing of *sevillanas*: whereas *sevillanas* are danced with sinuous, voluptuous sensuality, *flamenco* at its best is performed with intermittent outbursts of frenetic, hysterical passion. With a bad dancer such passion can verge on the ludicrous.

All *aficionados* are agreed that the greatest performances of *flamenco* require an element called '*duende*', a word which literally means 'fairy'. Lorca, quoting Goethe on Paganini, referred to *duende* as 'a mysterious power which everyone senses and no philosopher explains'; 'All that has black sounds has *duende*,' wrote a music critic after hearing Falla play his own *Nights in the Generalife. Duende*, Lorca emphasized, is very different from the muse, being violent, discordant, and only present when 'he sees that death is possible'. To perform *flamenco* with *duende*, technical virtuosity alone is not sufficient. Lorca's contemporary, Manuel Torres, a celebrated *cantaor* known to sing from the chest rather than from the throat, told a singer: 'You have a voice, you know the styles, but you will never triumph, because you have no *duende*.' Even if a singer has this quality, it is unlikely that it will be brought out during a public performance of *flamenco*, as these performances require a professionalism and discipline that are anathema to it. The most memorable performances of *flamenco* are nearly always the gypsy *juergas*, the spontaneous musical gatherings put on purely for the benefit of the musicians and a handful of *aficionados*.

Lorca undoubtedly glamorized the notion of *duende*, and gave it much more romantic mystery than it actually has. Drink and drugs are as likely to induce *duende* as deep spiritual passion, and Lorca himself suggested this in his description of a performance given by a singer called Pastora Pavón. At first she had sung beautifully, but had left the audience unmoved; only later, after drinking half a bottle of *aguardiente*, did she begin to hold everyone's attention, singing 'with scorched throat, without voice, without breath or colour, but with *duende*'. The *juergas* are notorious for the amount of drink and drugs consumed, and have often involved prostitutes. They also tend to last for hours and even days on end, the stamina required to endure them having frequently to be maintained with cocaine. Many of the *flamenco* singers, including the great Silverio Franchetti, have died of heart attacks, and Lorca and others have loved to stress that these were caused by the emotional intensity required of their performances. The excessiveness of their life-style seems a more likely reason. It is a life-style similar to that of many rock stars, but with the difference that in their case it reflects the gypsy and Andalusian philosophy of life brought to its ultimate conclusion. The *juergas* begin in a spirit of fooling around, but, as the hours wear on, the search for pleasure is carried to such a degree that it can turn into self-destructiveness. And this is perhaps when the *duende* enters.

Duende may be incompatible with commercial *flamenco*, but *flamenco* would not have enjoyed any great popularity, and might not even have survived at all, had it not been commercialized. Up to about 1860, *flamenco* had been restricted almost entirely to gypsy homes, and it was only after then that it came to be widely known. The years 1860–1915 are often referred to as the 'Golden Age of *Flamenco*', and correspond exactly to the period of the *cafés cantantes*. Cafés and bars began to allow private *juergas* to take place in their back rooms, and eventually arranged for *flamenco* artists to perform in public. One of the most famous of these *cafés cantantes* was the Café Silverio in Seville, which was founded by Silverio Franchetti in 1869 on his return from a long period in Latin America. Another well-known one was the Café de Chinitas in Málaga, a favourite haunt not only of musicians, but also of bull-fighters and poets; it is now a dress shop, but there is a plaque outside recording the days when Lorca loved to come here.

The new prospect of earning money from *flamenco* encouraged numerous gypsies to take up music. There was certainly a remarkable number of major *flamenco* performers in the second half of the nineteenth century. This was also the period which produced the first serious writer on *flamenco*, Antonio Machado y Álvarez, the father of the poets Antonio and Manuel Machado; he usually wrote under the pseudonym 'Demófilo', because he was a 'lover of the people'.

The considerable number of adherents which *flamenco* gained in the late nineteenth century was matched by a small but vociferous group of opponents. Among these were many of the writers and intellectuals belonging to the Generation of '98, including the philosopher Ortega y Gasset, who thought of *flamenco* as part of the 'southern copperware' which Andalusia employed to hide its real identity. Ortega y Gasset and many others who criticized *flamenco* had probably never witnessed any outstanding *flamenco* performance, for by 1900 commercialization had the inevitable effect of vulgarizing the genre. The success which *flamenco* artists began to enjoy abroad, combined with the international impact of Bizet's *Carmen*, led in Andalusia to countless gypsy shows intended primarily for tourists. A taste for '*flamenco* operas' developed, gypsies and dancers came to be increasingly self-conscious in their looks and performances, castanets and other accessories were introduced, and *cante jondo* came to be abandoned in favour of *cante chico*.

Manuel de Falla, with the assistance of Lorca and others, attempted in 1922 to halt *flamenco*'s decline by instigating a *cante jondo* competition in Granada. In his rules for competitors, Falla warned 'most earnestly that preference will be given to those whose styles abide by the old practice of the classical *cantaores* and which avoid every kind of improper flourish, thus restoring the *cante jondo* to its admirable sobriety, which was one of its beauties and is now regrettably lost'. The competition represented an important moment in Andalusia's cultural history, but it did little to stop *cante jondo*'s continuing decline. Walter Starkie made a pilgrimage in the early 1930s to the Triana home of a celebrated *cantaor* of the old generation, Fernando de Triana. He found the aged singer bitterly upset about recent developments in *flamenco*, ranging from the craze for castanets to the mixing up in dancing of the '*cuadro Andaluz*' with the '*cuadro flamenco*'. Then the singer got on to the subject of *cante jondo*. 'There are,' he said, 'only a few of us left here in Triana who remember the great old days of *cante jondo*, when gypsy singing was as different to Andalusian singing as brandy is to Jerez. When Niña de los Peines and a few others have gone there will be nothing to remind us of the proud, metallic harshness of the gypsy voice.' Fortunately the singer did not get to hear of the experiences while visiting Granada of an English contemporary of Starkie called Marguerite Steen. Steen found herself entertained in a cave in Granada by a group of gypsy boys who had never even heard of a *solea*. What is worse, they 'insulted' her ears with a rendition of 'Slow Boat to China'.

The *cafés cantantes* died out in the first quarter of the century, and were replaced by institutions devoted exclusively to putting on *flamenco* '*tablaos*'. These *tablaos* show *flamenco* at its most debased, but they have maintained its international popularity to this day; they are still one of Andalusia's major tourist attractions. The most popular centre of the *tablao* is Granada's cave district of Sacromonte, where in 1908 a cave night-club opened, called La Zambra. The place enjoyed an immediate success among the chic and wealthy, and more and more of the surrounding caves were subsequently transformed for the putting on of *tablaos*. Walter Starkie recalled how the Granada dancer Lola Medina 'enlisted the services of a well-known Madrid architect to create a sophisticated residence out of her cave and furnished it with illuminated alabaster baths and cocktail bars'. Starkie had known Lola as a plain-looking girl, but now she was 'a glamorous gypsy princess wearing the diamond bracelets and emeralds of the Duchess of La Rochefoucauld, her humble devotee, who humbly waited for her in her cave'. Today the Granada caves are used solely for *tablaos*, though these generally attract a rather less glamorous public than before. Every hotel will try to sell you tickets for a *tablao*, and I once had to take a group of young Americans to one of them. After being offered a glass of weak *sangría* to get us in the right jovial spirits, a group of understandably jaded and bored gypsies displayed some of the worst dancing I have ever seen, before finally encouraging members of our party to dance with them. The one excitement of the occasion came from the possibility of being pick-pocketed, or of being made to pay more than had originally been bargained for.

In the 1950s a renewed serious interest in *flamenco* was marked by the birth of the *flamenco* festival. The first festival took place in Córdoba in 1956, and was soon followed by others in Chiclana, Morón, Lebrija, Utrera, Jerez, and Mairena del Alcor, the latter founded by the town's greatest singer, Antonio Mairena. The rapid spread of these festivals was accompanied by the emergence of a growing number of critics and historians describing themselves as 'flamencologists'; it was a period, wrote Mairena, in which the intelli-gentsia was concerned with Andalusian gypsy singing. *Flamenco* fes-tivals are now held in the summer months throughout Andalusia, and usually take the form of a single, protracted concert, involving many musicians and dancers, among whom is always a local celebrity. Mairena himself described the festivals as offering 'the most spec-tacular but least genuine form of *flamenco*', and the phoniness of the occasions is emphasized by the way in which many of them are named after 'typical' Andalusian dishes, such as the *Gazpacho* of Morón, the *Potaje* ('stew') of Utrera, the *Caracol* ('snail') of Lebrija: these names serve only to highlight the myth that the gypsy has no food. None the less, they are surprisingly free of tourists, are well attended by both gypsies and *aficionados*, and offer an opportunity to hear often excellent *cante jondo*: without these festivals it is unlikely that the purest forms of *flamenco* would have survived. As with the *juergas*, the concerts are interminably long: beginning usually around midnight (about two hours after they officially should have done), they do not get really animated until around three in the morning, and last well into the dawn. The toilets are filled with men sniffing cocaine, but the festivals are also attended by families with small children who seem happy to endure the ordeal to the very end. It is important not to go to the festivals in the same spirit that you would go to a classical concert, for not even the greatest *aficionados* can comfortably sit for up to eight hours seriously engrossed in the music. The success of a festival depends much on the proximity of the bar to the stage. The first and best festival I went to, the *Caracol* of Lebrija, had an excellently situated bar where most of the musicians and *aficionados* spent the greater part of the night, interrupting their lively banter only by the occasional glance at the nearby performers. On occasions such as these, some of the character of the *juergas* survives into the festivals. I remember also a memorable scene at the *Potaje* of Utrera when the successful singer 'El Lebrijano', not scheduled to appear that night, spontaneously joined in the proceedings. A woman was singing on stage, and El Lebrijano stood up from the audience and sang back at her. In a drunken state, and continuing to sing, he advanced towards her, precariously balanced on a wall, from which he eventually fell and broke his arm. Even this incident did not stop his singing, which was quite magnificent and well appreciated by an equally drunk audience. Whether or not the *duende* took possession of him, it is incidents such as these that remind one that the best of *flamenco* is the unplanned.

Foreign visitors to Andalusia are constantly asking where the 'real *flamenco*' can be heard. Many journalists, including those from the BBC, end up by asking this question to Paco Lira, the quiet but charismatic owner of Seville's large and attractive bar, the Carbonería. Paco, a *payo* greatly respected by gypsies and musicians, is one of those people who is aware of everything which is going on around him, and can even overhear conversations across a crowded, noisy room. He knows more than anyone where the best *flamenco* can be heard on a particular night, but, sadly, his own bar is no longer the major *flamenco* centre that it used to be a few years ago. Every

Thursday night informal *flamenco* sessions are held in the bar, but the players are mainly young and inexperienced and the occasions outnumbered by poseurs and naïve young foreigners. Increasingly few bars in Andalusia allow *juergas*, the tradition having been killed off by the ubiquitous bar television and by the new licensing laws that permit only a few bars to remain open throughout the night. You are more likely to hear *flamenco* in a truly sympathetic environment in one of the private clubs known as *Peñas Flamencas*. It was at the Peña Flamenca at the village of Trebujena, near Sanlúcar de Barrameda, that I experienced the most exciting *flamenco* performance that I have yet attended. The occasion, unpromisingly, was a recital of '*flamenco* piano' given by an elderly music teacher from Seville, Pepe Romero. I would not have gone had I not met Pepe a few days earlier in Seville and been impressed by his sparkling and engagingly eccentric personality. He is largely unrecognized in Spain, though he has been referred to, much to his amusement, as the 'Chopin of *flamenco*', and has a small but passionate group of devotees, who feel that he is one of Spain's greatest pianists. I arrived at the concert an hour after its scheduled time of ten o'clock and found Pepe incongrously in dinner jacket and bow tie in the middle of an almost empty room. At midnight, with still only a handful of people present, he decided to begin playing, and within fifteen minutes the room began to fill with villagers, and was soon packed out. Never had I expected a piano recital to be interspersed with constant shouts of '¡Olé!' '¡Anda Pepe!', and other expressions of passionate enthusiasm; one old man was so carried away that he got up in the middle of the concert to thank Pepe for sharing with the audience his genius. Others were crying.

That the piano could lend itself so well to *flamenco* is an indication of the potential adaptability of the genre. Purists are critical of any changes to the *flamenco* canon, and yet change is perhaps needed if *flamenco* in its public form is to survive other than as an exotic entertainment or as a historical curiosity preserved by such institutions as the International Centre of Flamencology at Jerez de la Frontera. Some of the liveliest and most successful *flamenco* artists of today – the guitarist Paco de Lucía, the erstwhile heroin addict Camarón de la Isla, and the gypsy group Pata Negra – have all maintained a popularity through concessions to modern forms of music, Pata Negra even having gone as far as to combine *flamenco* with Rock. The artists who have resisted such modern innovations as the use of an electronic bass guitar, and have kept their integrity and purity of style, are once again facing difficulties in Spain. The audiences at the festivals are beginning sharply to decline, and many of the artists are forced to make a living abroad, where *flamenco* is largely understood in terms of 'Spanish colour'.

If the future of *flamenco* is at present in jeopardy, the singing and dancing of *sevillanas* is more popular than ever before, and a fashion for this music has caught on throughout Spain. In its commercial form, *sevillanas* combine folk with pop music, lyrics about sad love affairs with ones in praise of Seville, Andalusia or the processional virgin of El Rocío. I once went to a concert of *sevillanas*, which lasted as long as a *flamenco* festival but was completely sold out, and was far livelier if also more ridiculous than most of these festivals. The climax, at four o'clock in the morning, was the arrival on stage of a famous middle-aged group of musicians known as the Romeros de la Puebla. They emerged, out of a cloud of dry ice, dressed in the traditional leather gear of the horsemen of the Rocío; they began with a homage to Andalusia, and ended up with a song to the Virgin, during which many of the audience held up lighted candles. As an example of spectacular kitsch, this concert took some beating. But *sevillanas* should not really be seen in a concert performance, for they are essentially the songs and dances of everyday people rather than of professionals. Most people in Andalusia know how to sing and dance *sevillanas*, and foreigners are frequently surprised with the professionalism with which they are danced by the youngest children. Esperanza Flores, brought up during some of the worst years of the Franco period, told me that for the women of her generation these songs and dances were among the main means of expression and escape. Today you will often see people interrupting an afternoon's drinking or an evening *paseo* by bursting into *sevillanas*. Above all, however, it is in the *ferias* and in the pilgrimage to El Rocío that these songs and dances come into their own, performed by a myriad of women dressed in the gaily coloured *flamenco* costumes. Tourists at these occasions might be clicking their cameras and exclaiming at the quaintness of it all, but those involved are not performing for their benefit. They are perpetuating what must be one of Europe's liveliest, strongest and most genuine folkloric traditions.

6

FERIAS AND FIESTAS

'Great doings in the Cathedral, churches and convents, great consumption of incense, torches, oil tapers. I wonder how the lower orders manage to keep themselves, as every day seems to be a holiday.' Richard Ford's first impressions on reaching Andalusia in 1832 typify those of most people visiting the region today. Every possible occasion, religious or otherwise, seems an excuse for a holiday or *fiesta*, and it is often hard to imagine how any work gets done. Spectacular religious celebrations, noisy local festivals, bull-fights, gaudily striped marquees, women in polka-dotted costumes, men with wide-brimmed hats, gaily bridled horses, and perpetual singing, dancing and drinking, all feature prominently in travel-writers' accounts of Andalusia. Festive Andalusia is deeply seductive, but it is generally trivialized by writers, portrayed simply in terms of 'Spanish colour' rather than as the expression of a complex culture.

Wherever you go in Andalusia, and at whatever time of the year, you are bound to encounter some festival. Furthermore, the passion for festivals is increasing now that many of the restrictions imposed on them during the Franco period have been lifted. Events such as *romerías* (outings to a shrine) and parties known as *cruzes de mayo* were heavily frowned upon by Franco for their blatant mingling of religion with the purely secular. Carnivals, meanwhile, with their highly subversive element, were banned altogether, the one at Cádiz surviving only under a different name and at a different time of the year. The Cádiz carnival is now back in its original form, and is held once again in the second week of February. It is the first major festival of the Andalusian year, and one of the most local in its significance. Through the streets of the town parade raucous, costumed groups enacting humorous tableaux. The visual puns are extremely funny

and sophisticated, but virtually incomprehensible to anyone un-
familiar with the Andalusian brand of humour, or with local events
and personalities.

The festival season begins in earnest in the spring, which most
Andalusians consider to be the finest time of year. Seville certainly is
at its best during this period, bursting with flowers and redolent of
jasmine and citrus-fruits rather than of the rank odours that pervade
the town during the impossibly hot summer months. From Palm
Sunday to the Whitsun pilgrimage to El Rocío, the town is the scene
of near constant festive activity. The Sevillians are traditionally the
most pleasure-seeking of all Spaniards, and much of their year is spent
in anticipation of the Spring period, and remembering events that
have happened in previous festivals. Not surprisingly, Seville boasts
the two Spanish festivals best known abroad, those of its Holy Week
and *feria*.

Holy Week or *Semana Santa* is celebrated very differently in Andalusia from how it is in Castile, where the occasion is much more
sombre and mystical. Religious fanaticism plays a surprisingly small
part in an Andalusian Holy Week, and in Seville itself the religious
element of the occasion is far from being a conventional one. Most of
those taking part in the processions, or crying while watching the
religious images pass by, would never dream of attending a mass, and
frequently have a hatred of the church and its priests. Yet the emotions
that they experience during this week are integral to their lives. The
Sevillian obsession with Holy Week is evident in the many photographs of its processions and religious images that decorate the houses
and bars of the town: there is even one bar, El Joven Costalero, which
has a constant video show of the week (see page 342). Preparations for
the week take up most of the year, the sounds of bands practising for
it being heard every evening by the Torre de Oro.

When Palm Sunday finally arrives, the whole of Seville flocks to the
streets, and most of the bars in the town centre are open all day and
night. Hotel rooms for *Semana Santa* are booked up for months in
advance, yet to the ever-growing number of tourists who come to the
town during this week, the occasion must be a very baffling one.
Foreign tourists tend to stay around the cathedral, not realizing that
to get the most out of *Semana Santa* you need to be constantly on the
move and to be at particular places at particular moments. A good

knowledge of Seville's streets is obviously an advantage, and it also helps if you buy a daily copy of the newspaper *ABC*, which publishes a detailed guide to the day's processions and suggests the best places and times to watch them. Better still is to be guided by somebody from Seville, in whose company you will begin to become aware of the more subtle and mysterious aspects of the *Semana Santa*, such as the way an image is carried, the way in which it is decorated, and the emotional importance attached to it.

The *Semana Santa* processions are organized by lay confraternities (*cofradías*), who also possess the images that are paraded. There are on average eleven processions a day, each lasting between three and twelve hours, all passing through the cathedral, and beginning and ending in the church where the images are kept: the itinerary chosen by each confraternity rarely varies from year to year, and the slightest change made to it becomes a major talking-point. Up to Good Friday all the processions start from midday onwards, the mornings being the traditional time for the Sevillians to visit the images in their churches, where they will also receive a badge of the appropriate confraternity. *Semana Santa* begins in a particularly festive fashion, and a good place to be on Palm Sunday is at one of the open-air bars in the María Luisa park, through which passes the confraternity of La Paz. Monday, in contrast, is the most sober day of the week, at least two of the processions being completely silent. The festive atmosphere of Sunday does not fully reassert itself until late on Wednesday, which is when the Sevillians are officially free from work, the following two days being a public holiday in Spain. Maundy Thursday and Good Friday are the highpoint of the Seville *Semana Santa*. On Thursday morning the men of the town put on dark suits, while the women wear combs in their hair and black mantilla shawls. Most of the town is up all night, for no sooner do the Thursday processions end than the Friday morning ones begin, among which are those of the three most celebrated confraternities, El Gran Poder, La Esperanza de Triana, and La Macarena. There are so many people on the streets during this night that it can take up to an hour to do a walk that would normally be done in five minutes. By midday on Good Friday the Macarena procession finally enters its chapel, watched by cheering thousands. From now on the excitement of the *Semana Santa* begins to wane, the afternoon processions of Friday being less interesting than the morning ones, and the energy to watch them being considerably diminished. On Saturday there are only four minor processions, and on Easter Sunday the main event of the day is not a religious one but the first bull-fight of the season.

The Sevillians heavily dispute among themselves which are the best parts of the town in which to see a particular procession, but most are agreed that the processions are at their most beautiful at night (when the participants carry long candles), while passing along a narrow street, or while leaving or entering their churches. The most curious of these 'departures' ('*salidas*') and 'entries' ('*entradas*') are those of the confraternity of San Esteban, which take place along a narrow street crammed with people who have been waiting for up to two hours: the interest comes from seeing the processional images pass through the small ogee-arched portal of the church, a movement which requires exceptional skill. Other much appreciated moments of the *Semana Santa* include the Confraternity of El Museo passing alongside the Town Hall, the Esperanza de Triana crossing the Bridge of Triana, and the first rays of dawn illuminating the Virgin of the Macarena as it leaves the Calle Cuna and enters the Plaza Villasis. Outside the cathedral, on the Town Hall square, along the Calle Sierpes, and around the Campana, there is special seating for those wishing to watch the processions, but rights to these seats are frequently held by the same families for years. Whether the *Semana Santa* should be seen sitting down is another matter, for the processions are interminably long, with constant stops. The most comfortable way of seeing them is undoubtedly from the balcony of a private house, the owner of which will probably treat you indoors to drinks and food during the more boring moments. But *Semana Santa* should really be experienced while standing in the streets, jostling with the crowds, and becoming physically as well as emotionally involved in the occasions. As you move slowly from one part of Seville to another, the town is transformed into a vast stage set enlivened by thousands of actors, of which you are one: you see the place with fresh eyes, modest streets and squares that you might once have ignored acquiring in the excitement of the occasion a magical aspect.

The processions vary little in their make-up. First come row upon row of draped men wearing the same peaked hats used by the Inquisition and later adapted by the Ku Klux Klan in America. In

Seville these men are known as *nazarenos*, a reference to the Jewish sect to which Jesus belonged. Elsewhere in Andalusia they are called *penitentes* (penitents), a name which in Seville is used in reference only to those *nazarenos* who carry crosses; until the 1950s some of the *penitentes* would also bear chains, and, up to the early nineteenth century, would even flagellate themselves. Anyone can be a *nazareno* or a *penitente*, the only conditions being that you pay the annual membership fees of the Confraternity and sign yourself up for the processions several months in advance. There is no limit in age or in the number of members taking part: boys no more than four years old are frequently to be seen, and some of the processions have over 2,000 participants. Many people become *nazarenos* or *penitentes* as a genuine act of penance, but a love of spectacle and dressing up is a more common reason for doing so.

The longer a *nazareno* has belonged to a confraternity, the nearer he is allowed to the processional images. The wait for these images can seem endless, especially as a gap or *corte* often develops in the procession: a confraternity has to return to its church by a given time, though some of the confraternities prefer to pay a fine than to do this, that of the *gitanos* or gypsies being notorious in this respect. The longed-for arrival of the *pasos* (the processional floats bearing the religious images of the confraternity) is signalled by the appearance of men carrying long silver candlesticks known as *ciriales*: a stir of excitement runs through the crowd at this moment. Between the *ciriales* and the *pasos* are the church dignitaries, leading members of the confraternity, and enthusiastic members of the crowd, the latter walking backwards and sliding their feet along the ground, their eyes always fixed on the images. The *pasos* are nearly always two in number, the first always bearing a sculpture of Christ and the second an image of the Virgin. Behind the *pasos* is usually a band, and between them another double row of *nazarenos*. In Málaga – the Andalusian town most famous for its *Semana Santa* celebrations after Seville – the men supporting the *pasos* (the *costaleros*) walk on either side of the floats, but in Seville they are hidden underneath them. The *costaleros* were once all professional, but in recent years these professionals have been replaced by members of the confraternities, who are only too keen to undertake this most physically demanding of jobs. They suffer from infernally hot and claustrophobic conditions, their backs will ache for weeks afterwards, and their necks – on which most of the weight of the *paso* is placed – swell up and are rubbed raw. But all this is as nothing to the feeling that they experience of working together to carry as well as they can an image which they adore.

The respective merits of the processional images are much debated, and a tactless comment made outside the church of their origin could well lead you into a fight. Two of the most beautiful and famous Christs are those of the Salvador and the Gran Poder, the works respectively of Martínez Montañés and Pedro Roldán: both are life-sized representations of *Christ Carrying the Cross*, and it is a matter of personal taste and family tradition whether you consider the one to be more 'noble' and 'moving' than the other. The other outstanding and much revered Christ is that of the Cacharro, the masterpiece of the obscure late seventeenth-century artist Francisco Ruiz Gijón: tradition has it that for this portrayal of the crucified Christ the artist was inspired by the body of a gypsy killed in a knife fight in Triana. Other Christs feature in enormous and slightly ridiculous tableaux, for instance that of the *Lanzada*, in which the soldier driving the lance through Christ's body sits on top of a horse which could have come straight out of a funfair. An especially popular tableau is of *Christ before Pilate*, a processional float paraded by the Confraternity of the Macarena. Costumes comparable to those of the Roman soldiers in this tableau are worn by the men walking in front and behind it: these absurd 'centurions', who seem to be participating in an amateur drama, provoke much mirth among the crowd, and provide the necessary note of bathos prior to the arrival of the Virgin of the Macarena.

The processional virgins are all of identical composition, and are borne on elaborate baroque floats crowned by a canopy. Foreigners generally are unable to recognize the difference between the ex-pressions of these virgins, and cannot understand the fanatical devo-tion of the Sevillians to a particular one. The main rivalry is between the Virgin of the Esperanza de Triana and that of the Macarena (see page 118). The latter undoubtedly incites the most ecstatic reaction among the crowd, who always greet it with shouts of 'Macarena – ¡Guapa! ¡Guapa! ¡Guapa!' ('Macarena – beautiful, beautiful, beautiful!'). Intense emotion for all the processional images is express-ed most movingly in the singing of *saetas*. Sometimes a professional singer is hired to sing these most difficult of songs from a balcony near the entrance to the confraternity's church. Normally, however, members of the crowd burst spontaneously into song when the images pass by; sometimes the *saetas* are sung by people as an act of penance, in which case the singing is particularly bad and at the same time particularly moving. The finest *saeta* I have ever heard was sung by a woman in her late nineties, who was both deaf and blind and had to be told by the nurse who was with her when the *paso* had stopped so that she could begin.

The emotion generated by the processional images depends on factors that most foreigners fail to perceive entirely. Of particular importance is the way the image and its *paso* are adorned, the type of flowers that are placed on the float, the particular mantle which the virgin is wearing, and so on: it is common to hear the Sevillians make such comments as 'The Virgin of the Macarena is more beautiful this year than she has been for ages.' But above all it is the way an image is carried which can affect the enthusiasm of the crowd. Much depends on the competence of the man known as the *capataz*, who stands directly in front of the *paso*, shouts out instructions to the *costaleros*, and strikes a hammer telling them either to stop or to start. The skill needed by the *costaleros* to negotiate the portal of San Esteban (the *pasos* have to be moved by the *costaleros* on their knees) is evident to all. The other, more normal, manifestations of the *costaleros'* art are not so obvious. A *paso* lifted in a single swift movement, or carried smoothly, is much appreciated, as is the occasional spontaneous flourish, such as a rhythmical swaying to the band's music. A particular way of carrying a *paso* sometimes characterizes a particular confraternity, the Christ of El Gran Poder, for instance, always being carried with the same fast pace every year. Occasionally there is a complete departure from tradition: the full-circle turn performed by the Virgin of Montesión in the Holy Week of 1989 was admiringly commented on by the Sevillians for weeks afterwards. There are ultimately no fixed rules determining whether or not a *paso* is carried well or not, for, to appropriate Lorca's definition of *duende*, this is something which everyone feels but no one can explain. Foreigners tend to think of the Seville *Semana Santa* as a picturesque display of superstition and fanaticism by a culturally backward people. They are largely unaware of the refinement of the occasion, of the great degree to which it depends on *'arte'*, a word much used by the Andalusians and meaning not just 'art' or 'skill', but also 'grace', 'wit', 'intelligence' and 'subtlety', the attributes, in other words, of a highly sophisticated culture.

Depending on whether Easter falls late or early in a particular year, the Sevillians have between one and two weeks to recover from *Semana Santa* and prepare themselves for their *feria*, which can be described as the ultimate secular manifestation of the baroque spirit of Andalusia. The *ferias* of Spain have their origins in the market fairs held from the Middle Ages onwards with a view to selling and promoting local products. Today *ferias* exist almost exclusively for the pursuit of pleasure, and are comparable in their activities to village *fiestas*, or to those urban district festivals known as *veladas*, for instance the *Velá de Sant Ana* of Triana. The transformation of Seville's horse and cattle fair into a place of entertainment took place after 1847, following the example of the nearby town of Mairena del Alcor; Mairena del Alcor, in view of its pioneering position in the history of the Andalusian *feria*, always holds its festival several days before that of Seville. The Seville *feria* grew rapidly in size and popularity, and today occupies a vast precinct in the modern district of Los Remedios. Part of this space is taken up by fairground attractions, but the greater part of it is given over to *casetas*, or marquees. These *casetas*, lined along streets named after famous Sevillian bullfighters, were once all owned by individual families, though today they are largely paid for by companies, by societies, or by groups of families clubbing together; the number of *casetas* that are put up is strictly limited, but, with 1992 in mind, the rights to a *caseta* are being acquired by certain companies for exorbitant sums.

The women of Seville, traditionally frustrated at not being able to dress up as *nazarenos* in the *Semana Santa*, get their own back on the men by wearing *flamenco* or 'gypsy' costumes for the *feria*. These brightly coloured costumes featuring floral or polka-dotted material are worn for a maximum of two weeks in the year – for the week of the *feria*, for the *cruzes de mayo*, and for the pilgrimage to El Rocío. More women now wear *flamenco* costume than ever before, and the style of these costumes is improving slightly after a long period of decadence. When Esperanza Flores started making *flamenco* costumes in the early 1960s, she was virtually alone in being interested in style and design; at that time Seville high society spurned *flamenco* costumes as being vulgar, and Esperanza herself was once refused admission into a *caseta* for having one. Esperanza brought back good taste into the wearing of *flamenco*, and the costumes she makes herself are among the most sought after in the town. As a true artist, however, she refuses to commercialize her talents, and makes costumes usually only for friends, who allow her complete freedom to choose the materials and style.

Talk about *flamenco* costumes, combined with an intensive slimming programme, takes up much of the week prior to the *feria*. An equal amount of time is spent putting up the *casetas* and discussing how they will be decorated, prizes being later awarded to those *casetas* considered by a jury to be the most beautiful. The *casetas* – made normally out of canvas striped blue or red – are adorned inside with a baroque abundance of streamers, paper flowers, and gilded mirrors. The final touches to them are made on the Sunday, by which time people are already streaming into the *feria* precinct, even though the *feria* does not officially open until the Tuesday. On Monday night a sit-down banquet is organized for the associates of the *casetas*, and at midnight the *feria* is declared open by the turning on of a sea of coloured lights. From this moment onwards the colour, movement, and animation of the place become quite overwhelming.

The Seville *feria* is essentially one continual party lasting from Monday night through to the dawn of the following Monday. The whole of Seville is on holiday, and the town shuts down almost completely; on the instigation of the anarchic one-time director of the festival, José Luis Ortiz Nuevo, the Monday after the *feria* is now also a public holiday, and is referred to by everyone as 'Hangover Monday' ('*Lunes de la Resaca*'). A typical *feria* day begins around midday and continues until eleven or twelve at night, after which you might try and catch a couple of hours' sleep before returning to the *feria* at around two in the morning, where many remain for at least another six hours, enjoying before going to sleep a breakfast of chocolate and *churros* or doughnut fritters. By day the *feria* ground is packed with parading horses and riders, Andalusia being perhaps the part of Europe where equine culture is strongest. Women in *flamenco* costumes sit side-saddle behind men with leather breeches, grey waistcoats and wide-brimmed hats; other people ride around in horse and carriage. Despite the bustle of the streets, the life of the *feria* is centred mainly inside the *casetas*, which are used by their owners as places for inviting their friends and family; if you know many people in Seville, you can spend your day going from one *caseta* to another. Inside the *casetas* you will be treated to numerous *tapas* of ham, cheese, and shellfish, but rarely will you be offered anything lavish to eat, as this might dissipate the great stamina necessary to survive the *feria*. The main drink is sherry or *manzanilla* (see page 173), and every year journalists try and calculate how much of these fortified wines is drunk in the *feria*, the usual estimate being that this equals the same quantity consumed by the whole of Spain in one year. The effects of the drink are compensated for by the constant dancing of *sevillanas*. In the best *casetas*, music for this dancing is never provided by a gramophone. Instead a circle is formed around the dancers, with someone beating the rhythm on a drum, another person singing, and the others clapping their hands. In a handful of the more snobbish *casetas* belonging to Seville's high society, there continues the bizarre and condescending tradition of gypsies performing *flamenco* to men and women dressed in evening attire.

In the old days the Seville *feria* was crowded with turbaned Indian princes, Arab sheiks, bejewelled European aristocracy, and American film stars such as Orson Welles. Today it is still customary for foreign dignitaries and celebrities to visit the *feria*, but the *feria* is essentially a festival for the inhabitants of Seville, and the welcome given to outsiders is a guarded one. Families from Madrid have managed in recent years to acquire *casetas*, and these people are commonly thought by the Sevillians to be spoiling the character of the *feria*, as are the countless people from other parts of Spain who pour into the *feria* at the weekend. The *feria* is one of the great tourist attractions of Andalusia, and yet the tourists who come here will encounter one of the most private of public festivals, where full enjoyment is only possible if you can secure entry into the closely guarded private *casetas*. The owners of the *casetas* are more welcoming to foreigners than they are to other Spaniards, but it is rare for the foreign tourist without friends in Seville to be invited inside the *casetas* for more than a single glass of wine.

Acceptance into the superficially open but at heart very closed society of Seville is difficult for a foreigner. One person who managed this in the 1950s was a tall and kilted Scotsman known as 'Pepe el Escocés', who came to Seville every year for the *feria* and was invited into almost every *caseta*, where he delighted everyone with his vigorous if arhythmic dancing of *sevillanas*. He became such a feature of the *feria* that journalists used to report his arrival in Seville, indicating that this was a sign that the *feria* had at last begun. Acceptance like this demands the following of certain unwritten codes of behaviour. High spirits and wit are greatly admired, but excessive drunkenness and gauche behaviour are deeply frowned upon. Most people are slightly tipsy, but considering the amount of alcohol which is consumed in the *feria* it is surprising how rarely drunken brawls break out. Even drinking and enjoying yourself requires '*arte*' in Seville, and the *feria* must be one of the most inherently sophisticated of public festivities. Within the *casetas*, social and family barriers are broken down in the common pursuit of pleasure. Money is never talked about but is spent thoughtlessly, the private bills in the *casetas* amounting to hundreds of pounds a day. Wit flows as abundantly as the wine, and all the cares of life are temporarily put aside. No wonder that the Sevillians, with their ability to reject all material preoccupations, sometimes consider themselves to be the upholders of the spiritual values of Europe.

The notion of the *feria* as a highly sophisticated occasion seems to many people incompatible with the fact that it coincides with the principal bull-fights of the Seville year. Bull-fighting, a sport considered by most foreigners and a growing number of Spaniards to be the most barbaric of all sports, has for many years been a major component of all Spanish festivals, but it was originally an essentially Andalusian speciality. The rules of the game were drawn up in the mid eighteenth century in Ronda, a town which produced during that period one of the most legendary of all Spanish bull-fighters or *matadores*, Pedro Romero, whose last fight was given at the age of eighty-six. The bull-rings at Ronda and Seville are the oldest and most beautiful in Spain, the latter, known as the Maestranza, being a supremely elegant late baroque creation in white and vivid ochre. During the *feria*, fights or *corridas* are held in the Maestranza daily, and these are generally the most exciting fights of the year, as the bull-ring is always packed to capacity with a particularly enthusiastic audience: the mood of the crowd is vital to the enjoyment of a *corrida*. The one drawback of the *feria corridas* is that good seats have to be booked a long time in advance, and the price of the tickets – very high for all bull-fights – becomes ridiculously exorbitant.

The very attending of a bull-fight demands a certain amount of ritual. Ideally you should arrive at the Maestranza in a horse and carriage, and enjoy before the fight a glass or two of *aguardiente* in one of the animated bars beside the building. Do not get too carried away, however, as bull-fights are renowned as one of the few Andalusian activities that always begin exactly on time. To the sounds of a band and to general applause, the participants of the fight walk into the ring, preceded by two costumed men on horseback responsible for maintaining order in the Maestranza. The three *matadores* fight in order of seniority, and have to kill two bulls each. Directing the fight is the President, who sits behind a balcony facing the arch through which the bull enters the ring; the weight of each bull is recorded in a notice above this arch. The first moments of the fight give the *matador* a chance to assess the calibre of the bull, and to show off his own skill with the cape. After a few minutes without any blood being shed, the President signals for the *picadores* to be brought in. These men, mounted on horseback, carry long lances with which they gore the bull. Since the 1920s the horses have always been padded, thus sparing the spectator the once common sight of horses having their entrails quickly sewn up so that they can face the bull again. The skill of the *picador* is to stick the lance into the bull in such a way as to reduce slightly its energy without in any way destroying its fighting spirit. Then follow the *banderilleros*, men who run at the bull and have to place as elegantly as possible two coloured banners into its neck. Finally the *matador* is left alone in the ring with the bull, a moment of impressive silence. If the *matador* performs well with his cape, the band starts up to play in preparation for the kill. The *matador*'s reward for a good display of fighting is to be given the bull's ear, or both ears if his performance is thought to have been truly outstanding. In the latter case – a rare event in Seville, where the public is an especially demanding one – the *matador* is carried in triumph through the main gate of the ring. The bull's corpse meanwhile is dragged off to be cut up by eagerly awaiting butchers, who sell off parts of it to the town's bars and restaurants.

Many of the finer points of bull-fighting can be learned by observing the reactions of the crowd, who will shout out for a weak bull to be replaced, wave their handkerchiefs to demand that the *matador* be awarded an ear, and will constantly make such comments as 'the President knows his bulls', or 'good' ('*¡bien!*'), 'well done!' ('*¡bien hecho!*'), and '*¡olé!*' Furthermore, there are countless books in English on bull-fighting, generally written in an emotional, macho vein by those who claim to have a unique insight into the sport: two of the most famous English works on the subject are by Ernest Hemingway and the drama critic Kenneth Tynan, both of whom, incidentally, had relatively little experience of the Seville Maestranza. What you rarely read is that the great majority of the fights are very poor in quality, and that bull-fighting today has lost much of its former greatness. One of the reasons for the decline might be that the desire to escape from poverty was once the main spur to the *matador*, and that extreme poverty of this kind is no longer so widespread in Spain.

Currently at the top of the Spanish bull-fighting league is the Seville *matador* Espartáco, who is exceptionally brave and skilful, and can always be relied upon to give a good fight. However, he lacks *arte*, a quality which for many Sevillians can be found today only in Curro Romero, a native of the neighbouring town of Camas. Curro Romero, in his mid fifties but still fighting, is a living legend who already has a street named after him in the precinct of the *feria*. As cowardly as Espartáco is brave, he has been known to go to prison for his refusal to kill a particularly dangerous bull (failure to kill a bull constitutes a breach in the bull-fighter's contract). It is said that you never see Curro fight badly, for he either fights well, or not at all. Most of the time he does the latter, but occasionally he has moments of un-surpassed brilliance, an event which makes newspaper headlines: following a fight of his in the Seville *feria* of 1989, the front page of the *ABC* bore the enormous caption, 'CURRO FOUGHT!'. I was present at one such fight of his, and for little more than two magical minutes the crowd rose and gaped in astonishment, some people even starting to cry. No account can hope to explain exactly what he did in those two minutes, but the *arte* was immediately sensed, just as it is in the finest of *flamenco*, or in the truly successful carrying of a *Semana Santa* float. It is in rare moments such as these that bull-fighting transcends the level of mere butchery or sport to become one of the more sophisticated, moving and mysterious of human activities.

No sooner is the Seville *feria* over than the *cruz de mayo* parties begin. These are put on in private or communal *patios*, and in some of the town's smaller squares, for instance the Plaza de Santa Cruz in the Barrio de Santa Cruz. The essential component is a cross decorated with flowers, in front of which people in *flamenco* costumes sing, dance and drink. The parties are sometimes said to commemorate the discovery of the True Cross by St Helen, but parallels can be drawn with maypole celebrations and ancient fertility rites. The blending of the religious and the secular is certainly striking, though not as much as it is in the Whitsun pilgrimage to El Rocío, which brings together elements of the *Semana Santa* and the *feria* to create what is not only the culminating festival of the Andalusian year, but also the most fervently supported festival in Europe today.

The story of the pilgrimage goes back to the fifteenth century when a man from the Huelva village of Villamanrique discovered while hunting a miraculous image of the Virgin hidden in a tree. A small hermitage was built, known at first as Nuestra Señora de las Rocinas. Around 1600 the villagers of nearby Almonte claimed the Virgin as theirs, and changed the name of the hermitage to the Virgen del Rocío ('The Virgin of the Dew'; she is also often referred to as 'La Blanca Paloma' or 'the White Dove'). From around that time there began a regular pilgrimage to the shrine, attracting a growing number of people. Pilgrimages of this sort are known as *romerías*, of which there are a great many in Andalusia. All these other *romerías* are completed within a single day, but the shrine of El Rocío is so isolated that it takes a day simply to reach it on foot from the neighbouring village of Villamanrique. From at least the early nineteenth century pilgrims were setting off for El Rocío from various places throughout the provinces of Huelva, Cádiz and Seville, arriving at the Hermitage by Saturday after a journey taking up to four days. The journey or *camino* to El Rocío became as important a part of the *romería* as the celebrations at the Hermitage itself. The popularity of the Rocío pilgrimage has increased yet further in recent years. Up to as late as the 1950s there was just a scattering of houses around the Hermitage, the pilgrims all camping in their wagons. A significant proportion of the pilgrims then were wealthy young men with a love of horses and practical jokes, who would attempt to seduce the women pilgrims behind the plentiful trees that you pass through on the *camino*. The pilgrims to El Rocío today form a representative cross-section of society and come from all parts of Spain, including the Canary Islands. The hamlet of El Rocío has swollen to an extensive village, where houses are rented out for astronomical sums of money, and where an estimated half a million people congregate for the Whitsun celebrations. To many people, known as *rocieros*, the pilgrimage is the most important event of their year, and they are happy to devote to it all their annual savings.

The pilgrimage to El Rocío from the various villages and towns of Spain is organized by local *hermandades*, or 'brotherhoods', at the head of which is a majordomo. An annual meeting of majordomos (of which there were seventy in 1989) establishes the exact itinerary and timetable which each *hermandad* has to follow. The 'brothers' of the *hermandad* carry their belongings in decorated wagons, pulled today mainly by tractors; some of the older *hermandades*, such as that of Triana, still have the traditional ox-drawn wagons shaped like those that once crossed America's Wild West. At the head of the long line of wagons is always the *simpecado*, a banner of the Virgin transported under an elaborately decorated canopy pulled by oxen. In front of the *simpecado* go pilgrims on foot, on horseback, or in horse-drawn carriages. The women are all dressed in *flamenco* costumes, while most of the men have cloth caps, black sashes, braces and grey and black striped trousers known as '*pantalones rocieros*'. All the foot pilgrims carry large sticks, the ones of the women decorated with flowers and sprigs of rosemary. Rosemary (worn by the men in their caps) is as essential an attribute of the Rocío pilgrims as the scallop shell is for those going to Santiago de Compostela, and indeed a pilgrim on this route is referred to as a '*romero*' or 'rosemary'.

The three major and most traditional routes to El Rocío run from Sanlúcar de Barrameda, Huelva and Triana; most of the *hermandades* eventually join up on to one of these routes. The *camino* from Sanlúcar is the most beautiful, crossing as it does the Guadalquivir and the protected section of the Coto Doñana National Park; the Huelva route is the dullest, while the Triana one goes through the most varied scenery of the three. Whatever route is chosen, the last day and a half before reaching El Rocío is spent in a wild and virtually uninhabited area formed by the estuary of the Guadalquivir and called the Marismas. Covered in marshes, sand and pine trees, the area was turned by Alfonso X into a royal hunting-ground in the thirteenth century. Triangular in shape, the Marismas have a great deal of mystery attached to them, and many like to locate here the legendary Tartessus. At the centre of the triangle, surrounded by marshes, lies El Rocío, and it is quite possible that long before the place became a shrine to the Virgin, there was celebrated here an important maternity and fertility cult. Most people who come to El Rocío are convinced of the magical properties of the place, and claim to experience a great renewal of energy whenever they visit it.

I embarked on the pilgrimage with considerable scepticism, believing that the occasion would be little more than a colourful folkloric pageant set in attractive countryside. I remain sceptical about the cosmic energy which supposedly emanates from El Rocío, but my week on the pilgrimage was certainly one of the most unusual I have ever spent, and completely outside the realm of everyday experience. I went with a group of friends from Seville, who hired three wagons and attached themselves to one of the oldest of the *hermandades*, that of Umbrete. Umbrete is one of the prettiest villages in Seville's Aljarafe, and the one perhaps most obsessed with the Rocío. To prepare themselves to be *rocieros*, the children of the village have their own annual pilgrimage to an old pine tree near the village, a journey undertaken in miniature wagons and with a *simpecado* pulled by dogs.

Nearly a third of the village's 3,000 inhabitants took part in the pilgrimage which I was on. After an early morning mass in the village church, we set off, serenaded by the village band and warmly applauded by the remaining villagers. A man playing a pipe and drum accompanied the *simpecado* throughout its journey, and rockets were let off in front of it at all the key moments, such as entering a village or passing a chapel. Angelus would always be said in front of the *simpecado* at twelve o'clock each morning, and there were frequent stops for singing and dancing; at the end of each long halt the majordomo would shout out, '¡Viva la Virgen del Rocío! ¡Viva la Blanca Paloma! ¡Viva la Hermandad de Umbrete!' A strong emotional attachment developed between the pilgrims and the *simpecado* and among the pilgrims themselves. Conversations were easily struck up, and those of us on foot were constantly being offered food and drink by the people travelling in the carriages.

Only an hour into our first day we left the asphalted road, and for the next three days we followed tracks through the dust and sand. There was a sensation of leaving the twentieth century, and once we reached the Marismas I felt truly in another planet. The procession of *flamenco* costumes and gaily coloured wagons through ever changing countryside provided an endless succession of beautiful images, and it was hard to believe that you were not experiencing some strange dream. One of the many memorable moments of the outward journey was the crossing of the River Quema, where there is a tradition of baptizing all newcomers to the pilgrimage and giving them names such as 'the Duck of the Quema': even this parody of the River Jordan ceremony has the effect of reducing many of the pilgrims to tears. At the end of each day our eighty or so wagons would group together around the *simpecado*, near to where various other *hermandades* had encamped. Rockets exploded all night, and around the countless camp fires *sevillanas* were endlessly sung and danced, the rhythms provided not only by clapping and drums, but also by the shaking of special reeds.

We arrived at El Rocío on Friday afternoon, two and a half days after having left Umbrete. In the village the *hermandades* all have their own houses, in the *patios* of which the wagons set up camp in the fashion of some Arabian caravanserai. I stayed in the house of friends who were not really *rocieros* at all, but Sevillians who enjoy the Rocío for its spirit of conviviality and for the energy which they say the place gives them. The life-style they lead here is comparable to that which they lead in the Seville *feria*: a continuous round of drinking, eating, dancing, singing and visiting friends. The main difference is that a spirit of total anarchy rules in El Rocío, and you lose altogether any sense of time and social responsibility. The village itself is unlike anywhere in Andalusia if not in Europe, resembling a Wild West town gone mad, with thousands of horses parading up and down dusty streets lined with arcades. From Friday afternoon to Tuesday morning the pandemonium increases with the constant arrival and departure of the *hermandades*, events greeted by fireworks, and people rushing to the doors of their houses to sing to the passing pilgrims.

The religious functions taking place in El Rocío – organized by the *hermandad* of Almonte – lack both the moving simplicity of those of the *camino* and the sophistication of the Seville *Semana Santa*; what they do have are moments of quite primeval intensity. The present Hermitage is a white modern building in a curious neo-baroque style; as for the image of the Virgin kept inside, this is a stiff, hieratic object with no trace of the subtle expressiveness to be found in some of the baroque Virgins of Seville. Throughout the Saturday the *hermandades* take it in turn to file past the open doors of the Hermitage to pay their respects to the Virgin. Loudspeakers constantly shout out instructions to those taking part in the processions, a ridiculous touch which would be unthinkable in any religious occasion in Seville. The Sevillians and most of the *rocieros* have a low opinion of the people of Almonte (the Almonteños), whom they consider stupid, brutal and arrogant. The Almonteños are noted for their predominance of blonds, and there is a theory that they are the descendants of a band of Vikings who got lost in the Marismas.

The boorish behaviour of the Almonteños is noticeable to everyone on the night of Whitsun. Only they have the right to carry the Virgin, and they defend this right in a vicious manner. At an unspecified time in the early hours of Monday morning the Virgin is carried outside the Hermitage and around the main square. The scene inside the Hermitage before this happens is quite terrifying, a surging, hysterical mass of bodies sweating under tropical conditions. After a given signal the Almonteños (recognizable by their khaki shirts) jump over the railings protecting the Virgin and fight among themselves for the privilege of carrying her. For a long time, both inside and outside the Hermitage, the Virgin is rushed backwards and forwards in the anarchic fashion characteristic of El Rocío. The hysteria and crush of the crowd is unceasing, and when I was there the Almonteños smashed the cameras of two television crews who they thought had not paid enough for the privilege of filming the event. Miraculously no one has apparently ever been killed during this night. With the first light of dawn, the Virgin is finally carried in a slightly more orderly fashion and taken in turn to each of the houses of the *hermandades*. The magic of El Rocío reasserts itself, and as the Virgin becomes ever brighter in the rays of the rising sun, people are everywhere crying with joy, believing that she has looked directly at them and will grant them their every wish.

The *hermandad* of Umbrete began its return later that Monday, the chaos and violent emotions of the weekend giving way to the pleasures of human company and of being united in a common endeavour. The journey back was very different to the outward one, more leisurely and intimate. Our last night and much of the last day was spent in the grounds of an eighteenth-century estate, where, in the courtyard of the *cortijo*, midday mass was said to the accompaniment of *sevillanas*; after this there was a sharing out of a large cake to commemorate the appointment of next year's majordomo. We arrived in Umbrete shortly after sunset on Wednesday, welcomed by fireworks and cheering villagers. I had slept for little more than ten hours in the entire week, but the sense of well-being counteracted the exhaustion. Good friendships had by this stage been formed, and departure was a genuinely sad occasion. The shock later that night of being back in Seville and of returning to the twentieth century was a considerable one. But Andalusia from the spring onwards leaves you with little time for serious reflection. The *cruzes de mayo* were continuing, and there was much talk of the following week's Corpus Christi celebrations and of a special procession in which the Macarena was to be brought to the cathedral. From this time onwards there would also be weekly *fiestas* in every village surrounding Seville, and throughout Andalusia. Meanwhile, in a bar in Umbrete, a noticeboard conscientiously records the days left to next year's Rocío. 'How we suffer to enjoy ourselves,' said Esperanza Flores.

7

FOOD AND DRINK

It is inconceivable that people as hedonistic as the Andalusians should not take an interest in what they eat. Yet the Andalusians, more than all other Spaniards, have been constantly criticized by foreigners for the poverty of their food. The idea that Spanish food in general is poor is another of the myths about Spain propagated by the Romantic travellers of the last century. Even someone as impartial and perceptive as Richard Ford could instruct the traveller to Spain not to 'lumber himself with much batterie de cuisine; it is not much needed in the imperfect gastronomy of the Peninsula, where men eat like the beasts which perish.'

'Spanish cuisine,' concluded Benjamin Disraeli after a few weeks' stay in Andalusia, 'is not to my taste, for garlic and bad oil predominate.' Oil and garlic were what nineteenth-century travellers loathed most about Spanish food, and Andalusia is perhaps the Spanish region which makes the most use of these ingredients. To these travellers the ultimate culinary abomination was Andalusia's most famous dish, *gazpacho*, a cold soup featuring garlic and olive oil mixed in large quantities with water. Dundas Murray's description of his Andalusian servant making this dish has the tone of someone recording a barbaric practice: 'Of this savoury mess, he offered me a share; but half-a-dozen spoonfuls sufficed to satisfy my curiosity . . .' Gautier went even further in his criticism of this dish: 'In our country, no dog with the slightest breeding would deign to put his muzzle in such a mixture. It's the favourite food of the Andalusians, and even the prettiest of the women here have no hesitations in swallowing every evening large spoonfuls of this infernal brew.'

In the course of the present century the long-held prejudices against oil and garlic have slowly been dropped, and the healthy properties of a cuisine heavily dependent on them have come to be widely recognized. The once much despised food of traditionally poor Mediterranean regions such as Provence is today very much in fashion, and even Spanish food is becoming increasingly popular. None the less, the food of Andalusia remains remarkably little known, and it is still widely looked down upon, even in Spain itself. Elsewhere in Spain Andalusia is disparagingly referred to as the land of the 'fried fish', and before moving to the region from Madrid, I was endlessly warned about how bad and unimaginative the food there was. The food I ate in Andalusia turned out to be one of the great revelations of this constantly surprising region.

The widespread ignorance about Andalusian food is explained to a large extent by the lack there of any long-standing tradition for eating in restaurants. Until comparatively recently the restaurants of the region catered mainly for tourists, and offered few truly local dishes. Today there are a number of outstanding Andalusian restaurants, but even so you are much more likely to encounter good food not only in people's homes, but also in bars, modest roadside inns (*ventas*) and other seemingly unpromising establishments that few tourists would think of entering. A certain spirit of adventurousness is needed to be able fully to appreciate Andalusian food. Certainly you have to adapt to what must be the most idiosyncratic of European eating habits. The Andalusians eat later than all other Spaniards, and it is not uncommon to have lunch as late as five in the afternoon or to dine at midnight. If you do insist on eating in a restaurant at times to which you have been used elsewhere in Europe, you will probably end up in the blandest of establishments. But you must also remember that Andalusians frequently forsake conventional meals altogether in favour of the *tapa* or bar-snack.

Andalusia is the traditional home of the *tapa*. In some of the region's bars, particularly in the provinces of Jaén and Granada, you will automatically be given a *tapa* whenever you order an alcoholic drink. In all other bars, you will almost certainly be asked if you want one, and if you answer yes, the waiter will probably recite at great speed a long list which would baffle most Spaniards. The tradition of the *tapa* is usually said to have developed as a result of poverty and great heat, two factors that can make impracticable the eating of a large meal. The *tapa*, however, also reflects a highly sophisticated attitude towards eating and drinking. It prolongs the amount of time you can drink without getting drunk, and it turns a lunchtime or an evening into a protracted eating experience which does not leave you bloated; it never impedes the flow of conversation. Above all it offers you an opportunity to taste an enormous variety of dishes, a variety which is the hallmark of Andalusian food. Even when sitting down to a meal, at home or in a restaurant, the Andalusians tend to cover the table with a large selection of small dishes, all of which are shared out (the only thing which is not shared in a restaurant is the bill, which is usually magnanimously taken up by one person). With their belief in eating well but in tiny quantities at a time, the Andalusians can perhaps claim to be more advanced in their eating habits than most other peoples. While others have traditionally regarded them as a culinary backward people, they feel that most foreigners do not have the same understanding of food as they do. They are perhaps the most gastronomically conscious of all Spaniards, and it is not coincidental that Seville should have more gastronomic societies than Madrid, and that Andalusia should have produced such a food-obsessed poet as Baltasar del Alcázar (see page 108) and two of Spain's pioneering food historians, Doctor Thebussem (see page 309) and Dioniso Pérez (known as 'Post-Thebussem'), author of the excellent *Guía del Buen Comer Español* (1929).

That Andalusia should have such an excellent and varied cuisine should not really astonish if you pause to think of the region's traditional fame for natural abundance, its having both an Atlantic and Mediterranean coastline, the presence of the immensely fertile Guadalquivir valley, the bringing in of so many new crops and fruits by the Greeks, Romans and Moors, and the fact that Andalusia was the first European region to benefit from American imports such as the tomato and the pepper. In the history of Andalusian cuisine, a particularly important role was played by the Moors. Andalusia under the Umayyads was as advanced gastronomically in relation to the rest of Europe as it was in all other cultural and scientific fields: it must be remembered that the great Ziryāb – an innovator in pastries and the man who introduced into Europe a fashion for eating according to a rational sequence of dishes – was active in tenth-century Córdoba (see page 68). The Moors encouraged the Andalusians to flavour their dishes with spices such as saffron, pounded ingredients together to create fine pastes (the basis of many Andalusian dishes of today, such as *gazpacho*) and created a tradition in pastries and sweets. Numerous Andalusian specialities are wholly Moorish in origin, including *ajo blanco* (see below) and all the region's many almond and honey-based pastries and biscuits such as *alfajores* and *polvorones*. At present there is also great interest in Andalusia in the revival of Moorish food, and two of the region's most renowned restaurants specialize in this, the Molino de Lecrín near Granada (run by the Gastronomic Society of Granada) and the Caballo Rojo in Córdoba. Among the famed dishes prepared by the latter are lamb in a honey-flavoured sauce (*cordero a la miel*) and angler fish with raisins (*rape mozárabe*), two excellent examples of the Moorish love of combining sweet and savoury flavours.

The great size of Andalusia, the variety of its terrain, and the traditional isolation of many of its towns and villages have led to a range of cuisine perhaps unrivalled in any other European region. It would be impossible to list and describe all the region's specialities, and the best way to find out about these is to make a point of visiting village bars, where there will always be someone to advise you on *tapas* characteristic of the locality. In the following few pages I have given only the broadest outline of Andalusian specialities.

Gazpacho alone exists in countless variations. In its most common form it comprises a blend of tomatoes, peppers, garlic and stale bread to which olive oil and wine vinegar from Jerez have been added, the whole watered down to the required consistency. Most people make the dish today in an electric blender, but it is really at its best when the ingredients are slowly pounded by hand in a special terracotta bowl known as a *dornillo*; either way, the dish should be eaten as soon as possible after it is made, and cooled with cubes of ice. Diced cucumber is often served with it today, as are diced peppers, tomatoes, onions, eggs, and fried croûtons (a particular aberration). The dish is ideal for an Andalusian summer, and though now considered mainly as a starter, it was traditionally drunk after a meal to refresh the palate. *Salmorejo*, a Córdoba speciality, is a dense version of *gazpacho*, prepared without water; *gazpacho verde* comes from Huelva province and uses parsley and other green herbs rather than tomatoes. *Ajo blanco*, a white *gazpacho* from Málaga, is especially good and one of the most Moorish of Spanish dishes: made with blanched almonds, it is served either with peeled muscatel grapes, or, less commonly, chunks of honeydew melon.

Seafood and fish provide Andalusia with some of its greatest dishes, and are apparently consumed here in greater quantities than in any other part of Europe. The best seafood is from the Atlantic coast of Cádiz and Huelva. Sanlúcar de Barrameda is renowned throughout Spain for its prawns (*langostinos*), while Huelva is known for its shrimps (*gambas*), clams (*coquilas*), razor-shells (*navajas*), and, above all, crayfish (*cigalas*), the finest of which are the females, recognizable by their lack of a large appendage under the head, and the delicious coral-coloured roe inside. Seafood in this western part of Andalusia is usually cooked by boiling in water flavoured with oil and bay leaves; from Málaga eastwards, there is more of a tendency to fry the seafood on a hot metal plate. *Arroz marinera* is a saffron-flavoured seafood rice dish of soup-like consistency, made with the excellent rice from the Guadalquivir estuary (considered by many to be superior to that of Valencia).

Though the Andalusians are sneered at for their love of frying most fish in batter, considerable skill and excellent, spanking-fresh fish are needed for successful frying. The prerequisite texture is for the fish to be crisp on the outside and succulent inside. It is ironic that the English tradition for frying fish in oil – a tradition which has led to the saddest, soggiest results – was probably introduced into the country by English merchants who had lived in Jerez. The English fish and chip shops of today have certainly nothing in common with Andalusia's *freidurías*, where exquisite fried fish is sold throughout the day. The fish most commonly fried in Huelva and Cádiz are *lenguados* (soles), *pijotas* (whiting), *acedías* (small soles), and *salmonetes* (red mullet); Málaga meanwhile is celebrated for its fried *boquerones victorianas* (a kind of anchovy), and *chanquetes* (whitebait), the latter described by the painter Zuloaga as 'crisp sea-spray'. *Adobo* is any white fish fried after being marinaded in wine. A selection of all these fish is often served on large platters in restaurants and bars.

Despite Andalusia's reputation as the 'land of the fried fish', fish is prepared here in a myriad of different ways, ranging from being grilled over charcoal (this is how the *Malagueños* like to cook their delicious small sardines) to being stuffed with minced meat, tomato, parsley and breadcrumbs, as in *chipirones rellenos* (stuffed squid).

Three outstanding elaborate dishes are *raya al pimiento* (skate in a pimento sauce), *chocos con habas* (cuttle-fish with broad beans) and *hurta a la roteña* (white fish similar to bream, with peppers, onions and tomatoes); the first two are specialities of Huelva, the latter of Cádiz. The roe (*huevas*) of *chocos* and other Andalusian fish is frequently served in salads, and makes a popular *tapa*. Mention should finally be made of the region's tunny fish (*atún*), which has been caught since at least Roman times along the coast of Barbate de Franco and Zahara de los Atunes. The main catches of the year (the *almadrabas*) take place in late May and early June, and are extraordinary spectacles with some of the excitement and brutality of a bullfight, the fish struggling on deck as men lance at them with long knives. Throughout the year the bars of Barbate offer an enormous variety of tunny-fish *tapas*, including *mojama* (dried tunny-fish) and *atún encobellado* (tunny cooked in a wine and onion-based sauce). The most sophisticated of all Andalusian tunny-fish dishes is *atún mechado*, a speciality of the Huelva town of Isla Cristina, featuring tunny-fish minced with bacon, garlic and parsley, coated with flour and lard, and cooked in the oven with a sauce of onions, garlic, wine and herbs; it is served either hot or cold.

Few sheep or cattle are raised in Andalusia, and thus there is little tradition here for eating most meats; the idea of a large bleeding steak is at any rate anathema to the majority of Andalusians. Pig-raising, however, is common to many parts of Andalusia, and the Andalusians have a particular love of raw hams, as is evident from Baltasar del Alcázar's famous poem quoted on page 108. Del Alcázar specified in this work that the ham he liked most came from the Sierra de Aracena in Huelva. The Sierra village of Jabugo produces among the best hams in Spain, rivalled in fame only by those of Trevélez high up in the Alpujarras of Granada: the latter perhaps are better known abroad, but the former are the most popular in Andalusia. Granada province, however, is undoubtedly superior in its charcuterie products (*embutidos*), in particular its *chorizo* (spiced sausage), *salsichón* (salami) and *morcilla* (blood sausage). A great many of the bars and *ventas* of this area make their own charcuterie, including the Venta Bienvenido outside Monachil (Granada), where I once enjoyed one of the cheapest and best meals I have ever had in Andalusia (see page 286). Lovers of *morcilla* should also make a pilgrimage to the Málaga village of

Cártama, home of one of Spain's best-known brands of blood sausage. Another Andalusian speciality is bull's tail (*rabo de toro*), though this is not exactly what you most care to eat after a bull-fight, nor on a hot day, as it is a very rich dish served always in a thick and heavy wine sauce (this dish is very popular in Córdoba). Poultry and game are not Andalusian specialities, but you should try the partridge pâté of the Sierra Morena, much of which is tinned in the Jaén town of La Carolina.

Most Andalusian dishes are accompanied by a salad of lettuce and tomatoes, but rarely by any other vegetables. Vegetables are served mainly as dishes on their own, and take frequently the form of stews made with fresh vegetables and pulses. Spinach cooked with chick peas (known simply as *espinacas*) is a great favourite of western Andalusia, while in the early summer months you should try the wild asparagus known as *esparagos trigueros*, which are fried with garlic, coriander and bread soaked in water. Broad beans cooked with little pieces of cured ham (*favas al jamón*) are common to the Granada area. *Huevos a la flamenca*, a dish now found throughout Spain, was originally from Seville, and consists at its best of eggs cooked in a terracotta dish together with pieces of cured ham and a selection of the abundant vegetables of the Guadalquivir valley, including artichokes, asparagus and peas.

The most national of Spanish dishes is the *cocido*, a stew featuring a selection of meats, pulses and fresh vegetables, the whole served in between two to four separate courses. The exact ingredients and way of serving *cocido* differ from region to region, and there are numerous variations within Andalusia alone. The main difference between the Andalusian brands of *cocido* and those of other parts of Spain is that the former always includes cauliflowers and is served in no more than two courses: first come the vegetables with the cooking broth, and then the meats (usually chicken, mutton, *chorizo* and *morcilla*), which the Andalusians tend to cut finely on their plates to form what is known as *pringá*. *Cocido* was the only Andalusian dish enjoyed by Disraeli, but he made the bizarre claim that the vegetable medley included slices of melon. A humbler form of *cocido* is the *puchero*, which leaves out *chorizo* and *morcilla* and uses meat bones. The broth from a *puchero*, together with a sprig of mint, is dished out in great quantities during festivals, it being renowned as a great pick-you-up and a cure for hangovers.

Cheeses are always eaten as *tapas* rather than at the end of a meal in Andalusia. The region's cheeses – all made of goat's or sheep's milk – are hardly encountered outside their village of origin, the one nationally known brand being the sheep's cheese of Pedroches, near the Córdoba town of Pozoblanco. Most Andalusians end a meal with coffee rather than with fruit or dessert: however, a great after-meal treat in the summer months is the *chirimoya* or custard apple, grown around Motril in Granada. Pastries and sweets are traditionally eaten mainly around Christmas and Easter, and many of the finest specialities of this kind are unobtainable at other times of the year: if you find yourself in Seville during Holy Week you should try *torrijos*, which are slices of bread that have been steeped in white wine and honey, coated in egg yolk and then fried. Estepa near Seville is famous for its crumbly almond-based biscuits called *polvorones*; Cádiz and its neighbouring towns make a rich variant of *crème caramel* known as *tocinos de cielo*; the large, thin, cinnamon-coated *tortas* of Castilleja de la Cuesta are exported throughout Spain; and Medina Sidonia has a tradition for its *alfajores* (pastries made of lard, honey and almonds), dating back to Moorish times. The best places to buy all these sweet specialities are convents, Spanish nuns having been engaged in the making of these products since at least the time when St Teresa distributed the sugar and egg-yolk *yemas* to the poor of Ávila (the outstanding *yemas* of Andalusia are those of the convent of San Leandro in Seville).

Lager beer, served extremely cold and often taken away from you as soon as it begins to get warm, is Andalusia's most popular drink; the main brand is Cruzcampo, which is far preferable to the Castilian Mahon or San Miguel and is regarded by many Andalusians as one of Europe's best beers. Andalusia's table wines are nearly all white, and hardly any of these are marketed; examples are the excellent *costa* from the Alpujarra and the *mosto* of Umbrete, both of which are young wines that should be drunk not more than five or six months after the grapes have been harvested. The Sanlúcar firm of Antonio Barbadillo has recently had an enormous success with its marketing of Castillo de San Diego, a light white wine of no great character but which goes very well with all fish and seafood.

The fame of Andalusia as a wine centre is based entirely on its fortified wines, the ones from the Jerez area being traditionally Spain's most popular wines abroad, and the ones that gave rise to the word 'sherry'. *Fino* is the dry, classic sherry, the most popular brand being Tío Pepe; *amontillado* is mellower and darker in colour, while *oloroso*, the most matured of these sherries, is the deepest in texture, and can be slightly sweet. *Manzanilla* is a wine from the sherry area which can be made only in Sanlúcar de Barrameda, the cool sea-breezes of this town being essential to its fermenting process. This wine has a slight tang of the sea, and a reputation of tasting at its best not just in Sanlúcar itself, but in the part of the town nearest the sea; many also claim that it is less likely to leave you with a hangover than the wines of Jerez. The other Andalusian area known for its fortified wines is Montilla in Córdoba, but these are slightly coarser in quality. Most foreigners tend to think of all these wines essentially as aperitif wines, and indeed there can be few drinks that so perfectly complement *tapas*: many Andalusians can conceive of few things better than to sip a glass of *manzanilla* while enjoying one of Sanlúcar's celebrated prawns. However, sherry, *manzanilla*, and Montilla are also regularly drunk here as an accompaniment to a full meal, a tradition which has yet to catch on elsewhere.

Most of Spain's renowned brandies come also from the Jerez area, among the most refined being Carlos I and Gran Duque de Alba. Sweet dessert wines made in the Jerez and Montilla areas include Pedro Ximénez and Solera; but the dessert wines best known abroad are those of Málaga, which enjoyed a great vogue in England in the Victorian and Edwardian periods and of which the finest are those of the Bodegas Scholtz. A drink manufactured in various parts of Andalusia is *aguardiente* or anis, which can be both sweet or dry. Zalomea (Huelva), Rute (Córdoba) and Cazalla de la Sierra (Seville) are among the main places where it is made, the latter producing also an attractive cherry-flavoured drink known as *aguardiente de cereza*. Significantly all three places are in traditional mining areas, a glass of *aguardiente* being a necessary boost before a day's work in the mines. An early morning *aguardiente* will also be appreciated by those who have undergone the rigours of a characteristically Andalusian night of drinks, *tapas* and banter.

8

ROMANTIC ANDALUSIA

In the years 1811–12, at the height of the Peninsular War, a group of radical patriots took refuge in Cádiz and set up the Spanish Parliament or Cortes. They held their meetings in the baroque oratory of San Felipe Neri, an oval-shaped building encircled inside with balconies as in a theatre. When the French laid siege to the town in 1812, these patriots drew up a Constitution which was to have a major impact on European politics. This document, demolishing the basis of the old monarchy and upholding the sovereignty of the people, used the word 'liberal' for the first time in a political context, and became a model for future revolutionaries all over Europe. From the time of the Peninsular War, the attention of Europe was turned increasingly towards Spain, and in particular Andalusia, which was considered by some to be the liberal centre of the country. 'In no other part of Spain,' wrote George Dennis in 1839, 'is the liberal part stronger than in Andalusia. Whether this arrives from the great commercial inter-course with foreigners, from the vicinity of Gibraltar, or from the naturally independent spirit of the inhabitants, the fact is certain.' Foreigners tended to romanticize and oversimplify the Spanish politi-cal situation, often reducing it to a straightforward conflict between the forces of 'liberalism' and those of reaction. In any case, those tourists who came here in growing numbers in the nineteenth century had usually only a superficial interest in the politics of Spain, preferring instead to dwell on the country's exotic past and traditions. The tourists who passed through Cádiz seem certainly to have given little thought to the great event which had taken place in 1812 in the oratory of San Felipe Neri. Even the young Benjamin Disraeli had anything but politics on his mind when he visited the town in 1830. He had not even reached Seville, and yet already the sounds of opera were ringing in his ears. 'Figaro is in every street,' he enthused, 'Rosina on every balcony.'

The romantic rapture which came to affect all travellers to Spain in the course of the nineteenth century developed against a background of near constant political turmoil. Since 1700 Spain had been ruled by the Bourbons, and in 1762 the Spanish and French branches of the family had signed a family compact whereby their two countries entered a closer alliance with each other. The ruling Spanish king was then Charles III, under whose reign Spain at last appeared to be enjoying again an image as a progressive nation, in touch with the latest European ideas. Charles III's edict of tolerance towards the gypsies, his expulsion from Spain of the Jesuits, and his programme of land reform – which had included the establishment of the Sierra Morena colonies – were all acts fully in accordance with Enlightenment ideals. Reform ceased to be fashionable, however, after his death in 1788. His successor, Charles IV, a weak and unintelligent man, was given in a famous group portrait by Goya an appearance which has been described as that of a contented grocer. Power in Spain came largely into the hands of the king's minister Godoy, who enjoyed both the favours and the bed of the queen, María Luisa. Godoy, who failed to prevent the execution of the French king, Louis XVI, compromised with the French revolutionaries and eventually became actively involved in Napoleonic schemes. Off Cape Trafalgar, today one of the wildest and most beautiful spots on the Andalusian coast, the Spanish and French fleets came together in 1806 to attack the British, and retired shattered to Cádiz. Two years later an irate mob stormed Godoy's house at Aranjuez near Madrid. The overthrow of Godoy was followed shortly afterwards by the abdication of Charles IV, the flight of the Spanish royal family to Paris, and the arrival in Madrid of French troops under Murat, whose atrocities were later recorded in Goya's horrific *2nd of May*. One of the first deeds committed by the French on their coming to power in Spain was to suppress the country's monasteries and convents.

The events of 1808 provided a great dilemma for Spanish liberals. On the one hand they welcomed French revolutionary ideas, and on the other they resented a foreign power in their land. The Seville-born writer and theologian Blanco White escaped from Madrid to Seville in 1808 and was overjoyed to hear of the French defeat at Bailén by

General Castãnos. However, he reported that the news was received with mixed feelings by a liberal friend of his: 'To my friend and companion, whose anti-catholic prejudices are the main source of his mental suffering, the religious character which the revolution has assumed, is like a dense mist concealing or disfiguring even objects which otherwise would gratify his mind.' When finally the French, under Marshal Soult, succeeded in entering Seville, the local intellectuals collaborated fully with the invaders, the reformist priest and poet Lista even becoming a freemason and journalist in the Marshal's pay.

Humiliatingly, the Spanish nationalists had to rely greatly on their country's traditional enemy, the English, to oust the French. The Peninsular War dragged on until 1814, one of the main French defeats taking place at Borrosa in Andalusia. In 1814, with English help, the Bourbon monarchy was restored in the person of Charles IV's son, Ferdinand VII. Ferdinand VII, universally described by his contemporaries as an odious figure, agreed to abide by the 1812 Constitution, but soon repudiated this. He attempted to stifle all liberal opposition, introduced rigid censorship, and brought back both the Jesuits and the dreaded Inquisition. A revolt in 1820 led to a short period of liberal rule, which was concluded in 1823 after French troops had put Ferdinand back in power. He continued to be as repressive as ever, one of his notorious deeds being to order the execution in 1831 of a young Granada woman called Mariana Pineda, whose crime had simply been to sew a liberal flag and to refuse to denounce the people for whom she had made it. Transformed by popular legend into a woman of remarkable beauty and virtue, Mariana Pineda was commemorated a few years afterwards by a statue outside her house and was later made the eponymous heroine of an early play by García Lorca. In the play, Mariana's decision to go to the scaffold rather than betray her ideals causes particular dismay to her lover, whom she rebukes with the following words: 'Do you love Liberty more than you do your little Mariana? Well I shall be the very Liberty which you adore.' Other liberals of the time made comparable gestures of defiance against Ferdinand, but did so in more bungled and inglorious fashion. One of these people was the exile Torrijos, who in 1832 landed with a small force near Málaga, only to be immediately arrested. He had been accompanied by an Irish

adventurer, Don Boyd, whose execution, together with that of Torrijos, provided the British cemetery at Málaga with its first corpse.
The British, still not fully recovered from their rage at the unchivalrous
treatment of Mariana Pineda, were made virtually apopletic by news
of what had happened to Boyd. Richard Ford, however, took a
different view to his compatriots: 'Certainly,' he wrote, 'if anybody
of the party deserved shooting, it is a meddling *Foreigner*.'

To everyone's relief Ferdinand died in 1833, but not before ensuring
that on his death the country would be plunged into chaos. Three
years before dying he had married María Cristina, by whom he had
had his only children, both of whom were girls. Altering a law which
would have granted succession to his brother Charles, he had appointed as his heir his elder daughter Isabel. On his death María
Cristina had immediately stepped in as regent to Isabel, thereby
provoking the First Carlist War. María Cristina was forced to enlist
the support of the liberals, and was also lent a hand by the British,
again much to the disapproval of Ford. A treaty in María Cristina's
favour was signed in 1839, but the confusion of Spanish political life
only worsened, and continued to do so for the rest of the century.
Isabel II, who had been declared of age in 1843, was forced to
abdicate in 1868 following a rebellion raised in Andalusia by a group
of liberals under General Prim. In 1874 Spain experimented with a
republic, but growing anarchism in Andalusia and Catalonia brought
this to an end just over a year later, by which time the Second Carlist
War had broken out in the North.

It was in these latter years of the century that the great economic
decline of Andalusia was consolidated, thus turning what had once
been Spain's wealthiest region into one of the poorest. The loss of
Spain's Latin American possessions, which had begun after 1812, had
affected Andalusia more than any other Spanish region, but it had still
remained relatively prosperous up to as late as 1868: what with the
expansion of the region's mining industry, the development of its
ports, and the continued success of traditional industries such as
textiles, tobacco, olive oil and wine, Andalusia could even claim to
have been one of the most industrialized parts of Spain. Growing
political confusion, the ever greater involvement of foreign companies
in the region's industries, and the emergence of the region after 1850
as one of the main monarchist centres of Spain, were all contributory

factors in Andalusia's economic collapse in the late nineteenth century. In the 1880s a phylloxera epidemic spread from the vineyards of France to those first of Málaga and then of Jerez de la Frontera, sparking off in the latter town one of the most virulent of the many strikes that had repeatedly paralysed Andalusia's industries from the early 1870s onwards. The journalist and writer Leopoldo Alas was a witness, and described the way in which the protesters, in their fury, had lashed out at anyone who wore glasses and was well dressed. This was certainly a different rural world to the bucolic one of the early years of the century, as evoked nostalgically in Alarcón's *The Three-Cornered Hat* (1874).

Misery and backwardness were among the features that made the country picturesque for the Romantic traveller. Previously they had deterred many from coming here. Until the late eighteenth century Spain had not in fact been a country particularly popular with tourists: most of those who had visited and written about the place had been merchants, diplomats or politicians. In the mid eighteenth century Voltaire was writing that 'Spain is a country which we know no better than the wildest parts of Africa and which does not merit being better known.' Charles III's enlightened policies helped change European attitudes towards Spain, and encouraged in the last years of the century a sudden rise in tourism, as is made evident by the appearance of numerous detailed travel books about the country such as those by Jacob Twiss, Peyron, Swinburne, Townshend and the Baron de Bourgoing. Many of these travellers commented with admiration on such aspects of modern Spain as the excellent new road between Madrid and Seville, and the Sierra Morena colonies. A new, cheerful and optimistic image of Spain began to emerge, and Andalusia was the part of the country which most lived up to this image. The Spain of morbid gloom and inflexible moral codes gave way to a country much more in keeping with the free-thinking spirit of the Enlightenment, a country of great gaiety and sensuality, where everyone endlessly courted and indulged in such exuberant and provocative dances as the *bolero* and the *fandango*. The popularity of this new Spain was mirrored and furthered by the success of Beaumarchais's two plays, *The Barber of Seville* and *The Marriage of Figaro*. Beaumarchais had not even been to Spain, let alone Seville, and neither had Rossini or Mozart, who set these plays to music.

The Peninsular War, though hardly strengthening the lively carefree image of Spain, made more people aware of the country than ever before. Accounts of Spain written by foreign soldiers who had been involved in the war proliferated, heightening people's curiosity about the place as well as fuelling many British readers with a desire to visit the sites where their compatriots had excelled themselves: Dundas Murray was not alone among British travellers in touring battle sites such as that of Borrosa, armed with a copy of Napier's history of the Peninsular War. In the years following the war, knowledge of and enthusiasm for Spain were further increased by the large numbers of Spanish political exiles, most of whom took refuge in England: an especially large community of Spanish exiles grew up in the London district of Somers Town. Among the Spanish liberals resident in Britain was Blanco White, who had left Spain in 1810, subsequently dropping his Spanish name of José María Blanco y Crespo. A man of Irish parentage, he had been brought up as a Catholic in Seville but had become disillusioned with the faith around 1800: after converting to Anglicanism in England, he ended up a Unitarian. His *Letters from Spain* of 1822 are full of vivid details of Andalusian life in the early years of the century, and were much read by the English. With a critical eye, a loathing of Spanish fanaticism and superstitiousness, and a belief in the essential superiority of British over Spanish culture, he described at length such popular aspects of Andalusian life as bull-fighting and the Seville Holy Week. Of a particular event from the latter celebrations, he wrote: 'I have carefully glided over such parts of this absurd performance as would shock many an English reader even in narrative. Yet such is the strange mixture of superstition and profaneness in the people.' Blanco White succeeded in informing and fascinating the English, and also confirmed many of their prejudices about the Spaniards.

For all the interest that the Peninsular War generated, it was not until the end of the 1820s that tourists started visiting Spain in significant numbers. They had allowed a sufficient amount of time to pass for the country to recover somewhat from its ruined state, but not so much time as to prevent them from benefiting from its impover-ishment: one of the new incentives of a journey to Spain was the realization that there were countless works of art to be had for the smallest sums of money. Between 1829 and 1850 there were published a great range of travellers' accounts of Spain, including four of the most successful ever written: Washington Irving's *Tales of the Alhambra*, George Borrow's *The Bible in Spain*, Richard Ford's *A Handbook of Spain* and Gautier's *Voyage en Espagne*. The majority of the travellers were either British or French, not surprisingly, given their countries' vested interests in the country. A genuine adventurous spirit was still required of this generation of travellers to Spain, even though they generally much exaggerated their bravery with constant tales of bad roads and banditry. The appearance of Ford's *Handbook*, the ensurance of greater safety for travellers by the founding of the Guardia Civil in 1848, and the spread of the Spanish railway network after the 1850s made journeys through Spain increasingly easy for foreigners, so much so that in 1887 Disraeli's nephew, recollecting his uncle's trip in the 1830s, could write that 'in these days of easy travel the whole of this foreign tour reads almost like a romance'. In the second half of the century there was no falling off in the number of travel books on Spain, but the quality of these books fell considerably. The observations of Spanish life seem second-hand, and the attempts to stir the reader's interest with evocations of adventure and romance have an increasingly hollow ring to them. Spain had changed considerably since the 1830s and 40s, but attitudes towards the country remained those that had been formulated in that earlier period; some of these attitudes are still held today.

Andalusia continued to represent for Romantic travellers all that was most typical of Spain. But these travellers saw the region in a markedly different way to their predecessors. It was still a region of all-embracing sensuality, but this sensuality had lost some of its innocence; a mood of cheerful flirtatiousness had developed into one of dangerous passion. The region's Moorish past, which had interested eighteenth-century travellers in an essentially archaeological way, became now a reflection of this sensuality, a consuming obsession, an ideal of civilization, and, not least, an excuse for British travellers to air their anti-Catholic prejudices. Whereas earlier travel writers gave equal emphasis to the modern and traditional aspects of Andalusia, Romantic writers were far less impartial, and reserved their enthusiasm for those aspects of the region that for them made the place exotic and remote from the rest of Europe. Richard Ford was thinking above all of Andalusia when he described going to Spain as 'flying

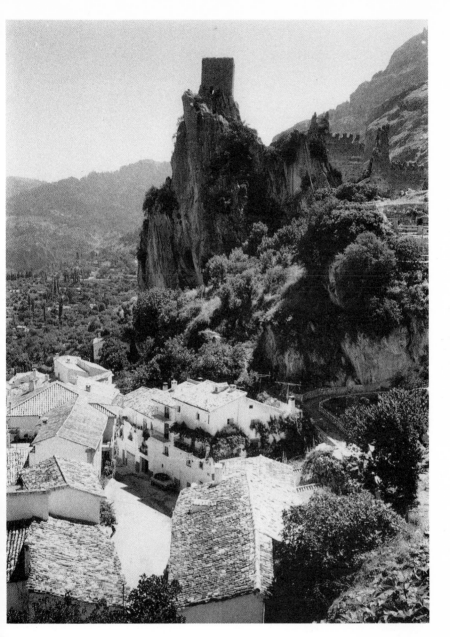

1 General view of Iruela (Jaén).

2 (*Left*) Plaque marking the modest beginnings of the Guadalquivir river in the Sierra de Cazorla (Jaén).

3 (*Below*) The Jaén Gate, Baeza (Jaén).

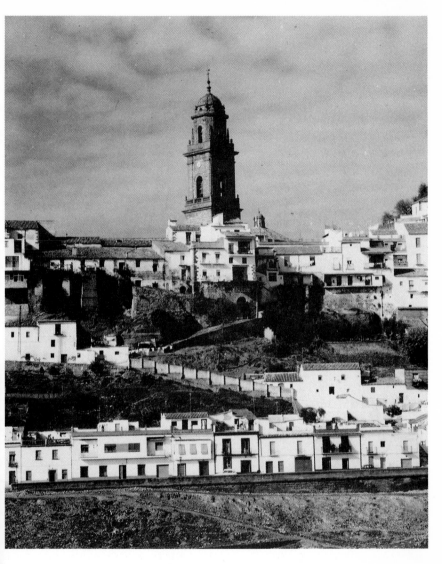

4 The village of Montoro (Córdoba).

5 The ruins of the Umayyad palace of Medina Azahara (Córdoba).

6 Inside the castle of Almodóvar del Río (Córdoba).

7 (*Above*) The seventeenth-century palace of the Marquis of Viana, Córdoba, seen from its garden.

8 (*Right*) On the Calle San Pedro, Osuna (Seville); the baroque palace of the Marquis of Gomera.

9 Esperanza Flores at the *feria* of Seville.

10 The confraternity of Los Negritos, Holy Week, Seville.

11 The brotherhood of Umbrete on its pilgrimage to El Rocío.

12 The entrance to the Seville *feria*.

13 (*Above*) Memorial to the bull-fighter Joselito by Mariano Benlliure, in the cemetery of San Fernando, Seville; the second bearer to the left is the bull-fighter friend of García Lorca, Ignacio Sánchez Mejías, who is buried alongside Joselito.

14 (*Right*) Roman necropolis, Carmona (Seville).

15 Castaño del Robledo, one of the many hidden villages in the Sierra de Aracena (Huelva).

16 The coast between El Rompido and Punta Umbría (Huelva).

17 (*Left*) The prehistoric rock shelter of Laza Alta, near Jimena de la Frontera (Cádiz).

18 (*Right*) The eighteenth-century palace of the Domecqs, Jerez (Cádiz); a statue of one of these 'sherry barons' is in the foreground.

19 View of the church of the Encarnación, from the medieval castle of Olvera (Cádiz).

20 Cave houses in Setenil de las Bodegas (Cádiz).

21 View of Ronda from the path leading to the Sanctuary of the
Virgen de la Cabeza (Málaga).

22 The fortifications of Ronda seen from the terrace of the palace of
Salvatierra.

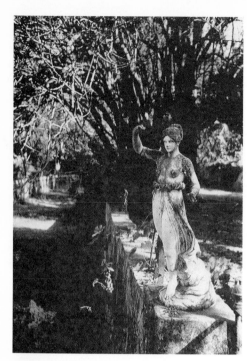

23 (*Left*) The eighteenth-century gardens of El Retiro, Churriana (Málaga).

24 (*Below*) Neo-Moorish market on the Calle Atarazanas, Málaga.

25 View from the Sanctuary of the Virgen de la Gracia, Archidona (Málaga).

26 The eighteenth-century octagonal square of Archidona (Málaga).

27 The baroque chapel of Santa María de Jesús, Plaza del Portichuelo,
Antequera (Málaga).

28 View from the National Park of El Torcal (Málaga).

29 (*Above*) General view of the Alhambra from the Albaicín, Granada.

30 (*Right*) The modern gardens of the Fundación Rodríguez-Acosta, Alhambra, Granada.

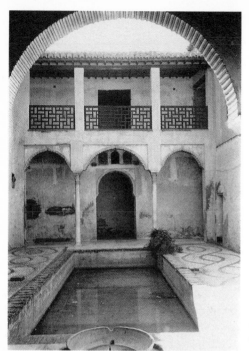

31 (*Left*) *Patio* and pool
in the Moorish Casa
Zafra, Albaicín, Granada.

32 (*Below*) View from the
summit of the Pico Veleta,
Sierra Nevada (Granada);
Mulhacén is on the left.

33 (*Above*) Fuente de la Teja, outside the village of Valderrubio (Granada), a favourite spot of García Lorca; the man in the foreground often met the poet here.

34 (*Right*) The view from García Lorca's bedroom and study at the Huerta de San Vicente, Granada.

35 (*Left*) Village scene in Busquístar in the Alpujarras (Granada).

36 (*Below*) View from the Alcazaba of Guadix towards the gypsy quarter of Santiago (Granada).

37 The village and Renaissance castle of Lacalahorra (Granada).

38 View of the gorge of Alhama, from behind the church of the Carmen, Alhama de Granada.

39 (*Above*) The Cabo de Gata at sunset (Almería).

40 (*Left*) The Moorish walls of Almería, seen from the Alcazaba.

41 The upper level of the Alcazaba of Almería, with Moorish tent in the foreground.

42 Mini Hollywood, Tabernas (Almería), the setting of many 'spaghetti westerns'.

43 The Renaissance castle of Vélez Blanco (Almería).

44 The view from the prehistoric cave shelter of Los Letreros, outside Vélez Blanco (Almería).

from the dull uniformity, the polished uniformity of Europe, to the racy freshness of that original, unchanged and unchangeable country.'

A striking feature of Romantic attitudes towards Spain is that travellers often criticized the place for the same reasons that they found it so exciting. They loved Spain for being 'unchanged and unchangeable' to the extent that they greatly exaggerated its backwardness; and yet they complained much of the time about poor inns, bureaucratic inefficiency, the laziness of the inhabitants, the lack of modern comforts and so on. They were stimulated by the sensual atmosphere of Andalusia, but frequently censured the women for the looseness of their morals. They were fascinated by the spectacular religious processions and other manifestations of religious fanaticism in the region, the painter David Roberts going apparently out of his way to put monks and priests in his Andalusian views. Yet they generally loathed the clergy and found excuses to criticize priests wherever possible: William Jacob even wrote that the pretty women of Andalusia were rarely to be seen in the streets because they were always being entertained in priests' houses. No visit to Spain, above all to Andalusia, could be made without going to a bull-fight. But few bull-fights could be seen without some reference to the barbarity of the sport, the sadism of the spectators, and so on.

British travellers – the most adventurous and noticeable of the foreign visitors to Spain – often prided themselves on their adaptability to Spanish manners. Richard Ford took to wearing traditional Spanish costumes, and thought that this was sufficient to hide his nationality and thus make him less of a prey to bandits. Clearly he loved the charade of trying to appear Spanish, as did many of the British travellers who later imitated his example. When Gautier went to a tailor's in Granada in 1845, he was told that the only people to buy such costumes were the English. The Spaniards' belief in the eccentricity of the English was constantly being confirmed. Dundas Murray had only to propose going on foot from Cádiz to Sanlúcar for a Spaniard to mutter 'mad Englishmen'; but, as Murray observed, 'in this quarter of the world Englishmen have the reputation of doing all sorts of odd things'. Ford wrote shortly after settling with his family in Seville that: 'The natives are interested and surprised at all our proceedings, and verily believe we have arrived from the moon.' Considering that the English had been the traditional enemies of the

Spaniards since the time of Philip II, the fact that the Spaniards regarded them at worst with bewildered amusement, and rarely in any hostile way, is remarkable. On the other hand the English were almost without exception patronizing towards the Spaniards, and convinced of their own superiority. These feelings usually rose to the surface the moment the British traveller entered Gibraltar. 'On again setting foot on British ground,' wrote George Dennis in 1839, 'to that thrill of delight which can only be experienced on passing immediately from a strange land to one's native soil, I felt added a pride, when with the neglected fortifications and squalid troops at the Spanish barrier fresh in my memory, I looked round on the clean, well-accoutred soldiery . . . Freedom in England, has brought knowledge, enterprise, wealth, power, in its train. Despotism, religious and political, has rendered Spain ignorant, superstitious, slothful, poor and impotent.' Willis Baxley put all this more succinctly in the concluding line of his own book of Spanish travels: 'Thank God I am an Englishman!'

Few of the British nineteenth-century travellers had actually much close contact with the Spaniards, and most of them were greatly dependent on the help and companionship of compatriots of theirs already resident in Spain. In Granada British visitors were often looked after in the first half of the century by General O'Lawlor, the lieutenant-governor of the province, and the man appointed by the Duke of Wellington to supervise the running of the vast nearby estate which the Duke had been awarded after the Peninsular War. Elsewhere in Andalusia the British could expect considerable hospitality from their consuls at Cádiz, Seville and Málaga. Brackenbury held the post at Cádiz during the 1830s and 40s; Julian Williams ('Don Julian') was consul at Seville during this time, and was later succeeded by his son Manuel; for most of the century the consulate at Málaga was run by members of the Mark family, beginning with William Mark. Bracken-bury, Julian Williams and William Mark had taken on the poorly paid job of consuls after having fallen in love with Andalusia in the course of working there as merchants. They were very knowledge-able about the area, and had amassed important collections of works of art, antiques, and curiosities. The arrival of British travellers offered a welcome opportunity to share their knowledge and en-thusiasm and to show their collections to people who they believed knew how to appreciate them.

Cádiz, Gibraltar, Málaga, Seville and Granada were the main centres around which the Romantic traveller's tour of Andalusia was usually based. Córdoba was visited quickly, being generally considered, in the words of Borrow, 'a mean, dark, gloomy place'; nor did it have any important foreign residents to take care of the visitor. Otherwise the traveller's attitude towards the Andalusian interior was very similar to that of today's tourist. Then, as now, travellers tended to visit few of the out-of-the-way towns and villages, and generally hurried between one main centre and the other. The one part of the countryside which many people made a special detour to go and see was the Serranía de Ronda, which was as popular then with the British as it is today. It was an area which managed to be conveniently near to Gibraltar while, with its savage aspect, notorious roads, and fame as a bandit centre, satisfying to the full the traveller's love of adventure. Describing a journey there in 1860, William Jacob wrote: 'It has not been unattended with fatigues, privations, and even dangers; but the scenes through which I have passed, the character of the people I have seen, and especially the bold features of the most picturesque country in Europe, will afford recollections which I shall dwell upon with pleasure through the remainder of my life.' Ronda itself, with its spectacular cliff-top situation, and its deep gorge cleaving the town in two, was the archetypal Romantic site. Owing to its isolated and wild situation Ronda was not thought at first to be a suitable place for the woman traveller, but in the second half of the century, a belief in the beneficial qualities of its mountain air led to the town gaining some of the character of a genteel health resort.

Though the Andalusian coast was not to be extensively developed until this century, the town of Málaga enjoyed an ever-growing popularity from the 1830s onwards, and by 1850 had become a thriving wintering resort for the British. Its consul, William Mark, who described the town as a 'Second Paradise', did much to encourage the British to come here. He was also able to allay British travellers' fears of dying on Spanish soil by founding at Málaga, in 1830, Spain's first British cemetery. Up to then Protestant visitors to this country had been treated at death like infidels, and in Málaga had been buried feet forwards on the beach. The locals had rather vague ideas about Protestantism, and were rather surprised by the cross which was put up at the entrance to the British cemetery; they did not know that 'these Jews' worshipped the same symbol as they did. The cemetery became an obsession of Mark's and he spent much of his life prettifying it. He had had to wait a long time for its first corpse, and, as Ford cruelly suggested, he might even have been secretly pleased by the execution in Málaga in 1832 of Torrijos's protestant companion Don Boyd: 'In heart,' Ford wrote in a letter, 'I believe he was as glad as a young surgeon to get a subject for his new churchyard. He has certainly a hankering after my wife's body, not her live body, but, hearing of her ill health, tried all in his power to get me to Málaga to have a pretty female specimen in his sepulchral museum.' When, shortly afterwards, a child of Ford's died and was buried in an orange grove at Seville, Ford doubted whether Mark would ever forgive him. However, it was not to be long before the cemetery began filling with the corpses of the British invalids who had come to Málaga to try and recover their health. As Málaga developed into a wintering resort (Augustus Hare wondered why so many invalids came here, as the place was thick with dust), the town acquired an elegant promenade with numerous trees planted by Mark. The cemetery meanwhile was further embellished by Mark's son and became quite a tourist attraction: Hans Christian Andersen, one of its many admirers, wrote that he could 'well understand how a splenetic Englishman might take his own life in order to be buried in this place'. Its former sea views have today been blocked by extensive modern development, but the cemetery is still a place of evocative charm, and much visited by an old-fashioned type of English tourist.

Granada and Seville were the foremost Andalusian destinations of the Romantic traveller, the former being praised above all for its monuments, the latter for its paintings and colourful life. Travellers to Granada would take a look at the Royal Chapel in the lower town, and the more adventurous of them would go to the gypsy quarters of the Sacromonte and the Albaicín. But their time would be largely taken up in the Alhambra, which Ford called 'that magical word which in the minds of Englishmen is the sum and substance of Granada'. Both the Alhambra and the adjoining gardens of the Generalife (an essential part of any Alhambra tour) had been left to decay ever since the late sixteenth century, and remained in a piteous state for much of the nineteenth century. Into the vast precinct of the Alhambra had moved a considerable population of gypsies and other impoverished people, while the palace itself had served as a military hospital and as a prison for both debtors and galley-slaves. After 1798 the palace had suffered further damage after being turned into an official residence of the Governor of Granada, who used much of the woodwork for fires and allowed farm animals to run around the halls. During the Peninsular War, the French invaders kept soldiers, prisoners, stolen goods, and dynamite here, and as a parting gesture, blew up eight of the Alhambra's Moorish towers. In 1811 William Jacob had predicted that 'without repair, to which the finances of Spain are inadequate, it will in a few years be a pile of ruins; its voluptuous apartments, its stately columns, and its lofty walls, will be mingled together, and no memorial be left in Spain of a people who once governed the peninsula'. Its ruined state, though causing alarm, undoubtedly contributed to its appeal for the Romantic travellers who started flocking here from the late 1820s onwards. Ford, in his magnificent descriptions of the Alhambra, relished the effects of bathos achieved through evoking one moment the sublime beauty of the place and then going on to observe such details of its decline as the sight of a group of galley-slaves converting part of the building into a storehouse for salt fish. He was there in 1831 and 1832, and at that time the Governor of Granada employed a peasant woman called Francisca de Molina to look after the palace with the help of her two nieces. 'Tiá Antonia', as she was called, made among the first tentative attempts to 'restore' the palace by clearing away the accumulated debris of centuries and by setting on their legs the famous lions of the Lions' Courtyard. Other, more important restoration campaigns were subsequently carried out, but Spain's constant political troubles in the nineteenth century led to equally numerous interruptions. Only after 1870, when the Alhambra was declared a national monument, was the future of the place finally safeguarded.

The Alhambra has always been regarded as one of the great wonders of the world, but in the seventeenth and eighteenth centuries many travellers were content simply to repeat the praises of others, and did not see the place for themselves. The Valencian writer Antonio Ponz, the author of the most detailed topographical account of Spain to be published in the eighteenth century, went to every part of Spain except Granada, as did the similarly meticulous French travel writer the Baron de Bourgoing. The French were in fact notoriously lax about visiting Granada, and several of the eighteenth-century accounts of the Alhambra are copied from other works. Characteristically it was the British who pioneered tourism to Granada in the eighteenth century. One of the few French writers to go there himself, Peyron, found in one of the Alhambra's rooms graffiti by the English writer Henry Swinburne. Swinburne and his companion Thomas Gascoigne had inscribed their names, a short poem and the date, 'January, 1775.' Another Frenchman, Nicolas Masiari, staying in Granada as a prisoner in 1792, wrote that 'the town and province of Granada are more famous than they are known. The English come to see the place to say that they have seen it, then rush away after having grabbed some of the stones from the palace of the Moorish kings, without even being stopped by the Spaniards, who merely register surprise that anyone should have come such a long way to look at stones.'

At this early date, the Moorish remains of the Alhambra were not the exclusive concern of travellers, the Renaissance palace of Charles V being apparently an equal source of wonder. William Jacob was lavish in his praise of this place, and in his *Travels in the South of Spain* of 1811 there appears an engraving in which the building dominates the Alhambra as it was never to do in views by later artists. With the fashion for orientalism which was soon to develop, Charles V's Renaissance addition was to be largely ignored. One of the great instigators of the new fashion was Chateaubriand, who came to the Alhambra in 1807, recording his visit with a signature in the gallery above the Court of Lions. 'It is,' he wrote of the Alhambra, 'one of those buildings from the Thousand and One Nights, that one sees less in reality than in dreams.' By 1826, when he published his Moorish romance set in sixteenth-century Spain and called *The Last of the Abencerrages*, memories of the Alhambra had indeed ceased to bear much resemblance to a real place. The enormous success of this book was soon rivalled by that of Victor Hugo's epic poem *Les Orientales* (1829), which turned orientalism from a fashion into a mania, and featured a beautiful evocation of the Alhambra, a place which Hugo had never seen. Two years earlier a little known English draughtsman, T. H. S. Estcourt, had published the first major series of engravings of the Alhambra, thus enabling the European public to have a much clearer idea of what the place actually looked like. Over the next few years many other engraved views of Granada were to appear, the most influential of which being those of David Roberts: as in his other Andalusian works, Roberts greatly exaggerated the proportions of both the buildings and the surrounding mountains, and in so doing enhanced the fairy-tale stature of the place. But the man who did most to influence foreign attitudes towards the Alhambra, and to fire travellers with an enthusiasm for seeing it, was a young American diplomat who arrived in Granada the same year that Hugo's *Les Orientales* was published.

Washington Irving, born in New York in 1783 of an English father, first came to Spain in 1826 to work for the American legation in Madrid. He had already earned a certain reputation as a writer, but in Madrid he dedicated himself to his first major work of scholarship, a biography of Columbus. His energy was prodigious, and when writing his biography he was known to rise sometimes as early as two o'clock in the morning, a time when most people in Madrid have usually not gone to bed. With a view both of completing this work and of researching another on the *Conquest of Granada*, he set off for Seville in March 1828. His travelling companion was a German called Stoffenegen, who 'having never before been so far to the south' was 'in continual transport with the luxurious indications of a southern climate'. Irving remained based in Seville for over a year, spending much of his time in the archives, and also going on a long excursion to the sites near Huelva associated with Columbus such as the Monastery of La Rábida. In Seville he spent much time with the Scottish painter David Wilkie, whom he had first met in Madrid and who was one of the most important of the Romantic artists to tour Spain. Irving was later to dedicate his famous book on the Alhambra to Wilkie, and in his preface to this was to recall how the two of them, in Seville together, 'were more than once struck with scenes and incidents in the street, which reminded us of passages in the Arabian Nights'.

In April 1829 Irving moved on to Granada, in the company of a Russian prince, Prince Dolorouki, Secretary to the Russian delegation. Over a month later Irving was writing to a friend to say how he and the prince were '*royally* quartered', the governor of Granada having offered them the use of his rooms in the Alhambra. 'Here, then,' Irving continued, 'I am nestled in one of the most remarkable, romantic and delicious spots in the world. I breakfast in the Saloon of the Ambassadors, among the flowers and fountains in the Court of Lions, and when I am not occupied with my pen I lounge with my book about these oriental apartments, or stroll about the courts and gardens and arcades, by day or night, with no one to interrupt me. It absolutely appears to me like a dream, or as if I am spell-bound in some fairy palace.' He and his Russian friend had virtually the palace to themselves, among the only other occupants being the Governor's housekeeper, 'Tía Antonia', and her two nieces. 'Tía Antonia', whom Irving described as a 'woman of strong and intelligent, though uncultivated mind', looked after the two guests with enormous devotion. When Prince Dolorouki eventually left, 'Tía Antonia' was most critical of Irving's decision to change apartments and to move into a remoter and more isolated part of the palace: she feared that he would be too vulnerable there to the many criminals and people of bad character who lived within the Alhambra precinct. Irving, however, was too enchanted by his new chambers to worry much about personal safety. These chambers, adjoining the gallery where Chateaubriand had signed his name, now form a small Irving museum, which can be visited only with special permission. After jostling with the crowds of tourists that daily throng the Alhambra, a visit to this museum affords a pleasant respite. The place comprises a suite of four small rooms, which differ from all other parts of the palace not only by their silence, but also by their sombre, murky and neglected character: suddenly you have an inkling of what the Alhambra must have been like in Irving's day. In these sparsely furnished rooms, dating back to the sixteenth century but thoroughly nineteenth-century in character, you will find the only furniture still left in the palace, including Irving's bed and writing-desk. The sitting-room juts out above the verdant northern slopes of the Alhambra hill, and from its window the writer's eyes must often have wandered over the rising line of fortifications up to the hanging gardens of the Generalife. While staying here, Irving completed his *Conquest of Granada* and began work on the book by which he is best known in Spain today, *The Alhambra: A Series of Tales*. In this book, today on sale in various languages throughout Andalusia, Irving combined romantic tales of the Alhambra's history with descriptions both of the place and of the memorable personalities whom he got to know there such as 'Tía Antonia'. Fact and fantasy were intermingled in the book, as they have generally been in the minds of the thousands of tourists who have come to the Alhambra in Irving's footsteps.

Summoned to work at the American legation in London, Irving left the Alhambra on 29 July 'after having passed between two or three months in a kind of oriental dream'. Two years after his departure, Richard Ford arrived with his family and English servants at Granada, and was also offered the possibility of staying in the Alhambra. The place was described to him as being in such a poor state that at first he was reluctant to take this up. '. . . As my children and English servants,' Ford wrote in a letter to his friend Addington, 'have no taste for the Moorish picturesque, but a great notion of the more humble gratifications proceeding from a comfortable home and well-appointed kitchen, I am rather inclined to put up with the unromantic reality of some good ready-furnished house.' In the end, however, practical considerations were outweighed by romantic feelings, though not before Ford had arranged for carpenters and decorators thoroughly to overhaul the rooms where he and his entourage were to be put up. This was the part of the palace where 'Tía Antonia' and her nieces lived, and they treated Ford no less well than they had Irving. Ford was a more restless traveller than Irving, and, while staying at the Alhambra, toured Granada and its surroundings rather more extensively than the latter apparently had done: he even made the arduous ascent up to the peak of Pico Veleta, accompanied by his wife, who thus became the first woman to do the climb. But, like Irving, he found the surroundings of the Alhambra to be so congenial that he took relatively little part in the life of the town below. Later travellers would nearly all try and stay on the Alhambra hill, and though the actual palace was soon to be no longer available to them as a residence, various hotels were to be built on the hill, including the Hotel Washington Irving, described in 1870 as 'the most comfortable hotel in Spain'. Visitors to Granada in the nineteenth century stayed in their ivory towers, ignoring as best they could the real world at their feet.

Of the French Romantic travellers to write about Granada, the most influential after Chateaubriand was unquestionably Théophile Gautier. Born in 1811 in Gascony, near the Spanish border, Gautier was always to pride himself on having a southern temperament and even Spanish looks. In Paris in 1829 he studied to be a painter, but he changed his vocation to writing after reading Hugo's *Les Orientales* and meeting the great man himself. Soon afterwards he started going around Paris dressed in Egyptian costume. By the end of 1839 he was beginning to tire of Paris, and toyed with the idea of visiting Turkey. A wealthy friend of his, Eugène Piot, suggested that they should go instead to Spain. Piot's motives for wanting to go there were not wholly romantic ones, for he pointed out to Gautier that as Spain had been impoverished by the Carlist War, antiques and works of art would be cheap to buy. They set off for Spain in May 1840, arriving in Madrid in June: by 1 July they were in Granada, and remained there until 12 August. They stayed in the lower town, and, unusually, did not have any regrets in doing so. Gautier was one of the first and last writers to describe Granada as a town of great gaiety and animation. Most people have usually commented on how dull the place is socially, but Gautier was in elated spirits, and was seeing everything through rose-tinted spectacles. He had found Madrid grim and provincial, but had started to become excited the moment he had crossed the Sierra Morena and entered Andalusia. Granada was his first taste of an Andalusian town, and it was the place in Spain which was to make the greatest impression on him: he dreamed one day of building a reproduction of the Court of Lions in his Paris garden.

After Granada, Gautier was able quickly to finish off the rest of Andalusia: three days were adequate for Málaga, two for Córdoba, and a week each for Seville and Cádiz; he was back in France by the beginning of October, his return having been prolonged by an enforced stay in Valencia. On the basis of what had been little more than a four-and-a-half month stay in Spain, Gautier wrote his best-selling *Voyage en Espagne* (1841). It is a book with many fresh and humorous observations, and is admirable for its open-minded attitude towards such reviled aspects of Spanish culture as food and baroque architecture. Yet at other times Gautier merely repeated by now hackneyed Romantic responses to Spain, and used too often as his visual point of reference the orientalist canvases of fashionable contemporary painters such as Delacroix and Decamps. Mario Praz, in his *Unromantic Spain*, put much of the blame on Gautier for 'faking a mannered Spain' which was later to be 'consecrated in the lyric prose style of Thos. Cook & Son Ltd'.

Descriptions of the Alhambra, after Gautier, became ever more delirious and tedious. The French painter Henri Regnault, visiting the place in 1869, was so overwhelmed that he was totally unable to do any sketching for several days. He concluded that the civilization of the Spanish Moors was infinitely superior to that of the West, and heavily criticized Charles V for having built within the Alhambra 'a horrible, enormous block'. Among the most purple passages inspired by the Alhambra were those by the once highly revered Italian author, de Amicis, author of the sentimental novel, *Cuore*. De Amicis, putting forward the oft-repeated idea that the architecture of the Alhambra is an expression not of power but of love and voluptuousness, wrote: 'There is thus a strong link, a harmony between the beauty of this Alhambra and the souls of those who have been in love at sixteen, when desires are dreams and visions.'

In view of Granada's development from the late nineteenth century onwards into a pretentious and ugly modern town, the oriental ecstasies that the Alhambra continued to provoke came to seem increasingly anachronistic. The magical name 'Alhambra' had by now been appropriated by theatres, cinemas and night-clubs throughout Europe, and the architecture of the place had been parodied in countless hotels and vulgar wealthy villas: a sewage works had even been built in London's Wapping with an interior inspired by it. It was left to Praz brilliantly to deflate the whole tradition of Romantic attitudes towards the Alhambra.

Reader I did not take up my abode between the magic walls of the Alhambra for four days and as many nights, with the tacit consent of the authorities, neither did I dwell there for several months attended by houris and escorted by valets descended from the Moorish kings . . . None of the bits of luck which fell to the lot of Washington Irving and Théophile Gautier was repeated for me. My mind was not haunted by any of the many delicious follies, pleasant whim whams, and gentle absurdities that the tearful Eduardo de Amicis claims to have thought and uttered between the Court of the Myrtles and the Court of the Lions. While visiting the Alhambra I did not tremble like an aspen leaf; while leaving it I did not tremble like an aspen leaf; while leaving it I did not bid farewell to all the illusions of youth and to that love which will never live again.

Seville's appeal for the Romantic traveller was altogether different to that of Granada. In the first half of the century, the town could boast Moorish monuments such as the Giralda and the Alcázar that were in a far better state of preservation than the Alhambra; moreover, the cathedral here was far more admired than Granada's and was indeed considered one of the finest in Spain. But the sightseer was drawn to Seville less for its architecture than for its seventeenth-century paintings. Murillo was still regarded as one of the greatest artists of all time, Velázquez was enjoying an ever-growing popularity, Alonso Cano was far more widely appreciated than he is today, and Zurburán had come suddenly into fashion after over a century and a half of neglect. Under these circumstances, Seville came to be thought of as one of the great art centres of Europe, as William Jacob wrote in 1811: 'Few places in Europe, with the exception of London or Paris, contain so many good pictures as are to be found in this city.'

Not content merely to look at these pictures, travellers made every effort to acquire them, and could do so at first with remarkable ease and minimum expenditure. Marshal Soult, occupying Seville at the time when its religious foundations were suppressed, began the collecting trend by ruthlessly requisitioning paintings; by the 1830s the Seville art market was as thriving as Venice's had been in the previous century. Two of the main collectors were the consul, Julian Williams, and the British businessman resident in Seville, Standish Hall. The former, who owned a renowned group of Murillos, was described by Irving as a 'man of great taste' and by Disraeli as 'the greatest connoisseur of paintings in Spain': it was under his influence and that of the Cádiz consul, Brackenbury, that Ford himself became a considerable collector, acquiring among other works a magnificent Zurburán of *The Martyrdom of St Serapion* (now in Dumbarton Oaks). Standish Hall, referred to by Ford as 'Maecenas Hall', was much more than a collector, being additionally a celebrated dandy, and the author of a biography of Voltaire: 'He is,' wrote Disraeli, 'a most singular character – a spoiled child of fortune, who thinks himself, and who is perhaps now, a sort of philosopher.' His collection, comprising both a wide range of Spanish old masters and numerous contemporary Seville works, was later to be offered by him to the British government in return for his receiving a peerage. The offer was turned down, and the collection ended up in 1841 in the famous Spanish Gallery founded by Louis-Philippe in Paris.

Louis-Philippe, a passionate enthusiast of Spanish art, had sent to Spain in 1835 a colourful personality called Baron Taylor to amass works of art for him. Baron Taylor, a Belgian-born soldier who had travelled extensively around Europe, spent two years in Spain, based much of the time in Seville. His mission was an enormous success, and when the Spanish Gallery was opened to the public in the Louvre in 1838 it caused a sensation, inspiring a fashion for all things Spanish. By this time, however, the people of Seville had begun to show concern at their rapidly disappearing heritage. With the further suppression of monasteries and convents in 1836, Dean Manuel López Capero tried to save as many works of art for the city as he could, and made these the nucleus of Seville's Museum of Fine Arts, which was established in the former monastery of La Merced. Without the intervention of López Capero, Seville's reputation as an art centre would have been greatly diminished, and the town would not have had an art gallery rivalled in Spain only by the Prado.

Fortunately Seville was not treated just as a repository of potentially lucrative objects. Travellers loved coming here for its people, social life, and festivities, generally regarded as the most lively and exotic in the whole of Spain. Colourfully dressed women and *majos* paraded the streets, the sounds of singing and dancing were constantly to be heard, and any excuse seemed sufficient for organizing an exuberant religious procession. The town's theatrical life was and still is notoriously bad, but in compensation the streets provided a constant human spectacle, and the whole place seemed to many like a living opera: nineteenth-century travellers were finding on every corner Figaro, Don Giovanni, and Carmen. One of the greatest promoters of Seville's charms was Richard Ford, who was also one of the few to write perceptively about its people, with their caustic humour, refusal to be hurried, and wild outbursts of childlike enthusiasm. Describing Granada, Ford wrote that 'to those who arrive from Seville, the inhabitants do not look either so well dressed, gay or intelligent. There are fewer *majos*, and the women are inferior walkers and talkers.' Ford had a passion for the Alhambra, but Seville was his favourite Spanish town, and it was here that he had decided to base himself when he first came to Spain in 1830.

The son of an eminent politician and an amateur painter, Ford was born in London in 1796. He studied law, but never practised, and in 1824 he married Harriet Capel, the pretty daughter of George, fifth Earl of Essex. Harriet was always in delicate health, and Ford thought that a stay in a southern climate would do her good. Most people in his position would have chosen to have gone to the French Riviera or Italy, but Ford, eccentrically, settled on Andalusia, a region which was still considered too wild to be wholly suitable for aristocrats travelling with their families, especially not for ailing women. Ford's interest in visiting Spain might have developed through his friendships both with the Duke of Wellington and with the British Envoy Extraordinary at Madrid, Thomas Addington, whom Ford had known since school days; he had also been much enthused by a talk on Granada given by Washington Irving in London in 1829.

Ford and his family and servants, including a nanny called 'Oggy', arrived in Seville in October 1830 and rented a house belonging to Standish Hall; they were to spend three consecutive winters in Seville, moving in their second year into a large sixteenth-century palace, the Palacio Monsalves. Ford had a letter of introduction from the Duke of Wellington to a leading Seville family, and with his evidently engaging manner was popular with most Spaniards. At the Palacio Monsalves he put on balls that were well attended by the local nobility, in particular one which was held in honour of the daughter of '*Míster Mark*' of Málaga. The Seville painter Joaquín Bécquer did a portrait of him wearing the *majo* costume of which he was so proud; another local artist, José Gutierrez, depicted him and his wife as seventeenth-century Spanish grandees. More than most other British travellers of his generation, Ford tried to immerse himself in Spanish life, and he is still remembered in Seville as one of the few foreigners to be accepted by the outwardly open though at heart closed society of this town. None the less, Ford's social life still revolved largely around the town's foreign community, a community which always looked forward to the arrival of visitors from abroad. Among those who came to see Ford in Seville were the collector Sir William Eden and the artist J. F. Lewis, for whom Ford was to arrange an introduction to the bandit king José María (see pages 20–21). To his regret, Ford was away from Seville when the French painter Delacroix passed by on his way to Morocco; Delacroix profited from his absence by openly flirting with Harriet. Ford at the time was on a lengthy and arduous sketching trip to Extremadura, one of several such excursions that he made from Seville. Like many of his compatriots, Ford had a passion for sketching, an activity which he described as being as incomprehensible to the Spaniards as reading. Outside Seville and

Granada sketching was met not simply with bewilderment but with deep suspicion, and was liable to have its perpetrator landed in gaol on charges of spying. Ford was much braver, more inquisitive and persistent than most other sketchers, and as a result came to know the Spanish towns and countryside more intimately than nearly all his compatriots. It was not until many years after leaving Spain that he was to put this knowledge to any great use.

Shortly before the outbreak of the First Carlist War, Ford, worried by the worsening political situation in Spain, decided to return with his family to England. Harriet and he had been having a difficult time together during the previous months, exacerbated no doubt by the growing isolation which she had experienced in the course of her husband's long absences from Seville. When they reached England in July 1833, they separated, he to move to Exeter, she to stay in London, where she was to die four years later. Ford purchased a house in the country, Heavitree House, and keenly refurbished it, indulging in the occasional Spanish touch: he decorated one of its towers with 'Arabesque lienzo' and confessed to Addington that the end result was 'prettier than the Puerta del Vino of the Alhambra'. Though he was never to return to Spain, Ford kept himself well informed about everything that happened there, and read all that he could on the country. In 1839 the publisher John Murray approached him for advice as to who should write the volume on Spain in the popular guide book series known as *Murray's Handbooks*. Under the influence of wine and a good dinner, Ford proposed himself, and soon found that he had taken on far more than he had bargained for. For the next five years he remained largely tied to his desk, dressed in a Spanish jacket of black sheepskin, and surrounded by growing piles of manuscripts and books. A very sociable person with a love of the good life, Ford had not the makings of a scholarly recluse, and in the end was thoroughly bored with the whole project. After the first edition had been withdrawn at great expense to incorporate changes suggested by Addington, the *Handbook* finally appeared in 1845. Despite being a two-volumed work densely printed in double columns, it was an immediate success, and the long, introductory section was soon afterwards reprinted separately as *Gatherings from Spain*, a work intended mainly for the armchair traveller; the *Handbook* itself was reissued numerous times in the nineteenth century, but is now available only in a Spanish edition.

By making the section on Andalusia the first and largest part of the *Handbook*, Ford greatly strengthened the misleading view that Andalusia is the quintessential Spanish region; he also shared and reinforced several other British prejudices about Spain, such as hatred for baroque sculpture and architecture. These cavils apart, the *Handbook* remains without doubt the best general introduction to Spain ever written, and one of the liveliest and most informative guide-books to have appeared on any country. Partly because of its healthy mixture of enthusiasm and down-to-earth observation, it conveys the feel of the country far more acutely than do the sentimental, high-flown ramblings of most travel writers on Spain; that it was written in England and so long after its author had left the country makes the achievement even more remarkable. Ford's prodigious scholarship is worn lightly, and the book is endlessly entertaining and shows no evidence of the tedium which such an encyclopedic task always entails. He kept himself and his readers amused by peppering his text with witticisms that make you want to laugh out loud. His turn of phrase was masterly. 'So great a literary achievement,' summed up a contemporary of Ford, 'had never before been performed under so unpretending an appellation.' Had the book been published today, it would probably scarcely have been reviewed, a distinction having now been made between travel and guide-books. The former are considered as literature, the latter are not.

Several other members of the British community in Seville tried their hand at writing about Spain and their Spanish experiences. Standish Hall brought out a dreary book on Seville in 1840, and Captain T. E. Cook ('not *the* Captain Cook', as Ford stressed in a letter to Addington) wrote two general works on the country. Ford had known Cook well in Seville, and found the man's first book on Spain to be not as bad as he had feared: its main failings for Ford were its artistic judgements, Cook being someone who did not know 'a Murillo from a mainmast'. A writer on Spain for whom Ford had unqualified admiration was George Borrow. John Murray had published Borrow's *Zincali: The Gypsies of Spain* in 1841, and it was quite clear from this idiosyncratic work that the adventures in Spain of the man who wrote it would make an equally fascinating read. Ford encouraged Murray to go ahead and publish these, and later wrote a letter to Addington referring to the 'extraordinary fellow

George Borrow, who went out to Spain to convert the *gypsies*. He is about to publish his failure, and a curious book it will be.'

Six foot three inches tall with a shock of prematurely white hair, a semitic nose, and a direct and aggressive way of looking at people, Borrow must have cut an eccentric figure in Spain; certainly he was the great individualist among the British travellers to the country, and the great outsider. The son of a recruiting officer, Borrow was born in 1803 and schooled in Norwich. In addition to his interest in gypsies, he developed an obsession with languages and the Vikings. With such a background he could hardly fail to turn to a life of roving, which began in 1824 when he abandoned his training as a solicitor and walked to London. Between then and 1833, the story of his life, as gleaned from his later autobiographical writings, is difficult to follow and even more difficult to believe. Prone to wild exaggeration, and to complete invention, Borrow none the less turns out demonstrably to be telling the truth when his tales seem least plausible. Possibly he went around the world before 1833, almost certainly he experienced life as a wandering tinker, and he travelled widely around Europe. In 1833 he found the perfect job to suit his travelling instincts when he joined the London Bible Society, the aims of which were to sell the Bible to as many countries as possible and in as many languages. The job took him around Russia between 1833 and 1835, and then to Spain shortly after his return from Russia to England. The Carlist War was at its height, and most British travellers of the time had the sense to be leaving Spain rather than going to it. Borrow was always at variance with the rest of society.

Borrow's first trip lasted until September 1836, but he was back two months later, this time visiting Andalusia for the first time. He went from England directly to Cádiz, where he took a room in the Hotel de Paris. Characteristically, he went out of his way to avoid the hotel's middle-class cosmopolitan clients. Unlike most other British travellers in Spain, he had no desire to meet his compatriots, and had a lifelong loathing for the niceties of British middle-class behaviour. In Cádiz he spent much of his time in coffee-houses and 'seeking out those parts of the town where the lower classes principally reside'. He went afterwards to Seville, and was not unnaturally drawn to Triana which he said 'is inhabited by the dregs of the populace, and abounds with Gitanos or Gypsies'. While at Seville he was delighted by a chance encounter with the Baron Taylor, a man whom he was always running into in various parts of the world, and whom he clearly regarded as a kindred spirit. 'Whenever he descries me,' Borrow wrote of Taylor, 'whether in the street or the desert, the brilliant hall or amongst Bedouin haimas, at Novgorod or Stambul, he flings up his arms and exclaims, "O ciel! I have again the felicity of seeing my cherished and most respectable B—".'

Borrow's second trip to Spain ended dramatically in Madrid, with his being thrown into prison as a result of his evangelizing activities. His imprisonment seems to have upset people in England more than it upset him, and he benefited from his stay in gaol by studying the dialect of thieves. Released in September 1838, he returned to England, but then set off again almost immediately to Spain, despite the by now wary attitude towards him of his employers at the Bible Society. On this third and final visit to Spain he was based mainly in Seville, which he described as 'this terrestrial paradise'. Unknown to the Bible Society and hardly in accordance with their conventional Christian morality, Borrow was joined in Seville by an English widow, Mrs Mary Clarke, with whom he lived out of wedlock for the rest of his time in Spain. This secret liaison is indicative of how nominal Borrow's work for the Bible Society in fact was, and he probably regarded it largely as an excuse for adventure and travel. Back in England in April 1840, Borrow broke off his association with the Society, married Mary Clarke, and devoted the rest of his life to writing. *The Bible in Spain* (1842), written in a solitary hamlet in a remote part of England, was immensely popular with the English reading public. In comparison with so many other travellers' accounts of Spain, Borrow's is startlingly original and unconventional; his emphasis is on his encounters with strange people, but even when he looks at places he does so in an unusual way, as for instance when he evokes the ruins of Itálica by concentrating on a vulture standing grotesquely over the pitiful corpse of a horse. He feels no necessity to praise at length the Moorish and other monuments to which his fellow travellers devoted so much of their tiringly romantic descriptive prose: the Alhambra is thankfully absent from the book. The most that he shares with other British travellers is his condescending attitude towards the Spaniards, above all to the Andalusians (see page 48). The Sevillians, however, bear no resentment towards him and remember him to this day as a loveable eccentric who sold his bibles in the town's flea-market. By a curious turn of fate, he is probably better known in Seville than he is today in England, and is still referred to by the endearing nickname of 'Don Jorgito'.

With so many foreigners describing Spain and the Spaniards, it is easy to forget that the Spaniards themselves turned their attention to the same exotic aspects of their country that intrigued their visitors. Seville in the nineteenth century played an important role in the history of *costumbrismo*, a movement in art and literature dedicated to the portrayal of manners and customs peculiar to the Spanish regions. The professed aims of its literary members were to record Spanish life in as impartial and objective a way as possible, avoiding the romantic embellishment common to foreign descriptions; in practice the writers tended to reinforce foreign stereotypes of the Spaniards. One of the leading writers in this genre in Seville was in fact of foreign extraction even though she always regarded herself as a Sevillian. Cecilia Boehl von Faber, who wrote under the name 'Fernán Caballero', was born in Switzerland of a German father and a mother who was half Spanish and half Irish. Her father, a Catholic convert, was a well-known Hispanist and German consul at Cádiz. Cecilia, after being schooled at a French pension in Hamburg, settled in Seville and lived there most of her life, marrying three times to members of prominent Seville families. Her literary reputation is based on *La Gaviota* (1849), which is set mainly in Seville and deals with the failed marriage of a German doctor to a fisherman's daughter: the latter falls in love with a bull-fighter, leaves her husband to take up a career of singing, and then, her voice ruined, returns to her home village to marry a barber. The book is filled with local colour, dwelling precisely on those aspects of Andalusia such as bull-fighting and beautiful singers that are essential to the region's picturesque appeal. Another example of Andalusian *costumbrismo* is Serafín Estébanez Calderón's *Escenas Andaluzas* (1847), a series of mannered though charming vignettes of Andalusian life. The author was born in Málaga but the finest of his essays are devoted to Seville, such as his account of dancing in Triana (see page 135). Colourful, light-hearted and filled with people prone to wild exaggeration, the Seville of Estébanez Calderón is little different to that evoked in countless accounts by Romantic travellers.

Seville was above all a centre of *costumbrista* painters. In contrast to their counterparts in Madrid, who took their lead from Goya and looked at Spanish life in a dark and savage fashion, the Seville *costumbristas* were sentimental, anecdotal, and heavily reliant on the local tourist industry. Their subjects were those that appealed to tourists – the Giralda, the *feria*, dancers, *majos*, gypsies, cigarette girls, and so on. The head of the school was José Dominguez Bécquer, who was so successful with tourists such as Ford that he sometimes had to employ a cousin, Joaquín, to help him out with his commissions. His two sons were Valeriano and Gustavo Adolfo, the former another well-known *costumbrista* painter, the latter Seville's leading nineteenth-century poet and the author of *Rime*, the most popular Spanish collection of poems before García Lorca's *Romancero Gitano*. Gustavo Adolfo had begun his career as a painter, and his decision to change to poetry had shocked his godmother, who had reputedly said: 'The English will always buy Andalusian scenes, but who will buy verses?' In the 1850s a Scottish painter and pupil of Wilkie, John Philip, came to Seville and emulated the local *costumbrista* school. His animated and brightly coloured canvases of Seville life earned him the nickname 'Philip of Spain' but were criticized by Ruskin for missing 'the wayward, half melancholy mystery of Spanish beauty'. The Romantic traveller needed ultimately a hint of tragedy to turn the brightly coloured surface of Andalusian life into a setting of great art.

It was left to a foreigner, Prosper Mérimée, to appropriate the subjects of Andalusian *costumbrismo* and create out of them a story which would seize the European imagination in a way which no Spanish work was ever to do. Mérimée first visited Spain in 1830, and came both to know Estébanez Calderón and to hear from an Andalusian family the story which many years later was to form the basis of *Carmen*. The first of his works inspired by Andalusia was *The Souls of Purgatory* (1834), which was a fictional account of a man with whom all travellers to Seville in the early nineteenth century were obsessed, Don Miguel Mañara. The music of Mozart's *Don Giovanni* fresh in their minds, these travellers came to Seville determined to find sites associated with Don Juan, and convinced themselves that Miguel Mañara and Juan Tenorio were, in the words of Hans Christian Andersen, 'unquestionably one and the same person'. The Hospital of La Caridad, founded by the man who came to be known even in Mérimée's story as 'Don Juan Mañara', was one of the high-points of the Romantic traveller's tour of Seville. Many of its visitors loved to speculate about what had happened to Mañara in his youth to justify his reputation as 'the worst man who had ever lived'. Mérimée, in his *Âmes du Purgatoire*, came up with an unconvincing story, as did Alexandre Dumas and various other Romantic authors who gave fictional treatment to Mañara.

Having exploited one of Andalusia's existing myths, Mérimée went on to create a new one in *Carmen* (1845). Before writing this he had returned to Andalusia to carry out archaeological research to determine the site of the battle of Munda, in which Julius Ceasar had defeated the followers of Pompey: his findings were to be published in the *Revue Archéologique* of June 1844. The narrator of *Carmen* is an archaeologist engaged in the same research as Mérimée had just done. On a field trip to the Serranía de Ronda he befriends an unkempt but well-educated man who is later revealed as a notorious bandit. The second part of the story finds the narrator in Córdoba, where he strikes up a conversation with Carmen, a beautiful gypsy whom he accompanies to her home. To his surprise the bandit bursts into the room and starts quarrelling with Carmen. He makes his escape. In the next and principal section of the book, the narrator is back again in Córdoba several weeks later, and discovers that the bandit has murdered Carmen and is shortly to be executed. Visiting him in prison, the narrator learns of the tragic story of the man, of how he had been a respectable army officer whose obsession with Carmen had led him into banditry, and of how he had killed her in a jealous rage over her flirtation with a bull-fighter. The story's concluding section is a general account of Spanish gypsies. Though based on a supposedly true story, and written up as if it were a historical document, *Carmen* manages to bring together every conceivable element which made Andalusia popular to the Romantic tourist, from banditry to gypsies, beautiful women to *majos*, dancers to bull-fighters, the Serranía de Ronda to the tobacco factory at Seville.

The tobacco factory, where the unfortunate hero of Mérimée's story first sets eyes on Carmen, was an essential component of Romantic Andalusia, and as obligatory to any visit to Seville as the cathedral. Travellers' fanciful conceptions of the place, when compared with the reality of the life which was led there, are an interesting reflection on the Romantic distortion of Andalusia. Early visitors to the factory had merely expressed wonder at the monumental dimensions of the building, at the efficiency with which it was run, and at the great number of people and mules employed there. By Mérimée's day the interest of foreigners was concentrated on four connected rooms at the very centre of the immense complex, for here were gathered a reputed 3,000 female cigar-makers, chattering away, their colourful street clothes hanging around the walls. One of Andalusia's great attractions was its beautiful women, and these four rooms, with their steamy, hot-house atmosphere, seemed to offer travellers unlimited possibilities for studying these women in a suitably sensual environment. Richard Ford greatly enhanced these women's reputation for animosity and provocative behaviour when he wrote that they were known to be 'more impertinent than chaste', and would sometimes smuggle out 'the weed in a manner her most Catholic majesty never dreamt of'; when A. C. Andros visited the place in 1860 he was turned away on the grounds that 'owing to the intense heat, the *eight thousand* females employed in making cigars are working in all but *puris naturalibus*'. The strong-minded, cheeky, beautiful and overwhelmingly sensual Carmen represented all that Romantic travellers had come to expect of the women of the tobacco factory. Naturally, the hopes being so greatly raised, numerous travellers came away bitterly disappointed, and went afterwards to opposite extremes to describe the women. 'I have never beheld such an assemblage of uglinesses,' wrote George Dennis. Willis Baxley, in 1875, considered that the complexion of Spanish women was never their strong point and that 'in the Tobacco factory it is absolutely repulsive . . . in this pest-house [the women] look as if they had breathed the deadly malaria of the Pontine marshes and were becoming prematurely mummified. Sallow, shrunken, shrivelled specimens of humanity, life seems to have but little hold upon the older of the operatives.' Baxley was one of the few nineteenth-century travellers to show a concern at the working conditions within the factory. According to him, the cigar-makers worked twelve hours a day with only an hour's break for lunch, which was provided in the building to lessen chances of smuggling; furthermore, the poorly ventilated, nicotine-filled atmosphere was thought by him to be very detrimental to the health, nicotine 'being among the deadliest of poisons'. The reward for all this hardship were the most meagre of wages, and only three years before the publication of *Carmen* the cigar-makers had gone out on strike to demand better pay. Yet for as long as the factory functioned, tourists would continue coming here in search of exotic beauty. As late as 1929 the sexual reformer Havelock Ellis, in an essay on Spanish women in his *The Soul of Spain*, was to describe the place as 'one of the most delightful spots in this delightful city, and one of the most picturesque'.

The impact of Mérimée's *Carmen* on European attitudes towards Andalusia was as nothing in comparison with that of Bizet's 1875 musical adaptation of the story. By this date the primitive, bandit-infested region which Mérimée had portrayed bore even less resemblance to reality than it had before. But when the opera was premièred critics savagely attacked it for its realism. Bizet did not live to see the work's prodigious success, and died shortly after the première, expiring on the very night when the principal singer, enacting the moment when Carmen foretells her own death, collapsed on stage. Four years later the opera was ecstactically received at Vienna, and in 1887 it created a sensation when first put on in Madrid. Nietzsche, shortly before dying, foresook his idol Wagner in favour of Bizet's *Carmen*. 'With *Carmen*,' he reflected, 'we take leave of the damp north, of all the mists of the Wagnerian ideal. This music possesses the limpid, dry atmosphere of southern climes.' Mario Praz was later to think that Nietzsche had finally gone senile when he said this, but the great man's opinion was shared by countless of his younger contemporaries, who turned towards the south, and Andalusia in particular, with renewed passion.

Music and dancing brought to Andalusia in the latter years of the century a popularity greater and more widespread than it had ever had. Bizet did much to spread the fashion for Andalusian music, even though the so-called Andalusian elements in his music had little to do with the region and were derived more from the folk music introduced into Europe by Cuban refugees. Unlike Bizet, the Russian composer Glinka had actually been to Spain, where he had befriended a gypsy guitarist during a stay in Granada in 1847. Andalusian gypsy music had a major influence on Glinka, whose works were in turn to affect the development of a national style in Russian music. In the wake of Glinka, and with Andalusia principally in mind, numerous European

composers wrote Spanish works, including Rimsky-Korsakov, Rubin-
stein, Saint-Saëns, Chabrier, and Lalo. Their knowledge of Spain itself
was often minimal, Rimsky-Korsakov basing his *Capriccio Españole*
on a three-day stay in Cádiz. A popular source of inspiration was the
Alhambra, and the '*Alhambrista*' music of foreign composers even
began to influence Spanish classical composers such as Pedrell, the
master of Falla. Confusion between what was genuinely Andalusian
and what was thought to be Andalusian developed in dancing too, as
dance-rooms called Alhambra proliferated in Europe and America, and
Andalusian dancers adopted foreign fashions, while foreign dancers
pretended to be Andalusian.

Ortega y Gasset wrote in 1927 that a craze for Andalusia and
Andalusian culture had dominated the history of nineteenth-century
Spain. The craze survived into the present century, though with the
difference that the romantic image which accompanied it was the
creation less of foreigners than of the Andalusians themselves.

9

POETRY AND WAR

Laurie Lee remembered Spain in the 1930s as a place where almost everyone was writing poetry. Spain is still such a place. In England few people will admit to writing poetry, let alone show it to you, but in Spain, as in other southern countries, poetry is shamelessly written by an exceptionally wide range of people. The passion for poetry is especially strong in Andalusia, where poems are penned on the slightest pretext, and people are constantly being presented to you as poets, even though they will rarely have had works published, or show any intention of doing so. In the 1920s and 30s Andalusian poets were in the forefront of what is sometimes referred to as Spain's second Golden Age. Keats's line about the poet being the unacknowledged legislator of the world has rarely rung so true as in those years, when poetry became enmeshed in politics, culminating in the Spanish Civil War, with the onrush of poets to the front and the political assassination of one of the greatest of all Spanish poets, Federico García Lorca.

Spain's transformation early this century into what Gerald Brenan described as a 'poetic klondike' must be set against the ever more fraught political history of the time. The twentieth century began only two years after Spain had lost in the space of a few months Mexico, Cuba and the Philippines: its economy had reached one of its lowest points, and the social unrest which had troubled the country for much of the previous century was worsening. *The Lost Grove* (1948), the autobiography of the poet Rafael Alberti, opens with the words: '1902 – year of great agitation and activity among the peasant masses of Andalusia, a year of preparation for the revolutionary uprisings to come. December 16 – date of my birth, on an unexpectedly stormy night.' Alberti's native region of Andalusia, a traditional stronghold of anarchism, now emerged also as a major centre of communism and was soon to produce in the Málaga-born José Díaz Spain's first communist deputy. At the same time the regionalist movement known as *Andalucismo* gained momentum, with intellectuals such as Blas Infante calling out not only for 'land and liberty' but also for a greater Andalusian autonomy. Seville's Ateneo, where Blas Infante held court, became a focus of this movement, the aims of which were further discussed in a series of important conferences held in the early years of the century at Ronda and Córdoba. *Andalucismo* was none the less to have more of a cultural than a political significance, one of the main barriers to autonomy being the continuing division between the eastern and western halves of the region.

Social unrest took on an especially savage character in Spain in the years between 1918 and 1923, with Andalusia and Barcelona being once more at the centre of the trouble. Spain's neutrality during the First World War, however, had led to a brief improvement in the nation's economy and to a revival of commerce, mining and agriculture. In Andalusia renewed capitalist investment had also been inspired by the prospect of the great Ibero-American Exhibition, planned for 1929. The idea for such an exhibition had first been mooted in 1910, and preparations for it had already got under way by 1914. The exhibition received a further boost following the collapse in 1923 of Spain's parliamentary monarchy and the coming to power of the right-wing dictatorship of Miguel Primo de Rivera. The dictator came from Jerez de la Frontera, and was thus keen to promote an exhibition which it was thought would bring back to Andalusia something of its Golden Age glory. Spain generally prospered in the early years of Primo de Rivera's rule, which at first was widely supported. The popularity of this rule was to wane as soon as the prosperity on which it was based began to be threatened: 1929, the year when the Ibero-American Exhibition opened, was described by the dictator's son, José Antonio, as 'the year of the dictator's agony'. Students and intellectuals had been largely unfavourable towards Primo de Rivera from the start, García Lorca, for instance, implicitly criticizing the dictator's rule in his historical play about freedom and political oppression, *Mariana Pineda* (1925). By the late 1920s those intellectuals who had been allies of the dictator, such as Ortega y Gasset and the poet Manuel Machado, changed their allegiance to the opposition. At a time when intellectuals had a potential influence on Spanish political life greater than ever before, the complete loss of their support was of particular consequence. The army and the king, Alfonso XIII, soon followed suit, and in January 1930 Primo de Rivera was finally forced to resign.

Spain's leading intellectuals of this time either belonged to or were heavily influenced by the 'Generation of '98', a group of writers who believed that the key to Spain's regeneration lay in the spiritual and ideological regeneration of the individual. The major poet associated with the group, indeed one of the most popular of all Spanish poets, was Antonio Machado. He came from a most talented Sevillian family, his father being the pioneering folklorist and student of *flamenco* known as 'Demófilo' (see page 140) and his brother, Manuel, also being an outstanding poet. The father – married to the daughter of a sweet-seller from Triana – was a middle-class intellectual who had actively supported the revolution of 1868. Shortly after the restoration of the monarchy in 1874 he had lost his job in Seville and had moved to Madrid, where in 1881 he had founded Spain's first Folklore Society. His family joined him there in 1883, when Manuel was nine years old and Antonio eight; he died of a stroke and overwork in 1893, aged forty-six, after having sailed alone to Puerto Rico to take up a post as a minor civil servant. Antonio and Manuel were both educated at Madrid's Institución Libre de Enseñanza, a revolutionary university which had recently been set up in protest against existing educational methods. As with so many Spanish writers and artists of their generation, both Antonio and Manuel continued their training in Paris, where they became involved in the bohemian life of the city.

The very antithesis of a bohemian life was led by Antonio after 1907, when he returned to Spain and took up a post as French teacher in Soria in northern Castile. In Soria he fell in love with and married the sixteen-year-old daughter of his landlady, but she died in 1912. Feeling unable to remain in the town any longer, he went on to teach at Baeza, a town filled today with his memories (see pages 253–4). The views towards the Sierra de la Segura enchanted him, but his mind was always drifting back to Castile and to his dead wife. The melancholy of these thoughts inspired the second part of his *Campos de Castilla*, a collection of poems evoking the loneliness and grandeur of the Castile landscape and reflecting on the decline of modern Spain. When he left Baeza in 1919 he went back to Castile, settling in

Segovia. Remembered by Alberti as a man whose appearance of a timid schoolteacher gone to seed was belied by a great dignity, Machado became a prophet-like figure to Spain's poets of the 1920s.

Whereas Antonio Machado felt an exile in his native Andalusia, his brother Manuel exalted this region, and in particular Seville, which he described as 'bull-loving, witty and animated'. In 1896 and 1897 he stayed with his mother's family in Triana, and during this period became obsessed by bull-fighting, frequented the famous *café cantante* of Silverio Franchetti, and enthusiastically attended the town's Holy Week Processions and *feria*; the poet Juan Ramón Jiménez claimed even to have seen Manuel – the son of an avowed atheist – dressed up as a penitent in the procession of the Brotherhood of Silence. Not long after his final return from Paris in 1909, he went to Seville to marry a cousin of his, to whom he had been unfaithfully engaged for thirteen years. Though they subsequently moved to Madrid, his poetry constantly harked back to Andalusian themes. His works, for instance his *Cantares*, were often inspired by the lyrics of *flamenco* songs, and can be seen as antedating many of the themes of García Lorca's poetry.

Juan Ramón Jiménez, known usually as 'Juan Ramón', ranks with Antonio Machado as one of the father figures of twentieth-century Spanish verse. The village of Moguer de la Frontera, where he was born and spent much of his life, was once exclusively a place of pilgrimage for those in search of Columbus associations, but has since become an obligatory destination for anyone seriously interested in Juan Ramón's works. This especially attractive village, rising gently above fertile plains a short distance away from the Río Tinto estuary, has lived off a combination of agriculture and fishing. Juan Ramón, the son of a wealthy wine-merchant, was born in 1881 in the 'Casa Grande', at 2 Calle de la Ribera. From this imposing, and now rather decayed, late nineteenth-century mansion, the young Juan Ramón endlessly observed his surroundings, his attention fixed above all on a house opposite, which he studied 'on clear evenings, during rainy afternoon siestas, at each slight change of each day and each hour'. Later the family moved to 10 Calle Nueva (now 5 Calle Ramón Jiménez), directly in front of a house where Columbus is reputed to have spent his last night before moving in February 1492 to the monastery of La Rábida (see pages 87–8). One of the poet's girlfriends was, curiously enough, Blanca Hernández Pinzón, a direct descendant of the captain who accompanied Columbus on his 1492 voyage (see page 88).

Schooled at a strict Jesuit college in El Puerto de Santa María, Juan Ramón later attended Seville University, harbouring ambitions at this stage of his life to become a painter rather than a poet. By 1899, when he went to Madrid, he had begun to concentrate on poetry and was shortly to become unofficial poet-in-residence at the Institución Libre de Enseñanza, where he met and befriended Antonio Machado. A supreme aesthete, with the sickly, languid temperament which traditionally characterizes such a person, Juan Ramón was to dedicate himself single-mindedly to poetry for the rest of his life. In 1905, after having spent much of the previous four years in sanatoria in Madrid and Bordeaux, he returned to Moguer and remained there until 1912. During this period he developed a particular passion for the countryside surrounding the village, and frequently buried himself in the family's country home of Fuentepiña, a twenty-five-minute walk from the centre. It was at this time that he wrote his best loved work, *Platero and I*, a series of prose poems dedicated to his mule, Platero. In this mixture of delicate observation and childhood memory, a detailed if rather sentimental portrait of Moguer emerges; quotes from the book are now recorded in ceramic plaques liberally placed in appropriate sites throughout the village. From 1912 until the outbreak of the Civil War he was largely based in Madrid, where he became closely associated with the Residencia de los Estudiantes, a progressive institution comparable to the Institución Libre de Enseñanza. He regularly returned to Moguer during the summer months, and like Manuel Machado, constantly evoked Andalusia in his poetry. After 1916 his poetry underwent a process of what he described as '*depuración*' ('purification'), whereby it was reduced to its self-conscious essence, to a state in which musical rhythms became more important than content.

While Juan Ramón's poetry aspired increasingly towards music, the music of Manuel de Falla blazes with images that have inspired poetry. Falla, another father figure to Spanish intellectuals of the 1920s, was born in Cádiz in 1876, spending his boyhood in a house in the Calle Ancha and later in the Fonda de Cádiz in the Plaza de la Constitución. His family moved to Madrid in 1896, and he studied music there under Felipe Pedrell, the composer who did most to influence the development of a Spanish national style in music. From Madrid Falla went to Paris, where he formed a life-long friendship with Debussy. The French composer was one of many in Paris who had been deeply impressed by a performance of gypsy singers at the Paris International Exhibition of 1900. Memories of their singing were later to inspire passages of his *Iberia Symphony*, which Lorca was to describe as 'a truly genial work in which Andalusian perfumes and essences dreamily float'; to Alberti, this symphony was a 'reflection by the most transparent composer in France on the exotic aroma of an imagined Andalusia'. Debussy was never to visit Spain, and it was his friendship with Falla that was later to help him in his two musical evocations of Granada, *Soirée en Grenade* and *La Puerta del Vino*, the latter based on a postcard of the Alhambra sent to him by Falla. Lorca found in the latter composition 'all the emotional themes of the Granada night, the blue remoteness of the *vega*, the Sierra greeting the tremulous Mediterranean, the enormous barbs of the clouds sunk into the distance, the admirable rubato of the city, the hallucinatory poetry of its underground waters'.

Gypsy and Andalusian themes permeated Falla's own work from the time of his *Vida Breve* and *Amor Brujo*, both of which were premièred on his return from Paris to Madrid in 1914. *The Three-Cornered Hat* (1919), a ballet version of Alarcón's tale of the Alpujarras, was intended for Diaghilev, who had also toyed with the idea of turning into a ballet Falla's piano and orchestral piece, *Nights in the Gardens of Spain* (1916): Diaghilev had conceived of the ballet in terms of a fiesta set at night in the gardens of the Generalife, the women wearing *mantillas*, the men in evening dress. Granada was perhaps the main influence on Falla's life and music, though it was not until after the death of his parents in Madrid in 1919 that he eventually settled there. In 1921 he acquired a tiny villa or *carmen* high up on the southern slopes of the Alhambra hill, and was to live here, together with his sister María del Carmen, up to 1939. This modest house and garden has been kept exactly in the state in which he left it, and is one of the most charming of Andalusia's small museums. In its white dolls-house rooms there are some costume designs by Picasso for *The Three-Cornered Hat*, a drawing by Zuloaga dedicated to Falla, various photographs cut out by the composer from books and a small design by him for a ceramic plaque to mark the site of the Granada pension where Théophile Gautier stayed. You will also find the composer's upright piano, and his monk's cell of a bedroom, adorned with a plain white cross above the tiny bed. Falla's was an ascetic and deeply religious household, and in his sister's bedroom are numerous sacred objects. To its garden, with its extensive views over Granada, there came in the 1920s and early 30s Lorca, Segovia and many more of the poets, musicians and intellectuals from Spain and abroad who gave to the town during this period a cultural life such as it had scarcely known since Moorish times.

The Moorish and gypsy Granada which inspired Falla and his circle contrasted with the ever more intrusive modern town of Granada, a place with a distinctly northern and unexotic character, sober and notoriously philistine. This latter reputation had already been acquired in the nineteenth century. Richard Ford referred to its people as stagnating in 'bookless ignorance' and remarked on how little they appeared to appreciate the Alhambra. From the nineteenth century onwards, these inhabitants have made little positive contribution to the appearance of the town and have distinguished themselves largely by destroying much of what they have inherited. A particularly insensitive act was the construction in the 1880s and 90s of the Gran Vía de Colón. This main street, lined with heavy and monstrously out-of-scale shops and apartments, radically altered the character of Granada, cutting as it did a great swathe through the town's Moorish and Renaissance centre. Angel Ganivet, an associate of the Generation of '98, wrote a book heavily critical of the urban changes to his native town, finding them symptomatic of Spain's spiritual decay. Juan Ramón Jiménez, visiting Granada in 1924, could not help contrasting the 'tempered mysticism and delicate sensuality' emanating from the town's Moorish monuments with the deeply inaesthetic nature of its present-day people. But the greatest critic of modern Granada was the man who, together with Falla, did most to animate the town during the 1920s, García Lorca.

'Granada is horrible,' Lorca wrote in 1924 in a letter to a friend. 'This is not Andalusia. Andalusia is something else. It's in the people. And here they're Galician. I, who am an Andalusian and an Andalusian through and through, sigh for Málaga, for Córdoba, for Sanlúcar la Mayor, for Algeciras, for authentic and high-toned Cádiz, for Alcalá de los Gazules, for that which is *intimately* Andalusia. The real Granada has vanished, and now appears dead beneath greenish and delirious gas lights. The other Andalusia is alive, for example Málaga.' Lorca, who in the early 1920s whimsically contemplated setting up in Granada a cultural centre commemorating the town's Moorish heritage, was entirely convinced that the decline of the place had set in after 1492. He was to put forward this view in a most outspoken fashion in an interview which he gave to the newspaper *El Sol* shortly before his death in August 1936. In this he spoke about 1492 as a 'disastrous event. An admirable civilization, and a poetry, architecture and delicacy unique in the world – all were lost, to give way to an impoverished, cowed town, a wasteland populated by the worst bourgeoisie in Spain today.' Such a statement as this served only to strengthen the resentment harboured by many in the town towards him. This resentment has survived in certain quarters to this day.

Granada and its surroundings are rich in places closely associated with Lorca's life, though until comparatively recently the visitor to these places might well have aroused local suspicion. In the immediate aftermath of the Spanish Civil War, Lorca was a virtually unmentionable name in Spain, and it was not until the mid 1960s that he was officially reinstated here. Even so, the opening in 1986, fifty years after the poet's death, of the memorial park to him at Víznar, and of the museum in the house where he was born at Fuentevaqueros, would have been unthinkable during the Franco era.

Fuentevaqueros, a prosperous village sixteen kilometres north-west of Granada, is a flat and architecturally unremarkable place set among fields of tobacco, sugar-cane and wheat, and backed to the north by grey, rocky mountains. It lies in the middle of 'El Soto de Roma', a vast estate awarded to the Duke of Wellington, though never visited by the Duke himself. The estate had lain idle for much of the nineteenth century, but towards the end of the century its economic potential had finally been realized by its English administrators, and the area had begun to be populated and to prosper. Lorca's father was a wealthy farmer, and his mother the local schoolteacher, a woman much loved in the village and still fondly remembered here. Federico García Lorca was born on 11 June 1898 in what is now 4 Calle Poeta García Lorca. The museum which now occupies this simple white building is beautifully and lovingly laid out, but the building itself has been heavily altered and modernized, and bears little resemblance to what it must have been like in Lorca's day. A small selection of family items has been gathered together in the house, including the cot used by the baby Lorca. Of similar sentimental interest is the *'geranio Vicenta'*, a pale-coloured geranium grown from the seeds of a plant which Lorca's mother, Vicenta, always kept in her classroom.

In 1907 Lorca's family moved to a village with the unfortunate name of Asquerosa, or 'Repulsive', four kilometres north of Fuente-vaqueros: in the 1920s the poet was to mount a campaign to have this name changed to the present one of Valderrubio. The Lorca home here, at 20 Calle Iglesia, is as full of character as the birthplace is lacking in it, having always remained in the family's possession and featuring much of its original furnishings, as well as a pleasantly decayed character (it is now leased to the local socialist party, the members of which will be glad to show you round, if you can find them). Two years after buying this place, Lorca's parents decided to install themselves in the very centre of Granada (in a house, now gone, on the Acera del Darro), and to keep their Asquerosa home merely as a summer retreat. In 1914, after a schooling in Almería, Lorca became registered as a law student at Granada University. As well as a budding interest in poetry, Lorca had by now developed his life-long passion for the piano and the guitar: a recording played in the Fuentevaqueros museum of Lorca accompanying the singer 'La Argentinita' on the piano gives some idea of his great facility as a musician. His cultural and intellectual interests were hardly satisfied by Granada University itself, let alone by his law course. But he did find stimulus in the *tertulias* or cultural gatherings that took place in the Café Alameda, a large café attached to the eighteenth-century palace now used by Granada's Town Council: the café itself has been replaced by the tackily decorated Cafés Coimbra and Chikito, the latter occupying the reading-room where the meetings were held. The Café Alameda group, known as the 'Rinconcillo', included among its members the art historian and author of the best guide to Granada, Gallego y Burín, and a colourful personality sometimes thought of as Granada's Oscar Wilde, Francisco Soriano Lapresa. The most significant contact Lorca made at the Café Alameda was with Manuel de Falla, whom he met in 1919.

Lorca joined Madrid's Residencia de Estudiantes in that same year, but he always returned to Granada during the summer months and was thus able to pursue his friendship with Falla. A mutual interest in puppets led in 1921 to their collaboration on a puppet show, first performed in the Lorca home at Asquerosa. A more significant venture was their organizing with the painter Zuloaga of the famous *cante jondo* festival of 1922, held in the courtyard of Charles V's palace and intended to halt the declining standards in *flamenco* singing (see page 141). This memorable and much publicized event attracted a wide range of listeners and performers, including the distinguished English Hispanist J. B. Trend, the American Romany gypsy Irving Brown, the guitarist Andrés Segovia, and two of the celebrated gypsy singers from the Café Silverio, Manuel Torres and Antonio Chacón. To accompany the festival, Lorca delivered his famous lecture on the *cante jondo*, a text combining historical and musical exposition with great flights of fantasy.

The deep popular roots that Lorca romantically claimed for the *cante jondo* were exactly those that he considered as nourishing his own verse. He felt an empathy both for the gypsies and for the countryfolk, among whom he had grown up. Undeniably he was a man whose charm communicated itself to all levels of society, and his work itself was loved by the people who had inspired it. A revelation for me was a visit to the Fuente de la Teja, a spring by a wooded river bank, situated a kilometre across fields from Asquerosa. In this quiet and enchanting spot sat a group of men drinking the spring water and talking. On a refrigerator were painted the words, 'Fuente de la Teja, where Federico García Lorca used to come and write.' In his summers spent in the early 1920s at Asquerosa, Lorca would sit for hours by this spring, his attempts at writing habitually interrupted in the late afternoon by the arrival of farm-workers, who gathered here when their day's work was done to talk to the poet, discuss with him their problems, and hear him recite. These occasions were vividly related to me by one of the men whom I myself met at the spring, a man in his mid nineties, partially blind and deaf, but with a perfect recollection of the young Lorca. The tradition of coming to the spring at the end of the day is still regularly maintained by the local men, and even though the great poet himself is no longer with them, the spirit of poetry has apparently lingered on among them. Before I left, the old man's son-in-law had opened the refrigerator and pulled out a cloth bag in which he kept poems written by himself in this very spot. There was a respectful silence as he then started to recite an ode to Spain's Socialist prime minister, Felipe González, a poem shortly followed by one inspired by Lorca, and telling of a young woman who forsook her husband so that she could come and meet the poet by this spring.

Though deriving inspiration for much of his verse from the countryside, Lorca had to look elsewhere for intellectual stimulus, and this he found in the 1920s above all in Madrid's Residencia de los Estudiantes. During this period the Residencia, or 'Resi', as it was often known, was the cultural centre of Spain, and certainly there was nowhere in Andalusia to compete with it, least of all Granada University. At the 'Resi' Lorca met Juan Ramón Jiménez, whose work he revered, and also befriended his fellow students Salvador Dalí, Luis Buñuel and Rafael Alberti. The latter had had, like Juan Ramón, early ambitions to be a painter, but had been side-tracked by poetry, and for a while enjoyed a greater recognition as a poet than Lorca. This happened after 1924, with the publication of his enormously popular *Marinero en Tierra*, a series of poems inspired by the environment of his native Cádiz. In 1927 Alberti, Lorca, and a number of their talented young poet contemporaries decided to celebrate the third centenary of the then disgracefully neglected Luis de Góngora, a poet whose pure aestheticism, constant use of metaphor, and delight in descriptions of colour and sounds was very much after their own hearts. This generation of Spanish poets, united in their admiration for Góngora, are generally known as the 'Generation of '27', though they are sometimes referred to as the 'Generation of the Dictatorship' and even as the 'Grandchildren of '98'. A significant number of them were from Andalusia, for apart from Lorca and Alberti, the group included Emilio Prados and Manuel Altoguirre from Málaga, and Vicente Aleixandre and Luis Cernuda from Seville.

The Góngora celebrations, comprising lectures and poetry recitals, were held not in Góngora's native Córdoba but in Seville, a town which Juan Ramón had described as the 'ideal capital of poetry'. Juan Ramón did not mean by this that Seville was a place filled with distinguished poets, but was thinking instead of the intense blue of its skies, the luxuriance of its vegetation, and the liveliness of its inhabitants. As a cultural and intellectual centre, Seville in the early years of this century was in fact scarcely more advanced than Granada. The mainstreams in European culture and thought had largely passed the town by, no one, for instance, paying any attention to the visit here in 1909 of the Dadaist painter Picabia or to that of the German poet Rainer Maria Rilke in 1912/13: Picabia's canvas inspired by the town's Holy Week processions, *Procession in Seville*, was far more original than any treatment of this subject by a native artist. Seville continued to be dominated by an increasingly anachronistic *costumbrismo*, which can be seen as much in the sentimental domestic dramas of the Quintero brothers as in the music of Joaquín Turina, the latter evoking such hackneyed aspects of Andalusia as the Seville *feria* and the procession to El Rocío.

The most exciting developments in Seville in these years were undoubtedly in the fields of architecture and town planning, the whole town being in a state of great activity in preparation for the Ibero-American Exhibition of 1929. The buildings that were being put up were by no means examples of the avant-garde, but instead were structures that reflected the growing regional pride of the Andalusians and that drew heavily on traditional Andalusian and, in particular, Moorish elements. One of the leading architects of the town was Espliau, who designed the Edificio Londres in the Calle de la Cerrajería, a splendid neo-Moorish pastiche with dazzling ceramics set against a white background. In 1916 Espliau won the competition to build the Hotel Alfonso XIII, which was intended as the main hotel for the 1929 Exhibition and the most luxurious hotel in Europe: Espliau's grandiose structure, rivalling in scale even the nearby tobacco factory, brilliantly combines Moorish with Andalusian Renaissance architecture, thus bringing together the two greatest periods in the city's history. A similar combination of styles characterizes the work of Anibale González, the architect responsible for the main exhibition buildings, most notably the monumental, curved mass of tiles, red brick, and towers which dominates the landscaped Plaza de América. As a setting for these buildings there was created the María Luisa Park, one of Europe's finest parks, comparable only to parks in Latin America in its jungle-like anarchy and vegetation. On the other side of the park to the Hotel Alfonso XIII grew up the wealthy residential area of El Porvenir, the name of which means 'the future', but the architecture of which looks back to Seville's past, the houses being in a traditional Seville style, white, adorned with black grilles, and centred around small jasmine-filled *patios*.

The visit to Seville in 1927 of Lorca, Alberti and this circle was certainly a major moment in their lives, and the optimistic mood of the town as it prepared for 1929 might well have had an added effect on them. Through Alberti Lorca met one of the more extraordinary personalities in Seville at that time, Fernando Villalón, Count of Miraflores, a Góngora-inspired poet who terrified Lorca with the speed with which he drove his car. A more important encounter was with Ignacio Sánchez Mejías, a bull-fighter who wrote plays and poetry and had a great interest in modern artists such as Picasso. While Sánchez Mejías yearned for the literary life, Alberti had a secret ambition to become a bull-fighter, though after a short practice bout in the ring with Sánchez Mejías he decided not to pursue this career. Alberti and Lorca became good friends with Sánchez Mejías, and one of their most memorable evenings in Seville was spent in the latter's house, where they were treated to the voice of the illiterate Triana singer Manuel Torres (the Niño de Jerez), who was to die in poverty only a few years later. News of the company which Alberti and Lorca were keeping in Seville reached the ears of Juan Ramón Jiménez, who was quite horrified, believing that through this association with Sánchez Mejías they had lost their way as poets: 'I have heard,' he wrote to a friend, 'that Alberti is involved with gypsies, banderilleros, and other low-living types.' Later in the year Lorca published his *Romancero Gitano* (*Gypsy Ballads*), the subject-matter of which bothered many of its more snobbish readers such as Juan Ramón and Salvador Dalí. However, it was this work which was to turn Lorca into the most popular of all Spanish poets.

Many of the Generation of '27 had their works published in Seville's *Mediodía*, which was described by Alberti as 'a somewhat offbeat poetry magazine started by a group of young people in Seville'. In March 1928 Lorca brought out in Granada a similar magazine called *Gallo*, and soon reported that it had created a great stir in the town, that the edition had sold out within two days, that a big fight had broken out in the university between the 'Gallistas' and 'Anti-Gallistas', and that everyone in the town was talking about it, in cafés, clubs and houses. This being Granada, however, the excitement soon died down, and, in the words of Lorca, 'in the two months between issues, Granada had regained her usual serenity and indifference'; there was not to be a third issue. It was high time for Lorca to broaden his horizons and to get away not just from Andalusia, but from Spain. In 1929, the year of the Ibero-American Exhibition, Lorca left for America. The exhibition itself turned out to be less of an event than the preparations leading up to it. Anibale González, its main architect, died two weeks after its opening, and Miguel Primo de Rivera, one of its most enthusiastic promoters, was experiencing the disastrous last months of his dictatorship. When the exhibition eventually closed, it left a saddened and bankrupted Seville. Sir Peter Chalmers-Mitchell, a former Secretary of the London Zoological Society, looking forward to what he hoped would be a quiet retirement in Málaga, passed through Seville shortly afterwards and went out to see 'the deserted and faded splendour of the unsuccessful Great Exhibition'. 'Few things,' he reflected, 'are more tragic than tattered splendour, whether it be of bright dresses or of painted pavilions.'

1929 was also the year that Gerald Brenan completed his last long stay at the Alpujarra village of Yegen, a place where he had been living periodically since January 1920 (see page 40). He had first come here with scarcely any knowledge of Spanish, and had intended his stay then to be merely a stage on a journey around the world. His yearning for travel had begun in his early teens, when he had run away from his conventional middle-class home and had set out to walk to Jerusalem in the company of an older and eccentric compatriot, Hope-Johnstone. At Yegen he tried to make up for his lack of a university education by devoting himself to reading and studying, concentrating in particular on classic literature and on the language and culture of Spain. Though friendly with the villagers, and very observant of their activities, he kept his distance from them and relied heavily on the company of visiting English friends. Even when travelling elsewhere in Andalusia, the future Hispanist had little close contact with the Spaniards and played virtually no part in the exciting cultural life of this period. In his description of Granada in the 1920s, he mentions having met Lorca but says that his encounters with him were too slight to be worth recording; instead he gives long accounts of the town's English community, the members of which lived in élitist isolation on the Alhambra hill. Hope-Johnstone came to live with him at Yegen, and he received several visits from members of the

Bloomsbury group, including Dora Carrington, who stayed here in 1920 when married to an old friend of Brenan's, Ralph Partridge. Brenan's passionate but essentially platonic affair with Carrington began then, and was to absorb much of his energy in the following years.

Brenan resolved to become a writer, and dreamt of being a poet or even a novelist, but he devoted much of his early literary output to long letters to the feckless Carrington. Finally, back in England in the mid 1920s, he embarked on a life of St Teresa of Avila and spent many hours in the British Museum Library. The book progressed slowly, and, early in 1929, he returned to Yegen, hoping that the place would provide the peaceful atmosphere in which to write it, yet soon becoming distracted by sexual frustration. For a man with an apparently enormous libido, an Alpujarran village in the 1920s might not on the surface seem the most promising place to be. Yet soon Brenan had embarked on an affair with a fifteen-year-old local girl called Juana, which turned out to be as physical as his affair with Carrington had been cerebral. Making love several times a day wreaked havoc on his biography of St Teresa, and Brenan later confessed that he was left in a state of mental lethargy. To recover, he went on a visit to the Seville Exhibition, but soon became involved there in other amorous adventures. Eventually, at the end of the year, he packed up and went off to England, leaving Juana pregnant with his child. Back in England, he married an American authoress, Gamel Woolsey, and attended to the funeral of Carrington, who had killed herself a few days after the death of her beloved companion, Lytton Strachey. Brenan was not to return to Spain until 1934, missing four critical and complex years in the country's political history.

With the resignation in January 1930 of Primo de Rivera, the most unpopular man in Spain became the one whose name adorned Seville's recently opened luxury hotel, Alfonso XIII. Later that year King Alfonso decided that it would be unwise to winter, as he normally did, in Málaga's Hotel Príncipe Asturias, the name of which was soon to change to the uncontroversial Miramar. Alfonso abdicated in April 1931, and Spain's Second Republic was declared. In the village of Mijas above Fuengirola, 'there was great joy', according to the local barber Manuel Cortes, shortly to be elected deputy mayor of his village. The people of Mijas were also to support the further swing to the left which occurred in December of that year, when Manuel Azaña came into power. Cortes, whose remarkable life was to be the subject of Ronald Fraser's *In Hiding*, was typical of many left-wing Republicans. An atheist, who welcomed the Republic's land and other reforms, and the introduction of civic marriage, he was none the less far from radical in his views, and was strongly opposed to communism. He and his kind were hardly the dangerous 'Reds' whom many believed to be now ruling in Spain.

Alberti related how in general Spain's intellectuals, authors and artists celebrated the advent of the Republic. For Lorca, who had recently come back from America, the first two and a half years of the Republic must have been particularly auspicious ones. In 1931 celebrations were put on at Fuentevaqueros to coincide with the naming of a street after him. After the election of Azaña, he was appointed the director of the government-sponsored theatre company, La Barraca, the aims of which were to employ university students to bring drama to the provinces, an enterprise typifying the initial progressive and optimistic spirit of the Republic. The only surviving film shots of Lorca – shown to visitors to the Fuentevaqueros Museum – are of the poet with smiling face travelling with his company to their next engagement. Such was La Barraca's success that it was invited in 1933 to tour Argentina, where it remained until the end of the year. A bleaker and more troubled Spain awaited Lorca on his return.

On 17 June 1934, Ignacio Sánchez Mejías was fatally gored at the bull-ring of Manzanares near Madrid, an event commemorated by Lorca in an ode with the insistently ominous refrain, 'It was exactly five in the afternoon.' The poem, one of Lorca's greatest, is full of foreboding:

> Oh white wall of Spain!
> Oh black bull of grief!

The political situation in Spain was rapidly deteriorating, Azaña's government having been ousted in November 1933 and a right-wing backlash having set in following the appointment of Lerroux as prime minister. Landowners, *caciques* and their allies were taking their revenge on those who had opposed them; the extreme right-wing party, the Falange, recently founded by Primo de Rivera's son, José Antonio, was growing at an alarming rate. The various left-wing opponents of Lerroux finally came together in January 1936 to form the Popular Front, which managed to defeat the Right in the elections held one month later. Manuel Cortes was made mayor of Mijas, an unenviable position at a time when his country was clearly heading for civil war.

The breakdown of Spain in the years immediately preceding the Civil War was dealt with in Ralph Bates's novel *The Olive Grove*, which is set mainly in the imaginary Andalusian village of Olivares. Bates, an English communist as opposed to anarchism as he was to the church, gives a detailed picture of Andalusian society, from the down-trodden day-labourer to the aloof landlord lost in his mystical day-dreams; at the centre of the novel are two friends, one a guitar-playing anarchist, the other an anarchist who becomes opposed to violence. The novel has many of the Romantic clichés of Andalusia, and a rather heavy-handed symbolism; but it has the advantage of being written by someone who had both extensive personal experience of working in an Andalusian olive grove, and an informed knowledge of the Spanish political scene. Most of the British who came to Spain during this period recognized the mounting political tensions in the country, but failed to take these seriously enough and continued merely to rhapsodize about the beauty and picturesqueness of the land that they were in.

The mood of Spain during the Easter of 1936, and the attitudes towards the country of the British traveller, are memorably evoked in Louis MacNeice's poem, *But They Remember Spain*. He describes attending a boring bull-fight in Seville, catching a cold on a rainy day in Córdoba, and failing to find the right light in which to take a photograph; he meets an obnoxious Cambridge don who shows off his Spanish by ordering anis at a café.

> But only an inch behind
> The map of olive and ilex, this painted hoarding,
>   Careless of visitors the people's mind
> Was tunnelling like a mole to day and danger.
>   And the day before we left
> We saw the mob in flower at Algeciras,
>   Outside a toothless door, a church bereft
> Of its image and its aura.

Chalmers-Mitchell, now happily settled in his retirement home at

Málaga, and enjoying life among the large British community there, remembered the spring of 1936 as 'a particularly beautiful spring', so much so that 'many who were in Málaga for the first time were considering buying or building villas for permanent residence'. There was,' he continued, 'much bridge at the club; golf on a rather ineffici-ent but beautiful course recently opened, motoring into the neighbour-hood, walks and mutual visits for luncheons or dinners or tea.' Living nearby, in the exclusive residential district of Churriana, were Gerald Brenan and his wife Gamel Woolsey. On the afternoon of 18 July, both Chalmers-Mitchell and Gamel Woolsey were sitting in their respective luxuriant gardens, the former reading a book, the latter resting after a lunch of fried red mullet. 'It was the most beautiful day of the summer,' she was to write in her memoir *Death's Other Kingdom* (1939). But suddenly shots rang out, and soon reports were coming in of buildings being set on fire. The temperature was 97° Fahrenheit; 'Not a good day for burning houses,' Woolsey reflected. Meanwhile in a garden on Granada's Alhambra hill, Baroness Nich-olson, recently arrived from a damp and depressing London, was being troubled by similar uncalled-for disturbances. She had come to stay with her daughter and Spanish son-in-law, and had up to now been thoroughly enjoying herself. 'The nightingales were singing in the Alhambra woods, the fountains were playing in the Gardens of the Generalife, and after a wet winter the countryside was extraordin-arily green, and dotted with clumps of wild pink oleander, which had an intoxicating fragrance. The sun shone on the *vega*, and on the snowcapped peaks of the Sierra Nevada. Who wanted to think of politics in such surroundings as these? Assuredly not I . . .' The young Laurie Lee, nearing the end of the Spanish idyll which he would record in *As I Walked Out One Midsummer Morning*, found himself on the Granada coast, at Almuñecar, on that fateful day of 18 July. 'There were no announcements, no newspapers, just a whimpering in the street and the sound of a woman weeping.'

On 17 July a military uprising led by General Franco had broken out in Morocco and had soon spread to the mainland. Three days later, the entire western half of Andalusia, as well as the town of Granada, had fallen to the rebels. Andalusia had been taken by surprise, but the suddenness of its capture had been very much in keeping with the region's response to invaders throughout its history.

Furthermore, the uprising had been almost universally supported by the great landowners of Jerez, Cádiz and Seville, whose wealthy estates were to provide food for Franco's troops. Romanticism and Andalusian machoism fuelled the enthusiasm for Franco among the younger landlords, some of whom were to form cavalry batallions with horses and riders harnessed as if they were going to the *ferias* at Seville or Jerez; one such young man, known as 'Cañoncito pum' ('little cannonfire') toured Seville's Aljarafe on 19 July frightening villagers into submission with the cannon he was carrying.

Seville itself, the first Spanish city to welcome Franco, was taken with insolent ease by General Queipo de Llano, who had simply walked into the city's military headquarters and put under arrest those officers who were too timid to join the revolt. Within hours he was delivering from here the first of his celebrated radio broadcasts, which were avidly listened to by everyone, less for their inspirational than for their amusement value. Gamel Woolsey was not alone in believing that the General gave these while under the influence of the local wine, for he had 'the cheerful wandering manner of the habitual drinker'. On one occasion, according to both Woolsey and Brenan, he referred to the 'villainous *fascistas*', and was quietly corrected by someone at his side: 'No, no, General, *marxistas*.' 'What difference does it make?' he apparently replied. 'Both are villainous.' Arthur Koestler, then active as a journalist, actually had the privilege of seeing the General at the microphone, in a decrepit, make-shift studio, prating like the buffoonish demagogue in Bertolt Brecht's *The Resistible Rise of Arturo Ui*. As examples of the contents of his broadcasts, Koestler quoted the following: 'The Marxists are ravening beasts, but we are gentlemen. Señor Companys deserves to be stuck like a pig'; 'I have given orders for three members of the families of each of the sailors of the loyalist cruisers that bombarded La Línea to be shot ... To conclude my talk I should like to tell my daughter in Paris that we are all in excellent health and that we should like to hear from her.'

García Lorca had returned from Madrid to Granada on 14 July and gone to stay at his parents' new estate, La Huerta de San Vicente, just beyond the town's western outskirts (see page 286). This house, the most beautiful of the surviving Lorca homes, was to remain in the family's possession up to 1986, and is still looked after by a man who has worked for the family for over forty years. It now lies within sight of the ugly modern apartment blocks that line Granada's wide street known as the Ronda, yet, miraculously, it is still shaded by trees and surrounded by orchards and fields. In Lorca's time, the Alhambra was clearly visible from the house, and the peace and beauty of the place must have been quite idyllic. Only four days after Lorca's arrival here in July 1936, the town entered one of the darkest phases in its history.

By 20 July the insurgents had captured Granada, encountering resistance only in the maze of streets in the Albaicín, which finally capitulated on 22 July. Surrounded at first on all sides by enemy territory, the Granada insurgents felt understandably insecure in their position, and responded by executing as many as possible of the town's potential trouble-makers. Every day, early in the morning, lorries would climb up the Alhambra hill carrying prisoners to be shot in the magnificently situated cemetery. William Davenhill, British Consul at Granada, closed his ears to this morbid convoy, which also passed right next to the Hotel Washington Irving, where many of the journalists and foreign visitors to the town were gathered. Baroness Nicholson, by no means a sympathizer of the 'Reds', came to dread these morning shootings, though they were to provide her with the title of her memoir, *Death in the Morning*. To calm her nerves she drank endless cups of tea, much to the amusement of her Spanish son-in-law. 'The English are an extraordinary people,' he used to say. 'Always in a crisis they drink tea!'

Lorca stayed on at the Huerta de San Vicente until at least 9 August, then decided that it would be safer for him to move into the centre of the town. He chose not to stay with Falla, with whom he had recently fallen out after having dedicated to him his *Ode to the Holy Sacrament*, a poem which had offended the composer's religious sensibilities. Instead he went to a house at 1 Calle Argulo which belonged to the family of Luis Rosales, a writer friend whose brother was a prominent Falangist. Lorca believed that this connection with the Falange would protect him, but he was arrested on 16 August and executed either late on 18 August, or early on the 19th. The Nationalists attempted to minimize the outcry which news of his death might provoke by making the fake claim on 19 August that the 'Marxists' had murdered the Quintero brothers, a piece of news which might well have pleased playgoers of all political persuasions.

Reports that Lorca had been assassinated were not confirmed by the Nationalists, though after weeks of speculation they were eventually accepted as true by a horrified Europe. The first Spaniard to react to the news with a poem was Antonio Machado:

> He was seen to fade in air . . .
> Cut, friends,
> in stone and dreams, in Alhambra,
> a tomb for the poet,
> over a fountain where the water weeps
> and eternally cries:
> the crime took place in Granada . . . his
> Granada.

The reasons why Lorca was killed have been much discussed, and no easy answer can be given to the question. Unlike Alberti, a member of the Communist Party, Lorca was never actively involved in politics, though neither was he apolitical, as was later claimed during the Franco period: he was an enthusiastic supporter of the Popular Front. A poem of his portraying the Guardia Civil as a symbol of death and evil, and his homosexuality, might not have endeared him to certain Spanish circles; but it was probably his left-wing views combined with his outspoken comments on Granada's philistine bourgeoisie that were held most against him. His assassination was at any rate an acute embarrassment to Franco and his supporters, who were later to hamper all attempts to investigate the death. One of the finest sections in Gerald Brenan's *The Face of Spain* is an account of the author's search for the place where Lorca died. Local conversations led Brenan to conclude that Lorca was driven up into the mountains near Víznar and shot in an execution ground commanding an extensive view over the *vega*. Appropriately this site, known as the Fuente Grande, was by a spring which had been greatly admired by the Islamic poets of Granada, and around which various Islamic villas had been constructed. Brenan had been driven to Víznar by taxi, but the taxi-driver had become suspicious of him and the author had soon been intercepted by the local police. The taxi-driver who took me to Víznar in September 1988 talked openly about Lorca's death, and had even read the stimulating book on the subject by Ian Gibson, a work which had been banned during the Franco period. The man helped me to climb over the gates of the ugly commemorative park which had been opened in 1986 near a large luxury residential block. The circumstances of my visit to Víznar could hardly have been more different to Brenan's, yet the subject of the poet's death is still not without its controversy. A handful of extreme right-wing families continue to play a dominant role in Granada life, and I was even told about one Lorca expert who is given police protection every time he appears in Granada for a lecture or book-signing.

Mass executions such as those that took place at Granada were also perpetuated by the Nationalists at Seville and Córdoba: the commander in charge of the latter town, Major Bruno Ibañez, was in fact so brutal in his recriminations against the Republicans that finally he was removed from the town, the Nationalists fearing that he would end up by doing away with most of the population. Republican resistance in eastern Andalusia was centred mainly on the villages, which were the scene of constant reprisals by both left and right. Terrible atrocities, still vividly remembered in the villages today, were committed by both sides, though after the Civil War, blame for these was put almost wholly on the 'Reds'. The 'Reds' too were accused of the most appalling brutalities in Málaga, where they had managed to defeat the July uprising and to keep the town until February 1937.

Chalmers-Mitchell, who prided himself on being a neutral observer, wrote that the 'Reds' had behaved almost impeccably in Málaga, and that on his daily visits into the centre of the town he had witnessed no instances of cruelty on their part. Brenan, who was later to confess to a dislike of Chalmers-Mitchell, believed that the man had developed a pathological left-wing ideology as a result of an oppressive religious background in Scotland. Yet Chalmers-Mitchell, like Brenan and Woolsey, had sheltered a Nationalist family in his Málaga home, and had helped many other Nationalists to escape from the town. Whatever his political views, he was certainly a most intriguing figure, a parody of proverbial British implacability, refusing to be flustered at the height of a crisis, and dressed always in immaculate summer clothes with a fresh flower in his buttonhole. When the Nationalists were on the point of seizing Málaga, and most of the British community had been evacuated from the town, Chalmers-Mitchell decided to stay on there so as to be able to observe subsequent developments. Arthur Koestler, who had come to Málaga in January, bravely resolved to stay with him.

No one believed that the Republicans would be able to hold on to Málaga, least of all Koestler, who had driven up to the nearby Sierra de Torcal to examine the town's defensive measures. Here he had found one Captain Pizarro (a reputed descendant of the conqueror of Peru) seated next to a telephone which was intended to relay any news of an enemy advance: the captain had anticipated the likely event of the telephone not working by rigging up to the military post below a wire with a bell attached to it, but this wire was constantly being pecked at by birds. The Nationalists captured the town on 9 February, and both Chalmers-Mitchell and Koestler were arrested, thanks largely to the ungrateful behaviour of a Nationalist whom Chalmers-Mitchell had previously saved from the 'Reds'. Chalmers-Mitchell was released straight away, and he returned to England, but Koestler spent many months in prison and narrowly escaped execution. His experiences in prison were later to serve as the basis of his novel, *Darkness at Noon* (1940).

The Civil War dragged on until April 1939, the Republicans holding on to Almería and the eastern corner of Andalusia almost until the end of the war. Rafael Alberti and Manuel Cortes, the mayor of Mijas, were both fighting for the Republicans at Valencia when their side finally surrendered. Cortes returned to his home village, intending to surrender himself to the authorities, but then decided to go into hiding. Alberti was able to escape from Spain and emigrated to Argentina, the first stage of an exile which was to last until 1977. Most of Spain's prominent intellectuals, artists, musicians and writers were likewise forced to leave their country. Antonio Machado fled with his mother and other refugees to Collioure across the French border, but died there almost immediately. His brother, Manuel, from whom he had become estranged at the beginning of the war owing to their differing political views, had gone to Collioure to see him, and had arrived too late. Juan Ramón Jiménez escaped across the Atlantic and found temporary homes in Puerto Rico, Argentina, Cuba, Florida and, finally, Washington, where he was to die in 1958, eighteen months after receiving the Nobel Prize; as he had wished, a museum to him was later set up in his family home at Moguer, bearing both his name and that of his wife Zenobia, who had survived the news of the Nobel Prize award by only a few days. Manuel de Falla, too ill to leave Granada in 1936, left for Argentina at the end of the war and spent his last seven years in a beautiful hilly area of the country known as 'New Andalusia', the capital of which was Córdoba. Alberti went once to visit him there, and the two men recollected past times. On the subject of Lorca, Falla remained silent, until after they had exchanged their farewells, when he hesitatingly said: 'I'm sorry, dear Alberti ... I know such horrible things about that ... but my conscience prevents me from speaking.'

After the Civil War Andalusia, like the rest of Spain, was left an impoverished place, both physically and spiritually. Few Andalusian writers are worth singling out in the post-war period, the literary output of Nationalists such as José María Pemán – the author of a book on Andalusia – being singularly mediocre. Gerald Brenan paid a visit to the region in 1949, and recorded the sad impressions of his journey in *The Face of Spain*. These impressions, however, did not prevent him and Gamel Woolsey from returning to live in Churriana in 1953. Brenan was to stay in the area for much of his remaining life, dying in 1986 at nearby Alhaurín el Grande, after having been rescued by the Spanish government from the oblivion of an old people's home in England.

In the years that Brenan had spent in England he had finally found himself as a writer, his first important book being *The Spanish Labyrinth* (1943), an attempt by someone of slightly naïve political views to explain as simply as possible the complexities of the Spanish Civil War. Later, in *The Literature of the Spanish People* (1951), he had bravely taken on the whole literary history of Spain, a history of which the English-speaking world was, and still is, shamefully ignorant: once again the tone is that of an inquisitive enthusiast, who prefers his own spontaneous observations to years of painstaking scholarship. Not until 1957, four years after having moved to Churriana, did he finally publish *South from Granada*, the book by which he was to be best remembered. This account of Yegen and of his experiences in the village is admirably unsentimental, though it had the effect of inspiring a romantic yearning for Andalusian village life among many of its readers. The Andalusian people are among the most urban-minded in Europe, but, thanks partly to Brenan, the British came to believe that the 'real Andalusia' is to be found in the region's traditional rural communities.

South from Granada appeared at a time when the coast near

Brenan's home was beginning to be radically transformed by tourism. Torremolinos, described by one nineteenth-century traveller as 'a delightful small fishing village', was by now being taken over by pot-smoking beatniks, most of whom, according to Brenan, were New York Jews. Brenan, with his love of bohemian life, rather welcomed these new arrivals, especially the uninhibited young women, some of whom came to stay with him. However, when Torremolinos, Fuengirola and other coastal villages near Málaga began to be increasingly commercialized in the 1960s, even such a tolerant and adaptable foreigner as Brenan became deeply depressed. Manuel Cortes, having spent thirty-three years in hiding in his native village of Mijas, emerged in 1968 and saw this coastal development for the first time. The shock of seeing what had happened to the former fishing village of Fuengirola, immediately below Mijas, must have been a considerable one. To Cortes, who had known Mijas in its days of great poverty, there was at least the consolation that a new era of prosperity had begun. One wonders, though, what he would have thought of Mijas today, now virtually a suburb of Fuengirola and overrun by coachloads of tourists. Some of the older inhabitants can be seen leading these tourists around the chic white streets of this 'typical Andalusian village' on gaily bridled donkeys known as '*burro-taxis*'.

Laurie Lee, in a recent interview, regretted not only the transformation of the Spanish coast into a 'concrete cliff' but also other aspects of modern Spain. 'Spaniards,' he said, 'have been poisoned by soap, by *Dallas* and *Dynasty*, as have all the once culturally-clean peoples of Europe and the Middle East. They have lost their identity. They don't know where they are any more.' Many foreigners would love Spain to be the 'unchanged and unchangeable' country which Ford described in the 1840s. But Spain, since the death of Franco, has changed more rapidly than almost any other European country. Andalusia itself, reduced to a backwater during the Franco period, is now receiving vast funds from a government headed by a man who comes from Seville, Felipe González. With the Seville World Exhibition of 1992 in mind, Andalusia is currently being transformed into what will perhaps be one of the economic centres of Spain. A new international communications network is being constructed, and some even see Seville regaining the importance which it had in the sixteenth century.

Outside Seville there are those who resent the amount of attention which Seville is now receiving at the expense of other parts of Andalusia, and in Seville itself there is scepticism about 1992 in view of what happened to the town after the Ibero-American Exhibition of 1929. It remains to be seen whether the millions of foreign visitors who are expected to come to Andalusia in 1992 will have much of an interest in the modern aspects of the region. One can only hope that these new visitors will look beyond the familiar images of Andalusia and find a place which is not only romantic and exotic, but also sophisticated, complex, and with one of the richest cultural histories of any part of Europe.

IO

A GAZETTEER OF ANDALUSIA

Andalusia is a vast and perplexing region, much of it unknown even to its inhabitants. In the gazetteer below I have been able only to hint at the enormous variety of the region's attractions, and have made no attempt to write a comprehensive guide. My selection of lesser places is a personal one, and the information given under all the entries unashamedly idiosyncratic. Methodical tourism is alien to the Andalusian mentality, and the immense heat which affects the region for much of the year greatly reduces the amount of conventional sight-seeing which can be done. The leisurely pace and anarchic character of Andalusia soon take hold of the traveller, and I hope that the following pages will convince the reader that the region is best seen in this way, slowly, meanderingly, and with lengthy stops at bars to try out local food and drinks.

The gazetteer is arranged alphabetically, though frequently I have included under a single location a variety of villages, monuments and scenic attractions that can be conveniently visited from it. The references at the end of each entry are to the map printed on pages viii–x, but the reader is strongly advised to use the gazetteer in conjunction with Michelin Map No. 446 (*Andalucía. Costa del Sol*), which is clear, detailed, and well indexed.

I have avoided describing hotels, unless these are of historical or architectural interest, or have considerable character; a detailed list of Andalusia's moderately priced to expensive hotels can be had from any tourist office in the region. Those in search of cheap and basic accommodation should look for the letter F (standing for *fonda* or inn) placed outside a building; in many of the villages it is well worth inquiring if anyone has guest rooms or *camas*, as these are generally of excellent value and very friendly. Further hints about cheap places to stay are provided in the *Rough Guide to Spain*. I have referred to several restaurants with a long-standing reputation for excellence, though as I emphasized in the chapter on Food and Drink, the best food in the region is generally found in bars and *ventas* (roadside inns). The Michelin *Red Guide to Spain and Portugal* has a short selection of Andalusia's restaurants, while a fuller list is included in the *Gourmetour: Guía gastronómica y turística de España* published by the Club de Gourmets de España. Bars play a central role in the life of all Andalusian villages, and because of this I have decided to include a fair number of them, my emphasis being on those with eccentric and old-fashioned interiors, strong cultural associations, and renowned *tapas* or bar-snacks. I have given details of food and crafts specialities, indicating occasionally where these can be bought; a useful list of addresses for food products can be found in José Capel's *Comer en Andalucía* (Madrid, 1981), while the series *Guía artesenal de España* covers in detail the crafts of Jaén, Almería and Granada provinces. Every village, every town, every district of a town has its own festivals, and I have mentioned in the entries only those that are particularly unusual or famous. A detailed pamphlet on Andalusian festivals is published by the Spanish Tourist Board; for a comprehensive coverage of Andalusia's festivals, you should consult Rodríguez Becerra's *Guía de las fiestas populares de Andalucía* (Seville, 1982).

The best places for walking holidays in Andalusia are the Sierras of Aracena, Segura, Cazorla, and the Serranía de Ronda; thanks largely to the English influence, horse-trekking is becoming particularly popular in the latter area. The beaches in the province of Huelva are flat and sandy, and are so long that it is possible to find many secluded stretches. The least spoilt and most beautiful Andalusian beaches are between Conil de la Frontera and Tarifa in the province of Cádiz, and along the Cabo de Gata in Almería; their drawbacks are the often vicious Levante wind which blows in the former, and the parched, treeless austerity of the latter. The Costa del Sol, which forms the coastline of the provinces of Málaga and Granada, has an excellent climate and clean beaches of fine sand, but has otherwise little else to recommend it as a holiday centre; I make no apologies for my cursory descriptions of its resorts, which are described at length in numerous English guide books, for instance in the Harrap/Columbus *Everything Under the Sun* series. Skiing is possible in the Sierra

Nevada, but the slopes are unpleasantly overcrowded at the height of the season (from early December to late February).

Road travel in Andalusia is greatly improving in preparation for 1992, but is still generally slow, particularly the further east that you go: the drive from Seville to Almería can take up to ten hours. Most villages are linked to the main towns by bus, and those that are not can usually be reached at no great expense by taxi; however, most of the bus services are irregular, and have departure times that are inconveniently early for most tourists. There are good train services from Madrid to Huelva and Cádiz, passing through Linares, Andújar, Córdoba and Seville. The journey by luxury express train (Talgo) from Madrid to Huelva takes seven and a half hours, to Caídiz eight hours, to Linares three hours, to Andújar three and a half hours, to Córdoba four and a half hours, and to Seville six hours; at present a new line is being built between Madrid and Seville, which will reduce the journey between these two cities to two and a half hours. Elsewhere in Andalusia there are relatively few train lines, and buses are a faster and more efficient form of travel; however, it is well worth taking a train between Algeciras and Ronda, and between Málaga and Antequera, as these lines run through quite spectacular scenery. Very occasional boat services run along the Guadalquivir from Seville to Sanlúcar de Barrameda, but those that once linked the main coastal resorts have all been suspended, with the exception of the line between El Puerto de Santa María and Cádiz. By far the cheapest places to hire cars are in Málaga and along the Costa del Sol.

Most museums and archaeological sites are closed on Mondays and open on other days from 10 a.m. up to 3 p.m.; from October to June they occasionally re-open in the late afternoon. Cathedrals are usually open in the mornings from 9 to 1, and in the afternoons from 5 to 7. Only a handful of the churches have the same opening times as the cathedrals, the others being open only for services that usually take place between 8 and 10 in the morning or in the evening between 6 and 8. As a rule parish churches have their services exclusively in the evenings, and those attached to convents or monasteries only in the mornings; at other times of the day you can sometimes get to see the parish churches if you succeed in tracking down the parish priest or 'párroco'. Nuns and monks are generally less obliging than priests in

showing you their buildings, and at any rate most of the nuns belong
to closed orders and can only address you from behind a grille. In the
case of closed order convents that sell their own products, the correct
procedure is to ring the bell next to the grille and greet the nun with
the words, *'Ave María purissima'*; after asking for what you want,
you place your money in the rotating drum or *torno* which lies behind
the grille, and then wait until the product is delivered to you. The
countless castles of Andalusia mainly belong to their respective towns
or villages, and can be visited by asking for the key from the local
Town Hall or *Ayuntamiento*; office hours are between 10 and 3, and
between 6 and 8. When different tactics are required to get into a
castle, I have usually specified these, just as I have given details of
some of the more peculiar opening arrangements of other places.

Tourist offices are to be found in all the main tourist centres of
Andalusia, and will provide you with beautifully produced brochures
featuring excellent town maps. Where there is no tourist office available, maps, brochures and other information can usually be had from
the Town Hall.

ADRA: The last king of the Moors, the unfortunate Boabdil, stayed
in Adra immediately before leaving Spain for good. If he sighed when
fleeing from Granada, he would have sighed even more had Adra in
the fifteenth century been anything like the place which it is today.
Backed by black, depressing mountains, Adra can be recommended
only for those with a love of seedy ports. Should you wish to visit the
Moorish castle where Boabdil was put up, you will just be able to
make out a few remaining fragments lying off the Calle Castillo,
surrounded by dereliction and grey modern blocks. The lead-mining
town of Berja, seventeen kilometres inland, is similarly grim despite
references in certain guide-books to its 'magnificent' palaces.

To the east of Adra stretches the Campo de Dalías, flat land which
in recent years has been made exceptionally fertile owing to the
introduction of 'plastic culture' (see page 42). The N340 to Almería is
today virtually one long, featureless town. [4G]

ALCALÁ DE GUADAIRA, one of the liveliest towns on the outskirts
of Seville, is popularly known as Alcalá de los Panaderos ('Alcalá of
the Bakers') because it was from here that much of the bread for

Seville was baked. It is dominated by its massive Moorish fortress or 'Al-Kala', the largest surviving one built by the Almohads in Spain. The castle is incorporated into a slightly seedy public park, and you are free to wander around it and to climb its many disintegrating square towers. The views down the river Guadaira are delightful, but the ones towards Seville are obscured by industrial pollution.

Four kilometres to the south of the town off the C342 to Morón de la Frontera is another impressive ruin of a castle, the Castillo de Marchenilla,which has parts dating back to Roman times, and machicolated round towers of the fourteenth century; the place is now used as a warehouse. [3C]

ALGECIRAS: After driving along the Costa del Sol from Málaga, Algeciras comes as a pleasant relief: though it is an indisputably ugly town, at least it has a life of its own independent of tourism. Founded in Roman times, and occupied by the Moors from 713 to 1344, it has kept virtually nothing of its past and is cramped with dirty nineteenth- and twentieth-century blocks. Much of its life is centred around its port, the town being the main point of departure for those going to Ceuta, Tangier and other Moroccan towns. The place also boasts the first hotel on the Andalusian coast, the luxurious Hotel Reina Cristina, which is set in a large park on the western edge of the town. Sir Alexander Harrison, a British philanthropist, decided to build the hotel in 1890 after his firm, Henderson Associates, completed the construction of the Bobadilla to Algeciras railway. The architect of the hotel was British, and the building (gutted by fire in 1928 and extensively remodelled) has much in common with the Hotel Reina Victoria in Ronda. Two plaques on the reception desk record the signatures of some of the many famous and diverse guests who have stayed in the hotel, including Alfonso XII, Sir Arthur Conan Doyle, W. B. Yeats, Orson Welles, Ava Gardner, Cole Porter and Rock Hudson. [5D]

ALHAMA DE GRANADA: 'Oh for my Alhama', the refrain of a famous medieval ballad translated by Byron, was the supposed sigh of a Moorish king on losing the town to the Christians in 1482. The sadness caused by the loss is easy to understand, for the place is one of the most beautiful of Andalusia's small towns, and is situated in a landscape of classical nobility, featuring meadows, ravines, olive trees, streams and picturesquely shaped outcrops of rock. Approaching the town on the C340 from Granada, turn right two kilometres before the place and you will soon reach a tiny gorge formed by the fast-flowing Río Alhama. At the entrance to the gorge the river is spanned by a Roman bridge, just as it would be in a classical landscape painting of the seventeenth and eighteenth centuries. The small road follows the gorge as it descends into an oasis of trees shading a popular spa resort, the waters of which are apparently beneficial to those suffering from rheumatism. Enter the modern Hotel Balnearia and ask to be shown the Moorish baths (*termas árabes*), and you will be taken downstairs through the modern baths until eventually a door is opened and a great heat released ('Al Hamma' means in Arabic 'hot springs'). The dark and mysterious twelfth-century baths that lie behind the door comprise large horseshoe arches, dramatically spotlit and half-submerged in the steaming water. Some of the stones have Roman inscriptions, indicating the Roman origin of the baths.

The town of Alhama is perched on top of a rock ledge, and on its southern side looks precipitously down to a wide and deep gorge, lined at the bottom with mills following the verdant banks of the Alhama as it winds its way down from its source high up in the Sierra de Almijara. The best views are from the terrace behind the seventeenth/eighteenth-century church of the Carmen, a simple austere structure formed of massive blocks of stone; the much damaged but recently restored interior has draperies dramatically hung behind the high altar. The small, tree-lined main square is framed at one end by its Moorish castle, now a decayed private residence which in the nineteenth century was given toy-like battlements. A street by the side of the castle leads into the tiny, late medieval heart of Alhama, dominated by its parish church donated by Ferdinand and Isabella; in the sacristy there are vestments with borders supposedly embroidered by Isabella herself. The elegant Renaissance bell-tower at the eastern end of the church was designed by the famous Diego de Siloe (see page 97) and faces an enchanting small square with a well-preserved sixteenth-century warehouse or *póstigo*. Following the southern side of the church back to the town's main square you will pass the so-called Casa de la Inquisición, notable for its amusing Isabelline plateresque façade.

Nineteen kilometres along the C335 to Vélez-Málaga you pass through Ventas de Zafarraya, where there is a deep cleft in the Sierra de Tejeda which has served as a pass since ancient times. On the other side you enter the province of Málaga, and there are beautiful views over a verdant, fertile landscape down to the distant Mediterranean. [4F]

ALMERÍA, the most African of Spanish towns, feels cut off from the rest of Spain and was indeed, until comparatively recently, best reached by sea. Its heyday was during its period of Moorish domination. In the mid tenth century the caliph of Córdoba, 'Abd al-Rahmān III, had a great fortress and arsenal built here, and transformed the place into the most important maritime town in al-Andalus. After the fall of the caliphate in 1031, Almería became the capital of a Moorish principality rivalled only by that of Seville. Poetry and philosophy flourished here, and the town's economy prospered as never before through the expansion of its silk and ceramics industries. 'When Almería was Almería,' runs a famous old saying, 'Granada was but its farm.' The town was captured by Alfonso VII in 1147, and though regained by the Moors only three months later, it did not fare so well under its new Moorish rulers. In the century and a half following the surrender to Ferdinand and Isabella in 1481, the town's decline was compounded by a series of devastating earthquakes, one of which, in 1658, reduced its population to 500. The redevelopment of the local mining industry, and the construction of a railway line and a new port, led to a revival of the town's fortunes in the late nineteenth century, but the place has never been able to shake off its overpowering atmosphere of decay. Gerald Brenan frequented its notorious brothels in the 1920s, and pampered members of the film industry are based in the town while working at nearby Tabernas; the controversial Irish rock group, The Pogues, evoked in their recent hit, 'Fiesta in Almería', the tackiness of a drunken spree here.

The twentieth-century heart of Almería, with its beaches, luxury hotels, and regular grid of streets, is the eastern half of the town, which is separated from the western half by an enormous wide avenue known as the Ramblas. The main monument of interest in this part of town is the Archaeological Museum on the Calle de Javier Sanz. In its hospital-like rooms are displayed a remarkable series of prehistoric and ancient finds, most of which were donated by the eccentric Belgian engineer and archaeologist Louis Siret (see page 57); of special interest are the objects from the Bronze Age site of Los Millares (see TABER-NAS). The western, older half of town is bordered to the west by barren slopes falling directly down to the sea, and to the north by the tall rocky outcrop supporting the vast Moorish fortress or Alcazaba. Along the sea-front runs an elegant palm-lined promenade, sheltering the town slightly from its port. The main thoroughfare through western Almería is the lively Paseo de Almería, which runs diagonally off the Ramblas and, with its restaurants, open-air bars, and elegant turn-of-the-century buildings gone slightly to seed, bears a strong resemblance to the famous Canebière in Marseille. At No. 56 is one of Almería's finest nineteenth-century buildings, the neo-baroque Círculo Mercantil, a club which on the outside could easily be mistaken for an opera house; its bar has a splendid ceramic decoration.

The area of the old town in between the sea-front and the Paseo de Almería is filled with dark, dirty and decaying nineteenth-century buildings, and at night becomes a silent and threatening place, with the occasional prostitute and drunken sailor emerging from its sha-dows. For those in search of a cheap room with much character and minimal comfort this is the place to come to: the sinister Fonda los Olmos, on the Plaza Bendicho, is one of a number of old *hostals* that seem straight out of a realist novel of the last century. There are also various other establishments that appear to have changed little over the years, for instance the magnificent Bodega del Patio at 84 Calle Real. At the very centre of the old town is the squat and sturdy sixteenth-century cathedral, begun in 1524 on the site of a mosque which had been destroyed in the earthquake of 1522. The crenellations on its exterior, and the overall fortress-like appearance of the building, are due to Almería being constantly under attack in the sixteenth century from pirates and rebelling *moriscos*. The military character of the outer walls is belied by the Renaissance elegance and rich sculp-tural decoration of its west and northern portals. The original plans for the building were drawn up by Diego de Siloe (see page 97) but executed by Juan de Orea, a pupil of Pedro Machuca (see page 96). The interior is an appealing blend of gothic and classical elements, and there is a rather austere Renaissance cloister, shaded by palms. To the north of the cathedral is the seventeenth-century Plaza de la

Constitución, an arcaded square in a grand Castilian style but with dingy, ochre-coloured houses and sliding metal gates closing off some of its arches. On the Calle de San Juan, to the east of the cathedral, is the austere church of San Juan, where you can still see the *mihrab* (prayer niche) and some of the ornamentation from the mosque which stood on this site.

The Alcazaba, to which you climb from a rocky path leading off the Calle Almanzor, is one of the major surviving structures from the time of the Córdoba caliphs, and the most important Moorish fortress in Spain after the Alhambra. A pair of camels is sometimes to be found sitting next to the path, waiting for tourists to be photographed with them. The fortress is divided into three levels, the lower of which contains a luxuriant and neatly arranged park, a refreshing contrast to the grime and starkness of the town below. From its northern battlements the town's surviving Moorish walls fall down into a dusty, African-looking valley and then rise up over the hill of San Cristóbal. The second level was crowded once with Moorish palaces, baths, prisons and other buildings, but is now a parched, unshaded and empty space; an Arab tent has been set up in the middle, where you can squat down and drink mint tea served by men in Arab costume. The third and highest level has a tower bearing the arms of Charles V. The sensation which you might have had throughout your stay in Almería that you are not in Spain but in Africa seems confirmed by looking down over the northern walls and seeing immediately below you a group of Sahara gazelles running across a stretch of desert: the animals form in fact part of the Sahara Wildlife Rescue Centre, a research centre dedicated to the study of animals that are in danger of disappearing in their original habitat (this place can only be visited on previous application). From this part of the Alcazaba you can also see, to the west, the poor district of Almería known as La Chanca. The novelist Juan Goytisolo first became aware of this district following a climb up to the Alcazaba, and was later moved to write a powerful book publicizing the desperate plight of its inhabitants (see page 9). To tourists and artists, however, La Chanca is considered essentially for its picturesque qualities, which are indeed considerable: built under an arid mountain, it is a district where white walls and roofs clash with façades painted in every conceivable colour. The poverty has been ameliorated slightly in recent years, and most of the cave dwellings that rise above the patchwork of low, flat-roofed houses below are no longer in use. [4H]

ALMONTE, a dull small town in the middle of flat, pine-forested country, has as its main architectural attraction a fanciful late baroque church by A. M. de Figueroa, who was also responsible for the colourful church of San Juan Bautista at La Palma del Condado, sixteen kilometres to the north along the H612. The fame of Almonte derives entirely from the town's possession of the celebrated Virgin of El Rocío (see pages 159–64). The village of El Rocío, where this Virgin is kept, lies fifteen kilometres to the south, and is a curious place with the look of a town from America's Wild West. Dazzling and anarchic at the time of its celebrated Whitsun festivities, El Rocío has for the rest of the year a quality of haunting stillness. The large and ungainly neo-baroque sanctuary housing the Virgin is at its most impressive when seen from across the marshland in front of it. A beautiful six-hour walk can be made from El Rocío to the village of Villamanrique, about twenty kilometres to the north. On the way you pass next to a splendid late eighteenth-century *hacienda*, and go across the sands and pine forests of the former royal hunting district known as the Raya Real. The village of Villamanrique is a charming small place boasting a baroque palace set in a magnificent exotic garden; the present owner of the palace is heir to the throne of Brazil. [3B]

ALORA, a former Roman municipality and a Moorish possession until 1484, is a lively small town with a ruined fourteenth-century castle standing in isolation on a parched hill at the eastern edge of the town. From Alora a short round trip can be made to three most unusual places in Málaga province. Leave the town on the MA441 towards Ardales and you will reach, after a winding uphill journey of sixteen kilometres, the first of these, the tiny spa town of Carratraca. The waters here were known to the Greeks and Romans but then fell into disuse, to be revived after the sixteenth century. The heyday of Carratraca was the nineteenth and early twentieth centuries. Ferdinand VII had a small palace constructed here in 1830, three gambling halls were opened, and numerous celebrities came to stay, including Lord Byron, Alexandre Dumas, Gustav Doré, Juan Valera, Romero de Torres and Rainer Maria Rilke. Badly damaged during the Civil

War of the 1930s, the baths have been recently restored, but the appeal of the place lies in its distinctly faded atmosphere. Ferdinand VII's palace is now a delightfully old-fashioned and remarkably cheap hotel known as the Hostal del Principe. You can use the staircase of the hotel to reach the upper street of the village, on which are located the baths; an attendant will show you the tub used by the wife of Napoleon II, the Empress Eugenia de Montijo.

The mountainous and wooded landscape around Carratraca is known ridiculously as the 'Switzerland of Andalusia'. Its character is unmistakably Mediterranean, and becomes no more Swiss after Ardales, when you turn right on to the MA446, passing alongside a series of interconnected artificial lakes. After six kilometres take the road to the right marked El Chorro, and turn off it after two kilometres to the road leading up to the ruins of Bobastro, the former stronghold of the Moorish rebel leader, Ibn Hafsūn (see pages 67–8). Before reaching the top of the hill a sign on the right indicates the footpath to the 'Iglesia Mozárabe Rupestre', the evocative remains of the ninth-century church built by Ibn Hafsūn into an outcrop of rock. The ruins of his citadel are further up the hill, but these are scant and difficult to recognize.

The slightly sinister hamlet of El Chorro (which can be reached by train from Málaga) is the starting point for a walk which should definitely be avoided by those without a head for heights. In 1921, with the construction of the local hydroelectric station, a catwalk was built following the narrow gorge of El Chorro. This catwalk, known as the Camino del Rey, clings perilously to the vertical cliff and was once one of the great wonders of Spain. Today its condition is dilapidated, and there are the added thrills of the odd gap and missing portion of balcony. [4E]

ANDÚJAR, on the right bank of the Guadalquivir, is a prosperous market town and centre of light industries, with a long-standing ceramics tradition. Of the original Roman settlement of Iliturgi there survives a heavily restored bridge dating back probably to the time of the Emperor Trajan. Andújar developed considerably during the Muslim period, thanks to its proximity to Córdoba and to the strategically important Pass of Despeñaperros. Captured by Ferdinand III in 1225, it became the first walled town in Andalusia in Christian possession. The walls survive now only in small fragments, and the Moorish castle – of which the celebrated epic poet Jorge Manrique was governor – has gone altogether. The appearance of present-day Andújar is mainly modern and unprepossessing, though there still remain a handful of interesting old monuments centred around the ungainly Plaza de España. On one side of the square stands the sixteenth-century church of San Miguel, which has a fine classical plateresque west portal: the porch which shelters this has two splendid polychromed wooden angels supporting the roof. The Calle Feria leads from the Plaza de España into the most attractive corner of Andújar, the long and narrow Plaza de Santa María, which contains at one end a rather Italianate medieval bell-tower: this structure, renewed in the nineteenth century, probably replaced a minaret. The church of Santa María, which takes up one of the long sides of the square, is gothic in origin but was heavily remodelled in the seventeenth century. In the chapel to the left of the high altar is a characteristically stiff *Immaculate Conception* by Velázquez's teacher, Pacheco. The church's greatest treasure is in the second chapel in the left aisle. This, a *Christ in the Garden of Olives* by El Greco, would alone make a visit to Andújar worthwhile, and is indeed one of the few outstanding paintings still to be seen in a provincial Andalusian church: the work originally formed part of the church's high altar, but the panels were all sold off in the nineteenth century. Returning to the Plaza de España, turn right by the Town Hall and you will come to the Calle Maestra, at No. 16 of which is an amusing late Renaissance façade featuring boldly if crudely executed carvings, two of which are of Roman soldiers sporting feathered helmets; the façade, preceded by an overgrown forecourt, is in a sad condition and is all that remains of the building known as the Casa-Palacio de los Niños de Gomez.

The ceramics products of present-day Andújar are mainly of modern design, and there is only one remaining potter, of venerable age, who still produces the traditional blue and white Andújar ware. This man, José Castillo, lives at 7 Calle Alfarero Castillo, off the Calle Monjas: you can buy from him the amusingly shaped *jarra de estudiante* ('student's jug') so-called because apprentice potters used to make them to show their skill. Of far more elaborate design is the *jarra grotesca*, a jug in four elaborate pieces crowned by an angel with a hat thought by some to be imitative of that of Napoleon: this wonderful example of popular baroque seems originally to have been used in the making of some home-made liquor, but has now a purely decorative function. Other more modest pieces made by José Castillo include horses with riders, which are another traditional Andújar speciality.

The most attractive nearby village to Andújar is Arjona, fourteen kilometres to the south on the C3219. The Roman settlement here was the scene of martyrdom of the obscure Christian brothers, Sts Boroso and Maximilian. The two saints are commemorated by statues in the heavily restored late gothic church of Santa María, which stands in a charming, decayed square on top of the village; on the other side of this square is a seventeenth-century reliquary chapel containing the martyrs' bones and a gruesome collection of other relics. The views from the upper village over roof-tops and endless rolling expanses of olive groves are splendid. Another possible excursion from Andújar is to the sanctuary of the Virgen de la Cabeza, situated in a wooded mountainous setting thirty-one kilometres to the north of the town on the J501. Little remains of the original sanctuary, which was founded in the thirteenth century to house a miraculous statue of the Virgin; the present building is a bleak example of post-Civil War Spanish fascism. The drive here is magnificent, though, and on the first Sunday of every April a colourful pilgrimage is made to the sanctuary from Andújar. [2F]

ANTEQUERA, backed by steep, barren peaks, and with extensive views over flat fertile country, was known even to the Romans as the 'Ancient City', or Antikaria. On the northern outskirts of the town, off the Granada road, are three dolmens constituting among the most important prehistoric monuments in southern Spain (see page 55). The two nearest the town, the Cuevas de Viera and Menga, are in an enclosed precinct with the same opening hours as the town's museum (10–1.30 and 5–7). The Menga dolmen, which is reputedly about 4,500 years old, comprises a vast underground gallery supported by vertical monoliths and adorned at the entrance with engravings of symbols and human figures: the burial place probably of an important nobleman, it is the third largest monument of its kind in Europe. The Viera dolmen, opened for you by the guardian of the site, is thought to be of slightly later date, and consists of a long and narrow tunnel leading to a small burial chamber, into which you have to stoop to enter. If you have a car, the guardian will accompany you to the Dolmen of El Romeral, three kilometres to the north. This is the most recent in date and the most sophisticated of the three tombs, having two chambers domed in brick: the smallest of these chambers was a votive chamber, where offerings to the dead would be placed.

The medieval town of Antequera, captured by the Christians in 1410, was built on top of a hill but from the seventeenth century onwards expanded down into the plain. In the late sixteenth century the town had emerged as a flourishing cultural centre, the grammar school attached to the former collegiate church of Santa María la Mayor becoming an important focus for poets and humanists. Numerous fine churches and aristocratic palaces were erected from then right up to the late baroque period, turning the place into what is today one of the architectural showpieces of Andalusia. The town continued to prosper throughout the nineteenth century, but thereafter went into a sharp decline, from which it has been rescued only in recent years.

Heading west into the centre of the town from the Cuevas de Viera and Menga, you will pass the delightful small square of Santiago, containing the late baroque churches of Santiago and Santa Eufemia. Continuing west along the Carrera you will eventually reach the Plaza San Sebastián, with its late sixteenth-century parish church; just off the street leading to it is the town's excellent museum, attractively housed in the eighteenth-century palace of Najera and containing prehistoric and Roman finds, notably a Roman bronze of a nude boy known as the 'Ephebus of Antequera' (first century A D); upstairs are numerous religious works, including a stunningly lifelike portrayal of *St Francis* by Alonso Cano. The bustling Calle Infante Don Fernando leads north from the Plaza San Sebastián into the heart of nineteenth-century Antequera, opening up eventually into a square on which stands the town's attractive mid nineteenth-century bull-ring; half-way along the street is the Town Hall, occupying a late baroque monastery.

The Cuesta Zapateros climbs steeply up into the quietest part of Antequera. The Arco de los Gigantes (Giant's Arch) at the top of the hill was built to display a group of Roman sculptures and inscriptions, and is thus claimed to be Spain's oldest public museum; at any rate it typifies the humanist spirit of late sixteenth-century Antequera. Adjoining the arch are the ruins of the town's medieval castle (now turned into a formal garden, with good views of the lower town), while beyond it is the former collegiate church of Santa María, distinguished by a most elegant early Renaissance west façade in the form of a Roman triumphal arch. To the east of the square is the district of El Carmen, dominated by the church of that name, which has a fine eighteenth-century interior and one of the finest and most elaborate of Andalusia's late baroque altarpieces. Another masterpiece of the eighteenth century is to the west of the collegiate square, on the enchanting Plaza del Portichuelo: here you will find the brick porticoed chapel of the Virgen del Socorro (known popularly as the 'Portichuelo'), a very idiosyncratic building in a style which could only be described as baroque-*mudéjar*.

The outstanding natural attraction in the area is the National Park of El Torcal, fifteen kilometres to the south of the town off the Málaga road. This is a large area of bizarrely-shaped calceous rocks, which give the impression of being the work of some contemporary sculptor rather than the result of erosion. Leaving your car at the small hotel in the middle of it, you can follow one of two footpaths which encircle the park: the shorter of the two (marked with yellow arrows) takes forty-five minutes to an hour, the other (marked in red) about two hours. There are magnificent and extensive views over wild countryside down to the distant coast of Málaga. [4E]

ARACENA is the main town of a beautiful district of low mountains covered in oaks, cork trees, fruit trees and recently planted eucalyptus. The Río Tinto mines (see NERVA) made the Sierra de Aracena very important in ancient times, and the collapse of the mining industry in the second century AD led to a serious fall in the district's population. The district has maintained over the centuries a generally neglected character: the Arabs left few traces of their stay, and the main Christian monuments are the many splendid castles that reflect the frequent border disputes with Portugal in the early Middle Ages.

Dominating the town of Aracena is a bare hill crowned by a thirteenth-century castle and the church of Nuestra Señora de los Dolores, perhaps the finest medieval church in Huelva province. Begun at the same time as the castle, it was brought to completion in the fifteenth century and has a *mudéjar* tower with ornamentation inspired by that of the Giralda in Seville. The short track leading up to the church from the town passes through a charming sixteenth-century brick gate. The parish church of Nuestra Señora de la Asunción in the centre of Aracena was never completed and is now an exposed shell, revealing elegant Renaissance workmanship. The sixteenth-century Town Hall next to it is one of the oldest in Huelva province, and has an impressive main entrance designed by the Seville architect Hernán Ruiz II.

The principal tourist attraction of Aracena lies on the eastern outskirts. This, the cave known as the Gruta de las Maravillas, is entered through a modern building surrounded by tourist kiosks, shops selling local ceramics (of rather poor quality) and a group of hideous contemporary sculptures forming the grandly-named 'Museum of Contemporary Sculpture'. The cave extends right under the castle hill, and the compulsory guided tour of it lasts up to an hour. The place, with its underground lakes and garishly illuminated stalactites and stalagmites, resembles a film set, and indeed this place has been used for several films, including *Journey to the Centre of the Earth*.

Near Aracena there are a whole series of pretty villages hidden in woods, dotted with small orchards, and characterized by their wooden-beam houses supporting picturesquely askew balconies decorated with a riot of flowers. Among these are Linares de la Sierra, Fuenteheridos and Galaroza; two of the best preserved are Valdelarco and Castaño del Robledo, both with cobbled streets, the latter with a delightfully rustic wooden-beam bar ('La Bodeguita'). One of the famed sites of the area is the Hermitage of Nuestra Señora de los Ángeles, situated on a rock ledge in between Alájar and Fuenteheridos, with magnificently extensive views towards Río Tinto. The hermitage, to which an annual pilgrimage is made on 7 and 8 September from Alájar, was lived in for many years by the sixteenth-century philosopher, naturalist and theologian Arias Montano, who had previously been librarian at the monastery of El Escorial near Madrid: Philip II had an enormous respect for this mystic, and came to see him here (an obelisk records this visit). The climb between here and Fuenteheridos is particularly attractive, and there is an excellent viewing-point at the top of the hill. Two of the finest castles in the area are at Almonaster la Real and Cortegana; places of interest further away include AROCHE to the west, CUMBRES MAYORES to the north and

SANTA OLALLA DEL CALA and Zufre (see SANTA OLALLA DEL CALA) to the east. Pig-raising is one of the principal local activities, and you should not leave the area without paying a visit to the hill-top village of Jabugo, which produces some of the best hams in Spain: you can buy a whole ham, or just content yourself with a ham *tapa* in one of the local bars. [2B]

ARCHIDONA, the name of which is derived from the Roman 'Estelduna', meaning 'oil mill', is built against the slopes of a mountain and overlooks a landscape of olive trees extending towards the Guadalquivir basin. The most remarkable feature of the pretty town centre is the octagonal square built between 1780 and 1786 by Francisco Astorga and Antonio González Sevillano. Constructed with stones from the nearby Sierra del Torcal (see ANTEQUERA), the square has remained much as it was in the eighteenth century, the main modern addition being the unappealing arrangement of benches and hedgerows at its centre.

Just outside the village in the Loja direction is a tiny road leading vertiginously up the rock face to the mountain-top ruins of Archidona's Moorish castle and palace. Next to these scant but magnificently situated ruins is the Sanctuary of the Virgen de la Gracia, a simple, heavily restored brick structure which was originally a mosque; inside is a ceramic baptismal font of *mudéjar* design presented as a gift by Isabel la Católica.

Legend has it that a Moorish girl from the palace of Archidona fell in love with a Christian, and that the two of them, realizing the impossibility of their love, decided to commit suicide by throwing themselves off the prominent, isolated rock which stands half-way between Archidona and Antequera. This rock, known as the Peña de los Enamorados (Rock of the Loved Ones) is thought variously to have the shape of an embracing couple and a girl's head. [3E]

ARCOS DE LA FRONTERA: The spectacular position of Arcos is best appreciated when approached from the east along the C344 from Ronda. The town is seen from here to hang above a sheer cliff face, into the darker recesses of which dive the occasional kestrels. Fortunately shielded from view is the extensive modern development which has grown up on the western side of the town.

The history of Arcos goes back to Celtic times, though all of the town's important monuments date from after its capture by the Christians in 1250; as with the many other towns and villages in this area named 'de la Frontera' ('of the frontier'), the place once marked the limits of Christian territory. Almost all its hotels and restaurants are in the animated lower half of the town, lining the long main street. This street becomes progressively steeper as it climbs the hill, and eventually turns into the Cuesta Belén, which goes through the old heart of Arcos. This part of the town, very silent at night, is crammed with tall white houses, and beautiful palaces, convents and churches with crumbling stone façades. Continuing uphill from the Cuesta Belén, you will see on your left the charmingly decorated late gothic façade of the Convent of the Encarnación; on the right is the parish church of Santa María, to enter which you should retrace your steps a few yards and climb up the steps leading to the magnificent west façade, a masterpiece of the Isabelline plateresque style; the interior has splendid late gothic vaulting, impressive baroque choir stalls by Pedro Roldán, and a rich treasury with a dubiously attributed painting by Zurburán. Once outside again, make your way round to the church's southern side, which has an impressive eighteenth-century bell-tower facing a large open square. On one side of the square is the town's privately owned castle, while on the other side is the grand late eighteenth-century *parador*, which was once, ironically, a poor people's home; it hugs the cliff edge and has been closed down twice recently as a result of subsidence. On the side of the square directly opposite the bell-tower of Santa María is a balcony with a breath-taking view down the cliff. The church which you see to your left is that of San Pedro, which can be reached by following the street adjoining the *parador*. This church, perilously poised at the highest and narrowest part of the town, has a baroque façade and a late gothic interior with a striking fifteenth-century polychromed retable. The high-point, in two senses, of a visit to San Pedro is the climb up on to the roof, an experience not to be recommended to those with a fear of heights, for there is nothing to prevent you from falling; the view over the village and across to the Serranía de Ronda is quite exhilarating.

Directly below the town, and accessible from the C344, is a small artificial lake, where you can sail, swim or relax by the shaded shores. [4C]

AROCHE: On the western edge of the Sierra de Aracena (see ARA-CENA), this attractive village near the Portuguese border has at one end a ruined castle containing a tiny and rustic bull-ring, and an even more primitive local museum. Lovers of eccentric little museums should visit above all the Museo del Santo Rosario in the centre of the village. This is housed in a small room inside the private home of Paulino G. Diaz Alcaide, who styles himself official chronicler of the village. To reach the 'museum' you have to pass through his oppressively decorated sitting-room, where you might well encounter a pair of old ladies taking an afternoon siesta: once there you are confronted with a room lined from floor to ceiling with rosaries that have been sent to the charming and energetic Diaz Alcaide from all over the world, together with photographs of their previous and often famous owners: the rosary of President Nixon lies in appropriate proximity to that of General Franco. [2A]

AYAMONTE: On the estuary of the Guadiana and overlooking the Portuguese town of Villa Real de Santo Antonio, Ayamonte is a fishing port and sprawling border town. The modern, lower part of the town is filled with bars and restaurants, where you will find numerous tourists on their way to and from the Portuguese coast of the Algarve. The place has a slightly run-down character, rather like that of the boats that ply between here and Portugal; the boat service is likely to be replaced soon by a bridge, which might seriously damage the town's economy. The old town, a considerable walk from the port, rises on a gentle slope up to the sixteenth-century church of San Francisco, from the tower of which there is a good view over the Guadiana; the ugly, modern *parador* lies in an isolated setting a short distance from here.

Between Ayamonte and Huelva is a landscape of estuaries, marshland, long sandy beaches, and extensive stretches of pine forest; the coastal towns and villages are famous for their seafood, in particular for their shrimps, razor-shells, crayfish and clams. The nearest long beach to Ayamonte is that of Isla Canela, a modern resort at the southernmost end of a flat, marshy and treeless area lying between two estuaries. To the east is the more interesting, if also slightly sinister, town of Isla Cristina, which is both a fishing port and a resort containing a number of strange turn-of-the-century villas and other buildings: its bars and restaurants specialize in two unusual fish dishes, *raya con tomate* (skate in a piquant tomato sauce), and *atún mechado*, a magnificent tunny fish concoction (see page 170). East from Isla Cristina the coastline is backed almost uninterruptedly by pine trees; the Playa de la Antilla, one of the finest sandy beaches in the province, leads on to the long sandbank of El Rompido, which lies between the sea and the estuary of the Río Piedras, and is an excellent place for swimming, camping, and for being on one's own. Situated five and a half kilometres inland from the resort of La Antilla is the modern and very prosperous town of Lepe, known for its strawberries and for being the subject of Andalusian jokes; in 1988 the civic authorities responded with good grace to this latter reputation by instituting an annual festival of humour, which takes place in the last week of May. On the eastern side of the Río Piedras estuary is the tiny and very attractive village of El Rompido, which has charming bars situated on the jetties; a fishing boat can be hired to take you over to the sandbank named after it. An attractive and little spoilt coastline of dunes, trees and secluded stretches of beach extends from El Rompido almost all the way to Punta Umbria (see HUELVA). [3A]

BAENA, straddling a ridge in between gently rolling agricultural countryside to the north and wild hills and rock escarpments to the south, has a long and important history. Situated in an area rich in prehistoric finds dating back to paleolithic times, Baena was a major town in Moorish times, and in the fifteenth century had one of the largest populations in Andalusia. Baena was one of the Andalusian towns which suffered most from emigration; indeed, so many of its citizens left that a group were able to found in northern Spain a town known as 'Nueva Baena', or 'New Baena'. Most of its finest monuments are in the upper town. You can begin your tour from the Plaza de la Constitución, on one side of which is an elegant arcaded warehouse or *póstigo* dating from the eighteenth century; part of this is a cultural centre, and another part the Mesón Casa del Monte, a bar with excellent *tapas*. From the square the Calle Fray D. Henares leads up to the early sixteenth-century church of Santa Maria, the bell-tower of which incorporates what was probably the minaret of a mosque built by 'Abd al-Rahmān II. You are now at the top of the town's ridge, and should turn sharply left, passing alongside the ruins of a castle erected by the Moors on Roman foundations. The furthest point which you can reach is the early sixteenth-century convent of the Madre de Dios, notable for a beautiful *mudéjar* portal and a Renaissance choir. The *Semana Santa* processions of Baena are famed for their noise, and between the Wednesday and Friday of that week, the streets echo to the unbearably loud sound of up to 2,000 drums. [3E]

BAEZA, crowning a hill dotted with olive trees, has views of Úbeda to the east and the Cazorla range to the south. An important city in Roman times, then a Visigothic bishopric, Baeza became under the Moors the thriving capital of an extensive city state. As with Úbeda, its greatest period was the sixteenth century, when its population increased enormously and its economy, based on agriculture, cattle-raising and textiles, prospered as never before: it was in that period too that it acquired its university, which continued functioning until 1824. Though Baeza has not quite the same extent of architectural treasures as Úbeda, it is still one of Spain's outstanding Renaissance towns, and has the advantage over its neighbour in its not having been affected this century by ugly urban development (see page 99).

The Calle San Pablo leads from the town's eastern outskirts (where the bus station is situated) to its centre. Walking along it in this direction, you will pass on the left-hand side three small Renaissance palaces with impressive façades – the Casas Cabrera and Acuña, and the Palacio Cerón. On the other side of the street is the fifteenth-century church of San Pablo, where Pablo de Olavide, promoter of the Sierra Morena colonies, lies buried in an unmarked tomb. Further along the street, at No. 21, is the Hostal Comercio, a hotel which will appeal to the impecunious tourist with a nostalgia for the old days of Spanish travel. This extraordinarily cheap establishment, patronized by a largely ageing clientele, and with a lugubrious tiled decoration, seems to have changed little since the early days of this century when the poet Antonio Machado put up here: if you do not mind the feeling of being in a morgue, you should eat in its splendidly oppressive dining-room, where the food, incidentally, is far better value than that of any other establishment in this town. The Calle San Pablo takes you into the town's bar-lined main square, which, at night, is more animated than anywhere in Úbeda. The large and elegant arcaded building on its southern side was built in the sixteenth century as a place for the buying and selling of grain (the third floor is a modern addition). The square widens at its western end and leads into the tiny Plaza del Pópulo, a perfectly preserved Renaissance square centred around a fountain adorned with lions. The town's tourist office, one of the most attractively situated in Andalusia, takes up the southern side of the square and occupies the former Audiencia. It is flanked on one side by the old slaughterhouse and on the other by an arch attached to one of the town's several surviving gates, the Puerta de Jaén: the arch, known as the Arco de Villalars, was erected during the time of Charles V, and commemorates the suppression of the Castilian revolt of the *comuneros*. On the slopes behind the tourist office lies the quietest and most attractive part of Baeza, crowned at its highest point by the town's cathedral; at night the area is virtually deserted, the only animation being concentrated on the incongruous Pub Bar John Lennon, an unpleasantly decorated discothèque occupying a beautiful old house on the Calle de la Portada Alta. The Cuesta de San Gil ascends from the tourist office towards the cathedral. An alternative and much longer way of reaching this building from the Plaza del Pópulo is to go through the Puerta de Jaén and follow the path which skirts the top of the town's extensive fortifications. This path makes a loop through open countryside and takes you round the southern edge of the town, offering magnificent views of the Cazorla range. The southern stretch of the path has now been named after Antonio Machado, who worked as a teacher in Baeza between 1912 and 1919, and loved to walk along these walls. 'Land of Baeza,' he wrote, 'I shall dream of you when I cannot see you' (see pages 207–8). Leaving the Paseo Antonio Machado after passing the recent memorial to the poet, you will soon reach the cathedral.

Built over a former mosque, the cathedral was begun in the thirteenth century and has an attractive fourteenth-century window on its west façade. The joyfully light and spacious interior retains its late gothic chancel but was given a magnificent Renaissance nave by Andrés de Vandelvira in the mid sixteenth century. A twenty-five-peseta coin, placed in a box innocently marked 'custodia' in the left aisle, has a remarkable effect – to a loud musical accompaniment a door is mysteriously opened to reveal a stand revolving against a red velvet background and supporting an exceptionally elaborate early eighteenth-century silverwork custodia by the Córdoba artist Nuñez de Castro. You can recover from the shock of this experience by walking outside into the medieval cloister, the vaulting of which is the main survival of the old mosque.

The north portal of the cathedral rises on steps above a charming traffic-free square, the Plaza Santa María; adjacent to this building is the former Renaissance Town Hall, with Isabelline plateresque detailing. Standing in front of the austere seventeenth-century Jesuit Seminary on the north side of the square is a sixteenth-century fountain in the form of a classical triumphal arch: this crudely carved work, by the local man responsible for the town's water system, has an engagingly provincial character.

On the beautiful Cuesta de San Felipe, which leads down from the Plaza Santa María in the direction of the town's main square, is the fifteenth-century Palacio de Jabalquinto, the most striking and unusually decorated building in Baeza (see page 99). In complete contrast to this fantastically ornamental masterpiece of the Isabelline plateresque is the romanesque simplicity of the church of Santa Cruz in front of it. Further down the hill, on the left-hand side, is the former university building, which was founded in 1542 and transformed in 1875 into the Instituto de Enseñanza Media, the school where Machado taught French for eight years. One of the rooms, with sixteenth-century tiered seating, was originally the main hall of the university. Next to this is Machado's classroom, kept almost exactly as it was in his day, with the addition of a small collection of documents and photographs relating to his stay in Baeza, and a heavy covering of dust. After staying at the Hostal Comercio, Machado settled at 21 Plaza Cardinal Benavides, which lies just to the north of the main square. His house, marked by a plaque, looks across the Plaza to the richly decorated Town Hall, the most interesting building in the northern part of the town and one of the finest examples of the classical plateresque style in Andalusia. [2G]

BAILÉN, a town of largely modern appearance, is famous as the place where in 1808 the Spanish General Castaños defeated French troops under the command of General Dupont (this was the first serious setback in Napoleon's career. Castaños is buried in the gothic parish church of the Encarnación, which has a sculpture attributed to Alonso Cano.

The outstanding attraction of the area is the village of Baños de la Encina, which stands on a hill eleven kilometres to the north of Bailén, dominated by its excellently preserved Moorish castle. The charming small village has a fine fifteenth- to sixteenth-century parish church in salmon-pink stone; on the toy-like square on which it is situated is also an attractive early sixteenth-century Town Hall bearing a prominent coat of arms. From here you can obtain the key to the castle, which is a few minutes' walk away. Completed in the mid tenth century by order of the caliph al-Hakam II, it comprises fourteen square towers and a large round keep facing the village. You enter it through a horseshoe-shaped gate, and can climb up to the battlements, from which there are magnificent views across a rolling landscape of olive trees towards the distant and majestic profile of the Sierra de

Segura (see CAZORLA); at the eastern end of the castle you look down to a reservoir encased by barren slopes. [2F]

BARBATE DE FRANCO: In the middle of one of the most beautiful stretches of the Andalusian coast, Barbate is an ugly modern town which none the less has the attraction of being a place where fishing rather than tourism predominates. Tunny-fishing is the great speciality of the place, and in every bar you can savour a wide variety of tunny snacks. A beautiful small road (the 169) to the west of the town leads up a pine-coated hill before descending to the tiny resort of Los Caños de Meca. This resort has been built up over the last fifteen years, and until recently has attracted people mainly from Cádiz and Seville; though a growing number of Germans are now coming here, it is still an extremely quiet place for most of the year (the worst times for being here are summer weekends and the whole month of August). It has a reputation for attracting unorthodox people, one of whom, known to everyone as 'La Francesa', runs the resort's oldest bar, the Trafalgar (a few simple rooms, with or without doors, can be rented from her); the best situated bar, the Pirata, lies opposite, and stands perched above the beach. An attractive walk, climbing over rocks and nudists, can be made underneath the cliffs which stretch all the way to Barbate; the furthest point to which you can go is a place where jets of water from a spring shoot over the cliff face to form an excellent natural shower. An alternative trip in the opposite direction can be made either by car or on foot (half an hour's walk) to Cape Trafalgar of Nelson fame. The site is enchanting, particularly at sunset, but swimming far from the shore is dangerous owing to the strong tides; excellent sandy beaches extend all the way north from here to the old hill village and popular resort of Conil de la Frontera.

Ten kilometres to the south of Barbate is Zahara de los Atunes, which has a large and crumbling fortress on its extensive beach. Much of this area of the coast is owned by the army, and to continue to the ruins of Roman Bella at Bolonia (see page 61) you have to return to the main Cádiz to Algeciras road and turn off it after fifteen kilometres. To wander around the ruins you have to follow a guided tour, but they can well be seen from outside their wire perimeter. Bolonia itself has a scattering of bars, and a small, recently built hotel; the beach is magnificent, but suffers terribly from the Levante wind. [5C]

BAZA, in the middle of the wild, little-populated expanse of north-eastern Granada, stands in an oasis of cultivated fields surrounded by erosion and distant barren mountains. In 1971 there was discovered on the outskirts of the town a beautiful polychromed Iberian statue of a goddess; this work, known as the Dama de Baza, is to be found alongside the equally famous Dama de Elche in the National Archaeological Museum of Madrid. Under the name of Basti, Baza was the capital of the Roman province of Batestania; a Visigothic bishopric until at least the fourth century, the town was occupied by the Moors up to 1489. Baza has suffered periodically from earthquakes, and the present town has little of architectural interest. The main legacy of the Moors is the warren of small streets in the centre, and the tiny much-restored baths that lie in a basement in the former Jewish quarter behind the church of Santiago (the woman who looks after these lives at 19 Calle Caniles). The town has a curious annual event mentioned by Cervantes and dating back to the late fifteenth century, when a bricklayer discovered a miraculous image of the Virgin in a local church. The nearby town of Guadix quarrelled with Baza over the rights to possess this Virgin, and the quarrel is commemorated on 9 September each year when a man from Guadix, dressed as the buffoon-like 'Cascamorras', arrives at Baza and is prevented from taking the Virgin by a crowd who taunt and pursue him; returning to Guadix empty-handed, he receives a similar treatment there. The unfortunate man who plays the part of the 'Cascamorras' often does so as an act of penance, but he reputedly never gets badly hurt.

Eleven kilometres to the north of Baza is the bleak and ugly village of Zújar, which until recently had a spa hotel nearby, frequented, so I was told locally, by elegant German women; the spa waters had been used by the Romans. The construction of the Negratín Reservoir led to the pulling down of the hotel, and Zújar's main attraction now is the isolated lavishly coloured outcrop of rock to the north, bearing a distinct resemblance to Ayers' Rock in Australia. [3H]

BELALCÁZAR: Those who wish to know what travelling in Spain was once like should come to Belalcázar, a place redolent of a great past, yet in a romantic state of decay, and far from all tourist routes. It lies at the most northerly point of Andalusia, in an area in which the sobriety of the architecture and people is entirely Castilian in character. The old part of Belalcázar is built on high ground, facing to the north another hill on which stands the village's enormous and ramshackle castle. In the dip between the two hills is an old fountain where many of the villagers come to wash their clothes. A stony path overgrown with thistles leads through land strewn with olive trees to the castle, which is one of the most impressive not simply in Andalusia but in the whole of Spain. Constructed in the mid fifteenth century within Moorish fortifications captured in 1240 by Ferdinand III, the place was already known as 'Belalcázar' or the 'beautiful castle' by 1466; in the sixteenth century a plateresque palace was added. The home of the counts of Belalcázar up to the nineteenth century, the place was heavily damaged by Napoleon's troops during the Peninsular War. The present eccentric owner has admirably resisted offers by the Spanish government to purchase the place and turn it into a luxury *parador*. But, following a recent visitor's injury from falling masonry, he has blocked up the main entrance and thus made it impossible now for anyone wishing to look inside. Of the rapidly disintegrating exterior, the most distinguished feature is the impressively high keep, which is crowned with bizarrely decorated machicolations that appear to be the whim of some extravagantly imaginative if heavy-handed pastry chef. On the south side of the castle are elegant Renaissance medallions. The sad fragments of the earlier fortifications lie scattered and half-buried in the surrounding fields.

On the run-down main square of the village, the Plaza de la Constitución, is the massive church of Santiago, dating from the fifteenth century but with an eighteenth-century granite façade and bell-tower; the interior was gutted during the Civil War. The ruins of the late fifteenth-century monastery and church of San Francisco stand in farmland on the eastern side of the village; the beautiful late gothic shell of the church is remarkably complete, but is now used as a pig sty. In a hamlet on the southern outskirts of the village, off the C420 to Hinojosa del Duque, can be found the convent of Santa Clara de la Columna, which was founded in 1476 by the first Countess of Belalcázar. Nuns still live here, but with no money to repair the sadly decayed late gothic church and cloister; the convent can be visited during the mornings and late afternoons. [1D]

BUJALANCE: The Moorish castle dating back to the time of 'Abd al-Rahmān II lies in ruins, but the rest of this village is well preserved and has an attractive medieval parish church with delightfully intricate late gothic vaulting in the chancel. Next to the church is a most elegant late seventeenth-century Town Hall, and in the middle of the long, narrow and tree-lined main square is a statue to the painter and writer on art, Antonio Palomino: born in Bujalance in 1653, Palomino settled in Madrid, and is best known today for his biographies of Spanish artists, to which he dedicated the last years of his life.

The landscape around Bujalance is covered with an interminable expanse of olive trees. At Porcuna, a singularly unattractive village twenty kilometres to the west of Bujalance, is a modern parish church with paintings by that specialist in Córdoba women, Julio Romero de Torres (see page 46). Porcuna was known in Iberian times as Obulco, and it was here that there were discovered in 1975 the extraordinary sculptures now in the Museum of Jaén (see page 292). [2E]

CABO DE GATA: The lunar-like volcanic peninsula of the Cabo de Gata is one of the least spoilt and most haunting sections of Spain's southern coast. The Phoenicians referred to it as the 'promontory of cornelians and agates', a name which the Arabs translated as Cabpta-Gata. Driving to it from Almería, you will pass the small resort of Cabo de Gata, after which you follow a group of salt flats until you reach the tip of the promontory, marked by a lighthouse. From here there are wonderful views of the bleached mountainous coastline to the east. The coastal road begins to climb after the lighthouse, and then turns into a dust-track, just about manageable by car. After ten kilometres of uninhabited and treeless landscape you approach the small resort of San José, which is backed by an African-looking landscape of palms and cacti. The coast road north from here to the resort of Las Negras is asphalted, but after Las Negras a Landrover is needed; the ten kilometres from San Pedro to Agua Amarga, passing through the hippy resort of El Plomo, has to be done on foot. The whole coast of the Cabo de Gata is particularly popular with Germans, whose taste for nudism and primitive living accords well with the prehistoric surroundings. [4J]

CABRA, a Roman colony and later a Visigothic bishopric, is today a small town with much old-fashioned charm and a beautiful situation. Standing above a group of palms and cypresses at the western end of the town is the sixteenth-century church of the Asunción, adjoining which are ramparts, with views directly down to a rolling landscape covered with olive trees; in the distance, rising above the village, are barren peaks, one of which is crowned by the hermitage of the Virgen de la Sierra. On the other side of the Asunción is the former palace of the Counts of Cabra (now a school), which has a heavily restored *mudéjar* tower containing a gloomy neo-Moorish saloon. Off the tiny green square below the Asunción runs the village's main street, the Avenida Solis Ruiz. The grand but somewhat decayed early nineteenth-century house at No. 13, its yellow paint flaking away from its pilastered façade, was the birthplace of the novelist Juan Valera (1824–1905). Valera, a diplomat for much of his life, spent relatively little time in his native Cabra, but constantly featured the place and its surroundings in his novels.

Pepita Jiménez (1874), the first and one of the best known of Valera's novels, is set in Cabra and deals with the love affair between the eponymous heroine and an older man, a characteristic theme of Valera's writings. In the book the Hermitage of the Virgen de la Sierra at sunset is evocatively described. To reach the Hermitage take the C336 in the direction of Priego de Córdoba; on the outskirts of the town you will pass a natural spring shaded by trees, a popular picnic spot; the village's spacious swimming-pool is on the other side of the road. The winding, steeply ascending road to the Hermitage leads off to the left after seven kilometres. The Hermitage is supposed to be at the very centre of Andalusia, and there are extensive views on all sides, embracing both the Guadalquivir and the Sierra Nevada. Fourteen kilometres to the north of Cabra is the village of Doña Mencía, where Valera lived for several years, and which he featured (under the name Villalegre) as the setting of his novel *Juanita la Larga* (1895). His house is in the lower end of the village, at 6 Calle Llana, off what is now the Calle Juan Valera; at the end of his street is a ruined castle.

Heading east from Doña Mencía on the CO241 towards Luque,

after 9 kilometres you will reach the village of Zuheros, which has a toy-town atmosphere, complete with what appears to be a *papier-mâché* castle. The view from the top of this is over an uninterrupted expanse of olive trees. In the barren mountains in which the village is built is to be found the Cueva de los Murciélagos ('the cave of the bats'), where major prehistoric finds were made at the end of the last century (see page 54). [3E]

CÁDIZ: Encased in its sturdy late eighteenth-century defensive walls, the old town of Cádiz is surrounded on three sides by sea and joined to the mainland by a long and narrow strip of land. Cádiz claims to be the oldest town in the west, its origins being in the Phoenician settlement of Gaadir, which was founded, according to classical sources, in 1100 B C, only a few years after the end of the Trojan War. Used by the Carthaginians as a base for their military campaigns in Spain, Cádiz later prospered under the Romans and acquired a reputation for its lascivious dancing girls. Captured by the Goths in the fifth century A D, Cádiz entered a long decline, and was a place of little significance under the Moors. Trade with the New World revived its fortunes in the sixteenth century, but then in 1596 over a third of the town was destroyed during an English naval raid led by the Earl of Essex. Only after 1717, with the transference here from Seville of the Chamber of Commerce of the Americas (Casa de la Contratacción), was Cádiz finally established again as one of the leading Spanish towns. In 1812 the Spanish Parliament or Cortes was temporarily set up here, proclaiming on 19 March the first Spanish Constitution (see page 174).

Cádiz today is one of the most beautiful of Andalusia's towns, and yet it has been barely affected by tourism. Most of the old town comprises long, straight and narrow streets lined with tall eighteenth- and early nineteenth-century houses with projecting windows. Elegance is blended with evocative decay. The inhabitants of this lively town are the people with whom the Sevillians have traditionally the most in common. They are famed both for their wit and their gastronomy. Their celebrated carnival, held in February, is a riot of sophisticated humour (see pages 146–7), while their bars, restaurants and *freidurías* offer a delectable and imaginative range of fish and seafood.

The town's massive cathedral stands in the southern half of the old town, occupying a site in between the Plaza Catedral and the western seafront. Built between the seventeenth and eighteenth centuries, it has an interior notable more for its size than for its subtlety, and a west façade curiously fusing baroque movement and sober neoclassical detailing; attached to the building is a small museum housing a collection of opulent ecclesiastical silverwork and some dingy seventeenth- and eighteenth-century religious paintings of dubious attribution. On the south side of the Plaza Catedral is a medieval arch marking the entrance to the Barrio del Pópulo. This tiny district – all that remains of medieval Cádiz – is crammed with picturesque if filthy small streets and buildings, among which is the Meson del Pópulo, a dilapidated inn dating back to the early seventeenth century. On the highest part of this district is the former cathedral of Cádiz, now the Iglesia de Santa Cruz: built after 1260 over a mosque, this is an attractive small building with an interior remodelled in the early seventeenth century in a sober Renaissance style.

The Calle Campania leads north from the Plaza Catedral into the Plaza Topete, which contains a pretty flower market; the town's fish, meat and vegetable market lies just beyond, a nineteenth-century building surrounded by excellent bars. Heading north from here along the Calle Obispo Calvo y Valero, you will pass on the left-hand side the late baroque hospice of the Carmen, which boasts a signed canvas by El Greco of the *Ecstasy of St Francis*. Turn east shortly afterwards on to the Calle San José, and you will arrive at the oratory of San Felipe Neri, where the Cortes assembled in 1812; this celebrated historical site adjoins the town's excellent history museum, which is housed in a nineteenth-century mansion and contains documents connected with the Cortes, and a model of the city in 1777.

A few minutes' walk north of San Felipe Neri along the Calle Sacramento will take you to the town's splendid turn-of-the-century theatre, a neo-Moorish building in brick now named after one of Cádiz's best-known sons, Manuel de Falla. The elegant, ultra-modern *parador* (Hotel Atlántico) lies further north, on a site overlooking the sea; follow the sea wall west from here and you will soon reach a sign advertising the Faro restaurant, which is situated at the junction of the Calles Ecuador and Felix. This restaurant, the best in town, is one of the outstanding fish and seafood restaurants of Andalusia; if you do not feel like a full meal, you can enjoy delicious *tapas* at its bar.

East from San Felipe Neri, the Calle San José crosses the Calle Ancha, where at No. 18 is the Casa Mora, an impressive early nineteenth-century mansion, open to the public on Tuesday mornings. The Calle San José comes to an end in the Plaza Mina, a delightful square with luxuriant gardens. The house at No. 3, on the western side of the square, is the birthplace of Falla (plaque; see pages 209–10). The southern side of the square is taken up by the Museo de Cádiz, which has good collections of archaeology, ethnography and the fine arts displayed in a light, spacious and imaginatively modernized setting. The high-points of the archaeological section are two large and powerfully carved Phoenician tombs, one discovered in 1896, the other in 1980; the finest of the paintings are those by Zurburán, most notably a large *St Francis Receiving the Stigmata*, and a series of panels from the high altar of the Jerez Charterhouse, featuring Carthusian saints (see page 115–16). Leaving the square by the street off its south-western corner, you will pass a large art-nouveau bar and café (El Castellón del Tinte) and eventually come to the late eighteenth-century church of La Santa Cueva, where there is a heavily decorated chapel featuring sober frescoes by Goya. Due east of the Plaza Mina are the small and charming seaside gardens of the Alameda de Apodaca, while to the south-east is the large Plaza de España, dominated by a massive early twentieth-century monument celebrating the Cortes of Cádiz.

South of the old town of Cádiz is a district of residential blocks lining the sandy Playa de la Victoria, the continuation of which, the Playa de Cortaduna, follows the N1V all the way to San Fernando, a sprawling town of mainly modern appearance, but with a long-established naval base. Puerto Real, to the east of Cádiz, is a similarly unprepossessing town, founded as a port by Ferdinand and Isabella after 1492; it has a small archaeological museum, with interesting Phoenician finds. Chiclana de la Frontera, to the south of the Bay of Cádiz, is an ugly small town but has a celebrated *flamenco* festival in July. Nine kilometres to the west of Chiclana, along a tiny road, is Sancti Petri, a hamlet situated on an as yet unspoilt stretch of coast (a large resort is being planned). At low tide you can walk out to the Island of Sancti Petri, on which stand the ruins of a Roman temple dedicated to Hercules. [4B]

CARMONA: 'Like the morning star at dawn, so shines Carmona in Andalusia', Fernando III is supposed to have said after capturing the town in 1247. These words are now incorporated in the coat of arms of Carmona, a place which is indeed one of the most beautiful and interesting small towns in the whole of Andalusia. Built on a bluff projecting from the fertile Guadalquivir basin, Carmona was lived in as far back as neolithic times. Numerous finds from the Tartessian period have been uncovered here, and the place later developed as a major Roman town on the Via Augustus. Under the Moors Carmona was the capital of a city state, and in the late thirteenth century it became a favourite residence of the Castilian king Pedro the Cruel.

In the modern outskirts of the town, off the road leading to Seville, is an overgrown Roman theatre, and directly in front of this is the entrance to the necropolis used by the Romans from the second century BC to the fourth century AD (see page 61). Excavated in 1881, this remarkable and excellently looked-after site also has a small archaeological museum containing funerary offerings, bronze figures, busts and other finds from the area.

Walking towards the centre of Carmona from the necropolis you will pass just before entering the old town the church of San Pedro, a fifteenth-century church remodelled in the seventeenth century and given a bell-tower imitative of the Giralda in Seville; the interior is notable mainly for its sumptuously ornate mid-eighteenth-century Sagrario chapel, the work of A. de Figueroa. The old town of Carmona is entirely encircled by the walls constructed by the Romans and strengthened by the Moors. You enter through the impressive double gate of Seville (Puerta de Sevilla), which is attached to a well-preserved castle. Beyond, lining the steep slope on which this part of the town is built, lies a whole series of quiet streets bordered by palaces, convents, churches and numerous other buildings, mostly painted in a brilliant white. The Calle Prim climbs up the slope to the cheerful and shaded main square, off which stands a former seventeenth-century monastery which serves today as the Town Hall; you should go inside to see the Roman mosaic of Medusa discovered in 1929 and now placed in the main courtyard of the building. Continuing uphill along the Calle Martin I, you soon reach the priory church of Santa María, built between 1424 and 1518 over a mosque, of which the charming Courtyard of the Oranges (on the north side of the building) survives. At the opposite end of the town to the Puerta de Sevilla is the beautiful Puerta de Córdoba, a Roman gate flanked by octagonal Moorish towers and embellished with a splendid seventeenth-century triumphal arch. Nearby, at the highest point of the town, stands the castle which Pedro the Cruel transformed into a sumptuous residence, employing the same *mudéjar* craftsmen who worked for him in the Alcázar in Seville. The castle lies in a neglected, rubbish-strewn area of town, and was in a piteous state until comparatively recently. Now part of it has been drastically converted into a luxury *parador*, the main attraction of which is the extensive views of the surrounding countryside: non-residents can use its neo-Moorish bar and walk out on to its spectacularly situated terraces. [3C]

CAZALLA DE LA SIERRA is in the middle of a gentle and extensively wooded mountain area popular with week-enders from Seville. The town, founded by the Romans, has been much damaged by urban development this century, and lacks a central focus. The incomplete and massive church of Nuestra Señora de la Consolación is an architectural mess, though with interesting parts, notably a Renaissance chancel with strange honeycombed vaulting. The Calle Virgen del Monte in front of the church's northern portal leads you into the animated market area of town. In the middle of this, off the Calle Carmelo Meclana, is the former monastery church of San Francisco, which has now been turned into the cellar and sales outlet of a well-known brand of local *aguardiente*, Miura. Cazalla is famous for its cherry brandy, and at the Miura store you can taste one of the best examples of this while looking up at the crumbling baroque decoration on the church's ceiling. The former Charterhouse of Cazalla (founded in the fifteenth century but much altered in the eighteenth) has also been subject to a strange conversion: the chancel of the church now serves as the bedroom of its eccentric owner, who intends the monastic buildings to be used as an artist's studio.

Six kilometres to the south of Cazalla is the Hermitage of Nuestra Señora del Monte, which was built after 1756 in commemoration of an appearance made by the Virgin to a local shepherd. On 7 August each year a pilgrimage is made to this enchanting shaded spot overlooking a valley densely covered with oaks and olive trees; a tiny rustic bar has been placed at the side of this building. The cheerful, palm-fringed town of Constantina, twenty kilometres to the east of Cazalla, was an important colony in Roman times, but was much damaged during the nineteenth-century War of Independence; its main monument is its sixteenth-century parish church of La Encarnación, which has a beautiful if slightly deteriorated classical plateresque portal by Hernan Ruiz. Alanís, sixteen and a half kilometres to the north of Cazalla, has a castle sitting on top of the conical hill which rises above the village: the building, reached by an overgrown footpath, was built by the Moors, greatly damaged during the French occupation of 1808, and has recently been crudely restored. East of Alanís begins a winding and beautiful stretch of road (the C21) crossing wild, uninhabited countryside which becomes suddenly parched and bare soon after entering the province of Córdoba. [2C]

CAZORLA, on the western slopes of the Sierra de Cazorla, is a popular mountain resort, and the main base for excursions into the National Park of Cazorla and Segura. The bustling centre of the town has a largely modern aspect and betrays little of Cazorla's formidable history, which goes back to an Iberian settlement of the first century BC and includes a period as one of Spain's earliest bishoprics, founded by St Isacius. West of the Town Hall, however, Cazorla has a completely different character, and you descend into a district of picturesque white houses clinging to the sides of a ravine. The centre of this very quiet part of town is the beautiful Plaza de Santa María, which has a Renaissance fountain and the imposing ruins of a sixteenth-century church designed by Vandelvira. Thrust up high on the steep rocky slopes above is the tower of the Moorish castle of La Yedra.

On the northern outskirts of the town, on the road to La Iruela, you will find the main information office of the National Park of Cazorla and Segura, where you will be provided with details about hunting, fishing and other activities that you can do in the park. The village of La Iruela, only one kilometre from Cazorla, is known for its basketwork (ask for the house of Esteban). At its far end is another sixteenth-century ruined church (Santo Domingo de Silos), also perhaps designed by Vandelvira. The ruins of the castle next to this, perched almost implausibly on a near vertical pinnacle of rock, seem to be the figment of a stage-designer's imagination; it is just about possible to climb up to it, though a certain skill at rock-climbing is an advantage. The road beyond the castle continues its relatively easy ascent into the National Park. Once over the pass you can turn right to the modern *parador* of El Alcantado, or take the unasphalted road below this to the source of the Guadalquivir (see QUESADA). The most popular route through the park is to head left four kilometres before the turning for the *parador*, and follow the J704 in the direction of Segura. Shortly before reaching the reservoir of El Tranco you come to the Torre del Vinagre, which has stuffed animals, photographs and other objects relating to the park; next to this is a garden bringing together the diverse flora and fauna of the region. On the southern end of the reservoir is an area unappealingly named the Cynegetic Park, which is a wild-life park with a path leading to a viewing balcony where you might see in the far distance some rather bored-looking red deer. [2G]

CÓRDOBA: Built on the northern banks of the Guadalquivir, underneath the Sierra Morena, Córdoba rose to fame in Roman times when it became the capital of Baetica, the largest town in Spain and the birthplace of Lucan and Seneca. The Moors made it the capital of al-Andalus, and between 755 and 1031 it was ruled by the Umayyad dynasty. In the tenth century, under the caliphs 'Abd al-Rahmān III and al-Hakam II, Córdoba enjoyed a reputation as one of the great cities of the world in terms of size, the splendour of its architecture, and the vitality of its cultural and intellectual life. The decline set in after the fall of the Umayyads, and was consolidated by the capture of the town by the Christians in 1236. For much of its subsequent history travellers have tended to describe Córdoba as a sad, bleak and empty town, living off memories of its past (see page 74). However, since the Civil War of 1936–9, 'the distant and lonely' town evoked by García Lorca has developed into a thriving commercial town and one of the major tourist centres of Spain.

At the heart of present-day Córdoba is the bustling but ugly Plaza de las Tendillas, which has, attached to one of its tall and pretentious buildings, a much loved clock chiming *flamenco* music. From this square, the Calle Jesús María begins the gradual descent into the Córdoba of postcard fame, passing, before leaving the modern town, the tiny Bar Correo, famous for its stock of white wines from Aguilar de la Frontera. Finally you come to the Jewish district or Judería. This is an area of simple white houses with flowers spilling over balconies, window-sills and *patios*. Almost all these houses seem now to be tourist shops, selling postcards, knick-knacks and the leather and silver goods for which the town has been famous since Moorish times. At the height of summer, the narrow streets of the Judería become unpleasantly crowded with tourists; late at night the area empties out almost completely, its stray tourists becoming an easy prey to muggers.

At the southern, lower end of the Judería, near the river, is the Mezquita or Great Mosque, the town's principal attraction (see pages 70–72). Most of the tourist groups are led into the Callejón de las

CÓRDOBA

Flores, a tiny cul-de-sac from which you can see the former minaret of the Mezquita framed by floral balconies. The minaret, which can be climbed, stands on the northern side of the building and overlooks the large, dusty courtyard known as the Patio de los Naranjos. Entering the Mezquita through the door on the south-eastern corner of the courtyard, you will find yourself in the part of the mosque added by al-Mansūr at the end of the tenth century. Turn right from here, and you will soon reach the original mosque, dating back to the eighth century. The ninth-century extension is to the south, and, beyond this, in the south-eastern corner of the building, is the section built by al-Hakam II in the tenth century; this last section is the most elaborate in its architecture and decoration, and contains the third *mihrab*, the *maqsūrah*, and a thirteenth-century *mudéjar* chapel, called the Capilla Villaciosa (see page 72). The sixteenth-century cathedral in the middle of the Mezquita is a remarkable structure mingling late gothic and Renaissance elements, with eighteenth-century carved choir stalls that blend well with the intricate ornamentation of the rest of the cathedral.

Córdoba is famous for its gastronomy, and off the north-western corner of the Mezquita a tiny alley leads to one of Andalusia's most famous restaurants, the Caballo Rojo, which specializes in Hispano-Moorish dishes such as lamb with honey. At the entrance to the alley is the modest Bar Mezquita, which has enjoyed for many years a reputation for its anchovies in vinegar (*boquerones en vinagre*), the excellence of which is attested by numerous newspaper cuttings around the bar's walls. West from here are an extensive section of the medieval walls (behind the Calle Maimonides), a charming fourteenth-century synagogue, and the Museo Taurino, a rather characterless modern display of local crafts and bull-fighting souvenirs; a number of these souvenirs are of the Córdoban bull-fighter of the 1960s and early 70s, El Cordobés, better known for his gimmickry and rock star presence than for his artistry. At the northern end of the Judería, on the Calle Barroso, is the church of San Juan, attached to which is an impressive ninth-century minaret.

Running down the western side of the Mezquita is the Calle Torrijos, on which stands the Episcopal Palace. This building, marking the site both of the Palace of the Roman and Visigothic governors of Córdoba and of the original Moorish Alcázar, features today the spacious Diocesan Museum, which is worth a visit largely for its well-restored baroque setting; the adjoining Casa de Expósitos or Foundling Hospital, containing the town's tourist office and a restful bar, is used in July and September by Paco Peña's guitar school and during these two months echoes with the sounds of *flamenco*. The new Alcázar, begun by Alfonso X in the late thirteenth century, is entered from the Calle Almódovar de los Ríos, just to the south of the Episcopal Palace; its main interests are its Roman mosaics and beautiful gardens. The Calle Torrijos leads into a tiny square featuring a curious late baroque monument to St Raphael and a Roman gate restored in the neo-classical period. Córdoba's celebrated Roman bridge, below the gate, crosses an especially beautiful stretch of the river, overhung with greenery, and cradling the evocative ruins of Moorish mills. The views of the town from the tower on the opposite bank are quite magnificent. The tower itself, known as the Torre de la Calahorra, now has a museum evoking Córdoba's Moorish past with the aid of maquettes, changing lighting, music and pretentious commentary.

The area to the east of the Mezquita has much of the charm of the Judería, but with fewer tourist shops. On the Plaza de Jerónimo Paez – reached from the Mezquita by following the Calle Encarnación – is a Renaissance palace with an attractively ornate façade and a cool, *patio*-dominated interior housing the town's Archaeological Museum; among the museum's most important finds are those from the caliphs' summer palace at Medina Azahara. The narrow Plaza del Potro, further east, is one of Córdoba's most delightful small squares, and comes down almost to the river. The house at the top of the square belongs to the guitarist Paco Peña, and is the headquarters of his guitar school. On the square's western side is a building which was once the 'Potro Inn', an inn mentioned by Cervantes. Opposite is the former Charity Hospital, founded under the Catholic monarchs and now containing the town's Fine Arts Museum and a museum dedicated to the local painter Julio Romero de Torres (see page 46). A plaque outside the latter indicates that the building was the birthplace of Romero de Torres, and that he also lived and died here. The interior is dark and gloomy, rather like Torres's paintings, which are nearly all of naked Córdoba women. One of the artist's best-known works is *La Chiquita Piconera*, which features a sultry, provocatively clad girl stirring the ashes of a brazier; another work on show here is *Viva el*

Pelo, which is rapturously described in *1912 + 1* (1986), a novella by the Sicilian writer Leonardo Sciascia. The Fine Arts Museum includes other works by Romero de Torres, and a large painting of the *Last Sacrament* by his father, Rafael. A staircase with a *mudéjar* ceiling and sixteenth-century murals leads up to the holdings of old master works, which range from a fine *Christ at the Column* by Alejo Fernández to slight works by Zurburán and Goya.

The Calle Armas leads north from the Plaza del Potro to La Corredera, a large and remarkably run-down seventeenth-century arcaded square inspired by Castilian models. It is a short walk from here back to the Plaza de las Tendillas, passing by the side of the ugly modern Town Hall and the adjoining, much-restored columns of a Roman temple. Alternatively you could turn east from the Town Hall on to the Calle San Pablo and enter a fascinating but little visited part of Córdoba. Half-way down the Calle San Pablo, on the Plazuela de Orive, is the House of Villalones, a small and elegant Renaissance structure crowned by a loggia. The pleasant Plaza San Andrés, further down the street, features a late medieval church and another modest Renaissance house. Further east still, in distinctly seedy surroundings, is the very impressive gothic church of San Lorenzo, the west face of which has a beautifully ornamented rose window.

A five-minute walk north of the Plaza San Andrés will take you to what is one of the most enjoyable of Córdoba's architectural attractions. This, the Palacio de los Marqueses de Viana, is a fourteenth- to eighteenth-century building boasting no less than fourteen *patios* and gardens; the interior, which can be visited, is splendidly furnished and has a well-known collection of Córdoban leatherwork. In front of the nearby medieval church of San Agustín is a monument to the bull-fighter Manolete, and a bar – once much freqented by *matadores* – decorated with bull-fighting souvenirs and specializing in deep-fried *boquerones*. West from here, along the Calle Conde Prigo, is the Plaza de los Dolores, bordered by a seventeenth-century convent and adorned in its centre with a statue of Christ encased by black railings supporting lanterns; this square is particularly attractive at night.

The square backs on to the spacious Plaza de Colón, which has in its north-eastern corner a fifteenth-century brick tower forming part of the town's original fortifications. Called the Torre de la Malmuerta (Bad Death), it was reputedly built as an act of contrition by a nobleman who had killed his adulterous wife and her servants. Much of the western side of the square is taken up by the former eighteenth-century convent of La Merced (now the seat of local government offices), the most important and colourful of Córdoba's baroque buildings. The town's train station is a short distance away to the west, on the Avenida de América. Running south from the Avenida are a wide, park-lined avenue marking the town's western fortifications, and the Avenida del Gran Capitán, lined with Córdoba's finest modern buildings. At the southern end of the latter street is the church of San Nicolás, with a tall bell-tower which was once a minaret; the Calle Gondamar leads east from here back to the Plaza de las Tendillas.

An enjoyable round trip from Córdoba can be made to Las Ermitas (the Hermitages) and the ruins of the Moorish summer palace of Medina Azahara (see pages 73–4). The former – a group of hermits' cells – are situated high on the verdant hills above the town and command beautiful views of the Guadalquivir valley; the winding ten-kilometre road which leads to them passes through the luxurious northern suburbs of Córdoba, in which are to be found the town's *parador* and one of Andalusia's most fanciful discothèques, Scheherezade. From the Hermitages you can meander slowly west along the ridge of the hills in the direction of Medina Azahara; before descending to the latter you will pass the Bar Restaurante Cruce, an excellent lunch stop, where you can eat the wild boar which is hunted in this area. The ruins of Medina Azahara, attractively contained within gardens coloured by bougainvillaea, are best seen either early in the morning or late in the afternoon. Above the ruins is the sixteenth-century monastery of San Jerónimo (now a private residence), which was built with some of the stones from the palace. In the far distance, to the west, can just be made out the castle of Almodóvar del Río, sitting on top of a tall barren mound directly above the Guadalquivir river. This impressive if heavily restored castle, seventeen kilometres from Córdoba on the C431, can be visited; it is now rented out to the masonic society, Opus Dei. [2E]

CUMBRES MAYORES lies at the north-western extremity of Andalusia, and already the densely wooded hills of the Sierra de Aracena (see ARACENA) have given way to the starker more barren landscape characteristic of Extremadura. The village, which has the sombre aspect also typical of that region, has an impressive castle, the keys for which can be obtained from the house at 3 Plaza Portugal, directly in front of the building. The castle is entered through an enormously tall gate, beyond which you reach, to your surprise, an overgrown football pitch. The walk around the well-preserved battlements is rewarded by extensive views. [2B]

ÉCIJA, sunk in a depression formed by the river Genil, has inspired one of the silliest lines in the Michelin *Green Guide to Spain*: 'Écija . . . has a mild climate except in summer when it becomes so hot that it is known as the Furnace of Andalusia.' Once an important Roman settlement known as Astigi (the scant ruins of which can be seen on the town's outskirts), Écija developed in early Christian times as one of the main bishoprics of Spain and was reputedly visited by St Paul. Under the Moors it began to decline, but in the seventeenth and eighteenth centuries it flourished because it was surrounded by prosperous *latifundia*, the owners of which had palaces built in the town. The Lisbon earthquake of 1755 led to the rebuilding of many of Écija's churches, and it thus acquired a splendid series of late baroque church towers that have earned it the nickname of 'the city of towers'. Away from the ugly outskirts that have grown up alongside the main Seville to Córdoba road (the N IV E5), Écija has a quiet aristocratic character, with numerous attractive corners and monuments. The Avenida Miguel de Cervantes leads from the N IV E5 to the Plaza de España, the town's pleasant, palm-lined main square, adorned with a nineteenth-century fountain. The church of Santa María adjoins this, and is of interest mainly for its cloister, where a large collection of Iberian, Roman and medieval finds are casually displayed. The finest survival from the early Christian period in Écija is an Early Christian sarcophagus in the eighteenth-century church of Santa Cruz, on the Plazuela Virgen del Valle, to the north of the Plaza de España. The baroque monuments of Écija are the town's greatest attractions, though few travellers have hitherto been able to appreciate these: one of the few was Théophile Gautier, who was enraptured by what he described as 'the sublime bad taste' of the local architecture. Of the town's many baroque towers, the most spectacular is that of the church of San Juan Bautista, which stands to the east of the Plaza de España, on the Calle San Antonio: this fantastical tower is dripping with volutes and coloured with brilliant blue ceramic tiles shining against a background of red brick. The former convent church of La Limpia Concepción de Nuestra Señora (Las Descalzas), on the eastern edge of the old town, boasts the most elaborate of Écija's church interiors: the building was begun in 1511, but completely remodelled after the Lisbon earthquake and given its magnificent polychromed stucco interior, which oozes rococo forms. There are various impressive palaces in the town, the most charming and unusual being that of the Marqueses de Peñaflor on the Calle de Castellar (near the church of San Juan Bautista): dating from 1726, it has a curving main façade covered in eighteenth-century decorations and featuring a frontispiece crowned with salamonic columns; leading off its beautiful *patio* is an intriguing staircase with columns in red marble and an elaborate plasterwork ceiling. The outstanding palace in Écija is that of the Marqueses de Benameji (on the Calle Castillo, behind the Church of Santa María): now occupied by the army, it was built about the same time as the Peñaflor palace, and has a particularly imposing frontispiece in grey and white stone, supporting a gigantic coat of arms.

La Luisiana and La Carlota, two of the colonies founded in the late eighteenth century by Charles III and his minister Olavide (see LA CAROLINA), lie respectively fifteen kilometres to the west of Écija, and twenty-one kilometres to the east, both along the main Seville to Córdoba road. As with the other colonies, these are both laid out on a regular grid plan. La Luisiana, the smaller and less interesting of the two, has a tiny and pretty small square flanked by a modest Town Hall and a neo-classical church highlighted in pink. The Town Hall of La Carlota, standing beside the main road, is a more notable building than that of La Luisiana: faced with giant pilasters, it is a true structure of the Enlightenment in its mixture of grandeur and simplicity. On the other side of the road is an attractive eighteenth-century red brick coaching inn (Real Casa de las Postas), while further along the road is a statue to Charles III and Olavide, recording how these two men 'came to transform these sterile and deserted lands into productive villages'. Set back from the road is the harmonious Plaza de las Iglesias, dominated by a large parish church featuring a triple-arched portico, and two bell-towers. [3D]

EL CARPÍO: Near the uninspiring hill village of El Carpío in Córdoba province is one of Andalusia's most remarkable examples of turn-of-the-century industrial architecture. Take the main road (N IV E5) east from El Carpío for four kilometres, then turn on to the small CO412. After crossing the Guadalquivir on a dam flanked by neo-Moorish towers, you will find on the left-hand side of the road a gate marked Central Carpío. Go through this, and, taking care to bear always to the right (if you turn left you will end up in the private estate of the Dukes of Alba), you will reach an extraordinary electrical power station designed, like the dam, by Casto Fernández Shaw, an eccentric architect of British origin. Crowned by mosque-like domes, this neo-Moorish fantasy has, on its river side, a balcony supported by magnificent elephants' heads. The adjoining estate of the Dukes of Alba was where Goya stayed in 1796, enjoying an affair with the Duchess, who inspired several erotic drawings of his and is said to have posed for the *Maja Desnuda*. [2E]

EL PUERTO DE SANTA MARÍA stands at the mouth of the River Guadalete overlooking the heavily industrialized bay of Cádiz. Founded by the Greeks, it developed in the fifteenth century as a major port and wine-exporting town; today it is also a popular summer resort, much frequented by the inhabitants of nearby Jerez de la Frontera. The poet Rafael Alberti, who was born here in 1902, described the town rapturously in his sentimental autobiography, *The Lost Grove* (see page 205). Extensive modern development has heavily spoilt the place in recent years, but there is a pleasant old quarter which, with its regular grid of streets and late eighteenth- to early nineteenth-century houses, is highly reminiscent of that of Cádiz. The main church of the town is the fifteenth- to seventeenth-century Iglesia Mayor Prioral, which has an imposing classical plateresque south portal. Of great historical and architectural interest is the heavily restored Castle of San Marcos, a largely thirteenth-century structure built by Alfonso X ('The Wise') on the site of a Moorish watch tower and mosque: the monarch referred to the construction of this building in one of his famous *Cantigas*. The foundations of the mosque, together with some Roman columns discovered here, were incorporated into the castle's small and delightful church. In the nineteenth century the castle was lived in by a strange variety of people and as such inspired two novels by the *costumbrista* writer Fernán Caballero (see page 199).

The town's enormous but elegant bull-ring was built in 1880 and is much loved by bull-fighting enthusiasts: a ceramic plaque placed at one of its main entrances records the fighter Joselito as saying that 'he who has not seen bulls at El Puerto does not know what a bull-fight is like'. Another of the square's attractions are its *bodegas*, most of which can be visited: the oldest and prettiest is the seventeenth-century Bodega Terry on the Calle General Mola. In the summer months an enjoyable journey from El Puerto to Cádiz can be done on a small old boat called the *'vapor'*; the service has been run since its inception in 1929 by the same Galician family.

The beach resort of El Puerto is the western suburb of Valdelagrana, the chic appearance of which is belied by the industrial landscape which surrounds it. A nearby resort is that of Rota, fifteen kilometres further east, which has, on its northern side, good clean beaches that are fortunately out of sight of Cádiz's industries. Rota itself is an old village with a pretty central square featuring an austere fourteenth- to fifteenth-century church and a much restored castle; its most offensive feature is the American military base on its outskirts, which has the appearance of a gigantic prison camp. [4B]

ESTEPA: When the Romans entered Estepa in 208 BC they found that its inhabitants had burnt their own property and killed themselves, preferring this to surrendering to the enemy. To most Spaniards the name 'Estepa' does not recall this valiant action but instead the dry, fragile biscuits known as *polvorones* and *mantecados*, which are eaten generally at Christmas time and are manufactured in various small factories in the lower half of the village. The old town of Estepa, which lies higher up, is like a small and not so well-preserved version of nearby Osuna. The church of the Carmen, on the small but lively village central square, the Plaza del Carmen, has an extraordinarily elaborate baroque façade of 1768, comprising a rhythmical interplay of convex and concave forms in black and white stone. Walking from this square down to the village's cheerful main thoroughfare, the Calle Mesones and its continuation, the Calle Castillejos, you have good views of the rugged rocky crags of the Sierra de Machuca; at 18 Calle Castillejos is the fine eighteenth-century palace of the Marqueses de Cerverales, with an animated frontispiece made up of salamonic columns. Above the village stand the ruins of a castle, dating back to Iberian times, rebuilt by the Romans, and given its sturdy keep in the late thirteenth century.

Fourteen kilometres north of Estepa is the communist village of Marinaleda, notorious for its charismatic mayor, Sánchez Gordillo (see pages 15–16). [3D]

FUENTE OBEJUNA, a sad and sinister town in a depressed area of Córdoba province, is famous for its insurrection of 1489 against its tyrannical governor (see pages 13–14). The event was commemorated in a play by Lope de Vega, who is remembered here in the name of the main square and in a plaque opposite the parish church praising him for having 'celebrated the civic virtues of our citizens'. The governor's palace was pulled down shortly after the tyrant's death, and this church put up in its stead: in its delicate late gothic interior is a beautiful sixteenth-century main altar in polychromed wood, and an altarpiece containing painted panels of the Hispano-Flemish school. [1D]

GAUCÍN, with its eagle-nest setting and former notoriety as a bandit's lair, had an obvious attraction for the Romantic traveller. The bandits have now been replaced by the British, who have bought up whole streets in this picturesque and superficially unchanged village. There is an excellent cheap and old-fashioned *fonda* (the Nacional), and a British-run bar which the locals have the good taste to avoid. Jutting out on rocky ground above the ridge to which the village clings are the ruins of a castle, from which you can see as far as Gibraltar on clear days. Ten kilometres to the north, off the C341 to Ronda, is the hamlet of Benalauría, the castle of which encloses the village church and cemetery. The old road to the south of Gaucín (MA539) descends perilously to the coast, passing on the left the attractive village of Casares. [5D]

GIBRALTAR: The Rock of Gibraltar, one of the famed landmarks of the Mediterranean, was thought of in ancient times as one of the pillars of Hercules, and as such marked the western end of the known world. Its present name was acquired after 711 AD when the Berber leader Tāriq Ibn Ziryāb landed here and called the Rock 'Jabal Tāriq', 'the Mountain of Tāriq' (see pages 64–5). Under Moorish domination up to 1309, and then from 1333, Gibraltar was definitively captured by the Christians in 1462, an event which presaged the imminent collapse of the Nasrid dynasty. During the War of the Spanish Succession of 1704, the Rock was taken by the English, who in 1782 brilliantly defended it against the combined forces of the French and Spanish. Thereafter the British transformed it into a British colony, which it remains to this day. Spanish antagonism towards the British presence here led in 1969 to the Rock being made inaccessible from the Spanish mainland; access to the mainland was only re-established in 1985. In 1988 the Rock acquired further notoriety when British police shot down and killed three apparently unarmed Irishmen suspected as terrorists. The British government subsequently went to absurd lengths to cover up the facts of the incident, despite a great international outcry.

Gibraltar is an unquestionably ugly place, and for those who have been relishing the sensuality of southern Spain, the shock of arriving here from the mainland is a considerable one (see page 36). The architecture of the town is almost wholly English, and even the local ice-cream van plays 'Greensleeves' to remind you of the mother country. Yet for all the Englishness of Gibraltar the place has a curious hybrid character. The bilingual inhabitants speak a mixture of English and Spanish, and the streets are packed with a fascinating variety of peoples, from blond British soldiers to Jewish traders and veiled Moroccan women. The oldest and most interesting part of Gibraltar is North Town, the main street of which provides a constant human spectacle. Of this district's more obvious attractions, mention should be made of the neo-Moorish Anglican cathedral of 1821 (on Cathedral Square) and the Gibraltar Museum, which retains an English drabness despite incorporating an old Moorish bath. From the southern end of North Town you can take a cable car up to the top of the Rock. Walking down from here, along St Michael's Road, you will pass next to the gigantic St Michael's Cave, where ballets and other shows are sometimes put on; the look of this garishly lit cave is very artificial. Further down the Rock you will come to the Apes' Den, a popular meeting-place both for tourists and for Gibraltar's famous Barbary apes: the apes were probably first brought over from Africa by the Moors, and are the only tribe of monkeys living wild on the continent of Europe. The Queen's Road leads from near here to the steeply sloping northern half of the Rock, inside which an impressive series of defensive tunnels were dug out in 1782; these tunnels, which can be visited, are known as the Upper Galleries. From here you can walk back to North Town by way of the much restored Moorish castle, the phoniness of which is emphasized by the waxwork Moorish figures which have been placed on its battlements. [5D]

GRANADA: Built underneath the snowcapped peaks of the Sierra Nevada, at the easternmost edge of the fertile plain or *vega* formed by the River Genil, Granada is one of the most beautifully situated of all Spanish towns, and has been since the early nineteenth century one of the principal tourist destinations of Europe. This town of fabled reputation was actually an obscure place in ancient and early Christian times, and even under the Moors it only rose to fame after 1241 when Ibn Nasr, founder of the Nasrid dynasty, established here the capital of his empire (see pages 81–5). After its capture by Ferdinand and Isabella in 1492, the town was troubled by racial tensions, yet it continued to have a great cultural importance and was embellished by numerous splendid Renaissance buildings (see pages 92–8). Later the town became the main baroque centre of Andalusia after Seville, and among the distinguished figures of the period who worked here were the painter, sculptor and architect Alonso Cano ('the Spanish Michelangelo'; see page 112), the sculptor Pedro de Mena, the painter Sánchez Cotán and the architect Hurtado Izquierdo (see page 120). Cultural decline set in in the late eighteenth century and coincided with the town's growth as a tourist centre. In the 1920s the poet García Lorca and the musician Manuel de Falla brought new distinction to the cultural life of Granada, but both were depressed by the modern aspects of the town and preferred to dream about its Moorish past. By this date much of medieval, Renaissance and baroque Granada had been badly affected by insensitive modern development. To this day charming old corners of the town are being brutally pulled down.

García Lorca described the people of Granada as 'the worst bourgeoisie in the world', and for anyone coming to Granada from Seville, it is certainly striking how generally more dour and conservative the people here are. However, Granada has a far more animated university life than Seville, and the town's countless lively student bars help

partially to compensate for the place's inherently sober character. Moreover, Granada has the attraction of being a much cheaper place than Seville, and the renowned food of this area can be had in bars and restaurants at ridiculously low prices (particularly good are the hams, sausages, and broad bean dishes; see pages 170 and 171). Finally, for the sight-seer, Granada still has a vast amount to offer quite apart from the Alhambra. This gazetteer can only rush rapidly through the town's main attractions, and anyone with a knowledge of Spanish who requires a thorough guide to Granada should purchase Antonio Gallego y Burín's excellent and beautifully illustrated *Guía Artística de Granada*; the most detailed account available in English is the one in the *Blue Guide to Spain* (1989).

Most tours of Granada begin in the Alhambra, and many people come to the town without visiting any other monument. The main entrance and ticket office to this large complex are near the south-western corner of the Palace of Charles V. You could begin your itinerary by walking around the battlements of the Moorish Alcazaba, which date mainly from the late thirteenth century and take up the western corner of the Alhambra hill; the views are wonderful, particularly from the Torre de la Vela, which directly faces the Albaicín hill and is the highest point of the Alcazaba. After descending from the tower, follow the signs to the Nasrid palace, which is the most popular attraction of the Alhambra and was constructed largely in the late fourteenth century. The first main courtyard which you come to is that of the Myrtles (de los Arrayanes), which is dominated by a long narrow fishpond and has at one end the two-storied Hall of the Ambassadors (the largest room in the Alhambra). The next courtyard which you come to is that of the Lions (de los Leones), off which stand the two rooms of the Alhambra with the most intricate honey-comb domes, the Sala de las Dos Hermanas and the Sala de los Abencerrajes; the former, perhaps originally part of a harem, has a dome with an estimated 5,000 cells. The door through which you leave the Court of the Lions takes you into the Alhambra's gardens; once outside you should bear left and re-enter the Nasrid Palace through the gate leading into the Patio de Daraxa. The apartments on the upper level of this *patio* were used first by Charles V and then by Washington Irving (to visit them you need special permission from the Alhambra authorities). On the opposite side of the courtyard is an entrance taking you to the palace's marble baths, one of the quietest corners of the Alhambra.

Before heading east in the direction of the Generalife you should go inside the Palace of Charles V, if only to see its powerfully impressive round courtyard. The Museo Nacional de Arte Hispano-Musulman is housed in this palace, but it has been inexplicably closed to the public for several years; if you are lucky enough to persuade one of the museum staff to let you in, you will find a beautiful display of Moorish finds from the Alhambra, and excellent views down into the courtyards of the Nasrid Palace. The Museo de Bellas Artes, housed in the same building, is not always open, and rarely can you see all its rooms: its high-points are a powerful and very life-like head of San Juan de Dios by Alonso Cano, and one of the enigmatic and hauntingly simple still-lives by Sánchez Cotán, this one featuring carrots against a dark plain background.

Walking east towards the Generalife along the street flanking the southern side of the Palace of Charles V, you will pass first the sixteenth-century church of Santa María (built on the site of the Alhambra mosque; see page 93) and then the Hostal América, one of the most delightful places to stay in Granada (early booking is essential as it has only fourteen rooms). Further east is Granada's celebrated *parador*, built within a sixteenth-century Franciscan monastery over the site of a Moorish palace; fragments of this palace can be seen in one of the courtyards. A path hemmed in by trees and box-hedges takes you to a modern bridge connecting the Alhambra with the Generalife. The buildings within the Generalife have been heavily restored, and the interest of the place lies essentially in its gardens, an enchanting mixture of Moorish and Renaissance elements. Once back again into the Alhambra, you can return to the Nasrid Palace by following the path along the Alhambra's northern walls. The unreal stage-set quality of both the Alhambra and the Generalife is heightened should you visit these places at night, which is possible between 10 and 12 on Wednesdays and Saturdays.

To descend to the lower town of Granada from the Alhambra, you have to pass through the wooded park which covers much of the southern slopes of the hill. In the upper reaches of the wood, near the main entrance to the Alhambra, is the famous Hotel Washington Irving, which was thought in the late nineteenth century to be one of the most luxurious hotels in Spain; today the place has a gloomy, run-down character. More cheerful is the nearby Hotel Alhambra Palace, which stands just outside the wood and enjoys a magnificent panorama over southern Granada; this hotel, put up in 1910, is unfortunately a considerable eyesore from the outside, a monstrous neo-Moorish structure in garish purple. At the end of the narrow and very pretty Antequerla Alta, which runs east from the latter hotel, is Manuel de Falla's simple and evocative home (see pages 210–211), immediately above which is a concert hall bearing the composer's name. The tiny street to the west of the hotel, the Callejón Niño del Royo, has in it the Fundación Rodríguez Acosta, a remarkably original house and garden of the early years of this century, now functioning as a cultural centre and a residence for artists. Next to it is the Museo Gomez Moreno, an excellent but virtually unvisited museum opened in 1982. Within its white and strikingly modern interior is displayed in random fashion, and to a musical accompaniment, a very eclectic collection of works of art, including a fascinating group of Iberian figurines, a powerful *Lamentation* by Hugo van de Goes, and an outstanding small sculpture by Alonso Cano of *San Diego de Alcalá*.

From the Hotel Washington Irving, the Alameda de la Alhambra descends to the Cuesta de Gomerez, which will take you to the Plaza Nueva; you leave the park through the sixteenth-century Granados gate, the sides of which have been much damaged by coaches. An alternative way down is to make the steep descent from the Hotel Alhambra Palace to the Plaza del Príncipe. If you choose the latter route, you will find yourself in a fascinating part of town little visited by tourists. The Plaza del Príncipe itself is lined with open-air bars, and is a favourite meeting-point at night. Behind the square, at the eastern end of the Calle de los Molinos, is the tiny Bar Lopez Correa, an evocative eccentric survival from the early years of this century, its walls plastered with bizarre objects and newspaper cuttings. To the south is the beautiful square and early sixteenth-century church of Santo Domingo, the façade of which features a triple-arched portico covered in frescoes. West of the square, on the Calle Pavaneras, is the attractive sixteenth-century Casa de los Tiros, which has a modest museum and a collection of documents relating to Washington Irving; behind the building a maze of streets lined with Moorish houses and gardens climbs up to the Alhambra hill. The Calle Pavaneras leads west from the museum to the Plaza Isabel la Católica, an ugly modern square at the southern end of the turn-of-the-century Gran Vía de Colón (see page 211). Before reaching this square you will pass near the Casa de Vinos, a wine bar standing next to where the gate of the old Jewish quarter once was; the bar itself, very popular with students, has an excellent range of wines and a friendly atmosphere.

The Plaza Nueva, a few minutes' walk east from the Plaza Isabel La Católica, is surrounded by cheap hotels and has a number of open-air bars favoured largely by tourists. At the north-western corner of the square are the Bodegas Castañeda, a large and popular bar with a fascinating interior, a strong bohemian character and a variety of unusual cocktails. As you head east up the square you will pass on your left what is now the town's Law Court (originally the Chancellery). The building, one of the finest Renaissance structures in Granada, is in a majestic Italianate style and has a most elegant courtyard, perhaps designed by Diego de Siloe. Siloe was certainly responsible for the church of Santa Ana, a tall and stylish building dominating the eastern end of the square into which the Plaza Nueva leads, the Plaza Santa Ana. By now you have left modern commercial Granada and are suddenly back in a quiet part of town which has changed little since the time when it was admired for its picturesqueness by travellers of the Romantic era.

Behind the church of Santa Ana runs the fast-flowing stream of the Darro, which divides the Alhambra hill from that of the Albaicín. Walking up the delightful Carrera del Darro, you will pass first the extraordinary Moorish baths at No. 3 (see page 83) and then the Calle Zafra, on which stands an evocatively decayed fourteenth-century Moorish house built around a pool (this house, the Casa Zafra, is soon to be turned into a museum, but in the meantime the caretaker will be pleased to show you around). Just beyond this street is the elaborate classical plateresque façade of the Casa de Castril, a Renaissance house with a recently renovated interior displaying a selection of archaeological finds from the prehistoric to the Moorish period. The last street which you come to as you walk east along the Darro is the Cuesta del Chapiz, which climbs up to the Casa de Chapiz, a Moorish house which is now a centre for Moorish studies. East from here you leave the boundaries of the town and reach the gypsy cave district of Sacromonte, much visited by tourists on account of its appalling *flamenco* shows (see pages 141–2). Further to the east, in lonely isolation high above the narrow luxuriant valley of the Darro, is the austere seventeenth-century monastery of the Sacromonte, inside which is a small museum comprising a miscellaneous collection of documents and works of art, including an original letter by Pizarro, and an *Immaculate Conception* by Sánchez Cotán.

The quiet attractive heart of the Albaicín extends west from the Casa de Chapiz, and is an area covered in beautiful villas and gardens, all with superb views towards the Alhambra. The most renowned viewpoint is the terrace in front of the Church of St Nicolás, a place to which numerous people come at sunset; west from here is the fifteenth-century convent of Santa Isabel La Real, the church of which has a very fine gothic plateresque west portal and a particularly elaborate *mudéjar* ceiling (see page 93). For the *cruces de mayo* celebrations, held in the first week of May, the entire Albaicín hill is alight with candles. You can walk back to the lower town on the shop-lined Calderaria Nueva, where you will find the As Sirat, an atmospheric tea-room set up by one of the many Arab families who have moved to the Albaicín in recent years.

Incongruously tucked away behind the Plaza Isabel La Católica and the Gran Vía de Colón are the Royal Chapel and cathedral (see pages 94–8), around which are to be found an extensive pedestrian and shopping district incorporating the sixteenth-century Plaza de Bibarrambla and the neo-Moorish bazaar known as the Alcaicería (see page 82). The Alcaicería leads at its southern end into the Calle de los Reyes Católicos, on the other side of which is a narrow alley taking you to the Moorish Casa del Carbón (see page 82). The busy and unappealing Calle de los Reyes Católicos connects the Plaza Isabel La Católica with the Puerta Real to the west. Turn left at the latter square and you will reach a wide thoroughfare which splits into the Carrera de Genil and the Acera del Darro. Off the former is the eighteenth-century building now housing the Town Council (*Diputación*), attached to which is the Café Restaurante Chikito of Lorca and Falla fame (see page 213). The Casa Bar Enrique, on the Acera del Darro, is an old-fashioned establishment well known for its hams, cheeses, and stock of sweetish Alpujarra wine known as Vino de Costa.

The pleasant and narrow Calle de San Jerónimo runs north from the cathedral to the eighteenth-century Hospital de San Juan de Dios, passing by the shaded and intimate Plaza de la Universidad. Respectively to the west and east of San Juan de Dios are the monastery of San Jerónimo and the Hospital Real (now the main university building), two of the most majestic Renaissance buildings in Granada (see pages 95–6). Granada's Charterhouse, containing perhaps the most elaborate and dynamic baroque decoration in the whole of Spain, lies in the western outskirts of the town, a good twenty-five minutes' uphill walk from the Hospital Real (see page 120). As well as its baroque decorations, it has an elegant early sixteenth-century cloister and a large collection of seventeenth-century paintings, including many clumsy figurative works by Sánchez Cotán, who was a monk here.

The most popular excursion from Granada is up into the Sierra Nevada by way of the well-graded GR420; the road goes right to the summit of the Pico Veleta, though its last stretch is often closed because of snow; the spectacular descent down the other side into the Alpujarras is only practicable from July to September, and even so is slow and dangerous. The adventurous driver might also wish to ascend the Sierra Nevada on the beautiful but unasphalted Carretera de los Neveros, which begins to climb in earnest after the village of Monachil. If you lose heart at Monachil, you can always stop off at the Venta Bienvenido, an open-air inn on the outskirts of the village; here you will find outstanding home-made charcuterie, which you can wash down with the pleasant white wine from the adjoining village of Huétor Vega.

Those in search of places in and around Granada closely associated with García Lorca would do well to buy Ian Gibson's excellent, *En Granada, su Granada: Guía a la Granada de Federico García Lorca* (1989). The major Lorca site on the outskirts of Granada is the Huerta de San Vicente, which stands in miraculous rural isolation only a few minutes' walk away from the junction of the Calle de Las Recogidas and the vile Camino de La Ronda (see pages 223–4); the coaches parked in the nearby carpark need not worry you, as they have only brought passengers to the *flamenco* show held in the adjoining Jardines Neptuno. Further west, in the heart of the *vega*, are Lorca's childhood villages of Fuentevacqueros and Valderrubio, both of which are accessible by a bus which you can catch outside Granada railway station (see pages 211–14). The commemorative park at

Víznar, marking the spot where Lorca was probably assassinated, is best reached by taxi (see pages 225–6). [3F]

GRAZALEMA, the subject of Pitt-Rivers's classic study, *People of the Sierra* (1954), is today one of the most visited villages in the Serranía de Ronda. Stretched in a mountain fold against a background of picturesquely protruding rocks, Grazalema is a beautiful if perhaps over-prettified place. The lower road into the village (the C344 from Arcos de la Frontera) passes the main local workshop specializing in blankets, an industry which has been practised here since Arab times; there is a small museum attached to the building. The road continues into the pleasant main square, from where you can walk up the Calle Mateus Gago to the prominently positioned eighteenth-century chapel of San José. A viewing balcony is near the chapel, though in many ways the village is best seen from below. The village's swimming-pool, which you reach by continuing to drive along the lower road until you leave the village, has an especially good view of Grazalema, and indeed must have one of the finest situations of any pool in Andalusia.

Just above the village there is a camping site, the office of which will provide you with information about walks and horse-treks in the recently-created National Park of Grazalema. The drive through Zahara along the CA531 goes through particularly impressive scenery. Before reaching the spectacular pass of Las Palomas, you will pass on the left-hand side of the road the entrance to a forest of *pinsapos*, majestic pyramid-shaped pines of a type not found elsewhere in Europe (see page 4); to visit the forest, special permission is required beforehand from the Dirección Provincial de la Agencia de Medio Ambiente, Avenida Ana de Virgen, 3-30, 11009 Cádiz (tel: 274594/274629). After crossing the pass, the road descends in dramatic fashion to the village of Zahara, which hangs underneath a noble outcrop of rock. The tiny village main square has a baroque church and an excellent viewing-balcony; at the very top of the rock is the single remaining tower of a castle built by the Romans and renovated by the Arabs.

The C3331 south from Grazalema passes next to Benaocaz, where there is a small museum of local archaeology and ethnography. Eight winding kilometres further on is Ubrique, famous for the leather industry which the Moors established here. [4D]

GUADIX has the strangest appearance of all the towns of Andalusia. The old town, apparently covered in an orange-red dust, stands out against a background of rows of tufa pinnacles formed by savage erosion; in the far distance rise the snowcapped peaks of the Sierra Nevada. The prosperous Roman colony which existed here was converted to catholicism by St Torquatus and became one of the earliest and most important Visigothic bishoprics in Spain; the subsequent Moorish occupation lasted until 1489. Work was begun on the magnificent cathedral in 1510, on the site of the former mosque; it was not completed until 1796. The dark, late gothic interior was significantly altered by Diego de Siloe (see page 97), who also gave it its polygonal apse and the chapel of San Torcuato to the left of the chancel. Among the baroque additions are the fine choir and pulpit, and the west façade, which with its undulating cornices and rich plastic decoration is one of the most dynamic of any Spanish cathedral. In front of the cathedral is the arcaded Renaissance Plaza Mayor, which was largely rebuilt after the Civil War of 1936–9. A street at the far end of the square from the cathedral leads up to the whitewashed Renaissance palace of Peñaflor, from which projects a charming wooden balcony. Below the palace a street descends to the church of Santiago, notable for its classical plateresque southern portal. The door of the building attached to the Peñaflor palace takes you inside a nineteenth-century seminary, where arrows will guide you upstairs and outside into the courtyard of the fifteenth-century Moorish castle or Alcazaba. The courtyard is parched and overgrown and is used as a squash court by pupils from the seminary. From the heavily restored battlements there is an excellent view of Guadix's northern outskirts, where dwellings – similar to those where gnomes live in fairy-tale illustrations – have been scooped out of the picturesquely shaped mounds, with tall white chimney-stacks pushing through the ground above. This is still a notorious gypsy district, and tourists can expect considerable attention from the local children. Guadix and the neighbouring village of Purullena are famous for ceramics, and stalls selling these line the main road through the latter. At Guadix itself, on the Calle San Miguel, which runs between the Alcazaba and the cave district, an unpromising modern-looking shop called Bañart sells, together with toilet seats and bathroom accessories, the increasingly rare traditional local piece known variously as the *jarra accituna* or the *jarra de los pajaricos*. This earthenware urn-like object, the lid of which is usually crowned by a hen, has an exceptionally intricate eighteenth-century design and is one of the finest examples of the continuing baroque tradition in Andalusian folk art. [3G]

HUELVA: A Phoenician settlement, and later the Roman colony of Onuba, Huelva has a long history but a largely modern appearance, the town having been extensively destroyed in the Lisbon earthquake of 1755. The ugliest and least interesting of Andalusia's provincial capitals, Huelva is a heavily industrialized town with a flourishing port, which is used both by fishing fleets and by boats exporting metals from the Río Tinto mines; the shrimps from Huelva are famous throughout Spain, and increasingly expensive.

One of the few pre-nineteenth-century buildings to have survived in Huelva is the Convent of the Merced, which was founded in 1605; its church, dating mainly from the eighteenth century, has served as the town's cathedral since 1853, and is notable for its spacious and dazzlingly white interior. Following the Paseo Independencia east from the cathedral, you reach after a ten-minute walk the heart of turn-of-the-century Huelva, a dirty and cramped area, with numerous seedy bars, particularly near the port. Many of the old buildings have been pulled down in recent years, but several splendid monuments remain, including the imposing Gran Teatro (1923) on the Calle Vázquez López, the art-nouveau Clínica Sanz de Frutos (1911) at 26 Calle Rico, and the neo-Moorish railway station (1880) at the eastern end of the town. South from the station is the town's greatest architectural monument, the now disused Río Tinto pier of 1874, an impressive if rather decayed ironwork construction designed by the British engineer George Barclay Bruce.

The main thoroughfare running through the northern half of the town centre is the Avenida Martín Alonso Pinzón, which is lined with neo-fascist arcading. This avenue leads north into the Alameda Sandheim and into a quiet residential area. The Provincial Museum of Huelva is situated off the Alameda, and occupies a pleasant modern building in the middle of a small shaded garden. This excellently arranged museum is particularly interesting for its ground-floor archaeological section, which features fascinating finds from the Río Tinto mines; the fine arts section on the floor above has a mainly mediocre collection of paintings dating from the sixteenth to the twentieth centuries. The best of the modern works are by the local painter Daniel Vázquez Díaz (1882–1969), who is best known for his murals in the nearby monastery of La Rábida (see PALOS DE LA FRONTERA); one of his Cézanne-inspired canvases in the museum is a portrait of his poet friend Juan Ramón Jiménez (see MOGUER).

On a small hill just to the north of the museum is a small residential district known variously as the 'Barrio Obrero' or the 'Barrio Ingles'. Built by the British in the early years of this century for their employees in the Río Tinto mines, the architecture of this suburb is unmistakably surburban English, but with the difference that these incongruously situated houses have been painted in brilliant primary colours. Many of the Río Tinto employees had half-timbered bungalows at the nearby coastal resort of Punta Umbría, which lies to the south of Huelva on the western side of the Odiel; this spacious high-rise resort, now the most popular on the Huelva coast, has a district known as the Punta de los Ingleses, where a handful of these British-built bungalows still survive.

Three kilometres to the north of Huelva, on the road towards Gibraleón, is the heavily restored Sanctuary of Nuestra Señora de la Cinta, to which a pilgrimage is made every year on 8 September. One of the tile decorations inside the church represents Christopher Columbus, who is supposed to have taken part in one of these pilgrimages. On the southern outskirts of Huelva, at the confluence of the estuaries of the rivers Odiel and Tinto, stands an enormous and ungainly statue of Columbus, which was given as a gift to the town in 1929 by its author, an American sculptress called Whitney. From here it is but a short drive to the two main Andalusian sites associated with Columbus, the Monastery of La Rábida and PALOS DE LA FRONTERA. [3A]

HUÉRCAL-OVERA, the main town in the far eastern corner of Andalusia, is a place of little charm in the middle of a dusty landscape speckled with orchards and ugly modern farm buildings. The Holy Week processions of the town enjoy a certain fame for their exuberance and for the beauty of their processional images, carved by artists of the Granada school. There is also a castle here of such cube-like simplicity that it resembles a child's building block. A far more interesting castle is to be found in the village of Cuevas del Almanzora, which stands in an eroded landscape about twenty kilometres to the south: the building was put up in 1507 to protect the village from pirate attacks. During the *morisco* uprising of 1568–71, the *morisco* leader El Maleh made an unsuccessful attempt to besiege it; when the *moriscos* were eventually expelled from Granada by Philip II, many stopped off here on their journey to Castile.

Those interested in the history of nuclear disasters could head from Cuevas east to Palomares (see page 43), while pottery enthusiasts could go south to Vera. One of Vera's few attractive buildings, a late eighteenth-century warehouse, was recently pulled down to make way for a modern bank (the Banco Central), and the town's traditional earthenware of elegant Phoenician and Arab design is becoming increasingly difficult to find: mediocre examples of the engagingly simple local jugs and pitchers can be bought from a man known as Bernardino, who lives at 11 Calle Alfarería and is the son of a well-known potter awarded a medal by King Juan Carlos. The ugly industrial town of Albox, eighteen kilometres west of Huércal-Overa, is also celebrated for its pottery industries, its traditional crudely coloured and glazed ceramics being similar to those of NÍJAR. The most interesting monument nearby is the austere eighteenth-century sanctuary of Nuestra Señora de la Asunción, twenty-one kilometres to the north of Albox, high up on the impressively barren Sierra de las Estancias. The place, marking a spot where the Virgin made yet another of her miraculous appearances, is popular with Sunday excursionists, and there is a bar and restaurant at the side of the building. [3J]

HUÉSCAR, at the northern edge of an eroded plateau and immediately below the parched southern foothills of the Sierra de Segura, is one of the most isolated towns in Granada province. The sixteenth-century collegiate church in the town centre is an enormous and impressive structure, partially designed by the great Renaissance architects Alonso de Covarrubias and Diego de Siloe (see page 97) and brought to completion in 1599 under the supervision of Andrés de Vandelvira (see page 98).

The bizarre desert-like landscape south of Huéscar turns at sunset into an expanse of purples, oranges, reds, and lurid yellows. It is intercut with dried-up gorges lined at the bottom with citrus trees. Much of the landscape is pock-marked with caves, and on the southern outskirts of the village of Galera, seven and a half kilometres to the south of Huéscar on the C3329, there is a picturesque district of cave dwellings; a group of hill-top caves near these forms the important Iberian necropolis of Tútugi, dating from the fifth to the third century BC: some of the tombs have paintings representing battle and hunting scenes, but a local guide is needed to help you find these. A collection of Roman stones found in the area has been assembled in Galera's Town Hall. [2H]

JAÉN, surrounded by an undulating expanse of olive trees and backed by mountains, rises steeply up the slopes of a hill, crowned by a massive cathedral. The capital of the Spanish province with the largest number of olive trees, Jaén has lived off its olive oil production since Roman times, a period when it also knew prosperity through silver-mining. Under the Moors, the town became the centre of a small Moorish principality and acquired the name of 'Geen' or 'caravan route', a reference to the place's importance as a bridge between Castile and Andalusia. Ferdinand III captured the town in 1246, and its displaced Moorish ruler, Ibn Nasr, went to Granada to found the Nasrid dynasty (see page 81). Much of the old town, including its walls, has now been destroyed, and in its stead has risen a seedy modern town, poor, parochial and stiflingly dull at night. Tourists come here mainly to see its cathedral or to stay in the *parador* above the town, but Jaén has a number of other attractions that deserve to be better known.

The Paseo de la Estación, the grand avenue which climbs up the hill from the railway station to the town centre, represents Jaén's attempt to imitate a major city such as Madrid. Half-way up, on the right-hand side of the road, is a large early twentieth-century building into which has been incorporated the west portal of the destroyed church of San Miguel. The museum's little-visited collections are paltry in comparison with the grandeur of the building in which they are housed. The archaeological section, which takes up the ground floor, contains what is undoubtedly the museum's most outstanding treasure, a group of Iberian sculptures discovered in 1975 at Obulco, a site on the outskirts of Porcuna (see BUJALANCE): particularly exciting are the stones of fighting warriors, carved with great boldness and a feeling for form which is quite modern. In the first floor rooms are displayed the museum's paintings, which are mainly of the nineteenth and early twentieth centuries. For the lover of kitsch and of absurd, high-flown academic canvases, these rooms make for a most entertaining experience. The prize for the most absurd work must surely go to Moreno Carbonero's *Don Quixote and the Windmills*, a vast canvas dominated by a tumbling horse violently ejecting a skeletal Don Quixote. The other paintings include a large proportion of female nudes bordering on soft pornography, for instance a portrait of the actress Montserrat Güell, painted by a former director of the Prado, Sotomayor.

Leaving the museum and continuing uphill on the Paseo de la Estación, you pass by a twentieth-century sculptural group as monumentally awful as are many of the works in the museum: known as the Monument of the Battles, it commemorates the battles of both Las Navas de Tolosa (see LA CAROLINA) and BAILÉN. At the far end of the Avenida is Jaén's ugly main square, the Plaza de la Constitución, but, further uphill, the town begins to improve somewhat. In between the square and the cathedral are three fine palaces: the sixteenth-century Palacio de los Vilches on the Plaza de los Vilches, the seventeenth-century Palacio de los Vélez on the Calle Dr Ramón y Cajal, and the seventeenth-century Town Hall on the Plaza de San Francisco. This latter building, featuring an elegant arcaded courtyard, looks obliquely across its square towards the northern end of the cathedral. Attached to this side of the cathedral is the late eighteenth-century church of the Sagrario, which has a satisfyingly simple oval interior designed by Spain's leading neo-classical architect, Ventura Rodriguez (see also MONTEFRÍO). The cathedral itself is on the site of the town's mosque, which was transformed into a place of Christian worship in the time of Ferdinand III. In the late fifteenth century work was started on a new cathedral, but the walls that were put up soon showed signs of cracking and were pulled down. The present structure, begun in 1548 under the supervision of the great Andrés de Vandelvira (see page 98), was not completed until the end of the eighteenth century. The most striking feature of the exterior is its baroque west façade of 1734, articulated by a giant order of columns and flanked by towers: this majestic façade sensibly turns its back on the ugly lower town of Jaén, and looks up to the rugged castle hill. The cathedral's dark and heavy interior largely impresses more through size than detail. The Renaissance structure has suffered from later additions, though you can see Vandelvira's style at its purest and most harmonious in the barrel-vaulted Sacristy and adjoining Chapterhouse. Of the cathedral's furnishings, special mention must be made of the outstandingly lively and dynamic late baroque carvings in the choir, many of which are of gruesome martyrdoms. The Calle Maestra and its continuation, the Calle Martínez Molina, lead north from the cathedral into what remains of the old town of Jaén, and passes near the town's one surviving gate, the Puerta de San Lorenzo (on the Calle de los Almendros Aguilar). Heading off from the Calle Martínez Molina is the Calle Cañion, down which you will see a plaque recording the site of the parish church of San Pedro, where the guitarist Andrés Segovia was baptized on 24 March 1893; further on is the sixteenth-century convent of Santa Clara, with a west façade decorated with amusing if slightly unsophisticated classical carvings. A group of palms on the small Plaza de las Mujeres, on the northern end of the Calle Martínez Molina, shades the façade of the palace of Fernando Torres y Portugal. The building has recently been converted into a pleasantly laid out museum of popular crafts and 'international naïve art'. But its greatest attraction is the baths underneath it, which were discovered in 1914 and are shown to you by one of the museum's guides; these baths, the most extensive surviving ones in Spain, are traditionally thought to be the place where the Moorish King Alí was killed by his Moorish enemies in the eleventh century. An underground passage connects the baths with the Moorish palace over which was built the monastery of Santo Domingo. The monastery, founded in 1392, later became a university and a seat of the Inquisition; it has an excellently preserved sixteenth-century courtyard, and a church with a façade designed by Vandelvira. The nearby gothic church of the Magdalena, at the northernmost end of the town, is Jaén's oldest church. It is erected over a mosque, the minaret of which forms part of its bell tower. The stagnant pool in the church's romantically overgrown courtyard is also Moorish, and was used for ritual ablutions.

Ascending the narrow and pretty Calle Santíssima Trinidad, you will reach the Bar Sobrino Bigotes, in front of which is a path climbing steeply through rough and wooded terrain up to the town's castle. The path, though beautiful, is arduous and difficult to follow, and you might well prefer to go up to the castle by way of the much longer road to it. The thirteenth-century castle, built by Ibn Nasr, has one of the most commanding positions of all the many castles in Andalusia. A drastically renovated part of it now houses the *parador* where President Charles de Gaulle wrote part of his memoirs. A path runs beside the ruined section of the castle and leads eventually to a spectacular viewpoint marked by a large cross: far, far below is the cathedral, standing up like a giant above its diminutive surroundings.

Eight kilometres to the east of Jaén is the pleasant village of La Guardia de Jaén, which has an important necropolis. At the top of the village are the ruins of a Moorish castle dating back to the eighth century, and the parish church of the Asunción built by Vandelvira. The church was originally that of the monastery of Santo Domingo, the ruins of which lie alongside it and include the arcading and central fountain of its Renaissance cloister. [2F]

JEREZ DE LA FRONTERA, situated in the middle of flat agricultural country, probably dates back to Phoenician times. Known to the Romans as Xeres, this name was corrupted to Sherrish by the Moors, who stayed in the town until 1264; as with many other places in this part of Andalusia, Jerez received the name 'de la Frontera' around 1379 because it marked the eastern frontier of the Moorish Kingdom of Granada. The fortified wines of the area, already famous in the Middle Ages, were first exported to England in the late fifteenth century. Thereafter numerous English and foreign merchants settled here, many, such as the Domecqs, becoming members of the Spanish aristocracy; the father of the English art critic John Ruskin was involved in the sherry trade in the early nineteenth century, and through this connection his son met the first great love of his life, Adèle Domecq. The presence in Jerez of these so-called 'sherry barons' gave the place a character totally unlike that of anywhere else in Andalusia: snobbish, aloof and with people apeing the social manners of the English. To most Andalusians Jerez is essentially the home of the *señorito* or 'toff'.

Jerez is in fact a town of particularly sharp contrasts, and even in the Romantic period travellers commented on the contrast between the magnificence of its palaces and the dirt and squalor of many of its streets. Today it is a town with extensive and ugly modern development, spacious and verdant residential districts that could be in Florida, a ramshackle and run-down old part, and one of the most famous and intact of all of Andalusia's gypsy quarters. At the very centre of the town is the Plaza del Arenal, around which are to be found the town's most important monuments. To the south of the square, at the end of the Calle San Miguel, is the church of San Miguel, a building begun in an Isabelline gothic style and with a splendidly ornate late seventeenth-century tower attached to the west façade. The much restored citadel of Alcázar, dating back to the time of the Almohads, rises up on a mound immediately to the west of the Plaza del Arenal; its most interesting feature is on its northern side, a small and well-preserved mosque which was later made the chapel of Santa María la Real. Immediately below the chapel to the north is the former collegiate church of San Salvador (now the town's cathedral), a bizarre building dating from the eighteenth century but in a gothic style and with Renaissance decorative features. Through an arch on the northern side of the Plaza del Arenal is a tiny passage on which is situated the lively Bar Juanito, renowned for its *tapas*. Nearby is the quiet and charming Plaza de la Asunción, dominated by the simple fifteenth-century church of San Dionisio, notable for its elegant gothic-*mudéjar* bell-tower. The Calle Calvo Sotelo heads from here to the town's most beautiful Renaissance structure, the former Town Hall, now an archaeological museum.

The least spoilt part of old Jerez stretches from north of the cathedral up to the gypsy quarter of Santiago. It is an area full of attractive churches and elegant palaces crammed into a maze of tiny streets and squares, some with a semi-abandoned look. Jerez, with its large gypsy population, is a famed centre for *flamenco*, and in the Palacio Remartín on the Plaza San Juan is the Fundación Andaluza de Flamenco, Andalusia's major centre for the study and promotion of this music; the centre organizes festivals and conferences, and puts on regular exhibitions with material culled from its extensive archive. The Santiago quarter is a few minutes' walk from here, and has as its principal attraction the late fifteenth-century church of Santiago, Jerez's best preserved gothic building. It says much for the character of Jerez that this lively if slightly seedy district adjoins an area of grand late nineteenth-century villas grouped around an old-fashioned zoo.

The busy Calle Largas heads north-west from the Plaza del Arenal through the commercial heart of Jerez. At the junction of the Calle Santa María is the Café Cena Cirullo, a splendid turn-of-the-century building that was once a celebrated meeting-place. Continuing further along the Calle Larga, you will eventually reach the Plaza Cristina, on which is the grand eighteenth-century palace built by the Domecq family, a statue to one of whose members is to be found immediately in front of it. Shortly beyond the palace begins Jerez's most elegant residential district, in the middle of which are two of the town's most popular attractions, a Museum of Clocks (the Museo de Relojes 'La Atalaya') and the Royal Andalusian Equestrian School, housed in an eighteenth-century building. Jerez is as famous for its horses as it is for its wines and *flamenco*, and the school puts on daily horse-shows with riders dressed in eighteenth-century costume.

The main *bodegas* in Jerez are all in the centre of the town, and can be visited every weekday from 10.30 to 1.30; the Gonzalez Byass *bodega* is particularly interesting on account of its nineteenth-century ironwork structure, designed by Eiffel of Eiffel Tower fame. Every year in September, the wine harvest is celebrated by the crushing of grapes on the steps in front of the cathedral. This festival is as phoney as the famous horse-fair in June is élitist.

Five kilometres south-east of the town on the C440 to Medina Sidonia is the Charterhouse of Jerez, well worth seeing if only for its sumptuous exterior and verdant surroundings (see page 115). [4C]

JIMENA DE LA FRONTERA is an attractive hill village of Roman origin which is gradually being taken over by the British, many of whom work and do their shopping in nearby Gibraltar. Looming over the village is its large and ruined Moorish castle, which entered the possession of the Dukes of Medina Sidonia after being captured by the Christians in 1434. The road north from Jimena to Arcos goes through wild and mountainous country densely covered with oaks and cork trees. After fourteen kilometres a dust track to the left climbs up the Puerto de la Yegua, near the top of which is an isolated farm; from here it is about half an hour's walk through the trees and undergrowth to the fascinating rock shelter of Loza Alta (see page 55). Without the services of a local guide this shelter is difficult to find.

Following the C331 south from Jimena in the direction of Gibraltar, you will reach after twenty-two kilometres a turning to the right which leads steeply up to the extraordinary hill village of Castellar de la Frontera. This tiny place is entirely encased in its well-preserved fortress of Moorish origin. Captured by the Christians in 1434, the village was in such a primitive state by the 1970s that it was abandoned, its inhabitants being moved into the specially built Nuevo Castellar on the Gibraltar road. German hippies were later attracted to the place for the same reasons that forced its inhabitants to leave it: some of these Germans constructed ramshackle huts around the walls, and others took over the houses inside; soon graffiti began appearing in Spanish with the words, 'German drug-addicted swine out.' The village is exceedingly picturesque, but claustrophobic and rather sinister. From the balcony of its German-run bar there is a spectacular view towards Gibraltar. Following the recent draining of the artificial lake below, the corpses of two Germans were found, attached to each other by rope. [5D]

LACALAHORRA is an austere village under the grey shingle slopes of the Sierra Nevada. Its celebrated castle (see page 100), sitting heavily on a grey conical mound above the village, is excellently preserved and well worth making a long journey to see. The building, though uninhabited for many years, belongs to the Duke of Infantado, and is officially open only on Wednesdays, from 10–1, and 4–6; should you come here on any other day, the staff at the Town Hall will help you locate the caretaker, who might grudgingly climb up to the castle with you to open its gates. Begun in 1509 by order of a member of the powerful Mendoza family, it was completed only four years later. A Spanish architect, L. Vázquez, supervised the overall construction, but a variety of Italian architects, sculptors and craftsmen (including the Genoese M. Carlone) were employed to carry out the interior. The exterior, a square block flanked by round towers crowned by what appear to be observatory domes, is impressively stark and not unlike one of the neo-classical futuristic fantasies of the French architect Ledoux. The delicately arcaded and exquisitely ornamented courtyard inside – one of the earliest examples in Spain of the Italian Renaissance style – could hardly be more different in character to the exterior. Plants and flowers now decorate its staircase, but the rest of the interior is empty; you experience a certain poignancy and a child-like sense of discovery as you wander on your own through its bare rooms and up into its turrets. [3G]

LA CAROLINA, set back slightly from the main Madrid to Córdoba road, was the most important of the foreign colonies founded in 1768 by Charles III and his minister Pablo de Olavide (see page 22–3). It is attractively laid out on a regular grid plan, and has a neo-classical parish church adjoining the elegant palace where Olavide lived until his fall from favour in 1775.

Just before reaching the small village of Las Navas de Tolosa, four kilometres to the north of La Carolina on the Madrid road, you will see on the left-hand side of the road an unappealing modern memorial commemorating the celebrated battle which took place here on 16 July 1212 (see page 80). Represented in the over life-sized sculptural group by Antonio González Orea are Alfonso VIII of Castile, Pedro II of Aragón, Sancho VII the Strong of Navarre, Don López de Haro, and the Archbishop of Toledo, Don Rodrigo Jiménez de Rada, all of whom participated in this decisive victory over the Moors; the bronze figure in front of them is that of a shepherd who guided them across the well-guarded Sierra Morena. The surviving Moors supposedly escaped through the beautiful pass to the north of here, which henceforth came to be known as the Pass of Despeñaperros ('overthrow of the dogs'; see pages 5–6 and 20). [1F]

LANJARÓN, a spa town attached to the southern slopes of the Sierra Nevada, is famous for its mineral water, which is drunk all over Spain; impressively perched on a rock directly in front of the village is a ruined castle. At Dúrcal, a village sixteen kilometres to the north on the road to Granada, a steep dust track descends into a delightful green and wooded valley which forms a striking contrast to the arid mountains rising above it. There are various old mills here, one of which, the Molino de Lecrín, is the headquarters of the Granada Gastronomic Society, and has an outstanding restaurant specializing in traditional Granadine food. [4G]

LAUJAR DE ANDARAX: The eastern half of the Alpujarras is much less spoilt than the western half (see ORGIVA), but has a more barren landscape and less obviously attractive towns and villages. Of these

Laujar is one of the largest and most interesting. On the Plaza Mayor is an elegant late eighteenth-century Town Hall comprising three superimposed arcades. Next to this is one of the town's many charming fountains, put up during the reign of Charles III. The village looks south to the stark and arid range of the Sierra de Gádor, but lies on the slopes of the Sierra Nevada, which is densely forested in its upper reaches. On the western outskirts of the town is a steeply ascending asphalted road climbing up the latter range; the views are impressive, and there are a number of footpaths leading off into the forest. On the other side of the town is a popular picnic spot next to the shaded source of the River Andarax. [4G]

LEBRIJA, in the middle of hilly agricultural landscape, was founded by the Turdetanians, who left here many traces of their civilization: the National Archaeological Museum in Madrid has various figurines and exquisite gold candelabra from this area. Under the Romans Lebrija was fortified and became an important centre of pilgrimage, because of the cult of Venus and Bacchus being celebrated here. Present-day Lebrija is a place not of great beauty but of considerable personality. It is one of the main Andalusian centres of *flamenco*, and every year in July there is held here one of the best of the region's *flamenco* festivals, the *Caracol* (see pages 142–3). Of the local *flamenco* dynasties, the leading one is the Peña family, whose members include the singers La Perrata, El Perrate, and El Lebrijano (one of the most popular *flamenco* singers of today), and the guitarists Pedro Peña and Pedro Bacán. Another traditional speciality of the town is its earthenware, most notably its pitchers (*cántaros*), gazpacho bowls (*dornillos*) and water-carrying jugs with spout and handle (*botijos*). The main workshop of the town is that of Juan López Barragán in the Calle Luis Recogado. López Barragán, whose family have been potters as far back as he can remember, will happily give you a demonstration at his wheel. You can also buy from him earthenware at exceptionally cheap prices: the shape of the pitchers has remained unchanged since Phoenician times.

The parish church of Lebrija, Santa María de la Oliva, is also well worth a visit, and is indeed one of the outstanding churches of Seville province. Situated on top of a hill in the prettiest and oldest part of the town, the church was an Almohad mosque consecrated by the

Christians in 1249. The west end of the church is still clearly recognizable as a mosque, and is like a miniature version of Córdoba's Mezquita, with exquisite Moorish decoration in its various domes. The chancel and crossing were a sixteenth-century addition, but have elaborate star-vaulting of Moorish character. The superb high altar of 1643 was the first major commission of Alonso Cano (see page 112) and is notable for the life-like sculptures that he executed for it. The bell-tower dates from the eighteenth century and is one of many in Andalusia inspired by the Giralda in Seville. [4C]

LINARES: In this large and ugly town known for its car manufactories and copper and lead mines, the guitarist Andrés Segovia was born in 1894 and the bull-fighter Manolete was killed in 1947. The parish church of Santa María la Mayor was begun in the twelfth century and has Renaissance elements designed by the great local architect Andrés de Vandelvira (see ÚBEDA). There is a small archaeological museum which includes finds from the nearby Roman colony at Cástulo. But the main attraction of the town is the superbly ornate late baroque frontispiece of the former Hospital of San Juan de Dios (now the Palace of Justice). [2F]

LOJA, lying along a narrow stretch of the fertile Genil valley, was a Moorish town until 1486. Its ninth-century castle, once one of the most important Moorish fortifications in Spain, survives now in a most fragmentary state, and is largely hidden by the surrounding modern development. The town is best looked at from below, on the other side of the Genil. From this angle it is seen rising above fields, its buildings, and even the peeping battlements of its castle, framed against a background of barren peaks. Before crossing the Genil you should follow the river east until you reach, just beyond the outskirts of the town, a point where it runs in cataracts down a small gorge. This pleasant spot, known inappropriately as Los Infiernos, has a shaded picnic area with benches. The hamlet of Ríofrío, also by a shaded stretch of the Genil, lies seven kilometres to the west of Loja and is a popular stopping-off place for drivers coming to and from Granada; there are good bars and restaurants where you can eat trout from the local trout farm. [3F]

LORA DEL RÍO is a lively but unattractive market town with a pleasantly decrepit Town Hall (1730) in an extravagant baroque style; on the nearby Calle Federico García Lorca is another interesting early eighteenth-century building, the Casa de los Leones. The modest ruins of the Roman settlement of Arva lie ten kilometres to the west of the town, off the C341 to Seville. More extensive, and beautifully situated, are the remarkable Roman ruins of Mulva (see page 61), accessible only by a poor and unasphalted eight-kilometre stretch of road from Villanueva del Río y Minas, a village nine kilometres further along the C431 from Arva. [2C]

LUCENA, situated among hills covered in vines and olive trees, is an ugly small town with a centre crowded with modern apartment blocks. However, a stop here is rewarded by a visit to the parish church of San Mateo, where the Sagrario chapel, off the left aisle, is one of the exquisitely ornate masterpieces of the Andalusian baroque. The author of this chapel is anonymous, but it is appropriate that there should have been born in this town, in 1669, one of the most extravagant of Spain's baroque architects, Hurtado Izquierdo, who died at nearby PRIEGO DE CÓRDOBA (see page 120). Near the church are the dismal ruins of the castle where the unfortunate Boabdil – the last Moorish ruler in Spain – was briefly imprisoned by Isabel La Católica in 1483.

An attractive drive along the C334 leads to the white village of Rute, overlooking the reservoir of Iznájar. The village is known for its dry and sweet anis. The poet Rafael Alberti (see page 215) spent much time in Rute in the 1920s, staying in the house of his brother-in-law and producing a volume of verse entitled *Cuaderno de Rute* ('Rute Notebook'). [3E]

MÁLAGA: Founded by the Phoenicians, a bishopric in the sixth century and a flourishing town under the Moors, Málaga was captured by the Catholic monarchs in 1487 and subjected to terrible reprisals. The town's economy, badly affected by the Christian conquest, was further damaged by the expulsion of the *moriscos* after 1568; it was not to recover until the eighteenth century. With its beautiful position between mountains and the sea, its balmy climate, and its surrounding sub-tropical vegetation, Málaga developed in the early nineteenth century into a thriving wintering resort, especially popular with the English. The poet García Lorca once described Málaga as his favourite town in Andalusia, but the town was badly damaged in the Civil War. In recent years it has suffered even more under the hands of town-planners, who continue to this day to destroy most of the old and attractive parts of the town. The capital of the Costa del Sol, with an international airport famed for its cheap package flights, Málaga today overflows with tourists. The tolerance shown towards them by the exceptionally open and friendly people of Málaga is quite remarkable.

The town is divided in two by the seasonal torrent of the Guadalmedina, which in the summer months has a particularly unappealing aspect. The broad Avenida de Andalucía, lined with huge modern blocks, runs through the western part of town, slicing in half the district of El Perchel, which used to be the centre of Málaga's *flamenco* culture. The rest of this once delightful, ramshackle district, is slowly being pulled down, the most attractive of its remaining old and dilapidated streets being those in its northern half. At the western end of the Avenida de Andalucía are modern gardens containing the first monument erected in Spain (in 1978) to Málaga's most famous son,

303

Pablo Picasso, who was born here in 1881; next to this modest work has recently been placed an exceptionally energetic semi-abstract monument to Picasso by Ortiz Berrocal.

The continuation of the Avenida de Andalucía on the eastern side of the Guadalmedina is the shaded Alameda, an elegant promenade laid out in the nineteenth century, some of the trees being planted by the English consul William Mark (see pages 183–4). Near the western end of the Alameda, at the junction of the Calle Comisa, is one of Málaga's few remaining old bars, the dirty, dimly lit Casa Guardia, founded in 1840 and comprising a long narrow room lined with barrels; this is an excellent place to try Málaga's famous sweet wines (see page 173). The commercial district to the north of here is pleasantly animated and has numerous interesting nineteenth-century buildings, such as the neo-Moorish market on the Calle Atarazanas. A lone seventeenth-century survival on the Pasillo de Santa Isabel, overlooking the Guadalmedina, is the Mesón de la Victoria, a charming building housing what is perhaps Málaga's most enjoyable museum, the Museum of Popular Arts and Traditions.

At the very heart of commercial Málaga is the Plaza de la Constitución, which has a shopping arcade known as the Pasaje Chinitas; in the middle of this is a clothes shop with a plaque marking the site of the Café Chinitas, which was frequented by bull-fighters and singers, and commemorated in a poem by García Lorca. East of the square, you come to what is left of medieval and Renaissance Málaga, the principal monument being the cathedral, the oldest part of which is the Sagrario chapel on its northern side. The chapel, erected after 1487 on the site of a mosque, served as the town's cathedral until 1588; it has an Isabelline plateresque north portal and an exuberant Renaissance high altar in gilded wood. The present cathedral, begun in 1528, has an oppressively marbled interior of gothic proportions but classical detailing. Opposite the cathedral's heavy late baroque façade, completed in 1783, is the late eighteenth-century Archbishop's Palace, inside which is the gloomy Museo Diocesano with numerous old master paintings of dubious attribution, and a series of modern works in quite execrable taste.

Continuing east from the cathedral, you will soon reach the hill supporting the Moorish Alcazaba or citadel, at the foot of which is a Roman theatre in a sadly neglected condition. The rebuilt Alcazaba, dating back to the Umayyad period, has beautiful views, pools, luxuriant terraces and an archaeological museum featuring mainly Moorish finds. On the high and verdant hill to the east of the Alcazaba rises the equally much-restored Moorish castle of Gibralfaro, immediately below which is the town's modern *parador*.

A few minutes' walk north of the Roman theatre is the Museum of Fine Arts, housed in a delightful early sixteenth-century building combining *mudéjar* and Renaissance elements. The old master works on display here are not nearly as memorable as the nineteenth-century paintings, which will be much appreciated by lovers of academic kitsch; particularly striking is Enrique Simonet y Lombard's '. . . Y *tenía corazón*' ('. . . And she had a heart'), which portrays in morbid detail a doctor holding up the heart of a beautiful young girl, on whom he has just performed an autopsy. There are also some fantastical views of Granada by the Granadine painter Antonio Muñoz Degrain, best known as Picasso's earliest master. Picasso, represented here by some slight works executed when he was only fourteen, was born at 15 Plaza de la Merced, just to the north of the museum. His birthplace, marked by a plaque, forms part of an elegant late nineteenth-century terrace, the only old survival of a dismally altered square. Near the square the long Calle de la Victoria leads to the Plaza Victoria, beyond which is the Sanctuary of Nuestra Señora de la Victoria. This church, begun in 1487 on the site where the Catholic monarchs installed themelves during the siege of that year, was largely remodelled in the baroque period and has as its principal attraction a *camarín*, or small chapel, with exquisitely elaborate and joyful late baroque ornamentation. Near the Plaza Victoria, on the Calle Puerto Parejo, is the Bar Los Chulitos, which is renowned for its excellent fried fish and seafood.

The continuation of the Alameda to the east is the Paseo del Parque, which runs among trees and grass in between the town's port and the Alcazaba hill. The most interesting of the buildings on its northern side is the large neo-classical customs house. The town's bull-ring stands at the Paseo's eastern end, and near this is the English cemetery, now hemmed in by modern development (see page 183–4). An 11 bus from the Paseo will take you east to Málaga's resort district of Pedregalejo, famed for its seafood restaurants, nightlife and fashionable bars such as the Juan Sebastián Bar (a place reputedly popular with musicians!). Twelve kilometres further east along the much developed coastal road is Rincón de la Victoria, on the upper slopes of which is the Cueva del Tesoro, where paleolithic paintings have been found.

Málaga's airport is on the western side of the town, near the exclusive residential district of Churriana. Churriana boasts one of Andalusia's finest gardens, El Retiro. Laid out in the eighteenth century with pools and classical statuary, the garden is overgrown with sub-tropical vegetation, and has a most unusual sundial. Until very recently the place was in aristocratic ownership and had been allowed to go evocatively to seed, but it has now been bought by a German chemical company who are restoring it with Nordic vigour, intending to turn it and the surrounding buildings into an ambitious tourist complex explaining man's relationship with the environment. Gerald Brenan lived for a long time in Churriana, and spent the last years of his life on the eastern outskirts of Alhaurín el Grande, fifteen kilometres to the west on the C344 (see pages 228–29). His Alhaurín house, at 20 La Cañada de las Palomas, is now the seat of the Gerald Brenan Foundation; there is also a Sala Gerald Brenan and a complete collection of his works in the Alhaurín library. Ten kilometres north of Alhaurín is Cártama, known throughout Spain for its *morcilla* or blood sausage; you can buy excellent *morcilla* at 8 Calle Pilar Alto, a house situated at the top of the village, in between the ruins of a Moorish castle and the early sixteenth-century parish church.

The notoriously dangerous road between Málaga and Gibraltar takes you through some of the most depressing coastal development in Europe, starting off with Torremolinos (shortened by the English to 'Torrie'). Fuengirola, which comes next, still has its Moorish castle, as well as a small wholly Spanish district at the back of the town featuring some modest bars serving some of the best fish and seafood on the coast (most notably the Bar La Paz Garrido on the Avenida de Mijas). On the mountain slopes above Fuengirola stands the village of Mijas, where Manuel Cortes spent thirty-three years in hiding (see page 229); the village is now wholly given over to tourism, and has various ridiculous museums, such as one devoted to the 'smallest paintings in the world'. Marbella, twenty-seven kilometres west of Fuengirola, is the most up-market of the Costa del Sol resorts, and has preserved a surprising amount of its old town, albeit in a rather chic state; the pine-shaded district of Puerto Banus attracts the coast's yacht set. Estepona, twenty-one kilometres further west, has Spain's oldest nudist beach, yet it has also kept the character of a fishing village more than have any other of this coast's resorts. [4E]

MARCHENA, at the heart of the fertile Guadalquivir basin, but away from the major routes that cross it, is a lively, little-visited market town with various monuments reflecting an important past. Though the town suffered from considerable neglect and damage in the nineteenth and early twentieth centuries, its present citizens have done their best to look after what they have left, and have made every effort to ensure that a visit here is an enjoyable experience. The surrounding walls, built by the Romans, and extended first by the Moors and then by the Christians after Ferdinand III's capture of the town in 1240, have partially survived, together with some of their gates and defensive towers. The most impressive gate is the Puerta de Sevilla off the Calle Rojas Marcos, while the best of the towers is the nearby Torre de Oro, the interior of which (entered from the Calle San Francisco) houses a recently opened and beautifully displayed archaeological museum, where you will be provided with an excellent map and brochure about the town. In the centre of the old town of Marchena is the late gothic parish church of San Juan, which has a superb intricately carved high altar containing panels of the life of Christ by Alejo Fernández (see page 109); in a room above the sacristy is kept a series of nine canvases by Zurburán, commissioned in 1634 and completed in 1637. Nearby, on the edge of the walled town, is the vast precinct of the former palace of the Dukes of Osuna. The magnificent plateresque palace was pulled down in the early years of this century by the Duke's creditors, and it is even said that parts of the masonry went into the making of the town's bull-ring. All that remains in the precinct are the thirteenth- to fifteenth-century church of Santa María and the sorry remains of the town's castle.

Outside the walls, at 8 Calle San Pedro (an animated street leading off the Calle Rojas Marcos), is the town's casino or men's club. This turn-of-the-century building, incorporating a former Franciscan monastery, boasts a quite magnificent neo-Moorish exterior. [3D]

MARTOS, a well-preserved small town overlooking a landscape of olive trees, has had an important history. Known to the Iberians as Tucci, the town later became a Roman settlement and then a Visigothic bishopric. It acquired the name of Martos after the Christians captured the town from the Moors in 1225, on St Marta's day. From the now ruined castle which rises high above the town on a steep outcrop of rock were later thrown the brothers Carvajal, accused of murdering the favourite of Ferdinand IV, Juan de Benavides. The brothers protested their innocence to the end, and, failing in their pleas, eventually begged God that the king himself should die in thirty days' time; their wish was to be granted. A stone tablet commemorating the brothers is to be found inside the church of Santa Marta, which also boasts an intricate Isabelline plateresque portal. The parish church of Santa María de la Villa dates back to the thirteenth century but was extensively remodelled in the fifteenth, sixteenth and nineteenth centuries. Other attractions of the town include the Renaissance Town Hall (originally a prison, and featuring representations of Wisdom and Justice), and a fountain known as the Fuente Nueva, which was designed in 1584 by a pupil of the influential Roman architect Vignola. [2F]

MEDINA SIDONIA occupies a prominent hill-top setting in the middle of a landscape of rolling wheatfields extending to the Serranía de Ronda. Originally the Roman colony of Assido, and later a Visigothic bishopric, the town was designated 'Medina', or city, by the Arabs. The title of Duke of Medina Sidonia was awarded to members of the family of Guzman the Good, who had distinguished himself in the capture of the town in 1264. Today the place is one of the most dignified and least spoilt of the white hill villages of Cádiz province. Its main monument of interest, the parish church of Santa María la Coronada, is near the top of the village's very steep hill, on a small, dusty and neglected square of considerable character: the building was erected over a mosque, the charming courtyard of which still survives; the gothic interior dates mainly from the early sixteenth century and has an enormous carved retable by M. Turín and B. Vázquez. From the top of the bell-tower, a good view can be had of the village, but for a more extensive panorama, you should take the path which leads up from the church to the scant remains of the former Moorish castle and ducal residence. The main survival of the Moorish fortifications is the beautiful and well-preserved Arco de la Pastora at the bottom of the village, next to the road marked to JEREZ DE LA FRONTERA. The village's large and pleasant main square is half-way up the hill, and has a good cake-shop, the Sobrina de las Trejas, from where you can buy the village's celebrated biscuits and pastries: of particular renown is the honey and almond-based sweet known as '*alfajor*', which dates back to Moorish times and on which a whole book has been written by the pioneering historian of Spanish food, Doctor Thebussem, a native of this town.

A twenty-kilometre drive in a south-easterly direction will take you to the small village of Benalup de Sidonia, beyond which are two little-visited sites of great interest: the prehistoric cave of El Tajo de las Figuras (see pages 54–7), and the abandoned monastery of El Cuervo. To reach the first of these, continue driving west on the CA212 towards the Serranía de Ronda. After ten kilometres the cultivated fields on the left-hand side of the road give way to bracken, and you will find a metal gate: go through this and bear to the right as you walk up the hill in the direction of a crowning group of large rocks. At this stage you are almost certain to be intercepted by the shepherd responsible for guarding the rock shelter, who will lead you there himself; a rope is provided to assist in lifting yourself up to it. Back again on the road (a ten-minute walk from the rock shelter), continue driving east and, shortly before the twenty-fourth kilometre post, at the top of a hill, you will see on the right-hand side of the road a cluster of trees and a white wooden gate. Beyond the gate is a wide footpath which leads after an hour's walk to the monastery of El Cuervo. The walk is a delightful one, and for much of its length follows a shaded stream, next to which you will find an abandoned mill (shortly beyond the mill this stream forms a pool where you can swim). To get to the monastery you have to turn sharply left at the mill, and climb up a steep path laid by the monks. The extensive ruins of the monastery constitute one of the most moving sites in all Andalusia. Begun in 1717, using sandstone quarried from the northern slopes of the Sierra Blanquilla on which it stands, the monastery belonged to the order of Discalced Carmelites. An Italian woodcarver was employed for the woodwork and statuary, though he never completed his work here, dying in Cádiz in 1755 in the tidal wave caused by the Lisbon earthquake. The monastery was occupied by French troops in 1810 and abandoned in 1835. Today stray cattle wander among its ruins. Of especial beauty is the crossing of the church: the dome has collapsed, but the ring which supported it has survived, overgrown with vegetation and even sprouting a tree. In the wooded slopes behind the monastery are a group of hermitages. [5C]

MOGUER: Gently rising above a landscape of wheatfields, vineyards, orchards and olives, Moguer is the most beautiful and interesting village in the southern half of Huelva province. A dependency of NIEBLA until 1333, Moguer was entrusted in that year by Alfonso XI as a seigneury to Don Alonso Jofre Tenorio, Almirante Mayor of Castille. Close to the estuary of the Río Tinto, Moguer became prosperous not only through agriculture but through being an important fishing and maritime centre: numerous famous figures associated with maritime history and the colonialization of the New World have come from Moguer, including Juan and Pedro Alonso Niño, who were respectively the captain and pilot of Columbus's ship, the Niña. The village today produces famous pastries, and an excellent sweet wine known as Vino de Naranja.

Moguer's medieval castle is now a decrepit ruin standing over a garage off the Calle Castillo, but many other monuments from the village's past survive in excellent condition, most notably the former Convent of Santa Clara, which stands behind a white crenellated wall running the whole length of the narrow and charming Plaza de las Monjas. Founded in 1337/8 by Jofre Tenorio and his wife, Doña Elvira Alvarez, it served as a convent for sisters of the order of St Clare until 1898, and is now a museum, which you are obliged to visit with a guide. On entering you find yourself in a small brick cloister in a *mudéjar* style, beyond which is a much larger cloister, painted a brilliant white and lined with palms. Among the rooms that you are shown are the kitchen, the refectory, the sick room, and an enormous late sixteenth-century dormitory divided with rows of columns that once separated the beds and were hung with curtains. The high-point of the visit is to the church, which has various medieval and Renaissance works of art, most notably the alabaster tomb of the convent's founder and some painted Renaissance choir-stalls. An inscription in the right aisle records that Columbus said a prayer in the church on his return from his first journey to America.

Parallel to the convent of Santa Clara, off the Plaza de los Franciscanos, is the late fifteenth-century monastery of San Francisco, which sent off numerous missionaries to America in the sixteenth, seventeenth and eighteenth centuries. The parish church of Nuestra Señora de la Granada, in the Plaza de la Iglesia, is a late sixteenth-century building with a bell-tower clearly inspired by that of the Giralda in Seville. The most important building of this later period in Moguer, and indeed the finest neo-classical building in the whole of Huelva province, is the elegant Town Hall on the adjoining Plaza del Cabildo.

In front of the Town Hall is a large memorial to the man who did more than anyone else to promote the fame of Moguer, the poet Juan Ramón Jiménez (see pages 208–9). Moguer, with its quiet streets and elegant but decaying white houses, has changed little since the time when Juan Ramón wrote his most popular book, *Platero and I*, extracts from which are quoted on ceramic plaques marking the many surviving buildings and monuments associated with it. Born in 1881 at 2 Calle de la Ribera, Juan Ramón later lived at what is now 5 Calle Juan Ramón Jiménez. This house remained in the family's possession for a long time after the poet's death in 1958, and is now a delightfully old-fashioned museum, retaining much of the house's original furniture and decoration: among the many mementoes is the telegram announcing the award to the poet of the Nobel Prize. On the eastern edge of the town is the cemetery where he and his wife Zenobia are buried, and, nearby, off the Carretera San Juan del Puerto La Rábida, is the Casa de Fuentepiña, the country home where the poet wrote most of *Platero and I*. [3B]

MOJÁCAR, the most popular resort on the Almería coast, is rapidly developing a character comparable to some of the Costa del Sol resorts, and has on its outskirts numerous signs in English advertising such implausible-sounding places as the Spotted-Turtle Inn. The old town comprises flat-roofed houses rising up a hill, and would be attractive were it not now so phoney: most of the houses in the upper end of town are now luxury residences, bars, restaurants or nightclubs. As is the way with villages such as these, its charms were first discovered by artists and writers. Among the creative pioneers who bought houses here in the 1950s was Walt Disney, whose parents were Almerian immigrants to America; the cartoonist took great pains to disguise both his Spanish origins and his real name.

The coast road south from Mojácar to the popular resort of Carboneras starts to climb after ten kilometres and then heads inland, the coastline being at this point too steeply mountainous to skirt: just before the climb is a track leading off to the Playa de Macena, one of the most unspoilt beaches in the area. Just to the north of Mojácar is the coastal town of Garrucha, a place of little beauty, but none the less appealing for being more of a fishing port than a resort. [3J]

MONTEFRÍO, a village of much character, lies between two rocky outcrops crowned by churches. The lower of the two churches, that of San Antonio, is on the eastern edge of the village, off the GR212 to Illora. Begun in the sixteenth century, perhaps to designs by Diego de Siloe, it was not completed until the eighteenth century; it has a finely sculpted west façade and, in front of this, a terrace with an excellent view of Montefrío. The very centre of the town is dominated by the vast dome of the pantheon-like church of the Encarnación, by Spain's leading neo-classical architect Ventura Rodriguez; the structure is undeniably impressive, even if totally inappropriate for an Andalusian village, both in its scale and in its architecture. Behind the building a street climbs up past the Town Hall towards the church perched on the village's eastern rock, the Iglesia de la Villa (stop off at the house at No. 11 to collect the keys). The street goes through the prettiest part of Montefrío, and, once above the roof level of the houses, has excellent views over mountains and olive trees. The Iglesia de la Villa is Montefrío's oldest church and was built shortly after the Christian capture of the village in 1482; it stands on the site of a Nasrid castle which was pulled down by Ferdinand and Isabella.

The village enjoys a great reputation for its charcuterie, most notably its *morcilla* (blood-sausage), *chorizo* (spiced sausage) and *salsichón* (salami). Excellent home-made sausages can be tried at the Café Bar La Fonda near the church of the Encarnación; the *salsichón* there is especially good.

A fascinating and beautifully situated neolithic site, Las Peñas de los Gitanos, lies ten kilometres to the east of the village, off the road to Illora. A sign to it by the side of the road indicates a stony track which climbs up past a quarry. Bear left and follow the white-painted stones by the side of this track and you will eventually pass a small dolmen to your right, and reach what looks like a carpark. Beyond this is a large field with various prehistoric tombs. [3F]

MONTILLA, a town of unremarkable appearance set among gently rolling expanses of vineyards, is famous for both its fortified wines and its historical associations. The place is now generally recognized as the site of the celebrated Battle of Munda, where Caesar defeated the sons and supporters of Pompey. It was also the birthplace of Gonzalo Fernández y Aguilar (1453–1515), who distinguished himself in various fights against the Moors, and earned the nickname 'El Gran Capitán' in the course of his campaigns in Italy against the French. Also connected with the town is the Renaissance historian of Inca civilization, Garcilaso de la Vega ('El Inca'), to whom a small museum is dedicated. The son of the conquistador Sebastiano Garcilaso de la Vega and the Inca princess Isabel Chimpu Oclo, 'El Inca' was born in Peru in 1536 and came to Spain in 1560, where he entered the Church.

Fourteen and a half kilometres south of Montilla, in the direction of Antequera, is the attractive small town of Aguilar de la Frontera, also famed as a wine centre. Among its monuments are the elaborate baroque monastery church of the Discalced Carmelites, and the parish church of Santa María de Soterrano, dating mainly from the Renaissance period. Of particular interest is the octagonal and poorly maintained square of San José (1806), which was certainly inspired by the Plaza Ochavada in nearby ARCHIDONA. Fourteen kilometres north of Montilla, along the N331 to Córdoba, is the town of Fernán Gomez, which has an eighteenth-century Ducal palace comprising an elegant group of buildings arranged around a fountain. [2E]

MONTORO, built above a bend of the Guadalquivir, is one of the most attractive and least spoilt villages in Córdoba province. Of ancient origin, and occupied by the Arabs up to 1240, Montoro caught the attention of Isabel La Católica in 1480 when its inhabitants pooled their resources to construct a new bridge across the Guadalquivir and thus greatly improve the existing communications between

Castile and Andalusia. The women of the village even sold their jewellery to finance the bridge, which in consequence came to be known as the 'Bridge of Las Donadas' or 'the lay sisters'. From that time onwards Montoro was awarded numerous royal privileges. In 1986 King Juan Carlos was made honorary mayor of the village.

The village's main square, the Plaza de España, is especially delightful, dominated by the salmon-pink gothic-*mudéjar* portal of its parish church of San Bartolomé, and the classical plateresque façade of the former Ducal Palace (now the Town Hall); at No. 19 is a traditional inn (no longer in use) of a type rarely found today in Spain. The Calle B. Comacho, a tiny street to the north of the square, leads to the church of Santa María de la Mota, dating back to the thirteenth century; there are numerous pleasant little corners in this part of the village. The Calle Corredera, the village's main street, connects the Plaza de España with the Plaza L. Benitez, and at No. 73 is a dark, traditional village store selling excellent basketwork. Off the Plaza L. Benitez is the village's casino or men's club, where you can enjoy good *tapas* of deep-fried pigs' testicles (*criadillas*) and brains (*sesos*) while seated in an elegant turn-of-the-century *patio*. Near this is a museum devoted to the locally-born contemporary artist, Antonio Rodriguez Costa, who is claimed to enjoy an international reputation.

The splendid bridge of Las Donadas, designed possibly by the celebrated Enrique de Egas, links the village with its run-down suburb of Retamar. The road which climbs up from here towards Cardeña (the CO510) provides some of the best views of Montoro. [2E]

MORÓN DE LA FRONTERA, the centre of a Moorish city state in the eleventh century, marks the approach of the Serranía de Ronda. Built on a hill, its highest point is its ruined eleventh-century castle. Near this, in a small park with excellent views, is a statue of 1912 representing a plucked cock, an allusion to an unpopular sixteenth-century tax-collector nicknamed 'the cock', who one day was stripped bare and beaten up by the inhabitants of Morón: the phrase 'to end up like the cock of Morón' is still used in reference to people who make fools of themselves. Immediately below the castle is the attractive parish church of San Miguel, which was constructed between 1503 and 1730 and has a west façade of 1726 in a pseudo-Renaissance style. Wholly baroque is the magnificent early eighteenth-century west portal of the church of San Ignacio (La Compañía), which stands on a street to your left as you walk down the Calle San Miguel to the Plaza de Ayuntamiento, the lively junction of the town's principal streets. Morón is famed as a *flamenco* centre, and hosts each summer a *flamenco* festival known as the *Gazpacho*. A description of the *flamencos* of Morón forms the basis of *Flamenco: A Way of Life* (1967) by the American 'flamencologist' Don Pohren, who in the 1960s ran a *flamenco* centre in the town's outskirts. [3D]

MOTRIL, the largest town by the coast of Granada, lies three kilometres inland in the middle of flat fertile land squeezed in between the sea and barren mountains. Vines, and almond and citrus trees grow here in abundance, and it is one of the only places in Spain suitable for the cultivation of such tropical fruits as the delicate custard apple (*chirimoya*). But the principal local activity is based on sugar cane, as a result of which Motril is sometimes known as 'little Cuba': the cane is used in the manufacture of an excellent rum known as '*ron pálido*', which is rarely to be found outside Granada province.

The town of Motril is mainly modern and uninspiring, and the ruined castle which once belonged to the mother of the Moorish king Boabdil is of little interest; the equally unappealing port of Motril is a holiday resort particularly popular with the inhabitants of Granada. The nearby old village of Salobreña is a far prettier place than Motril, and rises up above the surrounding fields on a rock shaped like a ship. Further west from Salobreña the mountains come down directly to the coast; the next important town and resort is Almuñecar, a long sprawling place dominated by a rock supporting its Moorish castle, inside which is the local cemetery. Laurie Lee stayed in the town at the end of the journey which was later to inspire *As I Walked Out One Midsummer Morning*; he disguised the place under the name Castillo, but is now commemorated by a plaque in its centre. East from Salobreña the coast becomes increasingly arid and depressing the nearer it gets to Almería province. [4F]

NERJA, a coastal town of sub-tropical vegetation at the foot of the beautiful Sierra de Tejeda, must have been a paradise before being 'discovered' by the British in the late 1950s and turned into a vulgar resort with uncontrolled villa development behind it. Its finest feature is its 'balcony of Europe', a small palm-lined belvedere jutting out into the sea; the view to the east is particularly attractive and takes in a rocky coastline overhung with palms and set against a background of wild mountains. The best beach is that of Burriana, on the eastern edge of the town.

The N340 east from Nerja to Almuñecar (see MOTRIL) is the most beautiful stretch of road along the Costa del Sol, and twists its way above small rock-lined coves and jagged capes. Three kilometres along it is the Cave of Nerja, which was discovered in 1957, conveniently just in time for the beginnings of the tourist boom; the cave is continually packed with tourists, and, with its garish lighting, seems almost as artificial as that of St George in Gibraltar.

The hill village of Frigiliana, six and a half kilometres above Nerja, at the end of the MA105, is exceedingly pretty and has magnificent views down to the coast; but the place is so spotlessly white and clean that it resembles less of a real village than the cover of an estate agent's brochure. In fact, like all the nearby hill villages, it is overrun by foreign settlers, most of whom are avid readers of the glossy English-language magazine, Lookout. The English influence in the village is clearly evident in the ceramic plaques stuck to the walls of many of the houses and bearing rather fatuous historical information. At the top of the village is an English-run bar with a terrace and exotic garden.

There is a fifteen-kilometre dust track leading from Frigiliana to Cómpeta, but if you are driving by car to the latter village, it is quicker and safer to head back to the coast, take the Málaga road for eight kilometres, and then turn north on to the MA137. The climb proper to Cómpeta begins after Torrox, a village largely filled with Germans and Scandinavians; the road begins then dramatically to wind its way up the mountain, the slopes of which are covered with vineyards. The pretty old village of Cómpeta, from which the sea is visible in the far distance, is known for its sweet wines. The Danes and English now living in the village almost outnumber the remarkably tolerant and friendly local population; at the time of writing there are three foreign-run estate agencies here, and two English-run bars. Behind the village the mountainside turns into the wild shrubland of the National Reserve of the Sierra de Tejeda. [4F]

NIEBLA: Surrounded by walls dating back possibly to Tartessian times, the small town of Niebla makes a most striking first impression when seen from the N431 between Seville and Huelva. Its exterio᾽ appearance bears witness to its rich past, and its strategic importance. Known to the Romans as Ilupa, Niebla became a bishopric under the Visigoths, and was later the centre of a small Arab *taifa* or city state; it was captured by Alfonso X in 1257. An English archaeologist, E. M. Whishaw, lived here in the early years of this century, and wrote a strange and fanciful account of Niebla's origins entitled *Atlantis in Andalusia. A Study of Folk Memory* (1929).

Niebla, at close quarters, may not quite live up to your initial impressions of it. The walls turn out to be in poor condition, and crudely restored in parts; on the other side of the town to the N431 the walls slouch down to a rubbish-strewn railway track and the sinister blood-red trickle of the Río Tinto. Inside the citadel is a friendly but unattractive town of mainly modern houses. Interesting archaeological finds have been made at Niebla, and certain guide-books refer to the town's archaeological museum, but of this there is now no trace. The one delightful monument here is the church of Santa María de la Granada, on the other side of the main square to the Town Hall, from which the key to the church can be had. You enter through a charming irregularly-shaped *patio* which is probably the remaining section of a tenth-century Mozarabic church. The building was transformed into a mosque by the Almohads in the thirteenth century; the modest interior has elaborate late gothic vaulting, and Mozarabic brickwork. The castle of Niebla is attached to the perimeter wall facing the N431, and every September hosts a festival of theatre and dance. The local craft of basketwork is at present being revived. [3B]

NÍJAR, an attractive small town by the standards of Almería province, is fringed by palm trees and orchards, and backed by the barren peaks of the Sierra Alhamilla; there are extensive views over the fertile Campo de Níjar to the parched mountains forming the CABO DE GATA. The place was given considerable notoriety by the writer Juan Goytisolo, whose travel book *Campo de Níjar* (1959) features a vivid account of the poverty of the area in the 1950s. The then mayor of Níjar, anxiously trying to develop his town, publicly expressed his desire to string up Goytisolo 'by the balls'. He need not have worried about the possible negative consequences of the book, for the town is now a fairly prosperous place drawing numerous visitors from the coast. The main attractions are the extremely cheap hand-made ceramics and textiles to be bought here. These crafts have been practised in the town since Moorish times, and their primitive designs, though very modern in appearance, have also changed little since then. The rugs are coarse-textured, while the ceramics are crudely glazed and painted in motley colours. Most of the town's craft shops are situated on the Calle Real de las Eras, in the lower half of the town, near the post office. [4J]

OLVERA: '*Mate a tu hombre. Y vete a Olvera*' ('Kill your man and fly to Olvera') ran an old saying, coined at a time when Olvera was a notorious bandit's lair. It enjoys a magnificent hill-top situation in the middle of a landscape of jagged outcrops of rocks and rolling hills covered in olive trees; the views to the south are dominated by the picturesque silhouette of the Serranía de Ronda. The village is disposed around a long main street which climbs up to the imposing seventeenth-century parish church of the Encarnación (which is best seen from the outside, the interior being somewhat bleak). On the square on which the church stands is a gate beyond which a path carved into the rock ascends steeply to the ruined castle (if the gate is closed, ask for the key at the house at No. 2 on the square). The castle was built by the Moors in the late twelfth century, and then renovated by Alfonso XI after the Christian capture of the town in 1327. The views down to the church and village are quite vertiginous. [4D]

OSUNA, one of the most beautiful small towns in Andalusia, is also one of the best preserved. Bordered to the west by fertile plains, and to the east by arid hills, the town has been barely developed on its outskirts and has hardly a single distracting modern building. It was not so long ago that a horse-drawn cart led you from the railway station to the town centre, and even today the town's main laundry service is operated by the nuns of the Convent of Santa Catalina (appropriately of the order of the Immaculate Conception). More surprisingly, considering Osuna's artistic and architectural wealth, the place has as yet scarcely been affected by tourism.

An important town in Iberian times, Osuna became known to the Romans as Urso and took the side of Pompey in the civil war against Caesar. Despite this, the town prospered more than ever after being finally subdued by Caesar, and enjoyed the privileges of being able to mint its own coins and having its own legislature: in the Archaeological Museum of Madrid are ten famous bronze tablets recording the town's statutes. Under the Moors the town lost much of its former importance, and only began to recover this after Ferdinand III's capture of the place in 1239. Given by Alfonso the Wise to the Order of Calatrava in 1264, the seigneury of the town later passed into the hands of the commander of this order, Don Pedro Girón. It was in the sixteenth century, under Don Juan Tóllez Girón, 4th Count of Ureña, that Osuna emerged as a major cultural centre, complete with a university, founded in 1548. In 1562 the Girón family was elevated to the title of Dukes of Osuna. The presence of aristocrats and wealthy landowners led to the creation of numerous fine palaces here right up to the late eighteenth century. Osuna still has the reputation of being an élitist place, and it differs from many other towns in Seville province by the persistence here of a very rigid class structure.

Osuna is built on a steep slope, and its main square and principal street are in the upper part of town. As you walk up the Calle Sevilla towards the main square the horizon is dominated by the west façade of the town's collegiate church, which stands in isolation at the top of the hill. Just above the square is the Mesón del Duque, a most attractive restaurant with a considerable reputation for its traditional Andalusian food. Continuing up to the church, you will pass the town's small and recently opened archaeological museum, housed in a tower which once formed part of the town's walls: inside is a collection of mainly Roman finds, including a fascinating display of medical instruments. The Convent of the Encarnación, founded in 1621 by the 4th Duke of Osuna, is further up the hill and can be visited: its most remarkable feature is its cloister, extensively decorated with ceramic tiles featuring amusing figurative scenes of minimal religious content, such as those representing the five senses. The north façade of the massive collegiate church rises above the convent, occupying the site of a church belonging to the town's former castle.

The collegiate church was begun in 1534 and richly endowed by the 4th Count of Ureña, who provided it with an abbot, four dignitaries, ten canons, and at least thirty-four other functionaries. Though not fully complete until the eighteenth century, the greater part of the building is of the early sixteenth century, and one of Andalusia's most harmonious Renaissance structures. The exterior is largely undecorated, apart from its classical plateresque west portal, inspired by a work by the Florentine artist Benedetto de Maiano and supporting a bas-relief damaged – according to Richard Ford – by French soldiers amusing themselves by taking pot-shots at it. The terrace in front of this portal stands above a slope densely covered in cacti, and has wonderful views of Osuna and the surrounding countryside. This is a particularly good place to come to at sunset, for as the sun disappears below the plain, the portal facing it, known as the Puerta del Sol, turns from ochre into a deep gold. The light and spacious interior with elegant piers in pale grey stone has the simplicity of a Florentine Renaissance church, with the exception of the late baroque chancel, a blaze of gold. The outstanding work of art inside the church is a dramatic *Crucifixion* by the leading seventeenth-century artist José Ribera. A series of four saints by Ribera can be seen in the Renaissance sacristy, which is visited as part of a guided tour around the rooms adjoining the church. These paintings are of exceptionally high quality, the canvases representing *St Jerome and the Angel* and *The Martyrdom of St Bartholomew* being among the finest in this artist's oeuvre: Ribera's characteristic emphasis on realistic detail such as wrinkles and veins is here combined with compositions of startling directness. Other high-points of the guided tour are the tiny and enchanting plateresque cloister, and, above all, the Ducal Pantheon below this. This burial place of the Dukes of Osuna takes the form of a church in miniature, and has some of the most exquisite Renaissance ornamentation in Andalusia: of the sculptures here, one of the most interesting is an anonymous polychromed relief of *St Jerome*, the saint's angular body having something of the realism and expressive pathos of Torrigiani's *St Jerome* in the Museum of Fine Arts in Seville.

Behind the collegiate church is Osuna's former university (now a school), a simple Renaissance structure with an unornamented arcaded courtyard and an attractive small chapel. The path heading north from here passes near the former monastic church of the Merced, which has a most intricately carved late baroque tower; at present the rooms surrounding the cloister are used by ceramic artists, but eventually they will form part of a hotel. Continuing along the path, you will eventually reach the town's old and impressive quarries, a surrealistic landscape crowned by the ruins of a sixteenth-century hermitage. Returning from the quarries, you can head back into the town centre by walking down the attractive Calle Granada, which heads on to the Calle Carrera, the town's animated main street. If you turn left in the direction of the town's main square you will pass the church of San Domingo, another of Osuna's Renaissance buildings founded by the 4th Count of Ureña. On the opposite side of the street is the sharply descending Calle de San Pedro, on which stand the two most splendid of Osuna's many baroque palaces. The higher of these is the former collegiate Chapterhouse, which has a frontispiece of 1776 featuring lively, undulating ornamentation framing a reproduction of Seville's Giralda. Further down the street is the palace of the Marquis of Gomera, with a dazzlingly white façade topped by an agitated, asymmetrical skyline inspired by German rococo illustrations. Another notable eighteenth-century façade is that of the Palacio de los Cepedas on the nearby Calle de la Huerta. [3D]

ÓRGIVA, lying in the valley in between the Sierra Nevada and the Sierra de la Contraviesa, resembles an Alpine town gone somewhat to seed. Off the main street, which is lined with open-air bars, is the twin-towered façade of its baroque parish church, and the decrepit medieval tower of the castle of the Counts of Sástago. Órgiva is the most important town of the western Alpujarras, and is the traditional starting-point for a tour of this region which was made famous in recent times by Alarcón's *Viaje a la Alpujarra* and Gerald Brenan's *South from Granada* (see page 40). Most of the villages are on the southern slopes of the Sierra Nevada, and are characterized by their flat-roofed wooden-beamed houses piled up on top of each other; in many of the villages you will find places to buy the beautiful rugs that have been made here since Moorish times (see pages 39–40). At the bottom of the spectacular, unasphalted road which descends from the Pico Veleta (see GRANADA) is the tiny 'Barranco de Poqueira', a steep and verdant river course along which are arranged, one above the other, three of the most popular villages of the region, Capileira, Bubión and Pampaneira. Capileira, the highest and most spoilt of these, has various hotels and craft shops, and – in one of its picturesque old houses – a museum devoted to local traditions, the Museo Pedro de Alarcón. The tiny village of Bubión shows fewer signs of tourism than the other two villages, but it now has a Sūfī centre and an English-run school offering 'contact with Spanish rural society'. The road east from Pampaneira drives above terraced fields with views over the range of the Alpujarras, the slopes of which have been made barren and arid by ruthless exploitation of its timber. Busquístar, a run-down but very attractive place, gives you a good idea of what the villages in this region were like in Brenan's day; you should walk down into the quiet lower half of the village. The next village, Trevélez, is, at 1,500 metres, the highest community not only in the region but in the whole of Spain (and one of the highest in Europe too). Numerous hippies settled here in the 1970s, and many tourists visit the place today, most of them attracted by its reputation for raw hams, which can be tasted in all the many village bars. To leave the tourist trail completely, head off ten kilometres after Trevélez on to the road leading to Cástaras, a parched and very poor village from where a narrow, unasphalted road leads to the similarly neglected village of Nieles. Shortly after Nieles you rejoin the principal road crossing the region and come eventually to Yegen, where Brenan lived, and which is just as ugly as he said it was. The house where he stayed, marked by a plaque, is at the top of the village and has been much altered in recent years. There is a small and pleasant shaded square in the lower part of the village, with a fountain and a Town Hall housing the 'Asociación Cultural Gerald Brenan'. The eroded landscape which comes into view at Yegen marks the beginnings of the eastern Alpujarras (see LAUJAR DE ANDARAX). [4G]

PALOS DE LA FRONTERA: Situated on the estuary of the Río Tinto, Palos de la Frontera is a friendly but characterless and heavily modernized village which attracts visitors purely through its associations with Christopher Columbus (see pages 86–9). Columbus set sail from Palos on his first journey to America on 3 August 1492 and returned here on 15 March of the following year; the village is now known as 'the cradle of the Americas'. Immediately before setting off, Columbus attended mass at the fifteenth-century parish church of San Jorge, which stands at the northern end of the town. He is supposed to have left the church through its southern portal (attractively decorated in a *mudéjar* style) and to have sailed from the bay immediately below; beside the bay is a medieval well ('La Fontanilla') around which a hideous small park has been built in preparation for the fifth centenary celebrations of 1992. The main village street is named the Calle Colón (Columbus Street), and as you walk south along it from San Jorge to the Town Hall, you will pass at No. 24 the house which belonged to Palos's most famous son, Martín Alonso Pinzón, who accompanied Columbus on his first voyage (see page 88). This house, the most distinguished in the village, is at present being turned into a local museum. On the southern outskirts of the town is the Avenida de la América, which is lined with ceramic decorations listing all the countries of the Americas. The road south from here goes through fertile agricultural countryside before reaching a magnificent forest of pines, in the middle of which, surrounded by luxuriant gardens, is the fifteenth-century monastery of La Rábida, where Columbus spent much time before first visiting America (see pages 87–8). [3A]

PEÑARROYA PUEBLONUEVO, a depressed coal-mining town with a neo-gothic parish church in brick, an overall covering of soot, and numerous abandoned buildings, has the atmosphere of an industrial town of northern Europe transposed to an incongruously sunny setting. Seven kilometres to the south on the N432 to Córdoba is Bélmez, a sinister small village with a Moorish castle dramatically thrust up on a tall pinnacle of rock; steps cut into the rock lead up almost vertically into the castle, from the top of which those not suffering from vertigo can appreciate an extensive view over the bleak and parched surrounding landscape. [1D]

PRIEGO DE CÓRDOBA, built at the edge of a plateau, underneath the highest mountain in Córdoba province, is surrounded by a landscape of ravines, olive trees and picturesque rock escarpments. Roman in origin, captured by the Christians in 1226 then recaptured by the Arabs in 1330, the town was definitively in Christian hands by 1370. In the eighteenth century Priego enjoyed an international reputation for its textiles, and it was during this period of great prosperity that this small town became one of the outstanding baroque centres of Andalusia, if not of Spain.

From the lively main square, the Plaza de Constantina, situated in an area of nineteenth- and early twentieth-century buildings, it is an easy walk to the town's principal monuments. Standing away from the other monuments are two great eighteenth-century fountains occupying a large and quiet square at the end of the Calle Río. This square slopes gently up a hill, and at its lower end is the Fuente del Rey, divided into two basins, the largest of which is lined with 139 grotesque masks spouting water at a sculptural group representing a lion struggling with a dragon (by J. Álvarez Cubero); the other basin has at its centre a group of Neptune and Aphrodite. Whereas this fountain takes its inspiration from the work of Italian baroque artists such as Bernini, the upper, more modest fountain, the Fuente de la Virgen de la Salud, is in an Italianate Renaissance style, with bas-reliefs featuring Venus, Neptune and the Hydra.

Make your way back to the main square by way of the Calle Río, and turn left on to the Calle Solana, which leads into the Plaza San Pedro. The church of San Pedro, a conventional seventeenth-century structure, is of interest mainly for its extravagant high altar designed by the great master of the Spanish baroque, Hurtado Izquierdo (see page 120). Izquierdo, who was born at nearby LUCENA in 1669, died at Priego in 1728; his only work here is his San Pedro altar, which, by comparison with some of the anonymous baroque creations of the Priego school, is a very rational affair. The Plaza de San Pedro backs on to the town's much restored castle of Roman origin (this has now been converted into private residences), the main façade of which overlooks the Plaza Abad Palomino, a square dramatically renovated in recent years in a rather questionable taste. At the far end of this square is the parish church of the Asunción, which on the outside is a modest sixteenth-century structure with an attractive but unexceptional Renaissance south portal. Nothing prepares you for the shock of its eighteenth-century interior, the finest in Priego and quite magnificent even in a European context. The ceiling of the simple sixteenth-century structure has been covered in an exuberant white stucco decoration, which has been whipped up to a frothing frenzy over the chancel. But the best is yet to come: the 1784 chapel of the Sagrario, entered through a door off the left aisle, is a circular structure ringed by a balcony supported by angels, the whole overwhelming in its size, its lightness, the vitality and complexity of its ornamentation, and the overall brilliance of its dazzlingly white and recently restored stucco-work (see page 121).

None other of the various seventeenth- and eighteenth-century churches of Priego is decorated to quite the same fanciful degree as that of the Asunción, though the stuccowork in the chapel known as the Aurora is also well worth seeing. This chapel stands at the end of the Carrera de Alvarez, a street running off the Plaza Abad Palomino. Behind the chapel begins the most beautiful part of Priego, a corner of the town which hangs directly over a cliff and embraces the tiny medieval quarter of 'La Villa', an area of narrow white streets behind the church of the Asunción. The street which hugs the cliff is popular with evening strollers and has wonderful views over the unmistakably Andalusian landscape below. [3F]

QUESADA has an attractive hill-top position directly underneath the highest peak of the Cazorla range, Mt Cabañas (2,028 m.). On the main square, housed in an unattractive modern building of makeshift appearance, is a museum opened in 1960 to display the works of the local painter, Rafael Zabaleta, who spent most of his life in Quesada. His own paintings, mainly of nudes and local scenes, are in a decorative sub-cubist style and would not look out of place in a tacky restaurant. But in the course of his life he seems to have made many important artist friends, and the museum has a photograph of him in the company of Salvador Dalí, and a room filled with lithographs dedicated to him by artists such as Picasso, Miró, Tapiès and Rafael Alberti; the key to this dire but curious museum can be had from the police station opposite.

The C323 south of Quesada leads up to the Sanctuary of Tíscar, impressively situated above rocks and olive trees and erected over a Moorish fortress captured by the Christians in 1319; inside is a much venerated image of the Virgin, and a painting by Zabaleta representing the annual pilgrimage to the Sanctuary of Quesada. Five kilometres beyond Tíscar a stony track, manageable in a strong car, climbs up through forest almost to the summit of Mt Cabañas and then descends to the source of the Guadalquivir. The source itself, marked by an inscription, is of sentimental rather than aesthetic interest, but the fast-flowing river into which it turns runs through the beautiful forested valley which constitutes the heart of the National Park of Segura and

Cazorla (see CAZORLA). Another, faster way of reaching the source from Quesada is to head north towards Cazorla and then turn off to the right, passing by the hamlet of El Chorro. This road is also unasphalted, but is in better condition than the other one. Before disappearing into the pine trees there are magnificently extensive views over an apparent infinity of olive trees. [2G]

RONDA, celebrated for its dramatic position, became one of the high-points of the Romantic traveller's tour of Andalusia. This town, epitomizing Romantic ideals of the sublime and the picturesque, took on in the late nineteenth century the character of a genteel mountain resort; today the place is overrun with tourists, and its old quarter seems more like a large museum than a real town.

Standing on top of an amphitheatre of rock, Ronda is cleft in two by the narrow vertiginous gorge of the Gaudalevín. The gorge, spanned by a late eighteenth-century bridge (the Puente Nuevo), divides the old Moorish town from the Christian district of Mercadillo, founded after the Christian capture of Ronda in 1485. Virtually all the town's hotels are in the Mercadillo district, including the Edwardian-looking Hotel Reina Victoria, built by an English company in 1906 and occupying a spectacular position at the edge of the town's cliff. The German poet Rainer Maria Rilke stayed here between January and February of 1913, occupying Room 208; if you ask for the key to this room, you will find yourself in a small Rilke museum, containing documents of his stay, including his bill, which reveals that he drank much tea and coffee, but no alcohol. There is a statue to Rilke in the hotel's beautiful grounds. Near these grounds, but separated from them by a locked gate, is the Paseo de los Ingleses, a spectacular path which heads south along the cliff to the turn-of-the-century gardens of the Merced, adjoining which is the second oldest bull-ring in Spain. Ronda occupies a critical position in the history of Spanish bull-fighting (see page 156), and an important museum to the sport is attached to the ring; every September, for the Ronda festival, a fight in eighteenth-century costume (a *corrida goyesca*) is put on here.

Once across the bridge and into the old town, turn left down the steep Calle Mario de Paredes, and you will pass on your left the so-called Casa del Rey Moro, built in 1709 over a Moorish palace. Further down on the right is the Renaissance façade of the Casa del

Marqués de Salvatierra; this homely palace, which can be visited, is crammed with antiques and pictures from the Renaissance to the nineteenth century, and has an excellent view from its garden of the town's eastern fortifications. Below the palace you leave the town, passing in turn a Renaissance and a Moorish bridge; at the bottom of the hill turn right along the river and you will come to the enchanting remains of some Moorish baths. Returning to the Casa Salvatierra, make your way back up the hill along the Calle de Mario de Salvatierra, at the top of which is the minaret of a former mosque. Nearby, within another mosque, is the sixteenth-century hall church of Santa María la Mayor, with an interior inspired by that of Granada cathedral. A few minutes' walk to the east takes you to the Casa Mondragón, originally the house of Ronda's last Moorish king, and later turned into the finest of the town's Renaissance palaces. Next to this is a terrace containing an open-air bar much loved by tourists on account of its cliff-side views towards the Puente Nuevo. Even finer views are to be had from the terraced gardens of the nearby Casa Don Bosco (20 Calle Tenorio); this early twentieth-century building is now a Salesian college, and visitors are welcome.

A further opportunity to admire Ronda's situation is provided by the rough path which descends steeply down to the river from below the Casa Mondragón. However, the best walk you can do outside Ronda is to the Hermitage of the Virgen de la Cabeza, a walk much admired by Rilke. From Santa María la Mayor walk south on the Calle Menez Nuñez, and leave the town by what was originally its main gate, the Puerta Almocabar (before reaching this you will pass the attractive late fifteenth-century church of the Espiritu Santo). On the other side of the gate you enter the modern Barrio San Francisco, the main building of which is the monastery church of San Francisco, adorned with an attractive Isabelline plateresque portal. Heading west from the church you will immediately come to the main road to the coast. Turn left, and just before passing the last house turn right on to the path leading through fields of olive trees to the Hermitage (about half an hour's walk). The views towards distant Ronda are superb, particularly in the late afternoon or early evening, when the sun's rays directly illuminate the town's cliff-face. The English painter David Bomberg, who first stayed in the town in 1933, lived in a farmhouse off this path in the 1950s. His expressive views of Ronda, like his ones of Toledo, are among the finest landscapes ever painted of Spain, though they were little appreciated in his time. An embittered and depressed man, he took to excessive drinking, eventually destroying his liver with cheap Spanish brandy; he was rushed back from Ronda to England in February 1957, but died shortly afterwards.

Two of the most popular excursions from Ronda are to the extraordinary prehistoric caves of Pileta (fifteen kilometres south-west, past Benaoján; see pages 53–4), and to the Roman ruins of Ronda la Vieja, sixteen kilometres north-west along the MA449 (see pages 60–61). [4D]

SABIOTE, a pretty unspoilt hill village with cobbled streets, is still largely surrounded by its medieval walls, from which there are beautiful views over olive trees to the nearby Sierra de Cazorla (see CAZORLA). In the centre of the village, at its highest point, is the parish church of San Pedro Apostól, which has a charming if crudely carved south portal in a classical plateresque style. The Calle Castillo descends from here to the castle and has two houses (at No. 1 and No. 3) with impressive sixteenth-century façades. The ruined castle, Roman in origin, then rebuilt by the Moors, is particularly striking for its massive Renaissance additions, with crumbling classical detailing of Piranesi-like proportions; Andrés de Vandelvira is said to have been responsible for these. The nearby main road leading from Úbeda to Albacete (the N322) runs parallel to the Sierra de Cazorla and hugs the summit of a long ridge in between the valleys formed by the rivers Guadalimar and Guadalquivir; there are excellent views on either side. Even more extensive views are to be had from the village of Iznatoraf, which lies just off this road, about thirty-three kilometres east of Sabiote. The village is perched on top of an exceptionally steep hill, and, with its maze of alleys lined with tall white houses, has a distinctly Moorish character. [2G]

SANLÚCAR DE BARRAMEDA: Lying at the mouth of the Guadalquivir, directly in front of the wild, tree-fringed expanses of the Coto Doñana, Sanlúcar de Barrameda has the character of a colonial town thrown up on some tropical coast. Vegetation pushes through the crumbling masonry of its convents, churches and palaces, its many vestiges of an impressive history. Yet Sanlúcar is not a sad place absorbed in nostalgic dreams of its past. The life which is led here is so lively, enchanting and special that it is easy to imagine the town as the setting of a novel by a 'magical realist' from Latin America.

A small agricultural village in Roman times, and then given its castle by the Moors, Sanlúcar was captured by the Christians in 1264 and entrusted as a fealty to Guzmán the Good, whose descendants were the powerful Dukes of Medina Sidonia. With its strategic position on the Guadalquivir, Sanlúcar became one of the major ports of Spain after 1492: Columbus embarked from here on his third journey to America in 1498, and for Magellan the place was the point both of departure and of return on his pioneering voyage around the world in 1519–22. The commercial prosperity and cosmopolitan life led here in the sixteenth century was quite remarkable, and its population even reached about 50,000 at a time when Madrid's was only 12,000. The town's decline set in in the early seventeenth century, but was almost halted once and for ever two centuries later, when Charles IV's infamous minister Godoy, who had a mistress here, was seriously considering turning the place into the capital of Spain. In the mid nineteenth century the Duke of Montpensier had a summer palace built here, and since then the town has been very popular as a summer resort.

A quiet place for much of the year, Sanlúcar becomes congested with holiday-makers in August, though few of these are from further away than Seville, let alone from abroad. Sanlúcar is not a place for those who love clean beaches and good swimming. Its appeal as a resort is for those who are happy to spend most of their days sitting in bars, talking with and observing people, sipping the excellent local fortified wine known as *manzanilla*, and tasting what must surely be among the best food in Spain. A great variety of vegetables are cultivated in the fields behind the town, while to the adjoining port of Bonanza are brought in daily a magnificent and celebrated range of fish and seafood: particularly famous are the *acedías* (small sole), *pijotas* (whiting), *cazón* (dogfish), *rape* (angler fish), and, above all, *langostinos* (prawns), for which people make a special journey to Sanlúcar. Almost every one of the town's countless bars serves the most excellent food, sometimes at ridiculously cheap prices.

Sanlúcar is divided into an upper and a lower town (El Barrio Alto and El Barrio Bajo), the former traditionally living off agriculture, the latter off fishing; it is often thought that the town's finest meat and vegetable dishes are to be found in the Barrio Alto, and the best fish ones in the Barrio Bajo. The oldest part of Sanlúcar is in any case set quite some way from the coast, and begins near the town's principal commercial thoroughfare, the Calles Ancha and San Juan. The axis of these two connecting streets is the town's main square, which is an excellent place to begin a tour of Sanlúcar. The square's only drawback as a starting-point is that you may find it difficult to leave it, for it is a charming and animated place lined on all sides with tempting open-air bars and cafés: one of the cafés is the Ibense, which was the original of a famous chain of Spanish ice-cream parlours founded in the early years of this century. From the Plaza head south past the Town Hall towards the upper town, and you will arrive almost immediately at the small square of San Roque: a small plaque on the chapel of this name records that Velázquez's teacher, Francisco Pacheco, was born at Sanlúcar (see page 110). If you look to your right at the end of the square you will see the convent of the Madre de Dios, where you can buy another local speciality, *tocinos de cielo*, which are tiny and very rich versions of *crème caramel*. In the mornings the Plaza de San Roque is a particularly animated place, for it adjoins the town's market building, which is one of the best in Andalusia both for its beautifully white interior, and for the staggering range of products on offer. The market can be entered from the Calle Bretones, the continuation of which, the Cuesta de Belén, climbs into the upper town, passing a low building adorned on the outside with some strange and badly eroded late gothic arches (the building is thought by some to have been a group of shops). Near the top of the hill, on the right-hand side, are the gates leading into the amusing neo-Moorish palace of the Dukes of Montpensier: the entrance lodge, inexplicably in the style of a Swiss chalet, is now used by the very friendly local police, who will gladly allow you to wander around the palace's small park and into its fantastical courtyard. Turn left at the top of the hill, on to the Calle Luis de Eguilaz, and you will find yourself in front of the church of Santa María de la O, which has a finely decorated gothic plateresque façade and an interior featuring a splendid *artesonado* ceiling. The church is attached to the palace of the Dukes of Medina Sidonia, which can be visited officially on Sunday afternoons or by trying your luck with the doorbell on other days: quite apart from its atmospherical sixteenth- to eighteenth-century interior, and wonderful views over the Coto Doñana, the palace has one of Spain's richest private archives, containing a vast amount of documentation relating to the Armada (the archive can be consulted on previous application to the Duchess).

The Calle Luis de Eguilaz, as it heads east towards the castle, passes *bodegas* on both sides. At No. 11 on this street is the house belonging to the largest *manzanilla*-producing firm, Antonio Barbadillo: the house has a charming courtyard adorned with a bust of the firm's founder; on the first floor are the firm's offices, where you can arrange to go on a tour of the *bodegas* belonging to it. The large Moorish castle at the end of the street is in a ruinous condition, but a pleasant flight of steps by its side leads you down into the lower town, depositing you eventually on the Calle Ancha. Every 15 August this street is covered with a brilliant 'floral carpet' made out of salt and coloured sawdust; the townspeople are up for most of the previous night watching and taking part in its assembly. At the eastern end of the street is the imposing Renaissance church of Santo Domingo.

North from the main square is a wide tree-lined promenade which leads down to the coast; many amusing and impressive turn-of-the-century villas can be seen in this part of the town, particularly if you head off to the right towards the end of the promenade and walk to the fishing district of Bajo de Guía. Bajo de Guía has a delightfully shabby character and many excellent bars directly overlooking the beach. The Bar and Restaurant Bigote, which has its own fishing fleet, is one of the most renowned places to eat fish and seafood in Andalusia. For a few days towards the end of August the Sanlúcar beach, right up to Bajo de Guía, is the scene of horse-racing, a tradition which goes back to the late nineteenth century and makes for an exciting spectacle.

At Bajo de Guía itself there are motor boats and a ferry service to take you across to the Coto Doñana. Landrovers on the other side will drive you along the Coto's wide sandy beach and deposit you at a place where the water is cleaner than it is at the actual mouth of the Guadalquivir; the beach, however, is dirty for the whole of its twenty kilometres. The pleasures of coming here are its quiet seclusion, beautiful views and wonderful array of shells; in the early evening you might even be surprised by the arrival of deer at the water's edge. In theory it is possible at low tide to drive your own car all the way to the popular modern resort of Matalascañas, but skill, bravery and a very strong car are ideally required to do this. To visit the interior of the Coto, you have to go on a guided tour by Landrover (tickets for this are available from the Hotel Guadalquivir in Sanlúcar; it is advisable to book a long time ahead in the summer months).

A small road following the Guadalquivir north from Sanlúcar leads, after four kilometres, to Bonanza, which is well worth visiting for its afternoon fish auction; further north still are salt flats and the haunting pine wood of La Algaïda. Nine kilometres to the west of Sanlúcar is the popular resort of Chipiona, which has clean though impossibly crowded beaches; the coast to the south of here includes the pleasant Playa de la Ballena, but this whole area is soon to be transformed into a massive holiday centre. [4B].

SANTA OLALLA DEL CALA: The extensive, well-preserved battlements that stand in isolation above the village of Santa Olalla del Cala make a powerful impression on those travelling between Seville and Extremadura along the N630. At the foot of this castle is an attractive fourteenth-century church with a horseshoe-shaped west portal. From here you reach the castle by clambering up a small rock face, entering through a hole in its walls. The castle, dating from after 1293, was heavily remodelled in the 1460s and used as the local cemetery in the last century. The north side of the hill falls down directly to stark, rolling countryside.

Fifteen kilometres to the west of the village along the C435 is the beautifully situated village of Zufre, which clings to the top of a hill and has extensively preserved sections of its original twelfth-century fortifications. Its large parish church in brick and pink stone is flanked by palm trees, and perched on the hill's edge. On its northern side is an enchanting small square with a fountain and a quaintly arcaded sixteenth-century Town Hall. [2B].

SEGURA DE LA SIERRA, at a height of over 11,000 metres, is a charming small village with panoramic views over the wild, mountainous and densely pine-forested landscape of this extreme north-eastern corner of Jaén province. As soon as you enter the village through its medieval gate, you will find on the right-hand side of the street the

Town Hall, a sixteenth-century building which was originally a Jesuit college; ask in here for the keys to the castle and to the Moorish baths. The village's tiny central square is shortly beyond the Town Hall, and you can descend from here to the small Moorish baths (in the basement of a house below the bakery), passing by an attractive sixteenth-century fountain adorned with the coat of arms of Charles V. Above the square is the village's only official accommodation, a cheap and beautiful old *hostal* tastefully decorated inside with antiques. Despite its little-spoilt look, the village attracts numerous holiday-makers in the summer months, and directly above the village is the sort of modern bar (the Bar Terraza Ben Issam) which you would expect to find in a sea resort; the views from its terrace are magnificent. An unasphalted road behind this winds its way up to the large, well-preserved castle at the very top of the mountain on which the village is built.

Twenty kilometres south of Segura is the village of Hornos, which sits on a steep outcrop of rock above the northern shores of the reservoir of El Tranco (see CAZORLA); there is a good viewing balcony next to the Town Hall. From Hornos the C321 meanders east through mountainous and little-populated countryside in the direction of Granada and Almería provinces; once across the Segura range, the forest thins out and the landscape becomes increasingly arid. At the village of Pontones, thirty-five kilometres from Hornos, a short, unasphalted road to the right leads to the source of the River Segura, now enclosed in a particularly ugly picnic area. [1H]

SETENIL DE LAS BODEGAS seemed until comparatively recently one of the lost corners of Spain. When I first came here in 1974 the stream that runs through its centre was little more than an open drain, and a popular diversion among the local children was to throw a stone at a bush to see how many rats would jump out; the neighbouring village of Torre-Alhaquime was then so inbred that its population appeared to consist mainly of the physically and mentally deformed. The area now shows signs of new prosperity, and a growing number of tourists are coming here from nearby RONDA. But Setenil will always be one of the most curious villages in Andalusia on account of its being bizarrely situated within the bend of a gorge formed by the River Trejo. A great many of the houses are actually tucked away in the gorge's caves and seem almost to be supporting the rock above them. As the name Setenil de las Bodegas suggests, all the old houses in the village have wine cellars, for at one time the place lived largely off viticulture; the phylloxera epidemic at the end of the last century killed off all the vines, and caused the economic slump from which the village has only just emerged.

The layout of Setenil is slightly baffling, though you will have a clearer idea of it if you walk up to its parish church, which stands in the middle of it and commands some of the best views of the town. The building itself has a dull, modern exterior but a fine late gothic interior with splendid vaulting: the vestry reputedly has an item donated by Isabel La Católica. Slightly lower down from the church is the local assize court, situated in the old Tribunal: it has an excellent *artesonado* ceiling surrounded by an inscription recording the victory of Ferdinand and Isabella over the Moors. [4D]

SEVILLE, the capital of Andalusia and the fourth largest town in Spain, has a long and distinguished history going back to Iberian times. Greeks, Phoenicians, and Carthaginians settled here, and, after 47 BC, the place became one of the leading towns in Roman Baetis. Julius Caesar stayed here, and in the neighbouring settlement of Itálica, the Roman emperors Hadrian and Trajan were born. The Visigothic archbishop San Isidro turned Seville in the sixth century into a major European centre of learning, and when the Moors first came to Spain in 732 they made the town briefly the capital of al-Andalus. In the eleventh century Seville was the most important of Spain's *taifa* or city states, and in the late twelfth and thirteenth centuries the town enjoyed enormous prosperity under the Almohads. Captured by Ferdinand III in 1258, Seville later became a favoured residence of Spanish kings, in particular Pedro the Cruel. But it was not until after 1492, with the discovery of the New World, that Seville entered the most important phase in its history, becoming in the sixteenth century one of the liveliest and most cosmopolitan cities of the Western world (see pages 100 ff.). Economic and political decline set in in the early seventeenth century, but this was also the period when there worked in Seville such remarkable artists as Velázquez, Zurburán and Murillo (see pages 112–17). When, in the nineteenth century, travellers started flocking to Spain from all over Europe,

Seville emerged as one of the country's major tourist centres, attracting people not simply because of its monuments and superlative seventeenth-century paintings, but also because it represented to these travellers all that was most attractive about Spain. It was a city of jasmine-scented sensuality, the birthplace of Carmen and Don Juan, and the scene of endless exuberant secular and religious festivities.

For most of the nineteenth century Seville remained surrounded by its medieval walls, and these looked out directly on to the Guadalquivir river and to the surrounding fertile plains. The walls have now largely been pulled down, large and ugly districts have grown up around where they once stood, and even much of the old centre has been damaged or left to decay. In many ways Seville today is the least liked of Andalusia's great tourist destinations, and certainly the least known. Tourists tend to enthuse over the cathedral and its surroundings, but often dismiss the rest of the city as being noisy, chaotic and run-down. Some people are also disappointed by the town's lack of any real cultural life: few classical concerts are held, drama is poor, cinemas are almost unattended, and the university is a slightly amateurish institution. To be able to enjoy Seville to the full, 'culture' has to be understood in the broader sense of the word, and not simply in terms of sightseeing and shows. As a place for leisurely socializing, lingering in bars, trying out delicious food, and being constantly entertained, either by festivities or witty conversation, Seville is perhaps without equal in Andalusia.

A great number of Seville's monuments remain unknown even to Sevillians. Much of the inner town is literally hidden, taken up as it is by the unexpectedly large grounds of private palaces and closed order convents. At present no satisfactory guide-book is available on the city, either in English or in Spanish; furthermore, anything that is written now about the city would soon need to be revised in view of the major urban modifications that are being planned for the World Exhibition of 1992. Below is only the most condensed account of the town's countless attractions.

The tourists who come to Seville are concentrated mainly around the cathedral and the Alcázar, a small but exceptionally attractive area in the south-eastern corner of the old town. The cathedral itself is so vast and so filled with treasures that at least half a day is needed to see it (see page 106). The main entrance to the building (the Puerta

Mayor) is on the cathedral's western façade, and is adorned with naturalistic late fifteenth-century carvings by Pedro Millán and Lorenzo Mercadante, who were also responsible for the carvings on the two flanking portals (the Puertas del Bautismo and del Nacimiento); early sixteenth-century carvings by Miguel Perrin decorate the portals of the eastern façade, while the northern Puerta del Perdón (the entrance to the Patio de los Naranjos) is a superb example of *mudéjar* craftsmanship incorporating elements of the original Almohad mosque (see page 106). Inside the cathedral it is easy to become disorientated in the cavernous gloom, and much persistence and good eyesight are needed to track down the numerous scattered works by artists such as Pedro de Campaña, Alejo Fernández, Morales, Murillo, Zurburán, Valdés Leal, Juan de Arce and Martínez Montañes. The one unavoidable work is the late gothic high altar, begun in 1482 by Dancart and said to be the largest and most elaborate in Spain. A selection of paintings, including one by Goya, has been gathered together in the Sacristía de los Calices on the southern side of the cathedral. Adjoining this, and far too rarely visited, are the Sacristía Mayor and the oval Chapterhouse, two impressive Renaissance structures designed by the great Diego de Siloe.

The Sevillians, while generally critical of the functions that take place within the cathedral, are enamoured of the building, and think that its one ugly feature is the crocodile carcass (known as the *lagarto* or lizard) which hangs, curiously, in a side chapel off the Patio de los Naranjos. They are not too keen either about climbing their beloved Giralda bell-tower (see page 81), and have the reputation of doing so only when they want to commit suicide; the view of Seville from the top of this former minaret is in fact well worth the climb. In between the cathedral and the Alcázar is the former Stock Exchange or *Lonja* (see page 105), an austere late sixteenth-century building now housing the Archive of the Indies (a selection of old documents is always on show here). Directly facing the southern side of the *Lonja*, on the Calle Santo Tomás, is the recently created Museo de Arte Contemporáneo, which puts on little-visited exhibitions and has a small permanent collection of twentieth-century Spanish art, notably abstract works by Zobel, Chillida, Millares, and Tapiès. The Alcázar and its gardens are entered from the adjoining Plaza de la Contratacción (see pages 106–7).

The Alcázar overlooks to the east the Barrio de Santa Cruz, which was the town's Jewish quarter, and is as much of a showpiece as is CORDOBA's Judería, but with fewer of the latter's offending tourist shops. With its maze of narrow streets, white walls covered in flowers, elegant black balconies and pervasive smells of jasmine, this is exactly how Romantic travellers liked to picture Seville, and it is appropriate that on one of the squares has been placed a statue to Don Juan Tenorio. Most of the bars in the Barrio de Santa Cruz are frequented largely by tourists, and the area is notorious for muggings in the early hours of the morning. The church of Santa María la Blanca, on the western edge of the Barrio, was originally a synagogue and has a gothic west portal surviving from this building; the interior was radically altered in an exuberant baroque style in the 1650s and has two outstanding canvases by Murillo. Also contained at one time within the old Jewish quarter was the nearby Calle Levies, on which stand the palace of Miguel Mañara of Don Juan fame (see page 119), and the Carbonería, a spacious bar which has played an important role in Seville's cultural life, and where you can hear *flamenco* every Thursday night (see pages 143–4). Behind the church runs a wide and ugly street which marks the site of the city's old walls, and is popularly referred to as the Ronda.

North of the Barrio de Santa Cruz the architecture of Seville retains many of the latter's features but becomes increasingly run-down. In the Calle Marmoles stand, above a stagnant rubbish-strewn pool, three enormous columns, the main survival of Roman Seville. Further north you are in the district known as the Alfalfa, which has, on the Calle Boteros, one of Seville's most unusual bars, the Garlochi. This small bar, open all night, is distinguished by a remarkable baroque decoration of flowers and religious images. East of here is the seventeenth-century convent of San Leandro, where you can buy famous egg-yolk sweets known as *yemas*. Walking from the convent east towards the Ronda, you will reach after a few minutes the Casa Pilatos, the most remarkable of Seville's Renaissance palaces (see page 107).

In the streets immediately to the north of the cathedral are a whole series of animated bars, including the Casa Bar Robles, well known for its *tapas*, and Antigüedades, the façade of which is adorned with ghoulish maquettes; of interest purely for its elegant setting is the Bar

Abades in the Calle Abades, a bar arranged with great style around a beautiful small *patio*. Some of the best views of the Giralda are to be had from the rooftop bars of the Bar Placentines (on the Calle Placentines) and the Hotel Doña María (on the Calle Don Remundo). The main street leading north from the cathedral is the wide Avenida de la Constitución, which ends by the town's plateresque Town Hall. West of this street are Mañara's Hospedal de la Caridad (see page 119) and, on the Guadalquivir, the Almohad defensive tower known as the Torre de Oro (now a small maritime museum) and the eighteenth-century Maestranza or bull-ring (see pages 156–7). The square on the western side of the Town Hall, the Plaza Nueva, is large and characterless, but that on the eastern side, the Plaza San Fernando, has considerable charm and elegance. North from the latter square is a pedestrian shopping district, the main street of which is the narrow and lively Calle Sierpes, shaded in the summer by awnings. Walking along this you should turn west down the Calle Gallegos to see the small chapel of San José, which has one of the more elaborate late baroque altars in Andalusia (see page 120). Turning east along the Calle Gallegos you will come to the delightful Plaza del Salvador, dominated by the large early seventeenth-century church of that name; in a side chapel is a celebrated polychromed statue of *Christ Carrying the Cross* by Martínez Montañés, a monument to whom is in the middle of the square (see page 117). The square has several open-air bars, including the Bar Alicantina, one of the most pleasant places to sit outside in Seville, and an establishment known for its justifiably expensive seafood *tapas*. Continuing north along the Calle Sierpes, turn east on to the short Calle de la Cerrajería, where you will find the Edificio Inglés, a turn-of-the-century Moorish pastiche by the same architect responsible for Seville's Hotel Alfonso XIII, Espliau. The building abuts on to the Calle Cuna, which runs parallel with the Calle Sierpes; at 18 Calle Cuna is the Palacio Lebrija, an eighteenth-century palace incorporating in its three *patios* magnificent Roman mosaics pilfered from Itálica. The Calle Sierpes comes to an end at the Campana, around which are a number of Seville's large shopping stores, including the Corte Ingles. The Campana forms part of a long thoroughfare which extends west to the Puente de Isabel II and east to the Ronda; it effectively divides the northern and southern halves of Seville's old town.

To the west of the Campana are the profusely marbled and poly-chromed Church of the Magdalena by Leonardo de Figueroa (see page 120), and the town's Museum of Fine Arts, the best in Spain outside the Prado and housed in the attractive early seventeenth-century Convent of La Merced (see page 118); disgracefully this remarkable museum, filled with works of the great seventeenth-century Andalusian artists, has been closed for several years for restoration. In between these buildings, on the Calle Bailén, is Bailén 34, a friendly, intimate restaurant, unmistakably Sevillian in its stylish awning decoration, and serving outstanding regional dishes. To the east of the Campana is the sixteenth-century university church, in whose spacious simple interior you can admire two exquisitely carved Italian Renaissance tombs by the obscure Genoese artists Antonio Aprile and Pace Gagini; the church also has a monument to the poet Gustavo Adolfo Bécquer, who, together with his painter brother Valeriano, is buried in the crypt here (see page 200). The Plaza Encarnación, on which the church stands, is a large, featureless and grubby square which also acts as a major terminal for Seville's buses. Further east, past the rather quieter and more pleasant Plaza de Cristo de Burgos, is the church of Santa Catalina, which has much fourteenth-century *mudéjar* work as well as a lavishly baroque eighteenth-century Sagrario chapel. The Bar El Rinconcillo, facing the church on the Calle Sol, is a famous bar with a splendid interior which has remained virtually unchanged since the late nineteenth century.

Much of the northern half of Seville's old town is poor and very decayed, but it also has numerous fascinating monuments and corners. Heading north from Santa Catalina, you soon reach the attractively simple medieval church of San Marcos, the parish of which was once largely made up of gypsies (see page 105); the gypsies still identify with this district and often crowd to its bars. It is typical of the great contrasts that are to be found in Seville that, immediately to the west of San Marcos, is the vast eighteenth-century palace and gardens belonging to the wealthiest and most distinguished of the town's aristocrats, the Duchess of Alba. Behind the church to the east are grouped the fifteenth-century convents of Santa Isabel and Santa Paula. The latter's church is entered through a large, pleasantly rustic courtyard, one of many such places in Seville where you suddenly feel far away from any city; the west portal has a polychrome Renaissance lunette by the Florentine Niculoso Pisano (see page 109). Santa Paula is the only closed order convent in Seville which can be officially visited, and the nuns take it in turns to show members of the public their small, atmospheric museum of ecclesiastical bric-à-brac; perhaps one of the best reasons to visit this convent is to buy the nuns' delicious home-made marmalade and other jams. The church of San Luis, one of the most exciting buildings by Leonardo de Figueroa, is reached by walking north from the church of San Marcos along the Calle Luis. The pompous exterior, imitating that of San Agnese in Rome, offers little hint of the colour and ornamental vitality of the interior, but sadly, prior permission is needed from the town council of Seville before being allowed inside. Continuing north, the surroundings take on a yet seedier aspect as you approach the chapel where the celebrated processional image of the Macarena is kept (see page 118). The nineteenth-century chapel of the Macarena adjoins the largest stretch of the town's old walls. Outside the walls, facing the chapel across a large square, is the enormous sixteenth-century Hospital of the Five Wounds (Hospedal de las Cinco Llagas), at present being converted into the seat of the Andalusian Parliament. A number 11 bus will take you north from here to the Cemetery of San Fernando, which has a small section reserved for both Protestants and atheists; but the great interest of this cemetery is in its early twentieth-century monuments, in particular the large and superb sculptural group by Manlliure representing the burial of the bull-fighter Joselito; one of the bearers carrying the coffin is García Lorca's friend, the poet/bull-fighter Ignacio Sánchez Mejías, who himself lies buried at Joselito's side (see pages 217 and 220).

Back again inside the city walls you should explore the part of the city which lies to the west of the street running between the Macarena and Santa Catalina. Due west of the church of San Marcos is the Calle Feria, which has a lively flea-market on Thursday mornings. Further west is the long and forlorn eighteenth-century promenade known as the Alameda de Hércules (see page 104), on the eastern side of which is the town's main prostitute area. West of the Alameda you find yourself once again in a more respectable part of town, the Barrio of San Lorenzo being indeed one of the most pleasant residential districts of Seville; in the large neo-classical chapel adjoining the church of San Lorenzo is kept Roldán's celebrated processional image of the Christ

of the Gran Poder (see page 151). North of this church, at the
northern end of the Calle Santa Clara, is one of the most remarkable
of Seville's forgotten monuments, the fourteenth-century tower of
Don Fadrique, which stands in peaceful, enchanting grounds attached
to the convent of Santa Clara; from the top of the tower you
have perhaps the finest of all views of Seville. A few minutes' walk
away is the Renaissance monastery of San Clemente, at present being
renovated in preparation for 1992; the monastery's grounds look
across the river Guadalquivir to Seville's Charterhouse, a much
damaged sixteenth-century structure occupying what was until recently an empty wasteland, but is now being transformed as the
site of the 1992 Exhibition. The bleak Calle Torneo leads south along
the Guadalquivir from San Clemente to the neo-Moorish railway
station known as the Estación de Córdoba. At No. 18 is the Joven
Costalero, a bar which is notorious for its intentionally tacky silver-
foil decorations and constant video-show of highlights from the
Semana Santa; the interior is certainly amusing, but this is not a
place to linger.

The famous former gypsy quarter of Triana, considered by many
people to be a separate township to Seville, lies south of the Estación
de Córdoba on the east bank of the Guadalquivir and has excellent
views over the river to the Maestranza, the Torre de Oro and the
cathedral. The district is no longer the poor ramshackle place it used
to be, and indeed becomes increasingly smart the further south you
walk in the direction of the modern district of Los Remedios. The
main street crossing through the northern half of Triana is the Calle
Castilla, which passes at its northern end next to the ugly neo-classical
church of Nuestra Señora de la O, worth a visit only for its famous
processional image of The Dead Christ. This much loved work,
carved in 1682 by Francisco Antonio Gijón, is known popularly as the
Christ of 'El Cacharro', and was reputedly inspired by the dead body
of a handsome gypsy singer who had been killed in a street brawl
outside the church. On the other side of the street to the church is the
Sol y Sombra, one of the city's outstanding tapas bars. The Calle
Castilla leads south towards the Plaza Alozano, next to which is the
Triana market, occupying the site of the notorious castle of the
Inquisition (see page 105). Opposite the market is a handsome turn-
of-the-century shop decorated with and selling the elaborate tiles and

ceramics for which Triana is traditionally famous; nearby, at the corner of the Calles Pages del Coro and Antillano Campos, is a beautifully tiled bar (Anselma) where guitarists and singers often meet in the evenings. The Calle Betis, which hugs the riverside in between the Puente Isabel II and the Puente San Telmo, is the fashionable heart of present-day Triana, being lined with bars, restaurants and night-clubs. A curiosity at its northern end, and a survival of the old Triana, is the eccentric barbershop called Los Pajaritos ('the Little Birds'), the exterior of which is covered by day with bird-cages.

South of the Puente de San Telmo, on the Seville side of the river, is a spacious, luxurious area of town incorporating the María Luisa Park, the luxury Hotel Alfonso XIII (see page 216), and the eclectic pavilions put up for the Ibero-American exhibition of 1929 (see page 216); two of the architectural pastiches in the park contain respectively the town's enjoyable ethnography museum and the extensive archaeological museum, the latter boasting a most striking horde of Tartessian jewellery from El Carambolo (see page 59). On either side of the Hotel Alfonso XIII are the old tobacco factory (see page 122) and the eighteenth-century palace of San Telmo, the frontispiece of which is one of the most elaborate of Leonardo de Figueroa's works (see page 120).

The most popular excursion in the immediate vicinity of Seville is to the dusty and shabby Roman site of Itálica, situated in and around the unprepossessing village of Santiponce (see pages 61–2). On the southern outskirts of the village is the impressive monastery of San Isidoro del Campo, which dates back to 1298 and was dissolved in 1386. Its church, rarely open, has a magnificent high altar of 1613 by Martínez Montañés.

The hilly land to the west of Santiponce is known as the Aljarafe, and is regarded with great affection by most Sevillians, many of whom choose to live here. Its appeal to the foreign visitor is less obvious, and its numerous villages include such unglamorous places as Camas, Valencina de la Concepcíon and Castilleja de la Cuesta, the latter being incongrously the birthplace of Rita Hayworth. Olivares, the home village of the famous seventeenth-century Duke of Olivares, has a beautiful and intimate arcaded square, while Umbrete has a large and impressive seventeenth-century church, and a reputation for its young sweetish wine known as *mosto*; between these two villages, near Villanueva del Ariscal, are the distinguished Bodegas Góngora, which have good table and fortified wines, an excellent brandy, and a cellar dating back to the Middle Ages. Near the village of Bollullos de la Mitación, in the southernmost part of the Aljarafe, are some outstanding eighteenth-century *haciendas* (most notably the Hacienda Torquemada; see page 12), and one of the district's most attractive sites. This, the isolated hermitage of Cuatrovitas, is notable for its well preserved Almohad tower, which was probably once the minaret of a mosque. [3C]

SORBAS occupies a dramatic site in the middle of one of the most dramatic landscapes in Europe. The old town stands high above its extensive modern suburbs and clings to the top of a high gorge which bites its way through an eroded landscape of primeval appearance. The desert which you are in continues west to beyond TABERNAS. To the north is the little-visited Sierra de los Filabres, which can be crossed on the C3325. From the south these mountains appear to be like peaks on the moon, but high up they turn out to be surprisingly wooded. One of the most attractive of the villages is that of Cóbdar, which lies in a narrow steep-sided valley underneath a massive rockface from which marble used to be quarried. [3J]

TABERNAS: The ruins of the castle where Ferdinand and Isabella stayed during the siege of Almería rise on a barren mound above the town. But the main interest of Tabernas is its bizarrely eroded surroundings. This landscape takes on a futuristic aspect at the nearby Central Solar (off the small road north to Senes), where row upon row of solar panels stand in the desert as if in some science-fiction film. Film-makers have indeed been favouring Tabernas for many years. Seven kilometres south of the town on the Almería road is 'Mini Hollywood', the oldest and most famous of several local re-creations of American villages of the 'Wild West'. This one was built originally for Clint Eastwood's *A Fistful of Dollars* and later used for 'spaghetti westerns' such as *The Good, the Bad and the Ugly*. Extras from the latter film decided to save the set as a tourist attraction, and today run the place themselves. Even without having to dress up in cowboy costumes, the men who work here look convincing as gangsters: at regular intervals during the day they stage in the village mock fights and hold-ups (the main scene of action is the saloon bar of the hotel). The more serious sight-seer should head north from here along the C3326 to Gergal, where there is an excellently preserved castle comprising a quadrangular block with round towers at each corner; the mountain which stands above the village is crowned by a German/Spanish-built observatory with the largest telescope in Spain. South from Mini Hollywood on the Almería road there is a turning to the right marked to Santa Fe de Mondújar. Before reaching the village, you will pass on the right-hand side the entrance to Europe's most extensive Bronze Age site, Los Millares (see pages 55–6). For the key to this you have to continue on to Santa Fe, which lies underneath the site and is reached by a narrow ironwork bridge perched perilously above the sinister landscape: the key is to be had from the bar in front of the Town Hall at the end of this God-forsaken village. [3H]

TARIFA, named after the Moorish leader Tarīf Ibn Malik, was the first Moorish possession in Spain (see page 64). The town, entered by a Moorish gate from the Cádiz to Algeciras road (E5), is filled with narrow streets that are congested with tourists. The heavily restored Moorish castle dating back to the tenth century (and rebuilt in the thirteenth) belongs now to the Spanish navy and cannot be visited; the best view of it is from the port. The town was captured by the Christians in 1292, but was subject to several counter-attacks during which the town was defended by Alonso Pérez de Guzmán. In an action foreshadowing that of General Moscardó's at Toledo in 1936, Pérez de Guzmán allowed his son to be killed rather than surrender the town: 'I prefer honour without a son, to dishonour with one,' he is supposed to have said. For this questionable gesture he received his name of the 'Good'.

The long sandy beaches east of Tarifa are very popular with wind-surfers; a particularly attractive stretch of dunes is to be found ten kilometres outside the town at Punta Paloma. The road west from Tarifa to Algeciras climbs up a barren mountainside and has wonderful views over to Morocco. [5C]

TEBA: On a barren hill rising above the village of Teba and the reservoir of Guadalteba-Guadalhorce stands an impressive and extensive castle, built by the Moors and dating back to Phoenician times. In 1330 Sir James Douglas, on his way to Jerusalem, took part here in a battle against the Moors. He was carrying with him a casket containing the heart of Robert Bruce, which he flung into the foray, swearing to follow after it. The casket fared rather better than he did, being afterwards recovered and taken to Melrose Abbey in Scotland, where it still lies. [4D]

ÚBEDA, built on the slope of a hill, looks out over a landscape of olive trees towards the imposing Sierra de Cazorla. The main road which runs along the top of the hill, through the northern outskirts of the town, was in ancient times a major line of communication between Andalusia and eastern Spain. It later fell into disuse, and Úbeda acquired a reputation for being cut off from the rest of the country. Today it still has an isolated character, and it is certainly one of the least visited of Andalusia's towns of major architectural and historical interest. The town's reputation for remoteness is reflected in the popular expression 'to wander off on the hills of Úbeda' ('*irse por los cerros de Úbeda*'), meaning to 'wander off the point' or 'to be distracted'. The origin of this expression is also connected with the apocryphal story of Alvar Fañez, a Christian knight who fell in love with a Moorish girl and as a result missed a critical battle at Úbeda. Asked by Ferdinand III where he had been at the time, Fañez replied: 'On those hills, sire . . .'

Despite its ancient origins, Úbeda did not develop into an important town until the arrival of the Moors, who encircled it with walls and built a castle here. After the Christian victory of nearby Las Navas de Tolosa in 1212 (see LA CAROLINA), the Moors from Baeza took refuge here, believing the town to be more securely defended than theirs. It fell to the Christians eight days later, but was not definitively captured until 1234, by Ferdinand III ('the Holy'). Numerous noble families were established by Ferdinand in Úbeda, twelve of whom are represented by the twelve lions in the town's coat of arms. Úbeda's period of greatest fame and prosperity was the sixteenth century, when its textiles were exported throughout Europe, and when members of its nobility held leading positions in the Spanish court. The

ÚBEDA

Iglesia de
San Nicolás

Hospital de
Santiago

C. OBISPO COBOS

CORREDERA DE SAN FERNANDO

PLAZA DE
ANDALUCÍA

Puerto del
Losal

Palacio de la
Calle de Montiel

Torre del
Reloj

Palacio del Conde
de Guadiana

Oratorio
de S. Juan
de la Cruz

Iglesia de
San Pedro

Iglesia de
San Pablo

PLAZA

DE MAYO

Real Monasterio
de Santa Clara

PLAZA DEL
AYUNTAMIENTO

Palacio de Vela
de los Cobos

Parador Nacional
'Condestable
Dávalos'

Sacra Capilla
del Salvador

Palacio de las Cadenas
(Ayuntamiento)

PL. VÁZQUEZ DE MOLINA C. BAJA DEL SALVADOR

Antiguo Pósito

Casa de las Torres

Palacio de Marques
de Mancera

Santa María de las
Reales Alcázares

Cárcel del Obispo

0   100   200   300m

Murallas y Puerta
de Granada

Iglesia de
San Lorenzo

EL ALCÁZAR

most renowned of these noblemen was Francisco de los Cobos y
Molina, who by 1529 was secretary to Charles V. He gained vast
wealth and was the virtual ruler of Spain during Charles V's absences
abroad, but eventually his greed for money and power led to his being
replaced as Charles V's secretary by Juan Vázquez de Molina, who
was also from Úbeda and to whose family indeed Francisco's mother
belonged. The Cobos and the Molinas, linked by various marriages,
dominated the life, culture and patronage of sixteenth-century Úbeda,
and it was through them that the town became one of the Renaissance
jewels of Europe. Their principal architect was Andrés de Vandelvira,
who was born near Albacete in 1509 and died in Jaén in 1575.

The prosperity of Úbeda declined dramatically in the early seventeenth century, and the town has few monuments of note after that
date. This century the town's fortunes have revived with the establishment of new industries and the expansion of old ones. The town has

347

grown considerably beyond its former walls, and its northern, upper part, including the main square (the Plaza de Andalucía), is a rather unprepossessing district crammed with tall dingy blocks. The most important old monument in this part of town is Vandelvira's Hospital of Santiago, which stands on the Calle Obispo Cobos, the main street leading from the town's bus station to the Plaza de Andalucía. Founded in the mid sixteenth century by Don Diego de Los Cobos y Molina, Bishop of Jaén, this vast little-ornamented building shows Vandelvira at his most austere, and is sometimes referred to as the 'Andalusian Escorial'. Also of interest in this northern part of town is the church of San Nicolás de Bari (Plaza San Nicolás), about a ten-minute walk uphill from the Plaza de Andalucía. Dating mainly from the fourteenth century, it has a playful late gothic south portal of 1509, and a superb west portal designed by Vandelvira; within its gothic interior you will find one of Vandelvira's earliest works, the Chapel of Dean Ortega Salido, the elaborate decoration of which forms a striking contrast to the simplicity of the Hospital of Santiago.

The Plaza de Andalucía lies just outside the town's former walls, and on its southern side there survives a tower from the old fortifications, the Torre del Reloj. Next to this, in the square's south-eastern corner, the narrow Calle Real descends into the old and peaceful heart of Úbeda. Half-way down, to your right, at the corner of the Calle Juan Pasquau López, is the Palace of the Counts of Guadiana, crowned by a richly sculpted Renaissance tower; in any other town this would be a building of major importance, but as you continue to wander around Úbeda, you will find countless other palaces like this. Opposite, at 45 Calle Real, is a large shop, Artesanía Blanco, which specializes in traditional local crafts, most notably basketwork and ceramics: the traditional Úbeda ceramics, produced here since Moorish times, are characterized by their dark green glaze. A short detour down the tiny Calle Juan Pasquau López will take you to the medieval church of San Pedro and the Convent of Santa Clara, where you can buy a wide range of cakes, biscuits and pastries. Continuing downhill along the Calle Real, you will reach at the end of the street, on the right-hand side, the Palace of Vela de los Cobos, which is crowned by an upper arcaded gallery, a typical feature of Spanish Renaissance architecture and a space intended for the women of the household to exercise without being observed from the street.

The Calle Real opens out into the Plaza del Ayuntamiento, dominated at its southern end by the free-standing Palacio de la Cadenas,
which was built originally as the Palace of Juan Vázquez de Molina,
and is now the Town Hall: the secular masterpiece of Vandelvira, it is
a relatively sober building attempting a conventionally classical ordering of its façades. Extending to the south and east on the other side
of the Town Hall is the Plaza Vázquez de Molina, one of the most
aristocratic of all Spanish squares, and lined on all sides with outstanding buildings. Before exploring it more closely, you should head west
down the Calle del Condestable Dávalos until you reach the charming
small square containing the profusely decorated twin-towered façade
of the Casa de las Torres (mid sixteenth-century; this is now an art
school, and you can walk freely around its beautiful courtyard).
Immediately to the south of here is a small section of the town's
southern walls, incorporated into which is the sixteenth-century
church of San Lorenzo. The walls look directly on to open countryside,
and from the terrace of San Lorenzo there are excellent views towards
the Cazorla range. Following the walls to the east, you pass by the
Granada gate and walk along a rubbish-strewn path until you reach
the Arroyo de Santa María, which will take you back to the Plaza
Vázquez de Molina.

The church which you come to immediately on arriving at the
square is that of Santa María de las Reales Alcázares, which once
formed part of the town's walls. In its attractive gothic cloister, once
the courtyard of a mosque, there is a plaque recording that when
Alfonso VII reached the walls of Úbeda in 1157 he placed his shield
here; you can still see this, as well as a nearby statue of the Virgin, left
here in 1212 by Alfonso VIII. Walking round the square to the east,
you pass in succession the former prison, the palace of the Marqueses
de Mancena and the old municipal warehouse. The square narrows in
its eastern end, and in its north-eastern corner is the long sixteenth-
century palace which once belonged to the Condestable Dávalos: it
was turned in 1930 into what is still one of the most impressive of
Andalusia's luxury *paradores* (it is also the only hotel in the old town
of Úbeda). Adajacent to it, proudly standing at the eastern end of the
square, is the most interesting of all Úbeda's monuments, the chapel
of the Salvador (see page 98). This was originally intended as the
private chapel of Francisco de Cobos, and was designed by Diego de

Siloe and executed, with considerable modifications to the original design, by his great successor, Andrés de Vandelvira. The chapel is entered through a door on the narrow Calle Francisco de Cobos, on which street can also be seen the side façade of Cobos's palace: the rest of the palace was largely destroyed by fire. Crossing a courtyard, you enter the chapel through its large and splendid sacristy, which was built by Vandelvira at an angle to the chapel, resulting in a curiously shaped door between the two spaces: Siloe would undoubtedly have favoured a more classical solution. Within the sacristy is a photograph of a statue by Michelangelo given as a gift to Cobos by the Venetian state, but destroyed during the Civil War of 1936–9. During this same war the chapel itself suffered much damage, but it is being patiently restored and is still one of the finest Renaissance ensembles in Spain. The tall chancel, with elegant coffering in its vault and late baroque gilding, is divided from the nave by a splendid Renaissance grille designed by Master Bartolomeu. The high altar, changed during the baroque period, features a carved and poly-chromed *Transfiguration* by one of Spain's most remarkable Renaissance artists, Alonso de Berruguete. Berruguete was trained under Michelangelo, and his style is notable for its pathos and expressiveness. His masterly *Transfiguration* is a characteristically agitated work, but, sadly, it was badly damaged during the Civil War, and only the Christ figure is original, the rest being skilful restoration.

To the east and south of the chapel the town comes to an abrupt end, suspended over a sea of olive trees. Heading north along the Calle Francisco de los Cobos, you will eventually come to the Monastery of San Juan de la Cruz, which was where the saint and poet St John of the Cross died of gangrene in 1591. Only a small part of this building is as it was in the sixteenth century, and its church (the first to be dedicated to the saint) was rebuilt after having been destroyed in the Civil War. The monastery houses a museum to the saint, with numerous documents and objects relating to his life, including the actual writing desk which he used; also displayed is a selection of the many books written on the saint, one of which is by Gerald Brenan. The museum has a singularly depressing atmosphere, complete with gloomily designed information panels imitating peeling leather.

North of the monastery is the horseshoe-arched Puerta del Losal, the town's north-eastern gate; beyond this runs the Calle de Valencia, lined with shops selling ceramics. To the west of the monastery is the large and pleasant Plaza 1 de Mayo, which has a bandstand in the middle; in its south-western corner is the former sixteenth-century Town Hall, while on the northern side is the church of San Pablo, an engagingly anarchic blend of gothic and Renaissance elements, with a beautiful late gothic portal of the Virgin facing the square. North of the church is a fourteenth-century house containing the town's small archaeological museum: the collections are well arranged but unremarkable, and the interest of the museum lies primarily in its enchanting *mudéjar* courtyard. Further north still is the wide Corredera de San Fernando, a busy commercial street which will lead you back to the Plaza de Andalucía. [2G]

UTRERA, a flat, dusty and ugly town, was very important in Moorish and Roman times, and even today is a place of considerable vitality and character. It is one of the main Andalusian centres of *flamenco*, and there live in the town two of the most established *flamenco* singers of today, the sisters Fernanda and Bernarda de Utrera. Every year in July the *flamenco* festival known as the *Potaje* is held in the small modern park alongside the sad fragments of the town's Moorish castle. Next to the park is the church of Santiago, which dates back to the late fifteenth century and has an exuberantly decorative if rather worn Isabelline plateresque west portal. A good example of the classical plateresque style is the west portal of the Church of Santa María de la Asunción, which stands in the small and shaded Plaza Enrique de la Cuadra: the portal takes the form of a triumphal arch with classical coffering framing a tympanum of the Assumption of the Virgin. In front of this church stands a modern monument to the poet, humanist and pioneering archaeologist Rodrigo Cano, born in Utrera in 1573 (see page 62). At El Palamar de Troya, thirteen kilometres to the south of Utrera on the N333, a basilica of monstrous proportions and hideousness is being erected to the dissident Christian sect of the Holy Face, which was founded after a supposed series of apparitions of the Virgin to four girls in 1968; the head of this sect – which lives mainly off the gullibility of foreigners, and is regarded as a great joke among the Andalusians – styles himself 'Pope Clement'. [3C]

VEJER DE LA FRONTERA, rising steeply behind the fishing town of BARBATE, is a sprawling village very popular with day-trippers from the coast. Occupied by the Moors up to 1250, it has a strong Moorish character and a maze of narrow white streets. You enter the upper part of the village through the original Moorish gates. Inside is the sixteenth-century parish church, which was built over a mosque. Near this, hidden by the surrounding houses, is a Moorish castle, with a horseshoe gate and recently uncovered Moorish plasterwork; the castle is now used by boy scouts, who will lead you on to its terrace, which has wonderful views of the village and surrounding countryside. Just outside the village gates is the charming, palm-lined Plaza de los Pescaítos, featuring nineteenth-century ceramic decorations in a Triana style. As at ARCOS DE LA FRONTERA, a bull with padded horns is let loose through the streets here on Easter Sunday. [5C]

VÉLEZ-BLANCO: The drive from the Sierra de Segura (see SEGURA) leads you through a lonely landscape of parched wheat-fields framed by bleached rocky peaks. Both Vélez-Blanco and the neighbouring Vélez-Rubio are in the centre of the major cereal-producing area in Almería province, and supplied grain to the troops of Ferdinand and Isabella during the last stages of the Reconquest. Vélez-Blanco, the smaller and more attractive of the two towns, extends under the rocky hill on which stands its famous castle (see page 100), which from the outside is one of the most impressive in all Andalusia. The original Moorish castle is a simple block connected by a bridge to a large polygonal structure built between 1506 and 1515 by an Italian architect, F. Florentini. The sixteenth-century bridge linking the Moorish and Renaissance structures was destroyed by the French during the Peninsular War, and rebuilt only recently. The most serious damage suffered by this castle, however, was to its Renaissance section, and was to be perpetuated by a descendant of the man who had commissioned this, Pedro Fejardo, Marquis of Vélez. The Marquis's descendant, fallen on hard times, sold off the castle's magnificent Renaissance bronze door and its entire marbled courtyard to a French antique dealer; the door ended up in a private collection in Paris, and the courtyard was eventually reconstructed in the Metropolitan Museum of Art, New York. The interior of Florentini's castle, patched up now with steel beams and concrete walls, has only the smallest fragments left of its original Renaissance decoration. It is worth a visit primarily for the views from the top of its tallest tower, and for the informative commentary provided by the energetic old man who looks after the building. This man, known to everyone in the town as 'Tío Perez', spends most of his day in the castle, and should you want to look inside, you need only stand under the bridge and shout out his name as loudly as possible; in case he is not there, he can usually be located in the Círculo de los Pensionistas in the town centre.

Just outside the village to the south, off the C321 to Vélez-Rubio, is a sign marked 'Cueva de los Letreros' (see pages 54–5). Turn right down a dust track, take the first turning to the left, and then the first one to the right. Up to now the track is just about manageable by car, but from now on you must walk. The prehistoric rock shelter of Los Letreros lies half-way up the cliff in front of you, and is reached by concrete steps carved into the rock. The very faint red and brown sketches inside, comprising abstract representations of men and animals, have been dated to 4,000 BC. The shelter is closed off by a metal grille, but the paintings – in so far as they can be made out at all – are visible from the outside. 'Tío Perez', might well offer to accompany you here and to open the grille, but he should be discouraged from doing so, as he is prone to throw water at the paintings to bring out the colour.

The principal monument of Vélez-Rubio is the large late baroque parish church of 1753, the most important monument of this period in Almería province. The majestic, richly carved façade is dominated by the huge coat of arms of the Marquises of Vélez, who had the church built at their expense. [2J]

VÉLEZ-MÁLAGA, one of the last Moorish strongholds to be taken by the Christians, lies in a fertile valley at the foot of a steeply mountainous district known as the Axarquía. The town, only four kilometres inland from the characterless coastal resort of Torre del Mar, is a large place with a prosperous and mainly modern look. The elegant and recently restored Palacio del Marques de Beniel is the seat of the recently inaugurated International University of the Axarquía, a summer school intended to give the town a new intellectual prestige. The old town of Vélez-Málaga rises up on a hill crowned by trees and the much restored tower of a Moorish castle. The church immediately below the tower is that of Nuestra Señora de la Encarnación. Originally a Visigothic church, it was used by the Moors as a mosque before being transformed back into a church after the Christian capture of the town in 1487. [4F]

FURTHER READING

GENERAL

In English

Acery, D., *Not on Queen Victoria's Birthday. The Story of the Río Tinto Mines*, London, 1914.

Brandes, Stanley, *Metaphors of Masculinity*, University of Pennsylvania Press, 1980.

Buck, Walter, and Buck, Walter, and Chapman, Abel, Unexplored Spain, london 1910.

Chapman, Abel, *Wild Spain*, London, 1893.

Fitton, Mary, *Málaga, Portrait of a City*, London, 1971.

Ford, Richard, *Handbook for Travellers in Spain*, London, 1845.

Fraser, Ronald, *The Pueblo*, London, 1973.

Gilmore, David, *The People of the Plain. Class and Community in Lower Andalusia*, New York, 1980.

Gilmore, David, *Aggression and Community in Andalusia*, New Haven, 1987.

Hall, Standish, *Seville*, London, 1840.

Josephs, Allen, *White Wall of Spain. The Mysteries of Andalusian Culture*, Iowa, 1983.

Lowe, Alfonso, *The Companion Guide to the South of Spain*, London, 1973.

Luard, Nicholas, *Andalucía, a Portrait of Southern Spain*, London, 1984.

Martinez Alier, J., *Labourers and Landowners in Southern Spain*, London, 1971.

Mountfort, Guy, *Portrait of a Wilderness*, London, 1958.

Pitt-Rivers, Julian, *The People of the Sierra*, London, 1954.

Praz, Mario, *Unromantic Spain*, London, 1928.

Robertson, Ian (ed.), *Blue Guide to Spain*, London, 1989.

In French

Lépidis, Clément (ed.), *Andalousie*, Paris, 1985.

In Spanish

Artola, M., *El Latifundio*, Madrid, 1978.

Bernal, A., *La Propriedad de la Tierra y las luchas agrarias andaluzas*, Madrid, 1974.

Bernaldo de Quiros, C., *El bandolerismo andaluz*, Madrid, 1973.

Burgos, Antonio, *Andalucía ¿tercer mundo?*, Esplugas de Llobregat, 1976.

Caro Baroja, *Los Pueblos de España, Ensayo de etnología*, Barcelona, 1946.

Cuenca Toribio, José Manuel, *Andalucía*, Madrid, 1982.

Díaz del Moral, J., *Historia de las agitaciones campesinos andaluzes*, Madrid, 1979.

Drain, Michel (ed.), *Los andaluzes*, Madrid, 1980.

Guía Illustrada de Andalucía, Madrid, 1984.

Infante, Blas, *El Ideal andaluz*, Madrid, 1976.

Javierre, José María, *Gran Enciclopedia de Andalucía* (10 vols.), Seville, 1979.

Madrid: Fundación March, *Tierras de España, Andalucía* (2 vols.), Madrid, 1980.

Martínez Alier, J., *La estabilidad del latifundismo*, Madrid, 1968.

Medina Molera, A., *Historia de Andalucía*, Seville, 1980.

Ortega y Gasset, José, *Teoría de Andalucía*, Madrid, 1944.

Pemán, José María, *Andalucía*, Barcelona, 1958.

Ramos y Espejo, *Andalucía de Fuente-Obejuna a Marinaleda*, Seville, 1985.

Sermet, Jean, *España del Sud*, Madrid, 1954.

Urbano, M., *Andalucía en el testimonio de sus poetas*, Madrid, 1976.

Zugasti, Julian, *El bandolerismo*, Madrid, 1876.

TRAVELLERS' ACCOUNTS

In English

Badcock, Lowell, *Rough Leaves from a Journal*, London, 1835.

Baxley, H. Willis, *Spain: Art-Remains and Art-Realities, Painters, Priests and Princes* (2 vols.), London, 1875.

Blanco White, *Letters from Spain*, London, 1822.

Bourgoing, J. F., *Travels in Spain* , vol. 3, London, 1789.

Boyd, Alastair, *The Road from Ronda. Travels with a Horse through Southern Spain*, London, 1969.

Brenan, Gerald, *The Face of Spain*, London, 1950.

Brenan, Gerald, *South from Granada*, London, 1957.

Byrne, William Pitt, *Cosas de España*, vol. 2, London, 1866.

Chetwode, Penelope, *Two Middle-Aged Ladies in Andalusia*, London, 1963.

Cook, Samuel E., *Sketches in Spain*, London, 1834.

Cook, Samuel E., *Spain and the Spaniards*, London, 1844.

Dennis, G., *A Summer in Andalusia* (2 vols.), London, 1839.

Havelock Ellis, *The Soul of Spain*, London, 1929.

Hutchinson, Marjorie, *Málaga Farm*, London, 1956.

Irving, W., *Diary. Spain, 1828–29*, New York, 1926.

Jacob, W., *Travels in the South of Spain in 1809–10*, 1811.

Lee, Laurie, *A Rose for Winter*, London, 1955.

Lee, Laurie, *As I Walked Out One Midsummer Morning*, London, 1969.

Meier-Graefe, *The Spanish Journey*, London, 1926.

Murray, E. Dundas, *The Cities and Wilds of Andalusia* (2 vols.), London, 1849.

Protheroe, Ronald (ed.), *The Letters of Richard Ford, 1797–1858*, London, 1905.

Scott, C. Rochfort, *Excursions in the Mountains of Ronda and Granada* (2 vols.), London, 1838.

Sitwell, Sacheverell, *Spain*, London, 1950.

Slidell, Alexander, *Spain Revisited* (2 vols.), London, 1836.

Swinburne, H., *Travels through Spain in 1775 and 1776*, London, 1779.

Thomas, R. M., *The Alpujarra: Notes of a Tour in the Andalusian Highlands*, London, 1903.

Ticknor, George, *The Life, Letters and Journals of George Ticknor*, London, 1876.

Townsend, Joseph, *A Journey through Spain in the Years 1786 and 1787*, London, 1791.

Tracy, Honor, *Silk Hats and No Breakfast. Notes on a Spanish Journey*, London, 1957.

Tracy, Honor, *Spanish Leaves*, London, 1964.

Trend, J. B., *Spain from the South*, London, 1928.

In French

Dumas, Alexandre, *De Paris à Cadiz*, Paris, 1846.

Gautier, Théophile, *Voyage en Espagne*, Paris, 1843.

Peyron, Jean-François, *Nouveau Voyage en Espagne* (2 vols.), London, 1782.

Taylor, Baron, *Voyage pittoresque en Espagne, en Portugal et sur la Côte d'Afrique, de Tanger à Tetoan*, Paris, 1827.

In Spanish

Alarcón, Pedro Antonio de, *Alpujarra*, Madrid, 1874.

Cela, Camilo José, *Primer viaje andaluz*, Barcelona, 1959.

García Mercadal, J., *Viajes de extranjeros por España y Portugal, desde los tiempos más remotos hasta fines del siglo XV* (3 vols.), Madrid, 1952.

Goytisolo, Juan, *Campo de Níjar*, Paris, 1959.

Goytisolo, Juan, *La Chanca*, Paris, 1959.

Grosso, Alfonso, *Por el río abajo*, Paris, 1966.

Ponz, Antonio, *Viaje de España*, vols. 16–18, Madrid, 1791–4.

PREHISTORY AND ANTIQUITY

In English

Bonsor, G. E., *An Archaeological Sketch-book of the Roman Necropolis at Carmona*, New York, 1931.

Breuil, Henri, *Rock Paintings of Southern Andalusia*, Oxford, 1929.

Knapp, Robert, *Roman Córdoba*, Berkeley, 1983.

Rothenberg, Beno, *Studies in Ancient Mining and Metallurgy in South-west Spain*, London, 1981.

Whishaw, E.M., *Atlantis in Andalucia. A study of folk memory*, London, 1929.

In Spanish

García y Bellido, *Andalucía Monumental. Itálica*, Seville, 1984.

Góngora y Martinez, M. de, *Antigüedades prehistóricas de Andalucía*, Madrid, 1968.

Maluquier de Montes, *La civilización de Tartessus*, Granada, 1985.

MUSLIM ANDALUSIA

In English

Burckhardt, Titus, *Moorish Culture in Spain*, London, 1972.

Chejne, Anuar, *Muslim Spain*, Minneapolis, 1974.

Goldstein, David (ed.), *The Jewish Poets of Spain, 900–1250*, Harmondsworth, 1971.

Grabar, Oleg, *The Alhambra*, London, 1978.

Irving, Washington, *A Chronicle of the Conquest of Granada* (2 vols.), London, 1986.

Irving, Washington, *The Alhambra*, London, 1986.

Jackson, Gabriel, *The Making of Medieval Spain*, London, 1972.

Montgomery Watt, *A History of Islamic Spain*, Edinburgh, 1965.

Whishaw, Bernard, *Arabic Spain*, London, 1986.

In French

Pérès, Henri, *L'Espagne vue par les voyageurs musulmans de 1610 à 1930*, Algiers, 1937.

Pérès, Henri, *La Poésie Andalouse en Arabe classique au XIème siécle*, Algiers, 1953.

In Spanish

Arjona Castro, A., *El Reino de Córdoba durante la dominación Musulmana*, Córdoba, 1982.

Bosch Vilá, J. (ed.), *Andalucía islámica*, Granada, 1980.

Guillen Robles, F., *Málaga musulmana*, Málaga, 1880.

Nieto Cumplido, M., *La mezquita-catedral de Córdoba*, Córdoba, 1976.

Sánchez-Albornoz, C., *La España musulmana según los autores islamitas y cristianas medievales*, Paris, 1985.

SIXTEENTH, SEVENTEENTH AND EIGHTEENTH CENTURIES

In English

Elliot, J. H., *Imperial Spain, 1469–1716*, London, 1963.

Kamen, H., *Spain in the Later 17th Century*, London, 1980.

Lomax, D. W., *The Reconquest of Spain*, London, 1978.

Perry, Mary Elizabeth, *Crime and Society in Early Modern Seville*, Hanover, N.H., *c.* 1980.

Pike, Ruth, *Enterprise and Adventure. The Genoese in Seville and the Opening of the New World*, Cornell, 1966.

Pike, Ruth, *Aristocrats and Traders: Sevillian Society in the 16th Century*, Ithaca, 1972.

Rosenthal, E., *The Cathedral of Granada. A Study in the Spanish Renaissance*, Princeton, 1961.

Rosenthal, Earl, *The Palace of Charles V in Granada*, Princeton, 1985.

Sitwell, S., *Spanish Baroque Art*, London, 1931.

In Spanish

Banda y Vargas, Antonio de la, *La escultura Sevillana del Siglo de Oro*, Madrid, 1978.

Bonet Correa, A., *Andalucía barrocca*, Barcelona, 1978.
Bonet Correa, A., *Andalucía monumental. Arquitectura y ciudad del Renacimiento al Barrocco*, Seville, 1986.
Dominguez Ortiz, Antonio, *La Sevilla del Siglo XVII*, Seville, 1984.
Gallego y Burín, A., *El barrocco granadino*, Madrid, 1956.
Hernández Diaz, J., *Arte y artistas del renacimiento en Sevilla*, Seville, 1933.
Modrales Pardon, Francisco, *La ciudad del quinientos. Historia de Sevilla*, Seville, 1977.
Orozco Díaz, E., *La Capilla Real de Granada*, Granada, 1968.
Orozco Díaz, E., *La Cartuja de Granada*, Granada, 1972.
Ruiz Lagos, *Illustrados y reformadores de la Baja Andalucía*, Madrid, 1974.
Sancho Corbacho, A., *Arquitectura barrocca sevillana del siglo XVIII*, Madrid, 1952.

NINETEENTH CENTURY

In English

Carr, R., *Spain, 1808–1939*, Oxford, 1966.
Hempel Lipschutz, *Spanish Painting and the French Romantics*, Cambridge, Mass., 1972.
Hutchinson, Marjorie, *The English Cemetery at Málaga*, Málaga, 1964.
Kaplan, T., *Anarchists of Andalusia, 1818–1903*, Princeton, 1977.

In French

Herr, Elena Fernández, *Les origines de l'Espagne Romantique, les récits de voyage, 1755–1823*, Paris, 1973.
Hoffmann, Léon-François, *Romantique Espagne, l'image de l'Espagne en France entre 1800 et 1850*, New Jersey, 1961.

In Spanish

Alberich, José, *Del Tamesis al Guadalquivir. Antología de viajeros ingleses en la Sevilla del siglo XIX*, Seville, 1976.

Bernal Rodriguez, Manuel, *La Andalucía de los libros de viajes del siglo XIX*, Seville, 1985.

Bernaldo de Quiros, *Colonialización y subversión en la Andalucía de los siglos XVIII–XIX*, Seville, 1981.

Estébanez Calderón, Serafín, *Escenas Andaluzas*, Madrid, 1883.

Reina Palazón, Antonio, *La pintura costumbrista en Sevilla, 1830–1870*, Seville, 1979.

Robertson, Ian, *Los curiosos impertinentes, viajeros ingleses por España, 1760–1855*, Madrid, 1976.

Ruiz Lagos, M., *Política y desarrollo social en la Baja Andalucía*, Madrid, 1976.

Santos García Felguera, Marín de los (ed.), *Imagen romántica de España*, exhibition catalogue, Palacio de Velázquez, Madrid, 1981.

Torres Martín, R., *La pintura costumbrista sevillana*, Madrid, 1980.

TWENTIETH CENTURY

In English

Alberti, Rafael, *The Lost Grove*, Berkeley, 1976.

Brenan, Gerald, *Personal Record*, London, 1974.

Chalmers Mitchell, Sir Peter, *My House in Málaga*, London, 1938.

Fraser, Ronald, *In Hiding – The Life of Manuel Cortes*, London, 1962.

García Lorca, F., *Selected Letters*, London, 1984.

Gibson, Ian, *The Assassination of Federico García Lorca*, London, 1979.

Gibson, Ian, *Federico García Lorca. A Biography*, London, 1989.

Monks, Joe, *With the Reds in Andalusia*, London, c. 1985.

Nicholson, H., *Death in the Morning*, London, 1936.

Woolsey, Gamel, *Death's Other Kingdom*, London, 1939.

In Spanish

Gibson, Ian, *En Granada, su Granada. Guía a la Granada de Federico García Lorca*, Barcelona, 1989.

Tussell, Xavier, *Oligarquía y caciquismo en Andalucía, 1890–1923*, Barcelona, 1976.

Tussell, Xavier, *La crisis del caciquismos andaluz, 1923–31*, Madrid, 1977.

GYPSIES AND FLAMENCO

In English

Borrow, G. H., *The Zincali: or an Account of the Gypsies of Spain* (2 vols.), London, 1841.

Brown, Irving, *Nights and Days on the Gypsy Trail through Andalusia and on other Mediterranean Shores*, New York, 1922.

Brown, Irving, *Deep Song*, London, 1929.

Clébert, Jean-Paul, *The Gypsies*, London, 1967.

Falla, Manuel de, 'Cante jondo' in *On Music and Musicians*, London, 1970.

García Lorca, Federico, *Deep Song and Other Prose*, New York, 1980.

Jones, Jo, *Paintings and Drawings of the Gypsies of Granada*, London, 1969.

Pohren, D. E., *Lives and Legends of Flamenco*, Madrid, 1975.

Pohren, D. E., *A Way of Life*, Madrid, 1980.

Pohren, D. E., *The Art of Flamenco*, Shaftesbury, 1984.

Quintana, Bertha B., and Floyd, Lois, *¡Que Gitano! Gypsies of Southern Spain*, London, 1972.

Sackville-West, Vita, *Pepita*, London, 1937.

Starkie, W. F., *Don Gypsy. Adventures with a Fiddle in Barbary, Andalusia and La Mancha*, London, 1936.

In Spanish

Barrios, Manuel, *Ese difícil mundo del flamenco, Semblanzas*, Seville, 1972.

García Ulecia, Alberto (ed.), *Las confesiones de Antonio Mairena*, Seville, 1976.

Grande, Félix, *Memoria del flamenco* (2 vols.), Madrid, 1979.

Machado y Alvarez (Demófilo), *Cantes flamencos*, Seville, 1881.

Mairena, A., and Molina, R., *Mundo y formas del cante flamenco*, Seville, 1979.

Molina, R., *Misterios del arte flamenco*, Seville, 1986.

Ortiz de Villajos, C. G., *Gitanos de Granada, La Zambra*, Granada, 1949.
Nuñez e Prado, *Cantaores andaluces*, Barcelona, 1904.
Sánchez, María Helena, *Los gitanos españoles*, Madrid, 1977.

FAIRS AND FESTIVALS

In English

Conrad, Barnaby, *Gates of Fear* (on bull-fighting), New York, 1957.
Epton, Nina, *Spanish Fiestas*, London, 1968.
Hemingway, Ernest, *Death in the Afternoon*, New York, 1932.
Willoughby, David, *Guide to Semana Santa, Holy Week in Seville*, Seville, 1974.

In Spanish

Burgos, Antonio, *Folklore de las cofradías de Sevilla*, Seville, 1972.
Burgos, Antonio, *La Romería del Rocío*, León, 1974.
Herrero, José Sánchez et al., *Las cofradías de Sevilla, historia, antropología, arte*, Seville, 1985.
Rodriguez Becerra, Salvador, *Guía de fiestas populares de Andalucía*, Seville, 1982.
Salas, Nicolás, *Las Ferias de Sevilla*, Seville, 1974.

FOOD AND WINE

In English

Casas, Penelope, *The Foods and Wines of Spain*, Harmondsworth, 1985.
Jeffs, Julian, *Sherry*, London, 1982.
Read, Jan, *The Wines of Spain*, London, 1986.

In Spanish

Alonso, Juan Carlos, *La cocina de Sevilla en su salsa*, Seville, 1988.
Briz, José, *Breviario del gazpacho*, Madrid, 1989.

FURTHER READING

Capel, José Carlos, *Comer en Andalucía*, Madrid, 1981.

Martínez Llopis, Manuel, *Historia de la gastronomía Española*, Madrid, 1989.

Pérez, Dionisio (Post-Thebussem), *Guía del buen comer Español*, Madrid, 1929.

Salcedo Hierro, Miguel, *La cocina andaluza*, 1979.

INDEX

Page numbers of main entries in the
Gazetteer are given in bold type

'Abbāsid dynasty, 75
'Abd al-Azīz b. Musa, 65
'Abd al-Mu'min, 80
'Abd al-Rahmān I (caliph), 66, 70
'Abd al-Rahmān II (caliph), 66, 68,
    250
'Abd al-Rahmān III (caliph), 67, 73,
    267
Abu 'Abdallah *see* Boabdil
Abu al-Kasim Ibn al-Arif (vizier), 78
Achila (Visigoth king), 64
Addington, Thomas, 194, 195
Adra, 42, **234**
agriculture *see also* land ownership
    cooperatives, 15
    'plastic culture', 42, 234
    SOC (workers' union), 15
    unrest, 12–13
Agrippa (Roman scholar), 56
Agua Amarga, 43, **258**
Aguilar de la Frontera, 267, **313**
Ahmad al-Yamānī, 69
ajo blanco (soup), 168
Alameda, 21
Alanís, **265**
Alarcón, Pedro Antonio de, 40, 178,
    321
Alas, Leopoldo, 178
Alba, Dukes of, 12, 274–5, 340
Alberti, Rafael, 205, 208, 210, 215,
    217, 228, 275, 302
    in Civil War, 220, 225, 227
Alcalá, 3rd Duke of, 110
Alcalá de Guadaira, **234–5**
Alcázar, Baltasar del, 108, 170

Aleixandre, Vicente, 215
alfajor (almond sweet), 309
Alfonso VI (king of Spain), 78
Alfonso VII (king of Spain), 80, 237
Alfonso VIII (king of Spain), 349
Alfonso X, 'The Wise' (king of
    Spain), 161, 269, 275, 317
Alfonso XI (king of Spain), 318
Alfonso XIII (king of Spain), 219
Algeciras, **235**
al-Hakam I (caliph), 72, 267
al-Hakam II (caliph), 69, 74, 254,
    269
Alhama de Granada, **235–7**
Alhambra *see under* Granada
Alhaurín el Grande, 306
Aljarafe, 161
al-Maqqarī (Arab historian), 73
al-Mansūr (Umayyad chamberlain),
    74
Almería (province)
    emigration from, 8
    established, 4
    isolation of, 19
    landscape, 40–43
    mining industry, 10
Almería (town), **237–40**
    Alcazaba, 73, 238, 239
    Brenan in, 237
    cathedral, 98, 238
    in Civil War, 227
    museum, 56
    taken by Christians, 85, 237
Almodóvar del Río (castle), 272
Almohad dynasty, 80–81, 334, 344